HAL BROGNOLA HAD BEEN CORRECT

unknown terrorist group had found a way to control the GPS network for the whole world. They were watching the world news and then shifting the GPS to cause a major disaster during anything that was already receiving major press coverage.

"And there's nothing America can do," the President raged, crumpling a report in a fist. "If we shut down our own GPS network, we're totally vulnerable. And if we try to shoot down enough satellites to collapse the GPS for the entire world, that would rightly be seen as a declaration of war!"

With a sigh, the President opened a folder to review the procedure to activate the remote-control device used to unleash the full nuclear might of the United States. If—when—the war did erupt, the nation had to be ready to defend itself from all aggressors, including former allies.

God help us.

Other titles in this series:

#26 FLASHBACK

#27 ASIAN STORM

#28 BLOOD STAR

#29 EYE OF THE RUBY

#30 VIRTUAL PERIL

#31 NIGHT OF THE JAGUAR

#32 LAW OF LAST RESORT

#33 PUNITIVE MEASURES

#34 REPRISAL

#35 MESSAGE TO AMERICA

#36 STRANGLEHOLD

#37 TRIPLE STRIKE

#38 ENEMY WITHIN

#39 BREACH OF TRUST

#40 BETRAYAL

#41 SILENT INVADER

#42 EDGE OF NIGHT

#43 ZERO HOUR

#44 THIRST FOR POWER

#45 STAR VENTURE

#46 HOSTILE INSTINCT

#47 COMMAND FORCE

#48 CONFLICT IMPERATIVE

#49 DRAGON FIRE

#50 JUDGMENT IN BLOOD

#51 DOOMSDAY DIRECTIVE

#52 TACTICAL RESPONSE

#53 COUNTDOWN TO TERROR

#54 VECTOR THREE

#55 EXTREME MEASURES

#56 STATE OF AGGRESSION

#57 SKY KILLERS

#58 CONDITION HOSTILE

#59 PRELUDE TO WAR

#60 DEFENSIVE ACTION

#61 ROGUE STATE

#62 DEEP RAMPAGE

#63 FREEDOM WATCH

#64 ROOTS OF TERROR

#65 THE THIRD PROTOCOL

#66 AXIS OF CONFLICT

#67 ECHOES OF WAR

#68 OUTBREAK

#69 DAY OF DECISION

#70 RAMROD INTERCEPT

#71 TERMS OF CONTROL

#72 ROLLING THUNDER

#73 COLD OBJECTIVE

#74 THE CHAMELEON FACTOR

#75 SILENT ARSENAL

#76 GATHERING STORM

#77 FULL BLAST

#78 MAELSTROM

#79 PROMISE TO DEFEND

#80 DOOMSDAY CONQUEST

#81 SKY HAMMER

#82 VANISHING POINT

#83 DOOM PROPHECY

#84 SENSOR SWEEP

#85 HELL DAWN

#86 OCEANS OF FIRE

#87 EXTREME ARSENAL

#88 STARFIRE

#89 NEUTRON FORCE

#90 RED FROST

#91 CHINA CRISIS

DON PENDLETON'S

STONY

AMERICA'S ULTRA-COVERT INTELLIGENCE AGENCY

MAN®

CAPITAL OFFENSIVE

A GOLD EAGLE BOOK FROM

WORLDWIDE®

TORONTO • NEW YORK • LONDON
AMSTERDAM • PARIS • SYDNEY • HAMBURG
STOCKHOLM • ATHENS • TOKYO • MILAN
MADRID • WARSAW • BUDAPEST • AUCKLAND

First edition December 2007

ISBN-13: 978-0-373-61976-4
ISBN-10:   0-373-61976-6

CAPITAL OFFENSIVE

Special thanks and acknowledgment to
Nick Pollotta for his contribution to this work.

CAPITAL OFFENSIVE

PROLOGUE

Sonora, Texas

Loose gravel crunched under the tanker truck's tires as it slowly rolled out of the darkness.

"Hold it right there!" the guard called out, raising a palm. With a stern expression, the big man stood at the entrance to the brick kiosk. "Right there, I said!"

With hissing air brakes, the massive vehicle rocked slightly as it came to a complete stop directly in front of the locked gate of the electrified fence. Coiled lengths of razor-sharp concertina wire along its top glistened in the reflected glow of the headlights.

On the side of the tanker was the name and logo of a famous fuel company, but the guard knew that was probably false. Everything short of an ice-cream truck had delivered materials to the desert warehouse. After working there for a year, nothing surprised the man anymore. Although dressed in civilian clothing, the U.S. Marine corporal was wearing a canvas military gun belt with a .45 Desert Eagle pistol at his hip.

Keeping a hand near his weapon, the Marine could see there were two people inside the cab, a big man sitting behind the wheel and a woman resting her head against the passenger-side window. The raven-haired beauty appeared to be sound asleep; he could hear her softly snoring.

Cautiously loosening the Desert Eagle, the corporal cast a wary glance at the delivery schedule tacked to a corkboard inside the brick kiosk and saw there wasn't a shipment due to the government warehouse for another couple of days. That wasn't unprecedented. Set behind the electrified fence, the massive Quonset hut that served as a warehouse was little more than a junkyard for spare parts and obsolete equipment. Whenever anything got upgraded, or outright replaced, the old equipment was sent here, to be labeled, numbered, indexed, stacked, listed and forgotten. There wasn't anything inside the warehouse worth stealing unless a person was looking for antiques. Everybody in his platoon considered standing guard here a punishment detail. Death by boredom. Although exactly who it was the soldier had annoyed he honestly had no idea.

"You folks lost?" the corporal asked, smiling politely. His relief had told him how a bunch of folks with cameras had stopped by once foolishly thinking this was the entrance to the famous Sonora Crystal Caves. It took him a full hour to convince the civilians that this was just a warehouse and not a tourist attraction. Civilians, he thought, were just about as useless as lips on a brick.

"Nope, not lost. Got a priority delivery," the driver said, flipping down the visor and pulling loose a sheath of papers held in place by a rubber band.

The corporal tensed at the action. But the driver stayed inside the cab and held the papers outside the window.

"A delivery at this hour?" the corporal asked suspiciously, slightly easing his stance.

The driver shrugged. "Hey, I just work here, brother."

A fellow Marine, eh? The corporal smiled. "I hear that." Accepting the papers, he quickly checked the documents and everything seemed to be in order. Just another load of miscellaneous equipment for the junkyard.

Tucking the papers into the pocket of his shirt, the corporal grabbed the stanchions supporting the sideview mirror and pulled himself onto the corrugated steel step and looked inside the cab. He didn't want to, but regulations were regulations, even out here in the middle of nowhere.

The driver raised both hands to show he was unarmed, and the corporal gasped at the sight of the sleeping female passenger. The buttons on her blouse were undone, the full breasts naked and exposed. One of the nipples was pierced, the steel ring glistening in the amber dashboard lights like gold.

"Okay, you're going on report, asshole," the corporal growled unhappily. "Bringing a goddamn hooker on a delivery run—" Suddenly he stopped talking and grabbed his throat with both hands, red blood gushing between his fingers.

Falling away from the truck, the Marine hit the ground hard, his head cracking against the pavement. Everything whirled for a moment, then he heard the door to the truck open. The corporal clawed for the Desert Eagle at his hip. As the gun cleared the holster, it was kicked from his grip and skittered away into the darkness. Then the driver knelt to stab him in the chest with what appeared to be a long sliver of glass wrapped in thick cloth.

The pain triggered adrenaline and the corporal savagely swung up an elbow to knock the makeshift knife aside, then he rolled over to frantically scramble for the kiosk.

Gotta make it…only a few yards, he thought. There were more weapons inside a locked cabinet near the minifridge along with a full medical kit. But more importantly, there was the alarm button on the desk. The telephone was useless; talking would be impossible with his vocal cords cut. With that realization, a wave of cold flooded the corporal, and he knew this wasn't some thrill-crazy lunatic, but a planned attack on a military site. Suddenly getting another pistol was replaced by the grim determination to hit the alarm button.

Stumbling into the kiosk, the corporal could see the alarm. But a heavy feeling was filling his body, and breathing was impossible, his chest aching from the need to pull in one more sip of air. Releasing the hand from his throat, the soldier saw crimson blood arch into the kiosk and instantly knew that a major artery had been cut with the first expert slash. Death was close. He had only a few seconds remaining. Summoning his last vestiges of strength, the corporal staggered toward the alarm button…but something pulled on his collar, hauling him back into the deadly night.

Tumbling to the hard ground, the dying soldier vaguely saw the grinning truck driver standing over him for a single moment, then the glass knife came down, stabbing into him again and again. Searing agony filled his universe, to be replaced with a soothing blackness that engulfed the Marine forever.

Standing erect, the frowning driver cast aside the glass knife and it shattered on the concrete steps to the small kiosk. "Sorry, brother," the big man muttered in guttural Spanish.

"Was he alone?" Lieutenant Henrietta Caramico demanded, leaning out of the cab of the truck, a silenced 9 mm Bersa pistol held expertly in her hand. The woman's shirt was still undone, her breasts swaying to the subtle vibrations of the big diesel engine.

"Yes, Lieutenant. There's nobody else listed on the duty roster," Sergeant Roberto Mendoza replied, squinting at the papers tacked to the corkboard above the desk.

"Good," Caramico muttered, her weapon sweeping the darkness for any video cameras. But the area was clean. Once again, she thought, Snake Eater had been right. Security here had been a joke. But then, the Americans didn't consider this isolated warehouse a chink in their national defense. Major mistake.

"Okay, let's finish this," the lieutenant snapped, swinging back into the cab. Holstering the gun, she began to hurriedly button her shirt closed.

Climbing behind the wheel, the sergeant revved the engine to build power and then shifted gears and charged for the wire gate. Sparks flew as the hinges were ripped away from the supporting steel posts and the gate crashed loudly to the pavement. Buckling the metal framework under its massive rubber tires, the heavy tanker rolled over the ruined gate and across the empty parking lot, steadily building speed.

"Zigzag a little," Caramico ordered, tucking the shirt into her pants. "Remember, we're supposed to be a runaway truck."

Nodding, the big sergeant did as requested and began to move erratically. He sideswiped a battered old VW Beetle, probably the car of the dead guard, then stomped the gas pedal to the floor and shifted gears. The speedometer just managed to reach forty miles per hour when the truck violently slammed into the Quonset hut. A headlight shattered and the tanker severely dented the corrugated steel siding. Braced for the collision, the man and woman were still almost thrown from their seats.

Allowing the engine to sputter and stall, the sergeant clamored out of the cab and went around to the rear of the tanker. The lieutenant was already there, smiling widely. Gasoline was rushing out of a break in the main feeder pipe, exactly where they had weakened the metal with acid only a few minutes earlier.

"Take care of our guest," Caramico said, walking briskly into the darkness.

Hunching his shoulder, Mendoza grunted. "Yes, ma'am." Climbing into the sleeper compartment situated behind the cab, the sergeant dragged out a corpse and stuffed the owner of the tanker carefully behind the steering wheel. When the position looked natural, Mendoza liberally poured whiskey over the body and tossed the empty bottle to the floor mat. It had been easy enough for the pretty lieutenant to strike up a conversation with the driver at the truck stop on the main road, then convince him to have a couple of sips of whiskey to put a trace of alcohol into his bloodstream. Caramico was a cast-iron bitch, but even Mendoza had to admit that his lieutenant was a real looker. The two had had sex in the sleeper compartment, and when the man was snoring afterward, she'd used a hypodermic needle to inject a bubble of air into his bloodstream. Death was almost instantaneous, but would be totally untraceable to modern-day forensics.

"All clear," Caramico reported, walking out of the gloom. "I dropped a few clues for the FBI to find tomorrow. Help them discover the identity of the terrorists, eh?"

"I dislike that word." Mendoza stepped away from the expanding puddle of fuel on the cracked ground. The rising fumes were starting to blur the air, and the reek was becoming intolerable. "We're soldiers, not criminals."

"And this is war," Caramico replied, retreating a few yards herself. "So shut the fuck up, and just do your job."

Biting back a response, the big sergeant opened and closed his scarred hands, but said nothing.

Lighting a cigarette, the lieutenant drew in the smoke with obvious satisfaction. Then she slowly exhaled and tossed the cigarette onto a crack in the dry pavement. The glowing tip resembled the eye of a demon in the shadow of the crashed truck. Splashing from the broken pip, the dark pool of gasoline was rapidly spreading across the parking lot, following the sandy cracks to head directly for the burning cigarette.

"How long do we have?" Mendoza asked nervously, licking dry lips. The man preferred timing pencils and fuses. Solid, reliable military hardware, not this makeshift nonsense. But subterfuge was what the general wanted. And orders were orders.

"Less than a minute," Caramico said slowly, estimating the expansion of the gasoline pool. The fuel seemed to be pouring out of the tanker faster than ever. Perhaps the minor crash had burst some of the internal seals.

In unison, the two soldiers broke into a run and were moving at a full sprint when they passed through the smashed gate and raced past the bloody corpse near the kiosk. A flickering light appeared from behind. Redoubling their speed, the man and woman frantically pelted into the desert and managed to dodge behind a large sand dune a split second before the ruptured gasoline tanker violently detonated.

Fiery light filled the night, and the very ground shook from the staggering force of the blast, the strident explosion rumbling across the flat Texas desert for countless miles. A heartbeat later, flaming debris sprayed across the desert, the sand dune shaking from the brutal impact on the other side.

Long moments passed before the force of the detonation dissipated. Brushing loose sand from their hair and clothing, the man and woman went around another sand dune and re-claimed the motorcycles they had parked there earlier that day.

Kicking their sleek bikes alive, Caramico and Mendoza paused for a moment to look to the north. Precisely on schedule, three bright pinpoints appeared above the mountains on the horizon.

"And so it begins," Mendoza remarked, his face a blank mask of control.

"No, this is how it all ends," Caramico corrected harshly, her eyes alive with pleasure.

Already moving at Mach Two, twice the speed of sound, a trio of experimental missiles streaked high in the evening sky, steadily moving away from one another as the war machines headed for scattered targets halfway around the world. Then, incredibly, they seemed to pause and rotate slightly to proceed in radical new directions.

CHAPTER ONE

Washington, D.C.

Dawn was just breaking over the capital city, and the White House, normally a beehive of activity at that early hour, was strangely quiet. Government aides rushed about without talking, telephone conversations were hushed and the Secret Service agents stationed at every door were grimly silent, their hard eyes constantly checking every identification badge. There were absolutely no tourists or news reporters anywhere in sight.

To the stoic people inside the Oval Office, the atmosphere was cool in both temperature and demeanor. The anxious members of the senior staff were perched on the two couches set in front of the fireplace, looking as if they were racehorses poised at the starting gate. Across the room, the President was sitting behind a massive hardwood desk, his fist clenched around a red telephone receiver. Ten years ago that would have been the hotline to Moscow. Now the secure line went directly to Beijing.

Openly cradling assault rifles, Secret Service agents stood in every corner, barely a ripple in their jackets from the body armor underneath. Outside the tall windows, armed helicopter gunships swept low around the capital building in a standard defensive pattern, then there came the low rumble of a full squadron of jet fighters streaking across the city. Through the glass panes of the door leading to the promenade, Marine One could be seen sitting on the manicured lawn between the Jefferson Mounds, the turbo props of the armored helicopter slowly turning as it stayed ready to fly the President to safety at a moment's notice.

The members of the senior staff knew that the vice president was already in the underground bunker at Camp David, and the Joint Chiefs were en route to Cheyenne Mountain, the headquarters for NORAD.

"No, Mr. Premier, the United States of America is not, repeat, not at war with China, or with anybody else for that matter," the President said in strained patience. The man's hair was tousled and his necktie was askew, as if he hadn't been to sleep in days. Yet he had only been awake for a few hours.

"Yes, I agree," the President continued after a short pause. "We do have to keep the incident from the general public…. Yes, rioting in the streets is a distinct possibility, I agree."

Frowning slightly, the President listened to the man on the other end of the receiver as he wearily poured himself a fresh cup of coffee from a steaming urn.

"No, that is not quite correct, Mr. Premier…. Look, Lu-Chan, I have absolutely no explanation about the missile misfiring." The President leaned back in his chair with a white china cup balanced in his hand. "We did help you shoot them down, after all. A dozen of our new ICBMs went wild, but we were able to self-destruct nine. Only three got away from us, and all of them were destroyed in-flight. We suspect a computer malfunction…. Yes, I agree, Lu-Chan. Machines are useful servants, but very poor masters."

The senior staff looked up sharply at the colossal lie, but said nothing. Nine missiles? Only three of the new ICBMs had been launched the previous night. But the careful distortion of the truth made the U.S. seem heroic and less like incompetent fools.

"I understand that hundreds of Chinese civilians were killed when the missiles came crashing down on that factory complex," the President stated, setting down the untouched cup. His voice was calm, but the tendons in his neck revealed the tension he was actually feeling. Red China was the last serious enemy to freedom in the world, but the gigantic nation was slowly becoming a valuable business partner with America. Soon enough, Communist China would crumble under the economic pressure to buy washing machines, DVD players and tractors, exactly as the Soviet Union had done several years ago. However, at the moment, the Chinese were still the only nation truly capable of nuking America off the map and their overly suspicious commander had to be treated with all due respect.

"This would have been much worse if the warheads hadn't been dummies," the President said, then abruptly stopped. There was an awkward pause. "Nonnuclear models," he explained patiently.

The Premier of Red China boasted of his excellent English and considered it a mark of distinction that he didn't need a translator like the American President. However, American slang sometimes confused the man terribly.

"I agree…we…yes, thank you, Lu-Chan." The President sighed deeply, his muscles finally relaxing. "I only wish that if the situation were reversed, I could also show such wisdom and restraint as yourself, my old friend.... Yes, absolutely. We shall talk again on this soon. Goodbye." Gently, the exhausted man hung up the red phone as if it were made of glass and a hurried gesture would shatter it into a million pieces.

"Well, sir?" Daniel Thursby nervously asked, wringing his hands. The senior domestic policy adviser had recently shaved and was neatly dressed. He looked almost too young to work in the government, yet in the halls of Congress, he was one of the most feared men in the nation.

"China has agreed to step down from Red Flag Five, their version of DefCon Five, and will no longer be preparing to launch missiles at us," the President stated, taking a sip from the tepid cup of coffee.

With audible sighs, everybody in the room eased their stance at the good news.

"Even if they did, sir, we could have stopped their missiles," Virgil McPherson stated confidently. Wearing a badly rumpled suit, the foreign policy adviser looked perpetually angry.

"All of them?" the President demanded pointedly, placing aside the empty cup.

"Greater than ninety-five percent."

The President tried not to frown. Which would mean only twenty or thirty million dead civilians.

"What was the breakage, sir?" Brent Morgan, the head of Homeland Security asked, easing his grip on a black cell phone. The entire White House was shielded against radio signals, but cell phones could be used inside the structure for relaying commands to staff while on the move.

"The estimated death toll is five thousand men, women and children," the President replied sternly, his displeasure at the cavalier euphemism patently obvious. "Although I'm sure that a lot of things—" he stressed the word "—were also smashed and destroyed. Our ambassador in Beijing will be receiving a bill within the day for the damages. Massively overinflated I'm sure, but we'll have to pay without complaining to maintain international goodwill."

"The one bright spot is that the Paris missile impacted on an empty apartment complex set to open next month," George Calvert, the secretary of the interior added, throwing his arms wide across the back of the sofa. "Not a soul was hurt. But the blaze from the crash spread to a nearby park and started a damn forest fire. The blaze is out of control and heading for civilian areas and oil refineries."

"Can we help?" Morgan asked. "Send some humanitarian assistance, try to earn some goodwill?"

Waving a dismissal, the other man snorted. "Hell, no! The Red Cross has already sent in disaster relief," he replied. "NATO, as well. But all American assistance has been flatly refused. The French are beyond furious, and are squealing like stuck pigs."

"Can we put any spin on this?" Thursby asked without much hope.

"Not a chance," Amanda Freeman said, shaking her head. The press secretary was wearing a neatly tailored dress suit sans jewelry. She wore polish, but the nails were kept short from her constant work on computers. "We have to take this hit politically." She frowned. "The Internet is burning with the tale, the bloggers are going nuts and the news cycle has already sunk its teeth into the story. The whole world thinks that we had a massive failure in our missile defense systems. We look like damn idiots, but at least nobody thinks we tried to start World War Three and failed miserably. Good thing the last missile hit the ocean."

Which was a lot better than letting them know the truth,

the President added mentally. The stealth capabilities of those missiles was being tested, not their accuracy. They should have been able to hit a phone booth on the other side of the globe! The very idea that three of them failed at the same time was beyond ludicrous.

"How are things at the United Nations?" Virgil McPherson asked pointedly. "I understand the Security Council has called a special meeting just to discuss limiting our—"

There was a knock at the door, then it opened and the President's secretary appeared. "Sir, the sandwiches have arrived," the elderly woman said quietly.

The dour expression on the President's face eased somewhat at the news. "Excellent. Send them right in."

"Yes, sir," the secretary replied. She left the Oval Office at a brisk walk.

"Sandwiches?" asked the senior policy adviser, glancing at the sideboard along the wall. It was stacked with enough food to feed a platoon of Marines for a week.

"Ladies and gentlemen, I want to thank you all for your diligent efforts," the President said, sitting straighter in his chair. "But now I need a few minutes alone to consider the matter."

"Leave? With so much on the table?" a junior speech writer asked in surprise, looking up from his laptop.

"Yes, thank you," the President said with a touch of impatience in his voice. "I'll confer with you again in an hour. Good day."

"Of course, sir, absolutely," Calvert said, rising from the couch. He shot the younger man a disapproving look. "We'll be in the Blue Room with the Cabinet discussing the matter."

Gathering their reports and files, the senior policy staff left the office, with the Secret Service agents following close behind. They also knew the difference between the President wanting to be alone and when he needed privacy.

When the office was empty, the President pressed a button on the intercom. Immediately the door opened and in walked Hal Brognola. Short, powerful, middle-aged, he looked like a Mafia capo or the CEO of a multinational corporation, instead of the director of the Sensitive Operations Group.

"By God, I have never wanted to see you less, but needed you more, old friend," the President said, standing and offering a hand.

"Sorry I took so long, sir, but traffic is a mess around DuPont Circle," Brognola replied, shaking hands, then taking a chair. "I heard about the missiles. What's the real story?"

The man was always two steps ahead of any conversation.

"I'll be brief." The President grimaced unhappily, starting to pour himself another cup of coffee. But the urn proved to be empty. "Last night at around 2:00 a.m., there was a test firing of three of our new StarDagger ICBMs. Absolutely state-of-the-art missiles theoretically capable of penetrating the defense grid of any enemy nation without their even knowing it occurred. The targets were located far at sea, a long distance from any foreign powers, and a safe distance from the commercial shipping lines…just in case anything went wrong."

"Which it obviously did," Brognola stated, templing his fingers. He didn't like where this conversation was going.

"Sadly, yes." The President started to speak, paused, then took a deep breath. "Almost immediately after launching, the missiles went wildly off course and hit Paris and Beijing. One landed in the Pacific Ocean."

"Where was that again?" Brognola asked, stunned. The news had talked about trouble overseas, but nothing like this. "Were the birds hot?"

"Thankfully, no." The President sighed, rubbing his face. "The missiles were only equipped with marker warheads, just a half ton of M-2 plastique."

Brognola knew that was enough high explosive to throw out a plume of water a hundred feet high, but not enough to do any significant damage to a major city. Maybe destroy a city block or two, but not much more than that. "How many people are dead?" he demanded gruffly.

"Hundreds. However, it could have been much worse."

"Not by much," Brognola replied curtly, shifting uncomfortably in his chair. Racking his memory, the man recalled that modern-day ICBMs didn't have a self-destruct and that their flight paths couldn't change from the primary target. It was a failsafe procedure to prevent an enemy from seizing control and turning the missiles back against America. Once launched, the warbirds were totally autonomous. "How far off course did they go?"

"The original targets were the Fifth Fleet in the North Atlantic, the third Carrier Group in the Sea of Japan and the Second Submarine Assault Group in the South Pacific."

The big Fed grunted in reply. Obviously the missiles hadn't veered slightly off course, but had completely changed direction and flown halfway around the planet in new directions. That smacked of outside control, not a malfunction. "Any idea what went wrong, sir?" he demanded gruffly.

"To be honest I have no idea," the President replied, spreading his hands. "Nor does anybody else. Only a wild guess. Every telltale was green, all telemetry was nominal, and yet…"

"Sabotage is the obvious answer, but how could anybody get to all three of them?" Brognola mused out loud, massaging his jaw. "Were they launched from the same base?"

"No."

"Then we either have a network of traitors scattered through the launch silos…"

"Not completely out of the question."

"Agreed. But if that's not the case, then logically, somebody has found a way to manipulate our long-range weapons systems."

"Sadly, that's also my conclusion." The President growled as if the notion put an unpleasant taste in his mouth. "Which means that until this matter is rectified, the nation is virtually defenseless. If we launch another ICBM, or even a long-range stealth bomb, it could go anywhere. Hit anybody from Manhattan to Melbourne. And the next time we may not be so lucky, and the civilian death tolls could be catastrophic."

"And if these saboteurs can also alter the course of other nations' missiles…" Brognola added grimly. The implications were staggering. "India fires at Pakistan, but hits London. The British launch at New Delhi and hit Moscow, and then they hit…" The man made an endlessly circular gesture. One wrong move by the U.S. could start a domino reaction that would bring about the long-feared apocalypse of the old cold war.

"I see that you've also come to the same conclusions as myself," the President said. "At the moment, every antimissile we have has been taken offline. We can't trust them anymore. Which leaves us with rail guns and lasers of questionable accuracy in the first place."

"Artillery would be better."

"Agreed. The Pentagon has all of our jet fighters on patrol around the continent watching for incoming missiles. But we can't keep them up forever."

"Especially if whatever is sending our missiles off course can also affect our jets, making them fly in the wrong directions to violate international airspace, crash into each other over populated cities…"

"…Or leave a wide-open breach for an incoming missile to fly through without hindrance," the President finished grimly. "We have the best combat pilots in the world, but men get tired, and when they need to rely upon their navigational systems…" There was no need to finish the sentence.

"What can my people do to help, sir?" Brognola asked bluntly, leaning forward in the chair.

"Find out what happen to those ICBMs and stop whoever is responsible from doing it again," the President stated, passing over a clear plastic jewel box containing a computer disk.

The shiny disk was marked with a brown stripe of high explosive. Open the jewel box incorrectly and the disk would violently be rendered useless. "This has the full technical readouts on the new missiles. Maybe your people at the Farm can find something useful. However, it is paramount that this remain top secret. If the public got wind of what was actually happening, there could be a national panic. Terrorists would attack U.S. bases overseas knowing that we can't properly defend ourselves. The stock market might crash, financially crippling the nation for decades, hundreds of companies could go bankrupt, closing down factories and sending thousands of people out of work." He grimaced. "It's a nightmare waiting to happen."

"Don't worry, sir, we won't let you down," Brognola declared, rising from the chair.

"You never have before," the President said, and started to add something more when telephone on the desk gave a soft buzz. The man glared at the device as if it were a live bomb, then lifted the receiver.

"Yes?" the President asked. He listened for a minute, then

replaced the receiver in the cradle. "Well, it just happened," he stated. "Two of our F-18 SuperHornets patrolling the oil fields of eastern Iraq got lost and accidentally crossed the boundary into western Iran. The mullahs are screaming violation of sovereign airspace and demanding punitive measures from the United Nations for our quote, 'rampaging aggression,' end quote."

"The enemy is escalating their attacks already?" Brognola asked uneasily. "We can expect a lot more of this, and soon."

The President opened a drawer and pulled out a folder marked with Top Secret seals and an explosive security tab. "Then stop wasting time talking to me and get moving," he commanded, sliding on a pair of reading glasses and opening the file to start skimming the pages.

With a nod, Brognola turned and left the Oval Office, his mind already working on the complex matter. A lot of people hated America for various reasons. However, he knew there were few groups who had access to the sort of highly advanced technology needed to pull off this sort of cybernetic attack.

Departing from the building, Brognola headed for the parking lot behind the Old Executive Building. Heavily armed Park Rangers were on patrol everywhere inside enclosure, while D.C. police officers patrolled the sidewalks outside.

The key to the matter was how somebody had seized control of an ICBM in flight. And sent a military jet a hundred miles off course, the big Fed noted. There were a hundred safeguards and multiple backups on both guidance systems. Yet it had been done. There had to be some sort of common denominator; a computer chip or software program.

Stopping at his car, Brognola looked skyward at the dark storm clouds gathering high overhead. In the distance, thunder softly rumbled. Unfortunately there was only one thing he knew of that they both used as a navigational aid, and if that was compromised, the entire world was in more trouble than he could even contemplate.

CHAPTER TWO

Tokyo, Japan

A heavy rain fell over the sprawling metropolis, the sky dense with rumbling black clouds. Blurred by the downpour, heavy traffic flowed like rivers of stars through the city streets, a million neon signs blazing in every imaginable color.

In the nearby harbor, the dark shapes of cargo ships, oil tankers and American warships loomed like metal mountains rising from the choppy ocean. Impossibly tall, slender skyscrapers thrust into the storm, lightning illuminating them briefly in silhouette. Many of the office buildings were alive with bright lights, the diligent workforce of the mega-corporations working through the wee hours of the night to assure their nation's future. The war for world domination had failed many decades ago, and the country paid a terrible price. Their attempt to financially control the West had also ended in total disaster, mostly through their own stupidity and greed, and now the Asian companies heroically struggled to try to repair the ghastly economic wounds.

Suddenly a low roar cut through the noise of the city and the storm. Then on top of an apartment building, a billboard advertising Green Apple cigarettes violently blasted into a million pieces of plastic and splintering wood as the prow of an American 767 jetliner punched through the flimsy obstruction.

Snarling curses, the frantic cockpit crew struggled to raise the lumbering aircraft, to change their course, regain the sky, their shock over not being at the airport dwarfed at their horror at the wall of mirrors looming directly ahead of them. What the hell were they doing downtown? How did they get this far off their flight plan?

Adorned with the name of the famous car manufacturer, the colossal skyscraper of chrome and steel swelled in front of the lost jetliner as it streaked across the broad city street, the pilot and copilot straining every muscle in their bodies as they fought the shuddering controls. Height! They needed more height! Before—

Lightning flashed as the jetliner and office building collided. The entire ninety stories of the majestic structure shook from the strident impact, then the rippling windows shattered as the crumpling 767 exploded into a deafening fireball. For a single horrible moment, the entire city of Tokyo was briefly illuminated in the hellish light. Then the building began to tilt to the side, cracks yawning wide in the exposed infrastructure.

Buffeted by the brutal shock wave, tens of thousands of people on the streets below looked upward in surprise, shouting at the nightmarish sight, then the rain of broken glass arrived and their cries became agonized shrieks. Hundreds of cars crashed into one another, spreading the destruction in every direction and plowing into countless horrified pedestrians.

More glass windows fell away as the trembling building began to collapse, crumbling into pieces like a sand castle. Chunks of smashed masonry mixed with debris, dead bodies, splintery furniture and burning pieces from the fuselage of the annihilated jetliner tumbled away into the rainy night. Crushing death filled the streets of Tokyo. An acrid cloud of concrete dust and roiling black smoke flowed outward from the building, the screams of the wounded and dying seeming to challenge the stentorian thunder of the raging maelstrom in the black sky above.

Stony Man Farm, Virginia

IN A RUSH OF WARM AIR, the Black Hawk helicopter landed in the middle of the freshly mowed field. The side hatch opened and out stepped a tall blond man carrying a nylon equipment bag. He was dressed in dirty denim pants, a flannel work shirt and hiking boots.

Keeping his head low, Carl "Ironman" Lyons tried to ignore the spinning turboprops only inches above his head, the breeze ruffling his short hair. Closing the armored hatch, the former L.A.P.D. detective waved through the bulletproof Lexan plastic window at the pilot of the craft. His hand still on the joystick, the pilot nodded curtly in return and promptly revved the massive Detroit engines back to full power.

As the Black Hawk lifted into the air, Lyons moved quickly across the smooth grass. Heading toward a rustic-looking farmhouse, the ex-L.A.P.D. detective noted the dozen men scattered about the grounds. Wearing denim overalls, the guards were trimming bushes, painting wooden shutters or taking soil moisture readings with handheld probes. Even though Lyons knew everybody in sight was heavily armed, he couldn't spot any of their weapons. That was both impressive, and a little annoying. The former cop had spent a lot of years on the mean streets of Los Angeles and usually could tag an armed man from fifty feet just from the way he stood and moved. Three pounds of steel strapped under your clothing altered a person's stance significantly to the trained eye. But not these men. Which was one of the many reasons they had been chosen from the top professionals in the nation to become a blacksuit, the elite soldiers who guarded the country's top antiterrorist headquarters, Stony Man Farm.

Stepping onto the wooden porch, Lyons pressed a hand to a sensor plate that resembled a smooth patch of wood. A moment later a small section of the wall cycled aside to reveal a keypad. He tapped in the entry code. There came a soft answering beep, then the armored front door swung aside with the soft hiss of working hydraulics. As he stepped into the building, the door closed behind him with a muffled boom.

Inside the farmhouse, the blacksuits were openly armed with pistols at their sides or carried in shoulder holsters. A softly beeping radar screen showed the departing Black Hawk heading for the horizon.

Hurrying on assorted errands, the men and women nodded to Lyons in passing as he strode for the elevator. Then he changed his mind and headed for the stairs. After six long hours in the Black Hawk he could use a good stretch of the legs.

Reaching the subbasement level, Lyons proceeded along a corridor. More blacksuits were down here, one standing on a ladder and fixing a light fixture, another dutifully running a waxing machine along the clean terrazzo floor. Both were wearing earphones and throat mikes, the constant chatter of the other guards a muted buzz from the miniature radios.

Passing the firing range, Lyons could dimly hear some sort of a machine gun yammering and took a guess that Kissinger was testing the new M-249 SAW. John "Cowboy" Kissinger was the armorer for the covert base, and there wasn't a weapon in existence that the lanky Texan couldn't fix, repair or modify for the field teams. Whatever was needed to get the job done, Kissinger had in stock.

The SAW was the latest addition to the Stony Man arsenal. Nicknamed "the Minimi" by NATO forces, the squad assault weapon had replaced the old M-60 machine gun as the standard support for a platoon needing suppressive firepower. An attached ammo box held the belt of ammunition, thus removing the possibility of tangling the feed, and also hiding from the enemy just how many rounds the gunner had remaining. Firing a much smaller 5.56 mm round, the M-249 was lighter, fired faster, farther and quieter. A lot of Marines were using them in Iraq, and nobody had complained about the weapons yet.

Turning a corner, Lyons saw Chief Buck Greene talking to a couple of unknown blacksuits.

Wearing sunglasses, with a massive Colt .45 revolver holstered at his hip, Greene resembled a drill instructor. Lyons almost smiled. Which was probably the whole idea. Veteran soldiers who would charge a chattering machine-gun nest flinched in horror at the memory of their miserable weeks at boot camp. Chief Greene was the man in charge of base security for the Farm, and he took his job very seriously. There was nobody better to have protecting your six.

Slinging his bag, Lyons grunted in passing, and Greene jerked his chin in reply. The men were friends and hadn't seen each other for a while, but when Barbara Price announced an emergency recall, that meant the blood had already hit the fan and there was no time for pleasantries.

Reaching the Conference Room, Lyons pushed open the armored door. Four people were hunched over a conference table reading security reports. On the wall was a video monitor showing maps of the world, the war status of the superpowers scrolling along the bottom. Additional screens displayed weather conditions around the planet and a vector graphic of orbiting satellites.

"About time you showed up," Rosario Blancanales said in greeting, laying aside a top-secret report.

Dressed is a three-piece suit of gray worsted material, Blancanales looked like a kindly banker rather than a professional soldier, and middle age had done nothing to soften his appearance of sheer physical strength. Called "The Politician" for his knack for fast-talking himself out of any trouble, Blancanales had salt-and-pepper hair and a million-dollar smile.

"Well, I was fishing in the Yukon," Lyons stated, dropping his bag on the floor.

"Yeah, yeah, always the same old excuse," Hermann "Gadgets" Schwarz said with a chuckle.

Wearing casual business attire, Schwarz looked more like the manager of a video store than the best combat technician in the world. General Electric had a standing offer for Schwarz to join the corporation at a staggering salary, but long ago the technical wizard had decided to use his talents for defending the nation instead of acquiring wealth. Nobody in his family truly understood the choice, but the call to duty was something only another soldier could ever really understand.

"Sweet Jesus, you smell like Baltimore Harbor at low tide!" Price scowled, wrinkling her nose. "Would somebody please pour a cup of Aaron's coffee over the man to kill the smell?" She was, of course, referring to Aaron Kurtzman, Stony Man's computer whiz.

"Can't. It might dissolve the concrete floor." Lyons grinned, taking a chair at the table. Then the smile dutifully vanished. "All right, I read the initial report on the flight over here. What's our current status?"

"Still at DefCon Five," stated Barbara Price, the Mission Controller for Stony Man Farm.

Crossing his arms, Lyons frowned. "Damn. Has there been another attack?"

"Tokyo, less than an hour ago," she replied, turning to gesture at a wall monitor.

"Son of a bitch," Lyons said softly, reading the scroll from CNN and the BBC. As civilian news agencies went, those were among the best. When the estimated death toll came into view, the man tightened his hands into hard fists, suppressing his rage. Lowering his head, the leader of Able Team paused in silent contemplation, then looked up again, his eyes diamond points of glacial fury.

"Any suspects yet?" he asked coolly, forcing his hands to unclench.

"Everybody and anybody," Blancanales replied with a dour expression. "This sort of thing seems out of the league for al Qaeda, the PLO or Hamas. Something like this must have required years of careful planning."

"However the hell they did it," Schwarz muttered angrily, studying a sheet of paper covered with technical information. There was a handwritten note for him from Brognola offering a possibility. But it was ridiculous. Utterly impossible, he thought. Thank God, because if it was correct, then America already had a gun to its head and the hammer was being pulled back to deliver the deathblow.

"We'll figure out the details after we shovel them into the dirt and read their operation files," Lyons declared. "By the way, where's McCarter? I'm surprised that Phoenix Force isn't also here." He paused. "Or have they already come and gone?"

Price nodded. "Hours ago. David McCarter and Phoenix Force are already at the Texas missile base checking into the possibility of sabotage," she said. "But it's just a feint to throw off the enemy. I'm also sending a couple of blacksuits to check the factory where the missiles were assembled, along with the U.S. Army train that delivered the warheads."

The members of Able Team looked at her disapprovingly.

"Agreed." Price sighed. "It's a long shot, but then, gambles have paid off before."

"So what is our assignment, another diversion?" Lyons asked, but then he saw her expression. "You found something." He stated the observation as a fact.

"Hopefully. Aaron found something odd a few minutes ago, just before you arrived." Price typed briefly on a small keyboard built into the wooden top of the conference table. The main wall screen changed from a view of the world to a satellite photo of southwestern America, then it jumped to a tight shot of Texas. Then again to a small town.

"The city of Sonora," Price declared just before the name appeared to scroll along the bottom of the screen. "Aaron and his cyber team were surfing the Internet, looking for anything odd around the time of the launch, when they discovered this." She tapped a button and a side monitor came alive with a newspaper headline from the Sonora *Gazette*. There was a picture of a smoking hole in the ground and several sheet-draped bodies. "Apparently an empty warehouse outside of town was blown up by a runaway gasoline truck at almost the exact same moment the missiles were launched."

"How far away from the launch site did this happen?" Lyons asked, studying the article for details. From the struts among the charred wreckage, he would guess the structure had been some sort of a Quonset hut.

"Roughly eighty miles."

"Interesting. Could the launch have been seen by anybody at the warehouse?" Schwarz asked, tapping a pencil on the table.

Price leaned back in her chair. "Bet your ass. An ICBM launch lights up the night brighter than a NASA space shuttle taking off. And there were three of them this time. Would have looked like the Fourth of July at Christmas."

"How sure are we that the warehouse was empty?" Blancanales asked pointedly. "Could the records have been faked?"

"At the moment, we don't know anything about the warehouse," Price replied honestly. "Aaron ran an inventory search, checked the deed, traced the utilities bills, everything we could think of, and his team has hit a stone wall. Nobody seems to have built the Quonset hut, nobody owns it and there were no customers. Yet the warehouse had an armed man out front in a brick kiosk."

That sounded like a guard station. "Dead?"

"Absolutely. Same as the truck driver. The preliminary autopsy indicates he was drunk, and that the guard was killed by flying glass."

"Which could be true," Blancanales said hesitantly. "However…"

"However, the driver was a Mormon, and they don't drink," she stated, sliding a sheet of paper into a slot on the desk. A wall monitor displayed the membership records from Salt Lake City, Utah. "That was a bad slip on the part of our saboteurs. And the guard…well, he seems to have died twice."

"Twice?" Schwarz asked with a frown. He knew what that meant, and it wasn't good.

"A spook," Lyons stated, rubbing his unshaven jaw to the sound of sandpaper on rock. "Interesting."

"We ran his footprints through the DOD." Price didn't have to tell the other people why. They all knew that fingers often got blown off in combat, or too badly mangled to read. However, footprints were just as reliable and inside an Army boot, they had a much higher rate of survival. "Apparently the guard was killed by a sniper near the Khyber Pass in Afghanistan four years ago, and then again yesterday."

"The corpse have a name?" Lyons inquired.

She snorted. "Aaron found fifteen and they have all proved to be fakes. This guy was so deep undercover that he could have been one of us."

There was a chilling observation. "That sounds like a CIA black bag operative," Blancanales mused. Able Team had encountered such men before. The Agency would have an operative pretend to be a civilian and get recruited into the military. Then they would arrange for them to be sent into the heart of the fiercest fighting happening at the time. When the operative arrived, there would be a switch and a corpse would take his place on the battlefield, followed closely by a nice mangling explosion, and the CIA op would faded away, his identify safely removed.

"Anything is possible," Price agreed, turning away from the screen. "Homeland Security, DOD, he's obviously a government agent."

"Yeah," Schwarz muttered, stroking his mustache. "The question is, which government?" The defunct KGB had been particularly fond of this trick, along with MI-5 in the United Kingdom and the Mossad.

"The guard could have been working for anybody," Lyons said, typing at another miniature keyboard set in the table and accessing a duplicate of the reports. He quickly flipped through the electronic documents. Nothing, nothing and even more nothing.

Just then, the intercom buzzed softly.

"Price," the mission controller answered brusquely, touching a switch.

"Bear, here," a gruff voice replied over the speaker. "My team just pulled in something hot."

"Excellent," Price said. "Send it over."

A moment later there came a soft hum from the table and a document extruded from the printer under the table. When it dropped free, she picked it up and briefly scanned the message. Then she paused and read it again, slowly and more thoroughly.

"It seems that the real owner of the warehouse is the DOD," she announced, sailing the sheet across the table. "And according to these top-secret inventory records, the Quonset hut was packed to the rafters with defunct electronics from the cold war. Mostly obsolete inertial guidance systems for ICBMs."

"Son of a bitch," Blancanales said, snatching up the sheet to read the report. "That's what used to steer our long-range missiles before we switched to GPS navigation, right?"

"Before we switched to using GPS," Schwarz said in a monotone, "an intercontinental ballistic missile was a hideously complex and staggeringly sophisticated piece of military ordnance. But not the warheads, of course. Atomic bombs were relatively easy to make. Slap two semicritical pieces of enriched uranium together and they exploded."

No, the difficult part was delivering the warhead on target, and on time, through the enemy defenses, halfway around the world, without having it veer off and explode in friendly territory. The trick was guidance.

The Pentagon had tried a lot of solutions to the problem, some of them quite bizarre, but in the end, the inertial guidance system proved to be the only viable solution to steering an ICBM at the time. Anchored by gyroscopes, and with fantastically detailed relays, an INS device could precisely deliver a two-story-tall ICBM anywhere with deadly accuracy. However, an inertial guidance system was hideously expensive to manufacture, almost a million dollars a piece, and each unit took nearly six months to construct. Even with computer automation. It was simply that complex a piece of equipment.

During the Reagan administration, the Pentagon had decided to scrap the INS and use the much cheaper GPS. A collection of telecommunication satellites had been launched around the world and placed in stable orbits in specific points above the spinning Earth. The satellites transmitted a complex code and could be read on a receiver to give your precise location on the ground. A civilian model of a receiver would give your location within ten yards, a commercial model within two yards. A military model was dead-on, bull's-eye accurate. Twenty years ago, the very existence of the GPS network had been beyond top secret. Nowadays, a person could buy a GPS device from the local electronics store to take on the family camping trip, and most of the better luxury cars came with the devices installed at the factory. It was commonplace. Ordinary. Mundane. There wasn't a plane, train, ship, submarine, missile or long-range weapon system in the world that didn't use the Global Positioning System as an aid to navigation.

"I thought the GPS network was untouchable," Price said suspiciously, "the access codes mathematically impossible to break."

"So did I." Schwarz sighed deeply. "But I guess these folks found a way. Some new approach, or technique, that we never thought of."

"Barb, you'd better call Hal and have him inform the President," Lyons stated brusquely. "The military is down to laser-guided weapons, dead-head rockets and heat-seekers for defense until further notice."

"All of them short-range weapons and pretty damn useless at stopping an incoming ICBM."

"Unfortunately, yes."

Without further comment, Price went to a phone on the wall and started punching buttons.

"Okay, if the saboteurs—or rather, the hackers—hit the warehouse before they stole the missiles," Blancanales said slowly, narrowing his gaze, "that means they're afraid we might fix this before a real war starts."

"Which certainly seems to be their goal," Lyons noted.

"Agreed. This seems to say that time is critical to them."

"Then we just have to move faster," Schwarz added somberly.

Deep in thought, Blancanales pulled in a long breath and let it out slowly. "Gadgets, any idea how long it might take for Jet Propulsion Laboratory to make replacement units?"

"I'm sure the templates are still in storage somewhere," the man said hesitantly. "Unless they were also in the warehouse. But even if they have to work from scratch, I'd estimate three months, maybe only two."

"No better than that?" Price demanded unhappily, hanging up the receiver.

Schwarz shrugged. "Hey, it used to take six months to build the things, and the very first model took years to perfect."

"All right, inertial guidance systems are expensive, rare and delicate," Lyons said, looking upward to stare at the featureless ceiling. "So let's use that to our advantage."

"What do you mean?" Price asked, reclaiming her chair.

"If we had more inertial guidance units, our ICBMs would be safe and the terrorists would be out of business."

Slowly, her face lit up. "So we make more of them. Hundreds more. On paper."

"Exactly. Then when the terrorists attack the fake warehouse," Lyons said, "we grab a few alive and twist the location of their base out of them."

"And how they're doing it," Schwarz added, gesturing with a finger. "That's paramount."

"Agreed."

Price said nothing. She could image what would be involved in the process. Able Team wouldn't torture a prisoner for information, no matter how badly it was needed, but there were a lot of ways a man could be forced to talk. Including letting him escape and following him back to his base of operations. However, that was used only when the situation was truly desperate. Sometimes, the "rabbit" would simply run, staying far away from his comrades. But then, nothing was certain in life except death.

Tapping on the intercom, Price said, "Bear?"

"Yeah?" the man replied.

"We need you to create a virtual warehouse full of INS devices," Price told him.

"What for?" Kurtzman growled over the speaker. "Oh, I get it. A trap. Sure. Where do you want it located? I know of a DOD warehouse in Columbus, Ohio, where we store nonsensitive documents. Easy enough to switch the inventory to guidance systems…no, that would be much too close. The warehouse has to be as far away as possible, but still on American soil."

"Good point. How about Puerto Rico?" Blancanales suggested, leaning forward in his chair. "I know for a fact that the U.S. government already has several long-term storage facilities on the island."

"Sounds fine," Kurtzman replied.

"As soon as you have the fake warehouse filed, I'll pull Phoenix Force off their inspection and have them order the technicians at the silo to prepare the other missiles for an emergency retrofit," Price said. "Then they'll take a standard military transport to Puerto Rico, requisition a cargo truck and drive off into the jungle, with a return flight scheduled for an hour."

"Why not helicopters?"

"The winds are too strong in some of the more remote valleys," she answered. "Besides, trucks are slower. Which gives the terrorists time to stage an ambush. So choose someplace appropriate, Aaron. Far from civilians."

"With plenty of combat room. I understand. No problem," the man replied, and the intercom clicked silent.

"How can we be sure the terrorists find out in time?" Blancanales asked, furrowing his brow.

"How did they learn about the first warehouse?" Price countered, typing on the keyboard. "Now, I want you three in Sonora, ASAP. These people would be fools not to have somebody watching the ruined warehouse to see who we send to investigate." She smiled coldly. "That's why I didn't send Phoenix Force there first. Make them sweat a little. Nervous people make mistakes."

"If I was any more nervous I'd need a change of underwear," Schwarz quipped.

"Again?" Blancanales retorted.

Ignoring the banter, Lyons pulled a .357 Magnum Colt Python from behind his back and swung out the cylinder to check the load. He closed the gun with a firm click. "How soon can Jack be ready to fly us down to Texas?"

"He's warming up a C-130 Hercules at Dulles right

now," Price replied, looking up from the keyboard. "Your equipment van is already being loaded. And a blacksuit has a helicopter on the front lawn waiting for you. Find me somebody, and burn the rope."

Stoically, the three members of Able Team rose from the table, gathered their personal belongings and headed for the door.

"Move fast on this," Price ordered in dismissal. "The numbers are already falling. You have no idea how close we came to the end of everything last night."

But the men were already gone, the armored door swinging closed behind them.

"Good luck," the mission controller added softly, returning to her typing. For a long while, the only sounds in the War Room were the soft patting of her strong fingers and the steady ticking of the mechanical clock mounted on the concrete wall.

CHAPTER THREE

Panama Canal, Panama

As the thick steel gates of the lock began to swing aside, the colossal *Pennsylvania* loomed in the opening, dominating everything with its sheer size.

"Back off!" the harbor master screamed into a radio microphone. The man was bent over a twinkling console in the control room of Lock Command. "Veer starboard! I said starboard, not port, you fool!"

But the American oil tanker continued irrevocably onward, the ship's computer totally confused by the conflicting information it was receiving from the channel markers and the GPS network. On the bridge of the *Pennsylvania,* the frantic captain was attempting to seize manual control of the huge vessel, but before he could, it was too late.

In a horrible groan of crushing steel, the prow of the ship crumpled against the open lock of the canal. The seams split, internal pipes burst and a tidal wave of thick, black crude oil gushed from the ship to spread across the surface of the water. The captain finally achieved control of his misguided vessel and applied full reverse, but driven by inertia, the million-ton tanker kept moving, sparks flying from metal grinding against metal. The bright spray touched the black torrent and the oil whoofed into flames. Rapidly, the fire spread across the water to lap against the walls of the open lock and spill into the next compartment of the waterway.

Still moving in the wrong direction, the wounded hull of the shuddering American tanker continued to yawn, the rush of oil dramatically increasing. Caught in the black deluge, a tugboat was capsized and several other ships became engulfed by the pool of fire—a Mexican fishing trawler, an Australian yacht and a gunboat of the Brazilian navy. The sails of the yacht instantly burst into flames, as did the nets of the trawler. With nowhere else to run, the crews took refuge from the conflagration belowdecks, but only minutes later their wooden hulls caught fire and men began to shriek.

Lurching into action, the Brazilian gunboat rushed to offer assistance. Sailors helped sailors; that was the rule of the sea. But, blinded by the dense smoke, the warcraft rammed directly into the trawler. The weakened hull splintered apart, exposing the vulnerable fuel tanks. As the oil fire reached inside, the gasoline lines caught like fuses, drawing the deadly blaze to the main fuel tanks.

Trapped between two of the locks, the *Pennsylvania* completely blocked the passageway as the crude oil continued to pour out, the internal safeties overwhelmed by the sheer amount of damage done to the crippled hull.

Standing along the side of the canal, behind an iron pipe safety railing, was a huge crowd of horrified civilians. The majestic passing of the international ships through the locks was always a big tourist attraction. Cameras flashed and cell phones took endless pictures of the mounting disaster.

In a thundering blast, the trawler exploded, the flying engine parts hammering holes in the gunboat, the oil flames seeping inside, spreading along the metal decks toward the ammunition lockers. Retardant foam gushed from the ceiling, and men dived forward to shut water-tight hatches, but it wasn't enough and the writhing flames reached the stores of munitions, washing across the missiles, shells and depth charges. For a single heartbeat it seemed that nothing would happen, then the Brazilian gunboat vanished inside a massive fireball, the deadly halo of shrapnel tearing the yacht into splinters, and riddling the hull of the *Pennsylvania* to actually increase the flow of crude oil into the beleaguered lock.

Behind the railing, a hundred tourists fell as bloody lumps, their shattered bodies torn to pieces, the arms and legs gone. The few wounded survivors began to scream for their lives. But the flashing of their cameras and cell phones never seemed to stop.

Bitter smoke was everywhere, Klaxons rang like gongs, sirens howled and the primary pumps for all of the other locks automatically shut down, closing the vital canal to all traffic until further notice.

Lujan, Argentina

WITH HEAVY TIRES HUMMING on the smooth roadway beneath the APC, a group of armed soldiers sat along the metal walls in cushioned jump seats, smoking and laughing. Suddenly there was a soft chime and a soldier opened a laptop to read the incoming e-mail. It took a few moments for the software to decode the garbled message.

"Good news, sir," the soldier announced in grim satisfaction. "We just took out the Panama Canal."

"Excellent," General Rolf Calvano replied without any warmth or feeling about the matter.

Staring out a viewport, the grizzled veteran watched the seemingly endless mob of fat civilians pass by the armored personnel carrier. The sheet of bulletproof Lexan plastic didn't distort the view in any way. More's the pity, he thought. It wasn't even market day and the noisy crowd completely choked the wide thoroughfare, spilling off the sidewalks and filling the streets.

As the APC stopped at a crosswalk, a dozen eager hands tried the handles, attempting to get inside to the passengers. But the driver of the military vehicle simply moved onward, the feeble attempts yielding nothing but frustration and the occasional bruised foot. In spite of its tremendous bulk, the APC was sporting slippers, rubber cushions, on the treads to prevent damage to the paved city streets, and also to any idiotic civilians.

Shouting loudly, everybody in the stores and along the sidewalks was offering items for sale. Scowling darkly, General Calvano felt distaste rise within him like the rank, sour bile that heralded vomiting.

"Too many people," he muttered. Food prices were becoming ridiculous, gasoline outrageous. There were housing shortages, and away from Buenos Aires, at least once a week the electricity went down. Not enough generators, not enough power lines, not enough cars, trucks, farms….

Like rats trapped in a cage, humanity was breeding itself to death. The truth was in every newspaper, every broadcast, on the Web, floating in the air. Overpopulation threatened the stability of the entire world, and when the end came it wouldn't be pretty. Natural resources were running short. The Americans were already embroiled in a war for oil. Soon, it would be for cropland. Worldwide rationing would follow, then food riots, civilians fighting one another like ants over scraps, and finally would come the ultimate horror of cannibalism.

The general grimaced at the very word. Cannibalism, the single, filthiest sin that it was possible to commit. To eat the flesh of your own kind was blasphemy beyond any salvation.

In spite of iron self-control, General Calvano shivered in remembrance of the bitter cold of that horrible month spent in the Andes, a young recruit trapped with his platoon in a cave by the unexpected avalanche. When the supplies ran out, the soldiers were forced to eat their boots, paperback books, anything possible. But as the slow days passed in an interminable march toward starvation, at last, straws had been drawn, and the killing commenced. At first a man voluntarily took his life, dying so that the others might live. But then it became a contest of the strongest, the meanest, and the true nature of Man had been brutally revealed to the young private in hellish clarity. Men were beasts, merely another form of animal, and would always revert to their base feral nature when it became a matter of survival.

As the foul memory welled, the general tried to block the taste, vaguely of pork, more like chicken. Acid flooded his gut at the horrid recollection, and he forced away the dark thoughts, denying their very existence. He alone had walked from the cave when a warm rain had finally melted away the blockage of deadly snow. He survived to walk a hundred miles through the barren hills until finding an isolated village and taking refuge near the blazing forge of the local blacksmith. As the teenager lay shivering on the dirty floor, his plan to save the world had been born. It had been crude, simplistic, but over the long years, the youth had become a man, and the plan had also grown in complexity and sophistication until it blossomed into fruition. Those American ICBMs had only been the first step toward salvation.

"Just too many people," Calvano whispered, the words thick with hatred.

The corporal driving the APC paid no attention to the mutterings of his commanding officer. As did the other soldiers riding in the rear. Brand-new FN-2000 assault rifles lay across their laps, the 40 mm grenade launchers slung beneath the barrels loaded with AP rounds and ready to be released at a moment's notice. They were the chosen elite, the personal guards for the leader of Forge.

Normally, officers in the Argentine army didn't have bodyguards, but then the 67th Battalion wasn't a normal unit, nor was Firebase Alpha. Once the soldiers had been told the truth, they eagerly joined Forge, and now worked for the general, the man who would become the unwanted savior of humanity.

Turning a corner, the APC nearly clipped a parked taxi-cab.The snoozing driver came to with a jerk and started to curse and wave a fist. The general knew that there was little chance of his losing a fare from the profanity. There were so many people, but everybody was walking. Cabs were expensive, while God had made feet for free.

If there really was a God, Calvano noted sourly, which he highly doubted. Enough prayers had been said over the centuries, and there had never been a reply.

Among the people thronging the sidewalks, Calvano noted drug deals happening, and instinctively reached for the 9 mm Bersa pistol holstered at his side. Then stayed his hand.

Not yet. But soon, the general noted. However, he marked the face of the traitor for later extermination along with the rest of the vermin and filth.

In a passing alleyway, Calvano saw a fat prostitute on her

knees, servicing a grinning customer in the reeking shadows, garbage strewed on the ground around them. Disgusting. A professional soldier, the general wasn't a prude, and very much in favor of recreational sex. He had a wife in Rosario and a mistress in Chivilcoy. But only the wife had been allowed to have children. After that, the general had gotten himself a vasectomy. The very minor surgery was virtually unheard of by the macho men of his backward country, and Calvano had been forced to fly to Canada.

Both of the children had been girls, which was fine with the general. Calvano wasn't a sexist like so many of his brethren. Argentine culture was an odd mixture of Spanish pride and German rigidity, along with a certain fine madness mixed into the gene pool from the tropical paradise they lived in, and were slowly paving under with concrete and asphalt. But his little girls were fine, safe with their mother in his farm to the north, far, oh so very far away from the coming apocalypse.

As the limo stopped at an intersection, a starving man in rags appeared and started to wash the prow of the APC with a squeegee dipped into a bucket of soapy water. Normally it would have been done to the glass windshield of a car, but the man diligently washed the armor while smiling with a gap-toothed grin.

Not just an old cloth, the general noted sourly. This poor man's job was to clean the dust from passing vehicles. He had found a way to survive. For that he applauded the man's ingenuity, even though he hated his very existence.

"Sir, should I…" the driver asked hesitantly, pulling a wad of brightly colored pesos from his shirt pocket.

"Drive on," the general commanded brusquely. "Give him nothing."

"Yes, sir," the driver replied, tucking the money away.

As the light changed, the APC surged forward, leaving the frustrated old man behind shouting obscenities and waving the squeegee in a threatening manner.

The sight made the general deeply sad. Calvano remembered when Argentina had been a beautiful land. The air and water had been clean, and crimes were few because justice had been swift. But the nation had started crumbling when the fat fool Peron and his wife took control, and was nearly bankrupt when they left. And the Americans had written a musical about the stupid bitch! he thought derisively.

Now there were homeless people living in cardboard boxes and under bridges. Crime was out of control, and food was becoming almost too expensive to buy. Only gasoline, made right there, was plentiful and cheap. A mixed blessing, as the smog was getting worse every year, even out on the ranchlands of the wide pampas. And smog brought lung disease, which meant more sick people, more hospitals, more taxes....

As the APC left the town, the roadway became clear of traffic and the driver dutifully increased speed until the lush green countryside was flashing past the military vehicle. Fresh, clean air came in through the louvered vents, and the soldiers joked about the lack of taste as they breathed in deeply.

Lost in his own thoughts, the somber general didn't join in the casual banter. Air pollution, water pollution...humanity was a cancer, eating itself alive, choking on the waste products and wondering what had gone wrong. Numbers didn't lie. World population was over six billion! India and China each had a billion, and soon so would other nations. In a high-secret report, the general had read about the S2 in Brazil acually rounding up their homeless people and machine-gunning them to death in warehouses late at night to try to curb the runaway poverty. Too many people and not enough jobs.

But population control wasn't the answer. New food technologies weren't the answer. Oh, no. Only the general seemed to understand the gravity of the situation. One man could live in a telephone booth, but not two, and certainly not five, ten…twenty… There were just too many people in the world. Unfettered and out of control. There was only one solution. Radical surgery. Amputation of the surplus population. There were six billion people in the world, so kill five to save one billion. The numbers were harsh and unforgiving, but acceptable. A soldier's burden.

Once, long ago, when fighting Communists from Chile trying to invade Argentina, Calvano had stationed a troop of men to hold a bridge at any cost while the rest of his battalion retreated to safety. A hundred men assigned to die so that a thousand could live. On paper it sounds like nothing. But he had looked directly into the faces of those brave men, those soldiers, when he told them to stay and die. And they had done as ordered. They stood the line and did their job, which saved the battalion. How could he do any less?

In sharp detail, Calvano still remembered the looks in their eyes as comprehension came. The flash of shock, the rage, the fear, and then the grim understanding of what had to be done. They died, or everybody died. It was that simple. There was no third option. The soldiers accepted the responsibility and stood their ground in a small foundry overlooking some nameless bridge. Long afterward, when the stripped bodies of his men had been recovered, Calvano found the last two soldiers lying behind a cold forge where they had made their final stand. There wasn't a bullet in their guns, and three of the rebels lying dead on the floor had been taken out by hammers. Hammers! Those heroic bastards had fought to the very end, beyond hope, beyond sanity, delaying the enemy at any cost.

And it had happened at a forge again. The young major took it as a sign from the Lord God, and that very night Forge was born. Soldiers determined to fight to the end at any cost, to give one last chance for a world gone mad.

Slowing to a halt to let a herd of cows cross the highway, the driver floored the APC and headed into the suburbs. Long stretches of track homes appeared, only to be replaced with green, rolling countryside that quickly became dense misty forest.

"Sir, we'd better take the back way in," the driver said, touching the radio receiver on his head. "There's a traffic jam on the continental highway."

"What's the problem?" the general demanded, frowning. His constant growing fear was that the Americans might send one of the covert assassination squads to kill him before the great task could be finished. He slept with a guard dog in his room, bars on the windows and a loaded assault rifle resting against the headboard.

"Some sort of crash on the Pergamino Bridge, sir. A truck hit a bus, and the cars behind plowed into them and…" He waved a hand in an expressive circle.

And everybody panicked, smashing into each other until cars were falling off the bridge like rats fleeing a burning ship, Calvano noted in repulsion. There was no room anymore, not even on the big roadways. Too many people.

"Do as you think best, Corporal," Calvano commanded, sitting back and pulling out a cigar from inside his uniform jacket.

"Yes, sir."

Lighting a match, the general let the sulfur burn off completely before applying the flame to the end. Drawing in the dark smoke with true satisfaction, Calvano pulled the fumes in his lungs until they threatened to burst, then exhaled twin streams through his nose. Tobacco was the only drug of which he approved. Nicotine kept a soldier's mind sharp, not befogged and stupid, like alcohol or marijuana. Hard drugs were strictly forbidden in the Argentine army, and in Forge their use was punishable by a public whipping for the first offense and a bullet to the head for the second time. Discipline was the key. The whole world simply needed more discipline! Calvano knew.

Veering off the main highway, the APC began a serpentine journey into the wild hills, leaving every trace of civilization behind. Located deep in the mountainous terrain, Firebase Alpha had once been a secret base of operations for the Communist rebels. But after clearing them out with VX nerve gas, General Calvano had then simply moved into the stronghold and taken over the place for himself, and Forge.

The deadly VX nerve gas purchased from a Russian arms dealer had proved to be most efficient, odorless and fast, but extremely painful. The rebels died screaming, ripping off their own melting flesh. Most of the Communists had used handguns on themselves to end the horrible agony. When Calvano rode unopposed into the camp the next day, only a handful of the rebels were still alive, grotesque twitching lumps on the ground. By his command, the troops encircled the dying rebels with wooden sawhorses and left them untouched to slowly die in the hot sun. Naked under the very eyes of God.

The base had proved to be a godsend. It was amazingly well stocked with weapons, fuel, food and communications equipment. The isolated valley was far from the annoying TV cameras of the news media, along with the watchful eyes of Argentine Military High Command. Hidden in the deep woods, the general had the privacy needed to build his private army. Out here in the wild forests of western Argentina, Calvano was king, free to do whatever he wished. There was no law, except his commands.

Surprisingly, the rebels had an underground bunker holding a staggering amount of hard currency, in very short supply in Argentina at the time, along with a tremendous supply of raw heroin they had been planning on selling cheaply to the decadent politicians and lawmakers to help corrode the fledgling democracy from within. Merely another good reason to kill every rebel without mercy, Calvano thought. He was only sorry that so many of them had perished so quickly from the VX gas. Criminals should pay for their crimes.

Debating the matter for only a few minutes, Calvano had taken all of the cash for Forge, and acquired an huge additional profit when he sold the narcotics to the gangsters of the Chilean underworld. In fact, the transaction had proved so profitable, the general regularly sent his private forces into Peru to raid the drug factories there and to seize more drugs to sell to Chile.

Let those fat fool idiots on the coast see to their own problems, Calvano noted callously. My only concern is Argentina.

Millions poured into the coffers of Forge, and a good thing, too. Constructing the other firebases had proved incredibly expensive, but vitally necessary. According to Professor Reinhold, there had to be a minimum of two uplinks to maintain their delicate control of the worldwide GPS network. The scientist tried to explain the technical details once, but the general soon became lost in the mathematical equations, and just took the matter on faith. Reinhold was one of them, a valued member of Forge, and fiercely dedicated to saving the human race from its own stupidity. Although unknown to the professor, there was also a hidden cache of VX hidden in the Black Fortress that the general could release by remote control. Just in case it was ever necessary to purge the mesa of rebellious personnel. Failure came from sloppy work, not a clever enemy, he believed.

"Here we are, sir," the driver announced, slowing at a gravel road.

Grunting in acknowledgment, Calvano dropped the cigar to crush it under his boot, then reached into his jacket to withdraw a small remote control. He pressed a few buttons and waited. After a moment, there came an answering beep and a tiny LED flashed green.

"You may proceed, Corporal," he said, tucking away the box once more.

"Yes, sir!"

Now the APC advanced onto the minefield, the loose gravel crunching under the weight of the heavy tires. Swinging around a copse of tall trees, Calvano looked closely, but only caught a brief glimpse of the large satellite dish antenna hidden among the dense greenery.

Passing a brick kiosk surrounded by a low sandbag nest, the general noted the Forge guards stood alert and wary, with hands on their assault rifles. Then he saw the woman.

"Hold!" the general bellowed, already rising from his jump seat.

Quickly, the driver braked the APC to a halt, but Calvano was out the sliding hatch before the vehicle had ceased rocking back and forth.

Walking across the blacktop, General Calvano scowled at the strange woman tied securely to a base of a metal flag pole. High above, the flag of Argentina fluttered in the soft breeze. Her clothes were in disarray, ripped and torn, the exposed skin underneath badly bruised. The nipple of one breast was showing, and it appeared to have been bitten. Gray duct tape covered her mouth. Weakly, she looked up from the ground with an expression of terror.

"And who is this?" Calvano demanded, pointing a finger at the cringing prisoner.

"Shelly Scoville, a news reporter from the capital," a burly sergeant said, snapping off a brisk salute. "We found her ID in her purse, along with a digital camera and a lot of memory sticks."

"We caught her trying to sneak into the base," another man added proudly.

Feeling hot anger building inside his mind, the general said, "And it seems she put up quite a struggle. How many of you did it require to capture the news reporter? Ten, perhaps twelve?"

The sergeant seemed confused, and looked around at his fellow guards. They were staying near the kiosk, as if distancing themselves from the man.

"I…we caught her easily, sir," the man said warily. "But I…we roughed her up some to make sure she was working alone, and didn't have any friends lurking in the woods."

"The woods around the firebase filled with proximity sensors and land mines?" Calvano asked pointedly.

"Yes, sir. I… That is…" The sergeant faltered, unsure of what should be the correct reply. "I was just doing my job, sir."

"We'll see about that," the general replied coldly, turning to the woman. On closer inspection, several of her fingers were broken, the nails bent back. "I assume she talked?"

"Yes, sir!" the sergeant answered smartly. "She's alone, working on a magazine article about forest fires and—"

The gunshot shattered the stillness of the forest, and birds took flight from the nearby trees as the dead woman slumped to the ground.

"We are not rebels, you stinking piece of filth! We're soldiers! And soldiers do not torture prisoners!" Calvano bellowed, then stopped. As she splayed on the freshly mowed grass, he could see there were fresh scratches along her inner thighs. The stockings were torn to shreds, and there was no sign of her underwear.

"Who did *that?*" Calvano demanded in a whisper, pivoting on a heel. The smoking Bersa pistol was still in his clenched fist, the ejected brass shiny near his boot like a fallen star. Then his voice came back in a strident roar. "Who raped a helpless prisoner on my base?"

The other Forge guards moved away from the sergeant, who suddenly started to sweat profusely in spite of the coolness of the day. "Sir, I…that is…" the man stuttered, then took hold of himself. "Sir, we haven't been to town in months, and since she was going to die anyway, I didn't see the harm in a little taste.…"

With a flick of the wrist, Calvano raised the gun again and fired. A neat black hole appeared in the forehead of the sergeant and he stumbled backward, blood and a sort of thin, watery fluid beginning to pour from the hole in his brain. As the sergeant's fingers twitched, the FN 2000 assault rifle stuttered, the 5.56 mm rounds stitching a line of destruction directly in front of the general and heading his way. As if he was carved from winter ice, Calvano didn't move, but instead fired twice more directly into the chest of the dying man.

Crumpling with a sigh, the soldier collapsed and went still.

"We are not killing four billion people only to put animals in charge!" the general stated furiously. His eyes held an insane look, and his gun swept the assembled men, pointing to each one in turn. Nobody moved. Then the 9 mm pistol was smoothly holstered.

"We are not terrorists, criminals or the American CIA!" the general continued. "We are soldiers! The saviors of the human race! And we do not torture prisoners, we kill the enemy! Period. Is that clear?"

The soldiers nodded quickly, saying nothing.

"Now bury her in the trees," Calvano said, turning his back on the guards. "And throw him into the ravine for the ants to eat."

As the guards rushed to obey, the general glanced at the waiting APC. His bodyguards were standing near the machine, their weapons at the ready, the driver at the gun turret, only his eyes showing behind the 7.62 mm electric minigun.

Feeling a rush of pride, General Calvano gave them a nod of approval, which was returned. Now those were soldiers, men of honor. There might have to be a thinning of his battalion after the nuclear war. There were just too many unreliables among the troopers.

Turning away from the APC, Calvano strode across the access bridge, his boots ringing against the corrugated aluminum. There was no safety railing for an invading force to hide behind, and a score of land mines were bolted to the underside of the prefabricated bridge in case an invading force needed to be stopped.

With a sputtering roar, the APC came alive and followed after the general, the bridge trembling slightly from the tremendous weight of the military vehicle.

Once past the sighing trees, Calvano smiled as Firebase Alpha came into view. A civilian might find the military installation rather drab and plain-looking, but to any combat soldier it was beautiful. The base was a sprawling expanse of squat concrete buildings surrounded by an electrified fence topped with razor-sharp concertina wire. An insulated fence formed a path of safety for the dogs padding around the firebase on patrol. Dimly seen soldiers watched with binoculars from behind the bulletproof glass of the tall guard towers, and there were subtle movements inside the dark concrete pillboxes at the corner of the electric fence. Canvas sheets covered the gunports, and there was no way to tell there was a 40 mm Vulcan minigun inside each squat redoubt.

More guards walked the flat roofs of interior buildings, and white whisps of mist rose from the ventilation fans of the command center, exhaust from the liquid nitrogen used to cool down the massive Cray SVG Supercomputer in the reinforced basement. The chief hacker for Forge had insisted on the installation of the SOTA hardware, and had proved its usefulness many times over. Nobody could properly pronounce his real name, so the soldiers liked to call the little man Snake Eater. Apparently he had been involved in some trouble in Calcutta a while back, and fled to Argentina. The computer expert had found refuge in the ranks of Forge.

Approaching the armored gate, Calvano snapped his fingers impatiently and the soldiers in the brick kiosk rushed to the control panel. As the APC lumbered to a halt behind the general, the solid slab of steel used as an anticrash stanchion descended from sight with the sound of working hydraulic machinery. Now, woven steel nets were raised, closing off the dog tunnel, and the gate loudly unlocked, then began to ponderously swing aside. The driver of the APC shifted the vehicle into gear, but Calvano didn't move.

Major Domingo San-Martin rushed toward the front gate from the command center. The short, heavyset officer held a sheet of crumpled paper in his hand. The general grimaced at the sight. That couldn't be good news.

"Sir…" Major San-Martin gasped, coming to a halt only a few feet away. "I saw you on the bridge—"

"What has happened?" Calvano demanded, snatching away the fax. The paper was covered in complex double lines of alphanumeric code, but the translation was written underneath each in red pencil.

"There is another…warehouse…sir," the man gasped.

The general went still. "Impossible."

"The Americans…are preparing all of their remaining missiles for a retrofit," he said, stumbling slightly over the odd term. "The inspection team in Texas is racing to Puerto Rico, and has a scheduled stay of only an hour." Color was returning to his face, and his chest no longer heaved.

So they did have more, Calvano thought. Or was it a trap? The Americans often acted stupidly but were rarely fools. If there were more warehouses with replacement INS units, Forge would have to shut down operations. Perhaps permanently.

"We could crash their place on the return flight," San-Martin suggested. "It would be easy enough to send a few commercial flights into their path."

"Which would send all evidence to the bottom of the sea," the general growled, crumpling the fax in his hand. "If there are replacement units in Puerto Rico, I need to know. Have Snake Eater assign a local team to handle the matter. They're to kill everybody on sight and destroy any INS units discovered. But I want a confirmation either way."

"Understood, sir." The major turned to go.

"And send Lieutenant Caramico back to Sonora," Calvano added.

The officer stopped and turned slowly. "But, sir, we specifically sent her away from the town in case the Americans tried to capture some of our people for questioning."

"Now we wish to do the same," the general stated. "The natural place to capture us would be at the warehouse, so have her avoid it completely. Watch the airport…no, the local law enforcement, police, sheriff, whatever they have. The CIA will certainly touch base with the people who were first at the scene of the fire. That will be the place to get prisoners for questioning."

"Questioning?" the major repeated slowly. He awaited clarification. It was a strange order coming from the general.

Feeling a mounting dread, General Calvano glanced backward at the guard post, the team of men burying the dead news reporter. Something trembled inside his soul, then died. This was a war for survival of the species. Sacrifices would have to be made. So he would perform the first. "Torture the Americans in any way necessary, but get me some answers."

The major smiled in relief. At least the kid gloves were coming off and the troops were free to do whatever was needed to save their beloved homeland. The rest of the world could die in flames, but Argentina would survive the coming holocaust no matter what.

"No problem, sir," Major San-Martin replied eagerly. "The lieutenant has Sergeant Mendoza with her. He's the perfect man for this sort of thing."

"Yes, I know," Calvano said. "And have the professor prepare for phase two."

"It will be my pleasure, sir." The major saluted, then sprinted toward the communications bunker.

There, it is done, Calvano noted, staring after the officer. I've crossed the line between soldier and terrorist. I am no longer an honorable man. Oddly though, a great weight was lifted from his shoulders at the decision, and the general felt exhilarated, almost intoxicated at the rush of total freedom. There were no more rules anymore, only results.

With a low rumble, the APC came alive and started after the general, the great machine advancing until it loomed over the man, casting him into a dark shadow.

CHAPTER FOUR

Makran Coast, Pakistan

"Red alert!" a voice boomed over the PA system of the U.S. Navy frigate as Klaxons blared. "Red alert!"

Erupting into action, the crew of the USS *Canton* scrambled for their posts even as the Phalanx guns at the bow and stern swung about automatically and started roaring at full blast. Guided by radar, the Vulcan miniguns vomited a fiery barrage of 40 mm shells at the incoming missile, the rapid-fire cannons spraying a wall of soft lead and steel pellets into the air.

With a violent concussion, the two LAW rockets fired from the hills along the rocky shore exploded in midair, peppering the sea with hot shrapnel until the water appeared to be boiling.

The crew cheered and quickly reloaded their weapons. Riding low in the choppy water, the USS *Canton* was anchored just off the desolate Makran Coast of Pakistan. There were no fishing villages along most of the coastline, the sea being far too heavily polluted from the oil refineries of Iran to the west and the steel industries of India to the east. But this section was possibly the worst. The coast resembled the lunar surface with bare jagged mountain covered by stiletto-like spires. There was only sparse vegetation, raggedy plants and leafy weeds struggling to stay alive in a hostile land, only a few randomly scattered acacia trees. Nearby was a gurgling mud volcano, the geological phenomenon endlessly pumping out waves of bubbling mud, the sluggish river of muck flowing along the cracked ridges and dissolving the sandstone formations on its way to the murky sea. Visibility was almost nil in the thick waters, and if there were any fish in the area, the sonar operator of the *Canton* couldn't find them. The crew knew they were still on the planet Earth, but had to keep reminding themselves of the fact.

On the bridge of the *Canton,* Captain David Henderson lowered his binoculars and grudgingly admired the strategy of the Afghanistan rebels. If they could get America embroiled in a shooting war with Pakistan, then the U.S. Navy would be hard-pressed to aid the NATO troops inside Afghanistan hunting down terrorist training camps.

"Ready a Tomahawk," Henderson said calmly as the bow Phalanx fired again. Then it swung to a new position and fired twice more.

Barely visible in the swirling steam of the mud volcano, another missile exploded, only doing damage to the ragged plants along the crumbling cliffs.

"And let HQ know we are under fire from the hills," the captain added over a shoulder. "These appear to be LAW rockets from the look of the contrail."

"Sir!" a man replied from the communications board inside the bridge. Swiftly, the man started to relay the information to the Pentagon via satellite.

Stoically, Henderson went back to watching the shore. LAW rockets against a frigate? The Afghans had to be desperate to try that. Even if they hit the ship, which was highly unlikely, the rockets simply didn't have enough power to punch through the armored hull. It'd be like throwing grenades at the Empire State Building.

"Tomahawks ready, sir!" a lieutenant reported crisply, with a salute. "On your command."

"Double check the coordinates," Henderson ordered, sweeping the coastline once more with the binoculars. "We want to hit that training camp outside of Safar, not the American troops encircling the damn place." Three hundred miles wasn't a long distance for a Tomahawk, but the old fortress the warlord ruled was small, and the troops in close quarters. The tiniest slip in the coordinates could spell a disaster.

On the stern deck of the *Canton*, sailors were returning fire at the snipers in the hills with an Armbrust. There was a snowy backblast of nitrogen flakes from the aft end of the launcher, and the rocket streaked away. But unlike the incoming LAW rockets, there was no smoke from the projectile to reveal its trajectory.

A few moments later there was a bright flash among the scraggly trees on a small cliff, and a fireball of white phosphorous spread across the ledge. Covered with flames, screaming men rose from behind the boulders to dash about madly. The sailors at the port-side gun emplacement opened fire with a .50-caliber machine gun and another Armbrust. In a muted crack, the ledge broke into pieces, slowly coming away from the sandstone cliff, bodies and boulders plummeting straight down into the gelatinous brown sea.

"Well done, men," the captain said, trying unsuccessfully to keep a tone of satisfaction from his voice. "Lieutenant, fire the Tomahawks!"

In a double explosion of smoke, two metal lids blew

open on the honeycomb on the main deck and a pair of sleek missiles lifted into the sky, then streaked away to disappear inland.

"Heading?" the captain asked, squinting after the Tomahawks. Funny, he actually thought that he could see the airborne missiles. But that was impossible. They were both much too far away by now to be spotted by the naked eye.

"Aye, sir," a lieutenant replied, hunched over the radar screen. "Missiles are at…" He paused to work the controls, the beeps strangely coming faster and faster. Then the men looked up in confusion and horror. "Sir! One of them is coming right back at us!"

"Don't be ridiculous," the captain demanded, turning away from the coastline. "Double check your instruments! It must be just another LAW coming in, that's all."

"No, sir, this is a Hawk!" the man replied, the beeps almost a single tone now, they were happening so fast. His hand hovered over the self-destruct switch. "Should I abort?"

Was the man serious? Henderson thought. Snapping his head back toward the craggy coastline, the captain briefly saw something moving in the air, coming straight for the frigate. He waited for the Phalanx system to engage, but the guns did nothing, the military software of the computer-guided radar strictly forbidding the guns to fire upon any Navy missile, even one coming straight for the ship.

"Abort!" the captain bellowed.

The lieutenant slapped the switch, but it was too late. Moving almost too fast to visually track, the Tomahawk slammed directly into the open hatch it had just launched from less than a minute ago.

A strident explosion shook the entire vessel from stem to stern, the fiery blast blowing out the portholes and causeways, throwing burning bodies into the sea. For a single heartbeat, Henderson thought the internal firewalls might just hold.

In a thundering staccato, the rest of the complement of Tomahawks detonated belowdecks, and the *Canton* lifted from the water and burst from within, the armored hull rent apart from the multiple trip-hammer detonations.

For several long minutes debris and corpses rained from the sky, hissing as they plummeted into the dirty water. But when the hellish rain eventually ceased, the USS *Canton* was gone, completely obliterated.

THREE HUNDRED MILES away from the coastline, the second Tomahawk cruise missile checked the GPS network and sharply veered around a tall mountain peak to flash down into a valley below, and then around another outcropping.

Running across the barren landscape, U.S. Army troops and tanks were steadily surrounding an ancient fortress carved into the rock of a hill. The resilient walls had withstood attacks by Alexander the Great, Julius Caesar, Napoleon and the Soviet Union. But now the rocks were cracked and weakening from the nonstop barrage of shells unleashed by the American tanks. A thousand Afghani fighters along the walls of the fortress were firing at the American soldiers with old AK-47 assault rifles, and doing very little to stop the steady advance.

The row of Abrams tanks fired again and a huge section of the sandstone palisade burst apart, the explosion and halo of rock splinters killing dozens inside the ancient fortress. Smoke and flame and blood was everywhere, and the screams of the dying men seeming to last forever.

Standing defiantly on the parapet, the Afghan warlord grimly watched the enemy come ever closer, knowing this was his last day alive, and that there was nothing he could do but try to die with dignity.

The Yanks will not pull me from some hidey-hole to parade on TV for the amusement of their fat children, the warlord raged internally, working the arming bolt of his Kalashnikov. I will die on my feet with a weapon in my hand like a man!

"Shar, incoming missile!" the bearded man cried from the old WWII radar console. A luminous green arm swept around the graduate screen, beeping softly.

The warlord raised an eyebrow at the pronouncement. Vaguely in the distance, he could see a streaking firebird, weaving a patch along the convoluted contours of the hilly land, avoiding the boulders and outcroppings as if it could see. Another Tomahawk so soon? So be it. Time to die. Damn the Americans and their technology!

Working the arming bolt of his assault rifle, the warlord started firing his weapon at the incoming missile. It wouldn't work, of course, but there was nothing else to even try. Only a few more seconds now....

Incredibly, the American missile flashed by overhead, streaking past the old fortress and rolling over to dive down and impact directly upon an Abrams tank rolling up the sloped hillside. The titanic explosion covered the landscape in fire and thunder.

But even before the mountain breeze cleared away the smoke, the warlord heard the terrible grinding noise of an avalanche. Still shaking from the concussion, endless tons of rocks and dirt came pouring down the side of the mountain to cover the startled American troops like a roiling blanket of death. The invaders disappeared from sight, then there came a series of dull explosions from under the rocks as the assorted munitions and ordnance of the Yankees detonated from the crushing weight of the devastating landslide. In a few minutes there was only a handful of American soldiers scattered about the valley.

"Ready the Jeeps!" the warlord bellowed, feeling his heart quicken with the taste of victory. "Charge the remaining troops and kill them all. Kill everybody you find! No prisoners! I want heads laid at my feet within the hour!"

"By your command!" A bearded man saluted and rushed off shouting orders to the troops.

"I rule Safar!" the warlord shouted at the sky, brandishing a gnarled fist. "Death to America! Death to all infidels!"

As the mob of screaming Afghan fighters came charging out of the old fortress, the few remaining American soldiers quickly made a defense circle and fought bravely, but it was all over in a few minutes. Without any support from the buried tanks, they were outgunned and outmanned. Soon, there were only still bodies strewed about the dusty ground. Then rusty axes began to rise and fall, gathering grisly trophies.

Utaudo, Puerto Rico

FLOCKS OF RAUCOUS PARROTS sitting in the tall banyon trees squawked loudly in protest as a VW truck rumbled past them on Route 111.

Smoking a cigarette, the armed driver ignored the noisy birds and shifted gears to take the steep hill coming ahead. The modified V-12 engine responded smoothly with a low growl of controlled power.

Although battered and dented, the truck was clean, and the smooth asphalt of the highway hummed beneath the six new tires, the outer rubber washed with diluted acid to make them appear old and worn. The ripped canvas sheet covering the sides of the vehicle had been expertly patched. The rear section was closed with a pair of hinged wooden doors instead of the usual loose flap, and several of the knotholes artfully were enlarged to now serve as crude gunports.

A passing police car paid the truck no attention, the uniformed officers completely unaware that twenty Kalashnikov assault rifles remained pointed in their direction until the natural rise of the landscape carried them out of view.

"Stupido." The driver sneered, casting the lit cigarette out the window and expertly starting another using only one hand.

"Did you really want them to pull us over for littering?" the man sitting in the passenger seat asked incredulously. A sawed-off, double-barrel shotgun lay in his lap. It was the perfect weapon to use inside the tight confines of the cab. Even at only a yard of distance, a man could miss with a pistol, but not with a twin load of buckshot. There were a series of small notches on the wooden stock, one for every fool who had shoved his unwanted face into the crew wagon of the Miguel brothers, and was promptly blown straight to hell.

"I am not afraid of the police," Esteban Miguel boasted hotly. But the driver checked the sideview mirror to make sure the officers were indeed long gone.

Shrugging in reply, Julio Miguel went back to watching for the exit. The sloped fields on both sides of the highway were heavy with tobacco plants, the broad leaves spreading wide to absorb the bright tropical sunshine. On the rubber floor mat between his shoes was an Uzi machine pistol, along with a canvas bag of spare clips and a plastic box filled with grenades.

When the call had come in through their agent in San Juan, the Miguel brothers had been uneasy about accepting the job. Nameless men asking for other nameless men to be killed on sight sounded like a sting operation by the U.S. authorities. Or worse, the military police. But then the bank confirmed the wire transfer of funds to their Swiss account, and the brothers dutifully gathered their full crew to head into the deep jungle mountains. It seemed like overkill, twenty guns to take out five tourists and blow up a building, but the client had insisted and paid the asked-for price, so who were they to complain? Besides, a job was a job.

We'd kill the pope, Julio thought, if the price was right, that is.

The cultivated farmlands fell behind and soon the truck was driving past a shimmering expanse of blue water. Hundreds of families were strolling along the public beach of Lake Coanillas, dozens of sailboats skimmed the low waves, and there seemed to be a endless supply of teenage girls in skimpy bikinis sunning themselves on the shore. The open display of young flesh was delightful.

"Perhaps afterward we can stop by for a snack, eh?" Esteban chuckled suggestively.

"Afterward," Julio promised, placing the shotgun down to check the load in the 9 mm Uzi machine pistol.

Cresting the top of a hill, the truck slowed and Julio pointed to the left with the shotgun. Esteban nodded and turned onto Highway 607. The new asphalt turned into old concrete, and the noise from the tires changed to a higher tone. The landscaping along the major highway changed into wildwoods of kapok, mahogany and tall palm trees. A few miles later the truck reached a gravel road. A wooden barrier marked it as closed from mudslides, but the brothers knew that was a lie. The rainy season was long over.

Slowing to a crawl, Esteban nosed the VW truck forward and knocked the wooden planks aside. They fell with a clatter and then he shifted into low gear and proceeded. From there on, things got tricky and conversation between the men ceased as Esteban concentrated on driving. There were no guardrails along this steep section of hilly road, and the ground dropped away sharply to a rampaging river. Composed entirely of rain water, the river had no name because it would be gone in a few weeks. But at the moment, the white-water rapids rose and fell in crashing waves against jagged boulders that dotted the rushing torrent like broken islands. A slip at this point, and even if the men survived the fall—highly unlikely—they wouldn't last a minute in the raging cascade.

Countless little creeks trickled along the steep hillsides like silver veins feeding life into the body of the tropical island, and the air became redolent with the rich smells of wild orchids and rotting fruit. Thankfully, the parrots could no longer be seen or heard. Then both men jerked as a monkey dropped from the trees overhead to land on the hood of the truck. The little animal screeched at them angrily, then scampered away, leaving a foul mess on the polished metal.

"I hate those fucking things," Julio snarled, lowering the barrel of his weapon.

"Then go live in Miami," Esteban suggested, curling a lip around the cigarette. "Get a skinny blond girl, pierce your ear and pretend you're from Cuba."

His brother's reply consisted entirely of four-letter words.

Chuckling in amusement, Esteban slowed the truck as he found the next turnoff, and thankfully put the dangerous river behind them. Now they only had to worry about the men they had been hired to kill. Probably DEA agents. Everybody hated those.

As they moved deeper into the mountains, the road became dirt, a path of crushed plants with a few rusting metal poles here and there to mark the trail. Eventually, the brothers had to consult a map, and finally use a GPS receiver to get their exact location and to locate the isolated valley they wanted.

The foolish American DEA agents had actually asked for directions to this valley from the local police. Idiots! The brothers didn't have any of the law officers in their pocket, but their sister was the radio dispatcher, and cops liked to chat among themselves. Everything the police knew, the Miguel brothers soon learned. The arrangement was expensive—their sister charged a fortune for her services—but·her flow of information had saved their lives and kept them out of prison many times in the past. A short burst of hot lead given to an eyewitness was much more economical than paying a million pesos to some San Juan law firm.

"This is as close as we can go," Esteban said, easing the truck to a halt below a poinciana bush. The plant rose thirty feet tall, its twisted branches spreading outward to form a fiery umbrella of impossibly bright red flowers. As he turned off the engine, the eternal sound of the jungle could be heard, rustling leaves, the tiny coqui frogs singing their mating song, and dripping moisture. Endless dripping.

"We're here, amigos!" Julio called, thumping a fist twice on the wooden wall separating the cab from the cargo area.

There came the clank of a bolt disengaging, and the rear doors swung open wide, exposing a group of armed men. While two stood guard, the rest jumped out, stretching their limbs and yawning after the long confinement. Then the guards closed the doors from inside and worked the bolts once more.

"How much are we getting paid for this?" one of the men asked, squinting at the dense greenery all around. His boots sank a good inch into the carpet of soft moss that covered the land.

The leaves of a banyon tree moved and a huge spider crawled into view with a wiggling lizard in its mandibles. The colossal insect crouched as it prepared to jump at the men, then scuttled away into the gloom.

"Not enough," another man replied curtly, easing his grip on the AK-47 assault rifle. "I hate the fucking jungle!"

Several other men agreed with the sentiment, and one of them spit in disgust.

"Shut up," Julio snapped, climbing down from the cab. "No more chatter until the job is done. And no smoking! That's an order."

The group of men grumbled softly, but complied. The bosses knew their stuff. The mercs had been in business for a long time and put a lot of people into the ground while the Miguel brothers were still alive and making steady money. It was hard to argue with that kind of success. Alive and rich was a winning combination.

"All right, let's spread out and find these fools and their secret warehouse," Esteban directed, loudly yanking back the bolt on an ungainly M-60 machine gun. The M-60 had been phased out of service by the U.S. military, replaced with the much lighter and faster M-249. But Esteban liked the big gun. The ventilated barrel and dangling ammo belt made it look as impressive as hell, and it threw down a thundering storm of .308 long AP rounds. The body armor of DEA agents stopped 9 mm rounds, and even .357-caliber bullets, but the oversize .306 armor-piercing rounds blew through the armor as if it were a banana leaf.

"Should be a couple of hundred yards to the north of here," Julio added, slinging an M-2 satchel charge across his back. "If we find the mainlanders, do nothing. Let them go inside the warehouse, then we'll blow it and do both jobs at the same time."

"What's the place look like?" a short man asked, thumbing a 40 mm round into the grenade launcher of the Russian assault rifle.

Tucking the sawed-off shotgun into a holster along his leg, Julio snorted. "What is this, downtown New York?" he snapped, picking up the Uzi machine gun. "We find a building, that's the one we want. Let's move out!"

Nodding agreement, the mercs checked their weapons and started along the crude path, their Kalashnikovs sweeping the lush greenery for targets.

Time passed slowly and the two hundred yards gradually became three, then four hundred. Suddenly the jungle broke and the group of men found themselves on a mossy escarpment overlooking a wide, swampy valley. Mist moved along the watery surface and bats hung from the banyon like grotesque fruit. There was no sign of any building, only dank muck and boiling swarms of buzzing insects.

"You sure we went in the right direction?" Julio demanded softly, scowling at the primordial morass in annoyance.

Resting the M-60 on a shoulder, Esteban pulled out the GPS receiver and checked the indicator again. "Yeah, this is it," he said slowly. "But there's nothing here, and never has been. So what the…oh shit." He dropped the receiver and used both hands to swivel the M-60 at the dense jungle.

"It's a trap!" Julio yelled, dropping to one knee and spraying the nearest greenery with a burst from the Uzi.

Snarling a curse, Esteban cut loose with the M-60, the big rounds chewing a path of destruction through the moist foliage. Instantly the rest of their crew hosed streams of copper-jacketed rounds in random directions, the spent brass from the chattering Kalashnikovs flying everywhere. The leaves violently shook in the dripping trees and birds erupted into the sky even as bloody monkeys tumbled dead to the mossy ground. Hot lead was poured into every bush and flow-ering tree, even the stagnant pools of water far below. But no-body fired back or shouted out in pain.

After a moment Julio called a halt and listened intently. The gunfire echoed along the swampy valley, but other than that, there was only silence. The jungle was momentarily still from the thundering barrage of military ordinance.

"What the fuck is going on here?" Esteban whispered nervously, digging into the nylon bag at his side to extract a spare belt of fresh rounds. With fumbling hands, he flipped open the breech and tossed away the last few remaining inches of linked cartridges, then laid in the new belt of fifty rounds.

Watching the greenery for anything suspicious, Julio licked dry lips. "Don't know, don't care," he stated forcibly. "Every-body back to the truck!"

Dropping spent clips, the mercenaries reloaded on the run, charging through the strangely quiet jungle. As the VW truck came into view, one of them tripped and went sprawling, his Kalashnikov sliding away into the damp bushes.

"Go get it, stupid!" Esteban snarled, then stopped as he saw a human eye blink in the carpet of leaves alongside the fallen man.

Faster than ghosts escaping from the grave, five large men in military-camouflaged ghillie suits erupted from the ground, the MP-5 submachine guns in their hands blowing flame and death. Five of the mercenaries died on the spot, the rest of the group diving for cover in the ferns and poinciana bushes.

"They're underground!" Julio bellowed unnecessarily, the Uzi spraying lead. One of the subterranean warriors dodged out of the way. But another took a full burst in the chest. Yes! However, the 9 mm rounds only tore off patches of wet fabric from the ghillie suits, exposing some sort of molded body armor underneath.

Snarling, Esteban added the yammering fury of the M-60 with the same results. The sight sent icy-cold adrenaline into his stomach. Body armor that could stop a .308 round? These weren't DEA agents, but U.S. Special Forces! What was going on here?

Spreading out, the five camouflaged strangers moved into the greenery, their weapons firing in short, controlled bursts. Screams of pain and bitter cursing came from everywhere. A grenade exploded, the fireball pushing back the jungle dampness for a searing heartbeat.

Bracketing the blast with suppressive rounds from the hammering M-60, Esteban knew that wasn't one of their grenades. It was something the Army called Willie Peter—white phosphorous—and it could roast the flesh from a person in under a heartbeat.

Constantly on the move, Kalashnikovs yammered in the gloom, the fiery flowers from the muzzles strobing in the thick foliage. The MP-5 submachine guns answered briefly in return, and more mercenaries shrieked into agonizing death.

Firing steadily, Julio backed toward the truck. When the Uzi clicked empty, he dropped the weapon to draw the shotgun. Crouching, the merc leader waited for a target. A shadowy figure lurched from the dripping vines and Julio gave it both barrels. In the bright muzzle flash, he was horrified to see that it was one of his own men. *Fuck!* Spinning, the mercenary tumbled back into the bushes, leaving a ghastly crimson trail.

Then a big man rose from the bushes, dropping a spent clip into his MP-5. Cracking the sawed-off shotgun, Julio frantically ejected the spent 12-gauge shells and shoved in fresh ones. Raising the shotgun, he saw that the other man was holding a crossbow, of all things. They fired in unison. The shotgun blast obliterated the plants alongside the big soldier, and Julio staggered backward, the long black quarrel from the crossbow sticking out of his shoulder.

Blood gushing from the wound, Julio tried to stanch the flow with his bare hands when he violently collided with a tree, the blow almost knocking him unconscious. He lost his vision for a time period, and silence filled the world.

Sight and sound returned with a vengeance, the jar shocking him painfully alert. Machine guns and assault rifles blazed away constantly all around him, then a grenade exploded nearby and Julio weakly looked up just in time to see his brother flying limply into the air, his arms and legs traveling in different directions. Fury filled his mind, but his body refused to obey and Julio slumped weakly against the tree, tears of rage coursing down his dirty cheeks.

A few moments later it was over. Only the five strangers were still standing, the bloody ground of the crude jungle path dotted with shiny spent brass and twitching corpses.

"T.J., give me a BDH," David McCarter ordered brusquely, reloading his MP-5 machine gun. "Calvin, see to that man! Everybody else, watch the perimeter."

The members of Phoenix Force moved without comment.

Gingerly checking his neck, McCarter found that he was bleeding slightly from a graze along the side where one of the mercs had come too close with a thrown knife. A former member of the vaunted British SAS, and now the leader of Phoenix Force, David McCarter was surprised a mercenary had gotten that close. Most professional soldiers held mercs in the same low esteem they did body lice, just something to crush when they got annoying.

Going to the panting leader of the Puerto Rican mercenaries, Calvin James looked down at the man and said nothing for a moment, watching how the blood came from the arrow wound. It was flowing, but not pumping. No arteries had been nicked, then. Good. This guy might just live if he cooperated. The tallest member of the team, Calvin James was a Navy SEAL, the field medic for the team and one of the best underwater demolitionists his teammates had ever seen.

"Drop the knife," James ordered, his accent a growl of pure southside Chicago. He was still holding the MP-5, but his finger wasn't on the trigger.

Looking down, Julio was surprised to see that he was holding a switchblade knife. He had no recollection of pulling the weapon. Forcing his fingers apart, he let the blade drop into the moss.

"Better," James said, slinging the weapon and swinging around a medical kit. "Now, I can stop the bleeding, but it's going to hurt. And I mean a lot."

"B-bah. I—I am not…not afraid," Julio wheezed, sweat running down his pale face.

"You should be," James replied stoically and, without another comment, he yanked the arrow free.

White-hot pain lanced through Julio, and he barely had a chance to scream before completely losing consciousness.

As the merc went limp, James pulled out a knife to start cutting away the crimson-soaked fabric so he could clean the wound.

With a Beretta in one hand and the MP-5 in the other, T. J. Hawkins warily approached McCarter, his expression grim.

"We've got a problem," Hawkins stated. "I count seventeen dead bodies."

Every member of Phoenix Force heard that over their earplugs and went instantly alert.

Standing with his back to a kapok tree, Rafael Encizo tightened his grip on the MP-5 just as drop of moisture fell from
the leaves above to hit the hot barrel. The water sizzled into
steam. A heavy, stocky man with catlike reflexes, Encizo was
less than handsome, his face carrying the scars of too many
battles. But the rough looks beguiled a razor-sharp mind.

"You sure about that?" Encizo whispered, studying the area.

Trying to appear casual, Hawkins scratched his nose.
"Definite."

"Shit." Gary Manning grunted at the pronouncement. The
big Canadian shrugged the massive bolt-action rifle strapped
across his back to a more comfortable position. Manning was
the sniper for Phoenix Force, and his weapon of choice was
the infamous .50-caliber Barrett rifle. The colossal weapon
fired a bullet that could penetrate most light-tank armor and
blow holes through brick walls from a mile away. The colossal Barrett was a deadly machine of distant termination, but
only in the hands of an expert marksman.

"Seventeen," Manning whispered, squinting at the still
forms scattered in the gory mud. "But I thought that Aaron
said the Miguel brothers always rode with a crew of twenty."

Down the jungle path, the headlights of the truck suddenly
came on, bathing Phoenix Force in a harsh illumination.

"They do!" McCarter yelled, moving and firing at the
same time.

As the team separated fast, the V-12 engine loudly came to
life and the truck started rolling forward, rapidly increasing
speed. From behind the vehicle, something even brighter
flashed and smoke puffed.

"Rocket!" James cursed, dragging the unconscious Julio
behind the massive tree for some protection.

The fiery dart of a LAW rocket streaked down the leafy

pathway and plowed into a stand of sugarcane. A split second later, a thunderous explosion tore the sweet plants apart, spraying debris into the misty sky.

Lumbering along faster, the truck kept coming, and now Kalashnikov assault rifles cut loose from behind the vehicle, the three ducking mercs only partially in view.

Bobbing and weaving among the dripping ferns, Phoenix Force arced through the jungle on both sides of the crude road, only to reappear and close upon the truck from opposite sides.

"T.J. and Gary, go!" McCarter commanded over the radio.

Rising into view, the two members of Phoenix Force hosed the truck with 9 mm rounds from their MP-5 submachine guns.

Forced to quickly take cover behind the moving vehicle, the three mercs pulled grenades from their pockets, clawing to get off the strip of safety tape holding down the arming levers. As the tape came loose, the mercs yanked out the arming pins.

That was when McCarter and Encizo stepped out of the ferns and stitched the three with prolonged bursts. Crying out in shock, the mercs threw their arms high as the copper-jacketed rounds tore them apart, the safety handles falling away free.

As the dying men collapsed, Phoenix Force rapidly took cover, and a split second later the grenades detonated, the entire jungle seeming to shake from the triple blast.

Crouching in the bushes, Hawkins grunted as something slammed hard into his belly. Slapping a hand to the spot, he quickly checked for blood, but his NATO body armor had stopped the shrapnel from penetrating. It had hurt, a lot, but he would live.

Continuing through the smoky trees, the truck jounced over the still corpses of the mercs lying in the bloody mud, until it wandered into the plants and rumbled away out of sight, the dripping leaves and flowery vines closing behind the vehicle.

"Anybody hurt?" McCarter demanded over the radio, slapping a fresh clip into his weapon. These three made twenty mercs total, but he was staying sharp in case the Miguel brothers had brought along some friends.

"No breakage," James replied, still kneeling alongside the unconscious leader of the mercenaries. He was in front of the man, protecting him from incoming rounds.

"And the area looks clear," Hawkins reported, scanning the jungle with IR goggles. The optical device registered heat sources, and aside from the Stony Man commandos and the sugarcane conflagration raging out of control, there was nothing within sixty yards that was bigger than an iguana.

"Stay sharp," McCarter directed, walking over to James and his patient. The Stony Man commando had the mercenary propped up against a banyon tree, and was just finishing off a temporary bandage around the ragged wound.

"What's his condition?" McCarter asked.

"He'll live," James said, adjusting the knot. Satisfied, he moved away from the man and reclaimed his weapons. Only a fool tried to heal an enemy with a gun at his side. "Just not sure how useful that arm will ever be."

"Can you wake him?"

James gave a curt nod. "No problem."

"Do it," McCarter ordered.

Pulling a preloaded syringe from the compact med kit, James gave the unconscious merc a combo shot of morphine, digitalis and amphetamine, a battlefield cocktail guaranteed to rouse the dead if the bodies were still fresh.

He'll have a splitting headache tomorrow, James thought, injecting the devil brew directly into a vein. But then again, the stupid son of a bitch is lucky to still have a head. Mercenaries he could tolerate. Drug dealers he could execute in cold vengeance.

His kid sister had died of an overdose of smack, and there weren't enough bullets in existence ever to balance the score.

With a low moan, Julio sluggishly came awake. "You…" the man mumbled in blurry recognition. "What did you give me?"

"Something for the pain," James said, putting away the empty syringe.

Along with other things to try to make me talk, Julio rationalized, waves of soothing warmth spreading through his arm and then his chest. The pain vanished, leaving him feeling slightly disconnected from reality. Then the memory of the fight, along with the death of his brother, came rushing back and he snarled in raw hatred.

"What do you want with me, gringo?" Julio demanded, his tongue feeling thick and awkward. "I tell you nothing. Nothing! Go ahead and haul my ass to jail. I will call my lawyers and be free in a day. A day!"

"That might be true, if we were the DEA or the police," McCarter said, glancing sideways at Hawkins.

Giving a wink, Hawkins recoiled from a corpse on the ground. "Hey, this guy is still alive!" he cried loudly.

"Too bad. We already have their leader," McCarter said. "So we don't need him."

"No problem, sir." Pulling his Beretta, Hawkins worked the slide and fired a couple of 9 mm Parabellum rounds directly into the chest of the dead man. The body jerked at each impact, almost seeming to die all over again.

The brutally callous execution caught Julio completely by surprise. These mainlanders were insane! Most definitely not U.S. Army, or even the CIA.

Crouching on his heels, McCarter lit a cigarette and offered it to the prisoner.

As if suspecting another trap, Julio hesitantly accepted and sucked in a ragged breath. He held the smoke for a long time, then let it out slowly. "Okay, okay, you win, I'll talk," Julio muttered grudgingly. "What do you want to know?"

"Don't want to know anything," McCarter said incredibly. "What you will do is send a message that this job was a total success. We're dead, and the warehouse was burned to the ground."

Smoking away steadily, Julio said nothing but his eyes narrowed in suspicion. "Why?" he asked, puzzled.

"Our business. And don't try to lie that it has to go through your sister," McCarter warned. "She is already in custody, and we've raided her files." Or rather Kurtzman and his cybernetic team had, the Briton thought, which was pretty much the same thing. "We know that she only relays information. Your brother runs the crew, but you make the deals."

In spite of the situation, Julio was impressed. At least the mainlanders weren't stupid enough to ask for the name of who they worked for. He had no idea. What a man didn't know couldn't be forced out by torture or used in court to bargain for an easier jail sentence.

"No, I run the crew," Julio lied glibly, dribbling smoke out of the corner of his mouth with every word. "My brother handles…handled the finances. You killed the wrong man. I don't know any codes."

"And who said anything about a code?"

The man frowned, puzzled and confused.

With a scowl, McCarter swung around the crossbow and pressed the razor-sharp tip of the quarrel against the bare throat of the wounded man. "Send the message," he stated in a flat monotone. "I won't ask again."

Rendered motionless from the presence of the barb, Julio had trouble taking his sight away from the crossbow. Instead of being made of wood like an ordinary hunting model, this was composed of slim metal tubing, with spare arrows attached to the underside. It looked lightweight and extremely deadly.

Feeling his mind starting to wander, Julio knew that lying would be almost impossible under the numbing influence of the drugs. And these men weren't trying to scare him. This was a straight deal: send the message or die. Fair enough.

Looming over the supine man, Encizo tossed a U.S. Army laptop onto the damp ground. "Get busy," he ordered.

Slumping in resignation, Julio slowly opened the lid and started to type awkwardly with his left hand.

Even though McCarter knew that Kurtzman was monitoring any outgoing signals on the Stony Man–issue laptop, he paid close attention to the coded e-mail. The ISP was for a Colombian Internet company known for not paying much attention to international law, the subject line was blank and the bulk of the message was total gibberish, created by Julio running a finger randomly across the keyboard. Only the last word was a carefully typed: "Success." Unexpectedly though, the screen name of the recipient seemed oddly familiar to McCarter. Snake Eater. Now where had he heard that name before?

CHAPTER FIVE

Argun River Valley, China

The ragged line of military trucks labored up the hillside, then came to a slow halt in a rocky field.

Staying in the idling vehicles, the company of Chinese soldiers watched the steep hill with sharp eyes, their gloved hands tight on the grip of their deadly QBZ-03 assault rifles. The 5.8 mm weapons gleamed with fresh oil, the short 30 mm grenade launchers set underneath the main barrel a dull matted black, resembling the eye of a Stygian demon. The afternoon air was cool in the mountain valley, and their breath puffed misty white from grim mouths.

Just over the next hill was the Ass of the Kurtzman. Not its official name, of course, but everybody knew what it meant. That was the route Broken Dragon company could take if they ever got the word to invade Russia.

Tugging his gloves on tighter, Lieutenant Xu Chang stood upright in the Norinco SPG and scowled at the horizon. And where the Russians would come boiling out if they ever decided to commit suicide and attack China, he thought. But nothing was in sight except trees and boulders, not a road, hut or farm. Somewhere a waterfall splashed.

Grunting in approval, Lieutenant Chang rested an arm on the big 155 mm barrel of the titanic howitzer and unbuttoned a flap on his heavy jacket.

Pulling out a GPS receiver, he carefully checked the exact position of Broken Dragon on the vector graphic map. According to the device, his company was a good kilometer from the border. Plenty of distance.

Smiling in relief, Chang tucked away the receiver. After the failed missile attack by the Americans, the Beijing high command had sent every border patrol to the very limit of the nation, watching for any sort of ground assault or covert invasion. The field lieutenant didn't think that very likely, but a good soldier didn't prepare for what the enemy might do, but for what they were capable of doing.

"All right, this will do!" Chang shouted, his words briefly visible in the cold. "Shut them down!"

In loose formation, the trucks, self-propelled guns and armor personnel carriers, turned off their engines. The vehicles were old, but serviceable, one of the 70 mm artillery pieces actually from WWII. But they chugged along the irregular mountain roads very well, even during the long rainy season. The mechanics at base kept every piece of equipment in top shape, even if an occasional bottle of whiskey had to change hands on the black market to get the needed parts.

As silence came crashing down in the valley, a gentle wind could now be heard whispering through the treetops and ruffling the flowery weeds.

Disdaining the short ladder, Chang hopped out of the vehicle and enjoyed the feel of solid ground under his boots.

"Sergeant Wu, establish a perimeter guard," he ordered, adjusting the collar of his jacket. "Ling, start lunch. Xi, begin the refueling!"

The soldiers moved with practiced ease. In short order, the valley was a bustling campsite. A group of mechanics began to haul canisters from a supply APC and started to fuel the trucks. Under the snapping voice of the fat sergeant, a dozen soldiers gathered branches from the nearby woods and spring-water hauled from the hidden falls. Soon, the smell of beef broth filled the air. Taking some heavy weapons from a 6x6 truck, another sergeant formed several groups of five and sent the patrols off to sweep the valley and hills.

Spreading out, the rest of the soldiers got comfortable on the grassy hillside. A couple of men started to clean their weapons, and several rushed to use the nearby bushes. A communications technician opened a bulky laptop and was quickly surrounded by grinning men as he surfed for pornography on the decadent Internet. A deadly serious chess game began between a private and a corporal, drawing in a larger crowd than the pornography. Everybody else started listening to music on miniheadphones attached to music players, smoking cigarettes or reading paperback books.

The valley was quite beautiful: thick green grass dotted with yellow flowers, along with some strange prickly plants that resembled a pitchfork and stood as tall as a man. Chang appreciated a lovely view, but much more importantly, the hillsides offered the company decent cover for the MRL trucks in case of trouble.

These were the most recent additions to the planned upgrading of the Chinese military. First, the high command had upgraded their rifles to the QBZ-03s, and then came new assault vehicles: trucks, APCs, MRLs and battle tanks such as the world had never seen before.

Which was how it should be, Chang noted with a swelling of pride. Machines were very important, but men won the wars.

Draped in canvas, the two MRL trucks were parked at opposite ends of the convoy, offering their vaunted protection to all. The multiple rocket launchers packed enough firepower to stop any possible invasion and send the fat Russians running back to their drunken orgies. Communists who turned capitalist? Disgusting, Chang thought. He had nothing against making a yuan now and then, but worshipping money as a way of life was a poor philosophy.

The crews of the MRL trucks considered themselves the elite of the company, and didn't mix with the rest of the soldiers. Which occasionally led to fistfights, but never in the presence of an officer. The truck crews were eating packaged rations from silver Mylar bags, while a burly technician did things under the canvas sheet. There was a lot of banging, and quite a bit of cursing, some of it extremely inventive. Apparently something wasn't behaving properly and the technician was attempting to correct the matter with sheer vulgarity, and a little help from a ball-peen hammer.

"This will keep you going until lunch, sir," a plump cook said, approaching with a steaming aluminum cup.

Nodding his thanks, Chang accepted the cup and lowered his pipe—his smoking was a rare luxury—to take a sip. Excellent. Beef broth was much better on maneuvers than tea to feed the belly and fuel the blood. An army traveled on its belly. Feed the troops and they would fight to the death for you.

The smell of the bubbling stew was spreading across the hillsides, and some of the men got out their mess kits to form a meandering line. In spite of the pipe and broth, the lieutenant's own stomach was rumbling in anticipation, but lunch would be brought to him. One of the sweeter privileges of rank.

Just then, the crowd of jeering men watching the porn stopped making noise as the communications technician touched the receiver in his ear and scowled darkly. With a curse, the technician slapped the laptop closed and started to run down the grassy hill toward Chang.

At the sight, the lieutenant felt the hairs on the back of his neck stand at attention. He didn't need twenty years of experience to know that soldiers didn't abandon their pleasure for anything less than trouble.

Stopping a few feet away, the technician threw a hasty salute. "Sir, we have air traffic coming from the west," the man declared, glancing at the rotating radar dish atop an APC. "Ten unknowns at thirty-five meters, 140 kph."

"Helicopters?" Chang growled, tossing aside the cup of broth. It hit the cold ground and steamed slightly. Grabbing the microphone hanging from his gun belt, the officer thumbed the switch.

"Alert," he said, the words booming over the PA system of the SPG. "We have incoming helicopters from the west. Take cover and prepare for battle!"

Instantly, the big pot of stew was kicked over to extinguish the campfire. Dropping whatever they were doing, the soldiers scrambled for their assault rifles and raced to take defense positions among the trees and boulders.

The rear doors of an APC were thrown open and a corporal started passing out RPG launchers and grenades. The crew of the big SPG released the holding clamps and the 155 mm howitzer whined with electric power as the cannon rose to aim down the valley. The canvas sheets were ripped off the MRL trucks, exposing the honeycomb boxes filled with red-and-green-tipped missiles. Hydraulics loudly hissed, and the MRLs pivoted about, one aiming toward the incoming helicopters, the other facing in the opposite direction in case this was a feint.

Sprinting over to the lead SPG, Chang stuck his head inside. "Corporal, tell HQ we have incoming unidentified aircraft!" he ordered brusquely. "Possibly Russians, but no visual yet. We will report again in ten minutes. If not, send in the MiGs."

"Sir!" the man answered, and turned to the radio built into the side of the SPG command-and-control.

"Tell them our exact location, then go silent," Chang snapped, grabbing a pair of binoculars. "Don't tell the enemy the vehicle is our command base."

Nodding, the radio operator was quickly setting the daily code on the scrambler, then promptly began to relay the message.

On a radar screen next to the radio, the luminous screen showed a flock of shapes moving fast along the valley. Suddenly the computer engaged and tags appeared under every blip identifying them as Russian Hind gunships.

"Base, we have a confirm," the radio operator said curtly. "Nine Russian gunships, classification Hind-D. Repeat, the Russians are approaching with gunships!"

Stepping outside, Chang pulled the .357 Norinco pistol from the holster on his hip. Dropping the clip, he checked the load, then slammed it back in and worked the slide to chamber a round for immediate use.

Only seconds later black dots appeared at the extreme end of the valley, moving fast and low over the fields of wildflowers and teasel.

Raising the binoculars, the lieutenant saw that the gunships were armed. The wing pods were fully loaded with AA and AM missiles, and minirocket pods, plus array bombs.

Softly, voices whispered in the lieutenant's earpiece about the readiness of Broken Dragon. The company was also hot and ready to go. Nervously, the man licked dry lips. Unless the Russians had one hell of an excuse, this was going to become one exciting afternoon.

Pausing a couple of hundred feet away from the Chinese convoy, the Russian helicopters spread out slightly into what was obviously an attack posture.

"Stop whatever you are doing!" a voice loudly boomed over a loudspeaker attached to the prow of the lead Hind. The words were in badly accented Cantonese. "You are on Russian soil! Turn around and go back, or you will be taken into custody!"

"Not likely," Wu snarled, thumbing a fat 30 mm brass shell into the breech of the grenade launcher of his QBZ assault rifle.

"Was that Cantonese? Do these idiots think we look like we're from Canton?" a private growled, disengaging the pistol-grip safety on the sleek Vanguard. The Russians were too close to risk using the heat-seeker function, so he switched the surface-to-air missile to radar guidance, putting his faith into the weapon techs at the Junin laboratory.

"Shut up, fool," Chang snapped in Mandarin, the official language of unified China. "Sergeant Xi, check your GPS, please."

Maybe I made a mistake? Chang thought. It's the end of my career if I made a mistake this huge!

"Sir, we're far on our side of the border," the sergeant reported crisply, double checking the electronic device in his hands. "No doubt about it, sir!"

Relaxing at the confirmation, Chang took the microphone from his belt and choose his words carefully. Russian was a difficult language to learn. Not as hard as English, perhaps, but still quite maddening with its bizarre syntax.

"Attention Russian invaders! You are mistaken!" the lieutenant loudly answered from the SPG. "We have checked our

GPS and you are over the border. Return at once, or we will be forced to open fire!"

"I repeat, you are on Russian soil," the pilot of the Hind thundered. "Leave immediately, or we shall be forced to shoot. You have five minutes."

"No, you have two minutes to get off Chinese land!" Chang snarled viciously, his hand tight on the microphone. "We will not yield to this feeble attempt to trick us into a retreat to show on your cable news shows. You are on the sovereign territory of China! Leave at once, or we will blow you from the sky!"

The helicopters did nothing for a long moment. "You now have three minutes," the lead Hind stated.

"You have sixty seconds!"

"Two minutes!"

Placing the microphone on the belt clip, Chang touched his throat mike and switched the transceiver on his belt to a general frequency. "Ready all guns," he instructed softly. "Prepare to fire on my command."

"Your time is up!" the Hind boomed, and the Russian machines began to drop lower to sweep forward in unison. "Throw down your weapons and surrender!"

Waves of adrenaline and nausea fought each other inside his stomach, and for a long second the lieutenant thought he was going to be sick in front of his men. Then a cold calm filled the officer and he touched the throat mike again. "All guns, fire," he commanded, the words puffy white.

Out of the MRL came pulsating stilettos of flame that moved across the honeycomb as the banks of missiles launched in rapid succession. As the rockets streaked down the valley, two of the Russian gunships opened fire with electric miniguns, while the rest moved quickly away. Half of the Chinese rockets were destroyed in midflight, but the rest hit the lead Hind broadside and it erupted into a staggering fire-ball, shattered glass, bodies and pieces of fiberglass shards spraying across the field in a hellish rain.

Now, the Chinese soldiers cut loose with their assault rifles, and the Russian gunships swept the miniguns along the line of parked vehicles. The barrage of incoming lead bounced harmlessly off the armed chassis of the SPC, APC and MRLs, but three of the trucks exploded. Shrieking in agony, burning men dashed from the wrecks, waving their arms.

Instantly the Chinese launched a salvo of ground-to-air missiles from the MRL truck, and one of the gunships deto-nated. Then the colossal 155 mm howitzer spoke, the report deafening everybody within a hundred feet. The shell hit an-other Hind, punching in the hull and coming out the other side before exploding. But then six of the remaining Hinds un-leashed missiles that slammed into the SMG and the lead MRL truck, blowing them off the ground in strident fury.

The Chinese troops sent more Vanguards airborne, but this time the guided missiles veered wildly into the hills, their radar jammed by the Russian gunships.

The last MRL took out another Hind, then it was also de-stroyed by a missile salvo. Darting about on the ground, the Chinese troops pounded the Russian with artillery. The gun-ships replied with rockets and a score of the Chinese died, torn into bloody bits.

Snarling curses, Sergeant Xi launched an antitank weapon at a Hind, the meager supply of Vanguard rockets already dispersed among the combat troops. The deadhead rocket streaked skyward and glanced off the armored side of a Hind to smash directly through the cockpit window of another. The interior filled with flames, and the gunship began to rotate, spraying its miniguns randomly, the heavy slugs bouncing off the other Russian helicopters. Then the rotor came off and spun away into the hills as the battered chassis dropped from the sky. The tons of metal crashed on top of a group of boulders, and the cargo of munitions detonated in a wild staccato of dull explosions. Hot shrapnel went everywhere, ricocheting off the rocks, and a dozen Chinese soldiers fell, their uniforms reduced to bloody tatters.

Explosions, acrid smoke, fire and screams filled the mountain valley as the deadly fighting rapidly escalated into total chaos....

Sonora, Texas

SHIFTING GEARS AT A TRAFFIC light, the unmarked van rolled through the intersection of the town and parked alongside the curb in front of the sheriff's office. The brick building was two stories high, the second-floor windows covered with steel bars set into the frames, not merely bolted to the outside as an addition. Clearly, this was the holding facility.

Stepping from the van, Carl Lyons approved. Setting the jail on the second floor would make it that much harder for someone to try to release a friend. Smart.

Slinging a nylon bag over his shoulder, Rosario Blancanales went to the sidewalk while Gadgets Schwarz pressed a fob on his key chain to set the security systems of the nondescript vehicle. The old van was their rolling command base on a mission, carrying an arsenal of weapons, medical supplies, fake ID, changes of clothing, burglary tools and a small electronics lab. Modified by Schwarz and Cowboy Kissinger, the vehicle was able to protect itself from car-jackers with electric stun guns built into the door handles, and BZ gas grenades hidden under the seats for anybody determined enough to get inside. If all else failed, any member of Able Team could trip the self-destruct with a simple phone call, and five blocks of thermite would instantly reduce the million-dollar vehicle into a bubbling puddle of steel.

Pushing their way through the door, the Able Team paused to soak in the deliciously cool air-conditioning of the sheriff's office. It was easily more than one hundred degrees outside, and stepping from their plane at the abandoned military airfield fifty miles outside of Sonora had been like entering a blast furnace. Even before the men had cycled down the ramp of the Hercules to unloaded the van, they were dripping with sweat and bitterly sorry they hadn't taken Kissinger's sage advice and brought along Stetson hats and neckerchiefs. There were only baseball caps and sunglasses in the equipment locker. Standard FBI issue. They didn't help much, but were a lot better than nothing.

During the long, hot ride into town, the Stony Man commandos noticed that every house they saw had a flower box, the colorful plants carefully situated under a wide awning for some vital shade. Water sprinklers formed shimmering rainbows as they struggled to keep the lawns green, and ivy seemed to be growing over everything that stood still.

Following a paper map bought at a gas station, the team found the sheriff's office.

Standing behind a waist-high wooden divider, the men of Able Team saw a large man sitting at a battered wooden desk, a pair of cowboy boots resting on top. The fellow was dressed in a loose tan uniform, and a shiny sheriff's badge was pinned to his shirt. A Sam Browne gun belt was wrapped around his waist, the J-frame handle of an old 1930-style revolver jutting from his holster. His black boots were polished to a high shine and had spurs. Completely bald, the man sported a large mustache with just a sprinkling of gray along the edges.

Somewhere a telephone was ringing, which the sheriff ignored. A moment later, the answering machine picked up the call and relayed a message about having no fresh information about the mysterious explosion of the previous night. The caller rang off abruptly.

Surreptitiously, Able Team exchanged glances. A lot of folks had to have been inquiring about the blast. With a nod, the men changed their story from being representatives of an insurance company. Pulling out FBI commission booklets, they opened them up and tucked the booklets into their belts so that the photo ID was clearly showing.

"Good morning," Lyons said, wiping his forehead with a handkerchief. "Sheriff Terrance W. Andrews?"

"That's me," said the bald man, lowering the newspaper he'd been reading. "What can I do for you DOD boys today?"

The smiles froze on the faces of the three Stony Man commandos.

Slowly, Blancanales removed his sunglasses. "Sorry, we're FBI," he started. But then was cut off by a laugh from the big Texan.

"Shoot, boy, that weird warehouse has been in our backyard for nigh twenty years," the sheriff said, putting his boots on the floor. The spurs softly jingled. "And the only folks who ever went there were in unmarked vans and wore dark suits." The big Texan laughed. "Only a damn fool would think it was full of used Army boots. DOD is the best guess down at Charlie's Bar and Grill. Although, the NSA is running a close second." His face got serious. "So what was it, a deep storage facility for defunct documents? Or full of dead alien corpses?"

Tucking his sunglasses into a shirt pocket, Lyons said nothing, but immediately raised his opinion of the county sheriff. This was the sort of lawman who had tamed the Wild West.

Tough as boiled leather and razor smart. They'd better stick as close to the truth as possible or risk blowing their cover completely.

"No alien bodies were stored here. Just secret documents," Lyons said. "But you didn't hear it from me."

Andrews shrugged, not particularly swayed by the admission.

"We could have been drug smugglers," Blancanales suggested, resting a hand near his fake FBI identification. The commission booklet was fake only in that Able Team wasn't working for the FBI. Everything else about them was real, including the identification numbers. A call to the FBI headquarters at Quantico would yield the service records of the three special agents in good standing, along with the matching photographs of the Able Team. The information had been uploaded into the FBI mainframe computers less than an hour earlier by Aaron Kurtzman's cyber team.

"Smugglers?" Waving that aside, the sheriff walked closer. "Nah, drug dealers dress much nicer than you three, and then always come into town looking for girls. We got girls, but not the kind they want."

"Girl Scouts?" Schwarz guessed wryly, peeking over the top of his sunglasses.

Stopping on the other side of the wooden barrier, Andrews chuckled. "Them's the ones. Well, come on, I got the crime-scene report over here."

Pushing open the gate in the divider, the law enforcement officer let the Stony Man team enter. He escorted them to a desk piled with papers and took the only chair. "Grab a seat, boys, there's plenty to go around."

Taking a wooden chair from a nearby desk, Lyons turned it around so that he could sit with both arms resting on top. "Were you the FOS?"

The sheriff arched an eyebrow. "First on scene? Hellfire and damnation, son, I was the only one here."

"Got any coffee?" Schwarz asked hopefully. The pot at a small table seemed cold and unused.

"Not at the moment. But there's beer in the fridge," the sheriff said, jerking a thumb. "Lone Star. Best damn beer in the world."

"I have a friend named T.J. who would heartily agree," Schwarz said, pulling four bottles from the small refrigerator. Inside was a lot more beer, several wrapped sandwiches and a dozen or so boxes of ammunition. The cold helped them last longer. Obviously, things were tight in Sonora, in spite of the local banners announcing a forthcoming major restoration and civic pride parade.

Schwarz passed around the bottles.

"That your grandfather's gun?" Blancanales asked, indicating the S&W revolver.

"Good eye," Andrews said, opening his beer and taking a pull from the bottle. "Ah, that's the stuff! But then, you boys have the look of combat soldiers rather than paper pushers from D.C. Y'all gonna tell me what was really in that warehouse?"

The men of the Able Team got comfortable in their chairs and drank some more beer. A minute passed, then another.

"Can we see the report now?" Lyons asked, inspecting the condensation trickling down the side of the dark glass.

"Yeah, thought so." The sheriff sighed in resignation, pushing over the folder. "Not much in it, really. Everybody in town heard the explosion at roughly midnight. Took me to until twelve-forty-five to get out that way 'cause..." Andrews paused, looking a little embarrassed. "I was with my lady friend, and you know how it is. Once a man is committed to a job, you can't just leave in the middle."

Sharing a good-natured laugh with the lawman, Able Team raised their bottles and clinked the glass in solidarity.

"You heard the blast while…romantically engaged," Blancanales said thoughtfully. "So everybody in town must have heard the explosion."

"Sure. Sounds travel far on the desert, especially at night. It rattled the china on the wall of the truck-stop diner and damn near gave old Mrs. Coply another heart attack. She thought it was the Rapture and ran outside in her skivvies to meet Jesus."

"Hallelujah," Schwarz said, riffling through the photographs of the ruins. "Nice work on the crime shots." There were a few pieces of what resembled the frame of a large truck mixed with the smashed bricks and smashed electronics. One body was lying on the sand, covered with a sheet. The driver of the tanker had only been recovered in small pieces. An attached note said that human teeth had been recovered twenty yards away.

"Used an old Kodak," Andrews said proudly. "Works every time. Digital cameras are shit for night work."

"No argument there," Schwarz replied.

"Any strangers in town?" Blancanales asked. "Maybe a busload of lost tourists?"

The sheriff said nothing, but slowly raised a single eloquent eyebrow.

"Sorry, had to ask."

Andrews shrugged. "Be fools if you didn't."

"Now, you found only the two bodies?" Lyons asked, leaning forward to rest elbows on his knees.

"Well, yes and no," the sheriff said, taking a long drink and then placing aside the empty. "There were only those two corpses at the scene, but that throat slash on the guard…" He shook his head. "Damn me for a fool, but that was no accidental piece of flying glass. Oh, it matches the window glass from the tanker, but it just happened to hit the guard exactly in the carotid artery? No way."

"So you think there was somebody else at the crash site?"

The sheriff stroked his mustache. "You tell me."

Skimming the reports, the Stony Man team gave no response, which the sheriff seemed to take as acquiescence to the theory.

"Besides, that blast was way too big for just ten thousand gallons of gasoline," the sheriff continued. "Must have been some explosives inside the warehouse, and from those burn marks, looks like the kind of thermite charges we used back in Nam. A paranoid man might think those were self-destruct charges that got triggered by the burning fuel."

"Any tracks leading away from the crash site?" Lyons asked, feeling slightly foolish. The sheriff had the whole matter nailed, but the man knew how to play the game and would pretend to be fooled until he was let into the case. Which would be never. Andrews was smart, but they were facing people who don't fight by the rules. Against these kind of terrorists, he would be completely out of his league.

"Tracks? Again, yes and no. Might have found some tire tracks other side of a sand dune that took the brunt of the detonation. That'd be where I would have hidden my escape vehicle. But with this wind, I was lucky to have found anything."

"Any idea what type of vehicle?" Lyons asked pointedly. "A Hummer or possibly an ATV?"

"My call would be a pair of motorcycles. BMW Explorer, most likely. They're silent, fast and can take the sand without choking."

He got all that from tire tracks? Schwarz thought. Placing aside the photographs, he tilted his head. "Okay, what color were they?"

"The name is Andrews, not Sherlock Holmes," the sheriff said, rising to get another round of beers. "I'm good, but not that fragging good."

Closing the refrigerator, the sheriff passed out the bottles, and added, "But if you want my guess," he said, twisting off the cap, "I'd say black, with the trim removed to keep down any stray reflections. Mexican stealth bikes. Illegal immigrants use them all the time to try to outrace the border patrol."

Laying down the folder, Lyons looked out the window at the gentle breeze blowing dusty outside. Any tracks would have been obliterated in less than an hour. It seemed the man had arrived just in time to get what little there was in the folder. That was a mistake on the part of the terrorists. They probably thought a small-town sheriff would be lazy and take his own sweet time getting there in the morning, and stumble about, ruining everything. But Andrews was as sharp as they came. Lyons glanced at the old 1930-style police revolver. The sheriff was probably the son of a son of a cop, and had crime-scene procedure burned into his bones.

"Any idea where they went?" Schwarz asked, inspecting a photograph of the sand. There was a dim impression of tire tracks, but it was almost impossible to tell for sure. Pulling out a Swiss Army knife, he thumbed out the tiny magnifying glass and squinted hard.

"Can't say for sure where they went," Andrews said, looking through the bottle and lost in thought for a moment. "But the most logical thing would be for them to head for the access road and take the highway out of here. They couldn't fly anywhere last night, what with the ICBM launch over at the military base. Their radar sometimes ruins TV reception. Everybody had to get cable a few years ago or never see Leno again."

"No planes or helicopters," Blancanales said thoughtfully. "Might have used a hovercraft."

"Or a radar jammer," Schwarz said, thinking out loud. They had encountered one of those before in a matter involving missiles.

The sheriff frowned. "A what? Who did this, the fucking KGB? Or them al Qaeda?"

The Stony Man operatives smiled in casual dismissal. However, the big Texan was closer to the truth than he thought.

"Well, thank you for all the help, Sheriff," Blancanales said, returning the folder. "I think it's time that we go check the crime scene now."

"Just wanted to see how the locals had run the evidence before checking it out firsthand, eh?" Andrews said with a knowing wink. "Make sure we're not morons taking souvenirs or running around with our dicks swinging in the wind, before you tried to analyze scuff marks and carpet fibers."

"Something like that," Lyons admitted honestly. Damn, the man was fast. "No offense meant."

"None taken. Would have done the same thing myself." As the sheriff tilted back his head to drain the bottle, a ripple of light passed across the room.

Instantly, the three Stony Man commandos froze their expressions, combat instincts honed in a thousand battles flaring to full awareness.

"Well, well, I'd say that you boys have been made," the sheriff drawled, rubbing the bottle against a cheek. "Somebody sure as shit seems to be watching us through binoculars."

Or the telescopic sight of a snipe rifle, Lyons thought.

"Keep smiling, and don't speak again," the Able Team leader said, rising laconically from his chair and offering a hand to the sheriff. His back itched from keeping it turned toward the window. "They might have a lip reader on the other end of the scope."

Giving a crooked grin, the sheriff nodded.

Suddenly, Lyons realized that was why Andrews had put the bottle to his cheek, to hide his mouth. Sharp. The man was icy cool and razor sharp.

"Got any enemies?" Schwarz asked, covering his face with a raised arm as he unnecessarily adjusted his sunglasses.

Bending at the waist, the sheriff dropped an empty into the wastebasket and put his back to the window. "Lots. But nobody with the balls to try to stir up trouble in my town," he said savagely, then turned around and rose, waving a hand toward the front door.

Moving away from the window, the men paused as the wall blocked any possible view of them from outside. Quickly, they pulled guns and checked the loads, working slides and clicking off safeties.

"Need a hand?" Andrews asked, tucking the S&W revolver back into the holster. "I know you DOD boys don't like to share the wealth, but I'm a hell of a shot. Got a squirrel once with this blunderbuss and think I can do it again with a man."

Lyons started to turn down the offer, then reconsidered the matter and slowly smiled. Yeah, maybe the big Texan could help after all.

WATCHING THROUGH THE scope of the FN-2000 assault rifle, Lieutenant Henrietta Caramico saw the front door of the sheriff's office open and three men walk out. Adjusting their sunglasses and baseball caps, they went to a van parked at the curb, started the engine and drove away toward the south.

"The warehouse is west of here," Sergeant Roberto Mendoza said through tight lips, an assault rifle cradled in his arms. "Think they're going to circle around from behind?"

"Only a fool would drive there directly," the lieutenant said, reluctantly lowering the weapon and turning off the computer-enhanced optics.

It would have been easy to kill the four men inside the building, but that wasn't the plan. If the general wanted prisoners, then that is what he would get. Once these DOD agents got far enough away from town, they would be taken captive by her team waiting in the sand dunes. So far, the Americans had done nothing clever or unexpected. This mission was a cakewalk. Soon enough, they would be back in the Black Fortress, watching the end of the world on television and preparing for the long journey home to Argentina.

Just then, the front door to the sheriff's office was flung open and the man dashed outside to a old Jeep in the parking lot. Starting the siren, he took off to the east, the light behind the grill flashing red and blue. Clearly something was happening to the west of here.

"Must be trouble at the airstrip," Mendoza muttered, shading his face with a raised hand. "Maybe a plane crashed." There was nothing in sight, no smoke or fire. Then again, it could be a simple bar fight or a stolen car.

Looking down at the brick building, Caramico powered up the optics and checked the office through the window again. The manila folder was lying in plain sight on a desk covered with empty beer bottles.

"Call in the rest of the team," she ordered, slinging her weapon. "Have them recon the warehouse and watch what the Feds do. I'm going after that file."

"Ma'am, is that wise?" the sergeant asked with a frown.

"We're here for information, aren't we?" Caramico replied,

climbing onto her BMW motorcycle. The big engine started with a barely audible purr. "You stay here and watch my back in case that old man comes back."

"And if he does?"

"Kill him," she ordered, pulling on a motorcycle helmet.

The acne-scarred soldier smiled in return, resting a hand on the knife at his hip. As a teenager studying to be a physician, Mendoza had quarreled with a teacher over a test grade, the fight ending with the other man dead and Mendoza on the run from the federal police. A few years later during the Dirty War of '83, Mendoza had used his detailed knowledge of human anatomy and deadly skills with a knife to aid the winning side and earn a full parole—if he joined the military. General Calvano had found Private Mendoza soon after that and recruited the man into Forge as the covert organization's unofficial interrogation expert. As word spread of his bloody handiwork, the Communists started to avoid Calvano's battalion, often canceling missions that had been months in the planning rather than risk being captured alive and given over to the brutal military inquisitor.

"I'll try to be inventive, Lieutenant," Mendoza promised, his dark eyes bright with inhuman delight.

"Just be quick." She grunted impatiently, swinging down the face shield. Her features were completely hidden. "The sooner we're gone from this wretched land, the better." Twisting the handlebar controls, Caramico rode away in a cloud of dust, and soon was moving stealthily among the acacia trees and juniper bushes.

With the hot wind ruffling his hair, Mendoza watched the lieutenant ride into the town through the telescopic sights of the FN-2000. Although he was a knife expert, the soldier was very impressed by the bullpup assault rifle.

The brand-new weapon was only part of the Argentinean government's attempt to try to propel the nation's military into the twenty-first century. Ten years ago, the army had been armed with whatever they could get their hands on, "grease guns" from WWII, M-1 rifles from the Korean War, Stirlings and so on. But with the abolishment of the South American debt, the nation suddenly had the financial ability to rearm the entire army into a single unified fighting force. The sergeant fondly remembered the last time his company had tangled with the rebels in the hilly Andes Mountains. It had been like stepping on bugs. All the Communists could do was scream and run. He got in a lot of practice with his blades that night, and soon the bodies were stacked like cordwood. It was a special time, and a cherished memory.

Adjusting the computerized controls on the optics, Mendoza tracked the lieutenant as she followed a bike trail through the park to avoid the open streets. The dorsal fin–shaped blade on top of the weapon contained a host of optical systems, telescopic, infrared and even a Starlite function, which allowed a gunner to clearly see the enemy in virtually no light at all. Just the faint glimmer of the distant stars above was enough.

Suddenly, an old man walking his dog was startled by the appearance of the lieutenant on her BMW, and seemed to be shouting at her. Pulling a silenced pistol from within her jacket, Caramico shot down the civilian along with his dog, and kept going.

"You should have saved him for me." Mendoza chuckled softly. "The elderly have little life remaining, so they cling to what's left with fierce determination."

"You are a sick bastard," a gruff voice said in Spanish from behind him, and he heard a metallic click-clack. "Now drop the weapon or I'll blow your fucking head off."

Instantly the big sergeant went motionless. There was no mistaking the ominous sound of a hammer being thumbed back into the firing position on a revolver.

CHAPTER SIX

Badlands, North Dakota

Reaching out a trembling hand, Edward Greenbaum grabbed hold of a jagged rock barely jutting from the sheer rock face. Testing the outcropping to make sure it could hold his weight, Greenbaum then carefully shifted his spiked boots and rose another few inches up the side of the towering mesa.

As he had read numerous times in journals and Web sites, North Dakota had some of the most barren and inhospitable regions on the face of the earth. In his younger days, Greenbaum had been to both the Sahara Desert and Antarctica. But for his money there was no larger expanse of nothingness than good old North Dakota.

It made the Nullabor Plains of Australia look like Disneyland, Edward noted, then forced his attention back to the climbing.

Some fools said mountaineering wasn't a sport, but it took more guts to climb a mountain than charge a defensive line in football. There were rules and laws preventing the fullbacks from inflicting too much damage. Even in hockey, there were referees and a penalty box. But mountains had no restrictions or limitations, and did everything in their power to kill off a climber. Shifting rocks, crumbling cliffs, high winds, blazing sun. Once when a line broke, Greenbaum had been forced to stand still as a colony of ants climbed through his clothing biting all the way.

"Not a sport, my ass," the man growled, pulling out a piton and using the hammer attached by a lariat to his belt to drive the steel pin into the rocks.

Gingerly testing the piton, he then clicked on the coupling attaching his rope to the new anchor, and eased the tension in his legs to rest for a minute. But suddenly, there was a sharp crack, and the rock beneath his boots broke away from the cliff face.

Instantly tightening his handholds, the man felt adrenaline surge through his body as his left leg swung free into space. Stay calm, he urged himself. Use fingers and palms. Heart against the stone. Use your body to stay in place. Friction is your friend!

Minutely adjusting his position, Greenbaum found a secure footing and stayed in place for several minutes just breathing in the cool, dry air. Whew, safe again, he thought. That had been close.

Wisely, the man had assaulted the penumbra side of the mesa. The morning sun casted cool, dark shadows, which meant he would sweat less, need less water, stay strong longer, and the rocks were less likely to sheer away.

Taking a judicious sip from the water tube at his collar, Greenbaum continued the perilous climb. Foot by foot, yard by yard, the man grimly moved across the side of the mesa, following the zigzag path of crevices and cracks. It was high noon when he finally saw the top of the Black Rock Mesa. Victory!

Reaching out, Greenbaum took hold of the edge and tried to lift himself, and felt it move slightly only a heartbeat before the rock splintered. As his handhold came loose, the man swung away from the rocks desperately clawing at the empty air. Digging in with his left hand, he spread his legs wide in an effort to brace himself fast. Eight hundred feet below there was only sand and rock. With his heart pounding wildly, Greenbaum tried to banish that thought as he felt the rope around his waist tighten, and then abruptly loosen. The piton had come free!

Frantically reaching for the cliff, Greenbaum unexpectedly heard footsteps crunching on the loose windblown sand and from out of nowhere a gloved hand reached down and grabbed his wrist in an iron grip.

"Hold on, I've got you!" a man shouted from above, the blazing sun casting his features into blackness. "Don't let go!"

"Don't get too close to the edge!" Greenbaum warned in response, tightening his hold on the stranger's forearm. The muscles beneath the cloth were like a bundle of steel cables. A fellow climber? he thought. Had to be. There was no other way to reach the top of Black Rock Mesa aside from using a helicopter.

Now with an anchor, Greenbaum levered himself upward, and got an elbow over the cliff. Another hand reached out to grab his climbing vest, and the climber let go with his left hand to claw the irregular surface of the mesa until finding a new hold.

Grunting in unison, the two men strained to the task, but the mountaineer was finally hauled over the precipice and onto solid ground.

"Thanks...." Greenbaum wheezed, breathing in the delicious smell of the hot sand and relishing the sheer joy of not holding on to anything for a second.

"No problem," the other man said with a chuckle. "Drink?"

A military canteen came into view, but Greenbaum waved it aside and got his own, savoring the vitamin-enhanced sport drink.

"Can't believe that I made it," he said, lowering the canteen and wiping his mouth dry on a hairy arm. "That was one bitch of a climb."

"A real bitch," the stranger replied, crossing his massive arms. "I would not have believed it possible that anybody could climb this thing. *Madre mia,* this is eight hundred feet high!"

"Nine hundred and ten." Pouring some of his drink into a palm, Greenbaum wiped down his dusty face. "So how'd you get up here?" he asked, squinting at the other fellow. "And who are you?"

"Reinhold, Sigerson Reinhold."

"Ed Greenbaum." He paused. "Er...Sigerson?"

Brushing back his hair, Reinhold shrugged. "Parents, what can you do, eh?"

Chuckling, Greenbaum rose to his feet. "Yeah, I know what you mean. I have a cousin named Hyman Bender. And the millionaire who created the Learjet, John Lear? He named his kids King and Chanda."

"No!"

"God's truth."

Laughing to the obvious lie, Reinhold took a look over the edge of the mesa. "So where's the rest of your party?" he asked, sounding concerned. "Are they on the other side? Or at your base camp?"

"There's nobody else," Greenbaum said, raising a hand to shield his face from the sun. Now that he could see the other fellow, he was a big man, wide shoulders and narrow waist like a professional dancer. "I always climb alone. It's more fun that way."

"Fun?" Reinhold turned from the open air. "Way out here? Isn't that dangerous?"

"Usually, no," Greenbaum admitted honestly. "But Black Rock Mesa is rather famous for being… How did you get up here again?"

"Helicopter," Reinhold said, flashing a smile. "Well, we really should get you back down to your truck."

"Motorcycle," Greenbaum corrected. "A sweet little Beamer Explorer. A ride down would be great. Don't often have that kind of an option. Just let me catch my breath first and do a scan."

The other man blinked. "A scan?" he repeated in confusion.

"Didn't make it to the top to go home empty-handed," Greenbaum said, pulling out his cell phone and activating the digital camera to take a panoramic view of the flat-top mesa for his Web site. Once on his Web site, this was going to become wallpaper for ten thousand climbers around the globe.

"Hey, folks!" Greenbaum called cheerfully, starting to turn in a circle. "Welcome from—"

A shot rang out and he felt a numbing blow to his hand.

In shock, Greenbaum saw the shattered remains of the cell phone fly away to bounce off the rocky ground and scatter over the edge of the mesa, spraying into the dry winds.

Spinning furiously, he gawked in surprise at the four men in camouflage-colored uniforms rising from behind a small pile of weeds and boulders.

"What the hell is going on here?" Greenbaum demanded angrily.

One of the men growled something in what sounded like Spanish, and Reinhold replied. Spreading out, the four men then worked the arming bolts on strange-looking assault rifles. Greenbaum knew something about weapons; he often read military adventure novels. But these things resembled something from a sci-fi movie, sleek and compact, with two different-size barrels.

"What is the Army doing all the way up here?" he demanded, suddenly feeling nervous. "Your helicopter break down or something?"

Without speaking, the grim men advanced, their weapons pointed directly at him.

"Look here, guys, if I stumbled onto some sort of Green Beret training mission, I can just go back down the mesa," the mountain climber offered, licking dry lips. There was a folding knife at his hip, good for cutting rope, but about as useful as a throw rock against these kinds of weapons. "Now, I'm a loyal American. I can keep my trap shut if this some kind of a cover thing. No problem there! You can trust me!"

Softly, the wind whispered across the top of the mesa, carrying away all of the accumulated heat of the distant sun.

Resting the stock of the FN-2000 assault rifle on a hip, one of the uniformed men spoke in Spanish again.

"Because I didn't want to waste half a day having you wash this fool's blood off the rocks below," Reinhold explained brusquely. "Now we know he is alone, and riding a BMW motorcycle. There is no need to torture a man, if he will give you the needed information willingly. It is wasteful and inefficient."

Utterly stunned, Greenbaum snapped his head toward the man who had rescued him only moments ago. Torture. What the hell was going on here?

Slinging the assault rifle over a shoulder, one of the soldiers pulled out a knife; the edge shone mirror-bright in the harsh sunshine.

Instantly alert, Greenbaum moved fast and kicked some dirt into the face of the soldier. Dropping the blade, the man staggered backward rubbing his eyes and cursing. Diving forward, the mountaineer grabbed the blade and came up slashing in a killing technique he hadn't practiced in twenty years. But the years spent in the dojo proved their worth, and a second man fell back, his hands gushing blood, the assault rifle tumbling free.

Grabbing the unfamiliar weapon, Greenbaum fumbled to find the safety, when Reinhold slammed the edge of his hand into his exposed throat. Hacking for air, the climber lost the weapon. But then Reinhold frowned as Greenbaum dropped into a Judo stance and lashed out a fist, thumb slightly extended for a killing blow to the throat. The professor nimbly dodged the blow, moving amazingly fast, and dropped into a crouch to sweep out a leg and send his adversary to the ground. He hit with a martial-arts cry, slapping the rock to absorb the force of the fall, and rolled over into a defensive stance.

The remaining two soldiers moved forward, but stopped at a command from their leader.

"Mine!" Reinhold snapped, lashing out a boot, the steel toe smashing directly into the bruised throat once more.

Unable to breath at all, Greenbaum scrambled away from the men, ripping open his jacket to reach for the pull-cords of the parachute strapped to his back. Gotta escape! Jump, catch the winds, dodge their bullets, move-move-move! he thought.

The mountaineer was only yards from the edge, leaning into the wind, when he collided with two more men in the strange desert uniforms. They seemed to come from out of nowhere. Then Greenbaum saw that their uniforms were different from the other soldiers, and hope filled his face for an instant. Until he saw their cold eyes and knew death had arrived.

Adrenaline fueled his muscles, and Greenbaum jumped for the edge, but was tackled hard to the rocky ground by one of the new arrivals. He rolled over to try to take both of them off the mesa, but more soldiers arrived, punching and kicking until he fell, panting, to the hot sand. Every part of his body hurt. Blood seemed to be everywhere, and the world was slowly spinning.

"Edward, Edward." The professor sighed in disappointment. "May I call you Ed? Alas, I truly dislike bloodshed. And you can still leave here alive." Reinhold paused to rub his bruised arm. "We know the man you are climbing with is an escaped convict. We only want him, not you, Ed. Not you. Stop protecting your friend. Tell us where he is, and you go free."

Dribbling blood from his mouth, Greenbaum looked up in fervent hope. "You…got wrong guy," he mumbled, more crimson bubbling out with every word. "Don't have a climbing partner…work alone. I'm…not the guy…you want."

Inhaling deeply, Reinhold nodded. "See? All you have to do is ask correctly and civilians will tell you anything you need to know."

In spite of the pain, Greenbaum couldn't believe what he'd just heard. Another trick? "No, wait! I lied! I have a climbing partner…."

Pulling a big automatic pistol from inside his shirt, the professor smiled. "No, you don't," he whispered, and shot the man in the side of the head. Blood and brains exploded across the sandy rocks, a few drops flying off into space and carried away by the dry wind.

"How many times do I have to tell you, always make sure the civilian is alone," Reinhold stated, holstering the 9 mm Bersa pistol. "Then you can execute the intruder."

One of the soldiers replied in fluent Spanish. They understood English, but their accent was so pronounced, it had been deemed wiser to not even have them attempt to pass as American soldiers. Even in California, it was painfully obvious these were foreigners.

"Yes, that's why I didn't simply let him drop before," Reinhold replied impatiently. "He might have reported to a Dakota park ranger which mesa he was planning to climb. If they came here and found a body—well, a stain at the bottom—then there would be an investigation. More rangers, maybe even police. But if a climber goes into the Badlands and simply disappears, it will be days before the authorities decide to check on his whereabouts. And by then, this will be over."

Still rubbing sand from his eyes, another soldier spoke.

"Yes, it will be good to go back home," the professor agreed. "Now take the body down the elevator and drive his vehicle off a cliff far away from here."

As the Forge soldiers got busy, Reinhold went to the collection of boulders and lifted a steel hatch painted to resemble the sandy rock. Climbing down the access ladder, the professor descended deep into the subterranean complex.

At the bottom of the ladder, the professor stomped his boots on the concrete floor to get off the sand. Tiny dust clouds billowed behind him as the man headed for the elevator banks. There were three sets of doors, but only the one on the left worked. The others were death traps for invaders. Readiness was all, as the general liked to say. True words, indeed.

Hitting the button for the communications center, Reinhold relaxed as cool air started blowing from the wall vents. Irritably, he rubbed the calloused edge of his aching hand. He never thought the short American would have proved to be such a formidable opponent. Rock-climbing enthusiasts were a lot tougher than expected. He'd have to make a mental note to remember that in the future. The man had been good. He grinned. Just not good enough.

Glancing at the security mirror set in the corner, Reinhold brushed back his prematurely thinning hair. He was middle-aged, but not weak. A strong mind deserved a strong body.

Gently slowing to a stop, the elevator doors opened with a pneumatic sigh and Reinhold walked past the armed guards standing behind a low barricade of sandbags. A lot of the equipment inside the mesa had been extremely difficult to smuggle into America, so it made only good sense to use as many natural materials as possible. Sandbags were one of the best barriers to gunfire, and a lot easier to transport than sheets of Lexan plastic or titanium-steel armor plating.

Passing a section of the tunnel lined with Claymore anti-personnel mines, the professor remembered how long it had taken Forge to find a suitable mesa, and then finish off the natural caves to make enough room for the power generators, barracks, storage facilities and uplink equipment. The FBI and Homeland Security were always on the prowl for munitions coming over the borders, but nobody thought twice about electrical equipment. Almost everything else had been purchased openly, or through a series of blind drops, unmarked cars passing each other in an empty parking lot in the middle of the night.

Bemused, the man smiled at the memory. It had taken three long years, but now Forge had a fully functional firebase situated smack in the middle of the continental United States.

A viper hidden in their bosom that would strike down the fat Americans, once and forever, Reinhold thought, showing a half grin. Their greed had destroyed the natural balance of the world, so it seemed only fitting for them to take the blame for the awful repairs about to begin.

The end was coming, nothing and nobody could stop that now. If there was some other way it could have been done, the professor would gladly have suggested the solution to the general. But this was the only answer. Billions of lives would be lost, but that would save a billion more.

Reaching an intersection, Reinhold nodded to the armed guards behind the next sandbag nest. One smiled and nodded, the other frowned.

"Password," he said in rather good English.

"What? Get out of my way, fool, I have no time for this nonsense," Reinhold began, starting forward.

But the soldier worked the bolt on his bullpup assault rifle. "Password," he demanded, leveling the deadly weapon.

From this angle, the professor could actually see the 40 mm AP round in the stubby grenade launcher situated under the main barrel. At this range, the stainless steel fléchettes in the antipersonnel shell would tear him into bloody gobbets. He knew that for a fact, having seen it done to some Communist rebels back in Argentina. The men had died never even knowing what happened. One moment they were alive and charging the Andes firebase, and the next they were gone, scattered debris on the snowy ground. Red on white. Wine spilled on a white tablecloth.

"Firestorm," Reinhold stated, feeling his stomach tighten slightly at the unpleasant prospect of his own demise.

"Pass, sir," the soldier said, raising the weapon and gesturing onward.

"Well done, trooper," the professor said, approaching the nest. "My compliments. I like to test my men, and make sure they are alert and ready."

"Ah, thank you, Professor," the soldier said awkwardly, easing off the arming bolt. "Just doing my job, sir."

"Indeed you were," the professor agreed, then he turned to

scowl at the other soldier. "On the other hand, you would have let me pass."

The man swallowed hard. "But, sir, I—"

"Ten extra watches standing guard and a reduction in pay for a week," Reinhold snapped. "Do it again, and you will leave this mesa by the stairs."

The soldier went pale. The stairs, that was their name for falling off the top of the mesa. Or being thrown off. "Yes, sir!" he said crisply, giving a stiff salute.

Pretending that he didn't know what it meant for a soldier to salute inside, Reinhold proceeded to a steel panel closing off the end of the tunnel. The men had to have their petty rebellions.

Going to a sensor plate set into the curved wall, Reinhold placed his hand on the dark plastic and kept still as the UV light scanned his finger and palm prints. There came a click, and a vector graphic of a keypad appeared on the plate. Tapping in the entry code, the professor waited while the steel panel slid aside on greased wheels. The double lock seemed a little like overkill, but better safe than sorry. An enemy might be able to fool one, but not both safeguards. The professor felt sure that nobody was getting into CNC without his express permission.

Inside command and control, the professor shivered slightly from the chill in the air. His breath didn't quite fog, but he was sure that it was close to freezing. However, the banks of Cray supercomputers that controlled the uplink array needed the low temperature to operate at their maximum levels. Tanks of liquid nitrogen were stored alongside the computers, a simple thermostat set to trigger more of the supercold liquid as needed. The system was simple, elegant and almost foolproof.

When they were setting up the apparatus, a technician had

accidentally gotten a finger sprayed with the liquid nitrogen, and before Reinhold could get the finger warm, the technician had bumped his hand and the finger shattered like antique glass. At the sight, the screaming man fainted dead away. Once the poor fellow had stabilized in the medical bay, the professor had sent him to the Firebase Alpha on a commercial flight out of Fargo, but knew that his career with Forge was in serious jeopardy. The general didn't tolerate fools gladly, and his anger was legendary. What Calvano had done to the rebels that his troops had captured during the '83 war had earned him the secret nickname Torquemada, after the ruthless priest in charge of the Spanish Inquisition who brutally tortured non-Christians into confessing their dealings with Satan. Oddly, the general found the nickname amusing. That disturbed Reinhold more than anything else about the head of Forge.

Circling the room was a series of high-density plasma monitors showing a panoramic view of the desert outside the mesa, and a few more monitors on a control panel gave views of critical tunnels and doorways. As the professor took his chair in front of the main console, he saw the squad of soldiers carrying out the body of the dead mountaineer in a body bag.

"Hello, sir, we saw everything on monitor nineteen," Erica Sabot said, the technician approaching with a clipboard.

A beautiful woman, her long auburn hair was tied back in a ponytail, and she wore no cosmetics. There were few women in Forge, and all of them had been chosen for their combat skills. Even the personal assistant for the general was a former Intelligence agent for the Argentine government and famous for her skill with a knife.

"A minor inconvenience," Reinhold said, accepting the clipboard. "I see the number six turbine generator is running a little hot. Better check the gauges and the needle valves. Those can sometimes stick from the condensed moisture."

Electricity was crucial at the mesa base to operate the massive computers needed to run the uplink. Stealing it from the local grid was impossible as the nearest power line was fifty miles away. Hacking into the GPS network was hard enough without adding power fluctuations to the equation.

"I'll check it personally, sir," Sabot replied. "Anything else?"

"Not that I can think of. Anything unusual spotted while I was dealing with our interloper?" the professor asked, gazing out the virtual-reality windows. Aside from the occasional ripple or flicker, it really did seem as if he were looking through glass at the rocky desert below. Another mesa rose on the distant horizon, and low-cresting foothills formed sandstone waves across the floor of the desert. Like a petrified ocean, with the waves caught cresting.

"No EM scans have been done of the mesa, no radar or laser sweeps, no burst radio transmissions, or anything similar, sir," another technician replied in English. Born in Argentina, the man had been schooled at Harvard and the conflicting accents were sometimes difficult to comprehend.

"Excellent. Thank you."

As the technician turned to leave, a red light began flashing on the main control board.

"Message from the Snake Eater, sir," a technician crisply reported, reading off the scrolling printer. "Our mercs in Puerto Rico have destroyed the secret DOD warehouse. No prisoners taken."

Thoughtfully rubbing his bruised ribs, the professor scrunched his face. "Thank goodness." The professor exhaled in relief. One planeload of INS units could have ruined everything.

"One problem, sir," the technician continued slowly. "He

believes the entire matter is fake, a bluff to lure us out into the open."

"Is this another of his hunches?" the professor demanded coldly.

"No, sir. The return flight time for the plane is wrong. If it was carrying a full load of INS units, it would move slower than the flight out there, but the return flight is marked as full speed."

That could be a simple clerical mistake, but perhaps not. He thought of the mountaineer. Danger often came from the most unexpected direction. "Is there a strong westerly wind?" Reinhold asked suspiciously. "Maybe the DOD is leaving their people behind to lighten the load?"

"No wind, sir. Clear sailing all the way to Texas," the tech replied. "And the manifest lists a full complement of people. Six and a pilot arrived, seven leaving."

The professor furrowed his brow. This could only mean that the Americans were already wise to their plans and Puerto Rico had been a trap! That return flight time was a bad mistake on their part. A very tiny one, to be sure. But a critical mistake all the same. Thank God Snake Eater caught the gaff. Once more, the little man proved his worth to the Great Project.

"Inform the general at once!" Reinhold snapped. "We must not send any personnel to try to destroy that plane when it lands in Texas! And destroy all links with Puerto Rico! Then recall our people in Sonora. The Americans must not get their hands on them at any cost!"

"At once, sir!" another technician said over a shoulder, his hands moving steadily across the complex controls. Indicators were starting to glow with power as accumulators for the satellite uplink slowly charged to operational voltage.

"And have Snake Eater send more mercs to the rendezvous point for Lieutenant Caramico and her people," Reinhold muttered angrily. "They are to help her reach North Dakota, where she is to dispatch them." He paused. "Unless the FBI is tracking them, trying to find our American base, then the mercs are to kill her and run for…Seattle." Where we shall have more mercs kill them upon arrival, he thought. What was it a politician had once said, you could always hire half of the poor to kill the other half? The supply of mercenaries was endless. There were just too many people. However, Forge was going to change that.

"But, sir, these are our people!" Sabot began, aghast.

"A necessary sacrifice," the professor said, waving the trifle aside. "We're going to murder five billion people. What does three more matter?"

The woman gave no reply and turned her face away from the professor so that he wouldn't see her dark expression.

"They're our own people," Sabot muttered, almost too soft to hear.

The rest of the technicians in command and control got busy. Safely relaying messages between the two uplink sites had always been tricky. First, the message had to be heavily encoded, then compressed to a microsecond squeal, and then relayed across the world to the Southern Hemisphere innocuously mixed into mindless Internet chatter. A recorded voice spoke normally while the ultrasonic message buzzed in the background like a housefly. The Snake Eater had designed the process, and so far it had proved to be unbreakable. The NSA and FBI monitored the Net for hidden messages in graphic files, but not audio files of rock songs, clips from porn movies, and the like. The technician in charge of communications had to admit Snake Eater was extremely clever, even if it did make her skin crawl to try to be respectful to the little foreigner. Calling the man "sir" tasted like ashes in her mouth.

But although she was born in Argentina, there was German blood in her veins and she understood the necessity of obeying orders. Life had to be controlled, or else there was only chaos. It amazed the woman that so few people ever seemed to understand this obvious fact.

Finished with the encoding, the chief technician mixed the tone with an audio file of children laughing at a birthday party, then tapped a few buttons.

ON TOP OF A MESA a mile away, the ground split apart, the sand pushed back by the sections of louvered steel. Spreading and expanding like a blossoming flower, the steel formed a large satellite dish. With a hydraulic sigh, a stubby beam antenna rose from the center and locked into place, then the dish began to track across the sky in a quick search pattern. After a few minutes, the Chilean telecommunications satellite was located and the terse message was beamed into space. Then the steel flower closed to disappear from sight as if it had never existed.

CHAPTER SEVEN

Sonora, Texas

"I said, drop the gun," the voice repeated harshly.

"My money is in my wallet," Sergeant Mendoza said. "Please, I'm just a surveyor for the county...." He tried to pretend to be scared, but it only sounded ridiculous.

"Nice try, son," Sheriff Andrews said contemptuously, pressing the muzzle of the S&W .38 into the back of the man's head. "Now drop that ray gun, Buck Rogers, you're coming with me."

"No. If I touch the second trigger, your hospital gets a 40 mm round dumped into the Emergency Room," Mendoza countered. "Perhaps it is empty, eh? But perhaps not. Now drop your weapon, or else I shoot."

"You'll be the first to die," the sheriff added in a graveyard voice.

Mendoza felt nervous sweat forming on his palms, but his heart was pounding deliciously. "But I shall not be the last," the big sergeant replied. "Drop it! I shall not ask again."

There was a long pause, then the gun was thrown onto the

rocky ground. But as the old revolver landed, the hammer jerked forward and the weapon discharged. Exactly as planned.

Caught by surprise, Mendoza flinched as the bullet ricocheted off a concrete block used to keep fools from driving off the hill. His grip loosened, and something hard slammed into the side of his neck. The impact jingled for some reason and the sergeant was thrown to the ground.

Rolling, Mendoza came up in a crouch with the FN-2000 at the ready. There was the small-town sheriff. His gun holster was empty, and the old man was wearing what appeared to be a lumpy bulletproof vest. Idiot! His hand already in position, Mendoza triggered the 40 mm grenade launcher.

Throwing fire and smoke, the weapon rocked backward. The shell missed the sheriff by an inch, slamming into the trunk of a tree. Bark and wood chips went flying as the whole tree shook, and the fat 40 mm round dug out a gouge bigger than a mauled fist.

Recoiling from the sight, Andrews waited for the shell to explode, not fully able to understand why he was still pulling in air. Had the shell malfunctioned? Then some dim recess of his mind dredged up the fact that grenades had to travel a certain distance before the warhead armed itself. It seemed clear that the tree had to have been just under that range.

Stepping forward, the sheriff kicked the assault rifle out of the hand of the bigger man, the spurs on his boots jingling from the hard blow. The weapon went flying and the man dived forward, catching the sheriff in a bear hug that drove him to the sandy ground.

Wresting for supremacy, the two combatants rolled over and over, kicking and punching. Unable to get a grip on his opponent's throat, Andrews tried to break the other man's nose with a head butt, but Mendoza turned his face at the last instant, then savagely bit the sheriff on the arm, drawing blood. Grimacing from the pain, Andrews spit in the sergeant's left eye and rammed a knee into his groin.

Both men knew that this was no friendly fistfight in the neighborhood bar, or a boxing contest with cash as the prize, but a bare-knuckle brawl to the death. Their weapons lay on the ground, but any attempt to grab a gun would leave that person vulnerable to a strike from behind.

Breaking apart, the two men scrambled to their feet and warily circled each other while gasping for breath. Both were bruised and bleeding, their clothing ripped and stained, but neither had any intention of asking for mercy or running away. They were here for the long count.

Needing more room to move, Andrews yanked off his bulky vest, and Mendoza tried for a grab. But the sheriff danced out of the way and hammered a gnarled fist directly into the man's kidney. Mendoza grunted from the impact, then rammed his elbow backward in a martial arts move. Andrews caught it full in the chest and felt a rib crack. Controlling his breathing, the sheriff put two more punches into the sergeant, then looped a slow overhand blow trying to lure the man closer. But Mendoza backstepped quickly, not falling for the obvious trap.

"Time to die, old man," the sergeant growled, pulling an Andes combat knife from a trick sheath strapped inside his sleeve.

"Not yet, son," Andrews snarled, lashing out with a boot trying for a vulnerable throat. The toe missed Mendoza, but the jingling spur caught his cheek, slashing the flesh open.

Ignoring the terrible pain, the sergeant thrust out his knife. But the sheriff moved out of the way as if dodging a rattlesnake. Then Andrews noticed a thin red line forming along his upper thigh and blood started seeping into his tan uniform. The son of a bitch was fast! the sheriff thought.

Snatching the handcuffs from the pouch behind his back, the sheriff threw them at the sergeant, then dived past the man and came up with his dropped revolver. Starting to turn, Andrews saw the sergeant gesture and cover his face with a raised arm a split second before the fistful of sand arrived. Firing twice blindly, Andrews scraped his face clean and opened his eyes just in time to see the other man grab the fancy assault rifle.

Trying one last time not to take a life, the sheriff drilled a round into the assault rifle. The computerized optics exploded into pieces, the blow almost making the sergeant drop the weapon. Spinning around into a crouch, Mendoza cut loose with a burst of rounds above the charging sheriff. But before he could swing the weapon downward, Andrews fired again directly into the sergeant's chest. Blood sprayed from the hit and Mendoza staggered, then trigged another burst, stitching the sheriff from knee to throat.

Thrown backward, Andrews tried to put another round into the big man, and only hit sky. With his life flowing out of the gaping wounds, the sheriff dropped to the concrete divider and fired again into the dust. Everything was getting hazy, and there was no pain anymore. The sheriff knew what that meant. Shock was setting in, and he was dying, every beat of his heart forcing out more precious blood. Only rage was keeping Andrews in motion, the old law officer grimly determined not to die alone on this nameless hill. He fired twice more, and hit nothing.

Grinning widely, Mendoza fired short, controlled bursts into the sheriff, driving the man to the ground never to rise again.

"You are lucky I had no time to question you properly," the

big sergeant said, dropping the spent clip and quickly reloading. "You and my little knives would have a good time, eh? Yes, I think so, gringo. A bloody good time."

The wind sighing over the grisly Texas hillock almost sounded like a whispery reply, then there was only silence.

Slinging the weapon over a bloody shoulder, Mendoza pulled the compact Kenwood radio from his belt holster to warn the lieutenant. Then he cursed at the sight of a gaping hole in the electronic device, the loose wires dangling free like jungle vines. The lieutenant was on her own.

"Good." Mendoza chuckled, putting his back to the town and heading for their motorcycles and the stores of medical supplies. If she died, he would be placed in charge of the mission. Then he would start having real fun.

PARKING THE MOTORCYCLE in an alley, Lieutenant Caramico paused and looked quickly around with her assault rifle at the ready. The soldier could have sworn that she'd just heard distant gun shots, but there was nobody in sight.

When the noise didn't come again, Caramico peeked around the building at the nearby hill, but again there was nothing visible. Hopefully the sergeant wasn't in trouble. Then again, the man could easily take care of himself. She felt only pity for anybody foolish enough to tangle with Mendoza. The only person to ever beat the sergeant in a fair fight was General Calvano.

Maybe it was the wind, Caramico thought, checking the 40 mm round in the grenade launcher. But she decided to move fast and get out of the town as soon as possible. The lieutenant didn't like covert operations. They weren't her style. Hit and git, as they said in the movies. She'd bust into the jailhouse, kill anybody there, grab the folder and go. Just like a bank robber in the Old West.

Easing through the front door, Caramico slipped into the office and glanced about. There didn't seem to be anybody lying in wait for her, but it was too dim inside to see clearly, so she lifted the tinted face shield of the helmet. The building seemed empty. She relaxed slightly. Excellent.

Stepping to the wooden divider, the lieutenant saw the file lying in plain sight on the desk only a few yards away. Rushing through the gate in the divider, Caramico grabbed the folder and paused to take a fast look inside. In cold horror, the lieutenant felt herself go pale at the sight of only blank papers. She riffled through them all, sending the plain white sheets tumbling to the floor. There was nothing here. What the— This was a trap!

Dropping the folder, the woman started to run for the door when she saw it, over by the file cabinets. Sitting on a wooden chair, where the wall hid it from outside view, was a small camera phone aimed directly at the desk, the display lid raised and a tiny red light blinking to show that the digital recorder was on and broadcasting.

And my shield is raised so now they know what I look like! Acting on impulse, Caramico stroked the trigger of the FN-2000 and a hail of 5.56 mm rounds smashed the camera phone apart. She hurried to the door, then touched the second trigger and the grenade launcher spoke. The fat 40 mm round streaked across the room and hit the file cabinets placed along the far wall. The distance was short, but just far enough. A strident blast rocked the building, shattering the window and setting off the fire alarm. Water gushed from the ceiling sprinklers, and from outside the building an alarm started to clang.

Leaving fast, the lieutenant knew that within a few minutes there wouldn't be a building left standing from the hellish heat of the military compound. Much less any hidden cameras she might have missed. Nothing could put out thermite except time, which was why she always carried a round with her. It just too damn useful.

Reloading the grenade launcher, Caramico heard a shout and turned, the FN-2000 pointed from the hip. A group of men were rushing her way from what had to be the local fire station. The distance was too far for the machine gun, so she launched the last shell. The HE round hit the street and detonated directly in front of the firefighters. Twisted bodies went flying and their shouts became shrieks of pain.

Now several doors opened and people timidly peeked out to see what was happening. A couple of men rushed out carrying commercial fire extinguishers. Ruthlessly, Caramico gunned them down with the assault rifle, then randomly peppered the storefronts with AP rounds until every civilian had ducked into hiding.

Satisfied that nobody else in town was going to hinder her departure, Caramico climbed onto the BMW slammed down her shield, started the engine and drove away, revving the purring engine to top speed.

Arching around a deserted apartment building marked for sale, she checked her mask, then pulled a Kenwood radio from a sheath on the bike. Clumsily tapping the access code onto the small keypad, Caramico thumbed the transmit switch. "Louie to the Dog Pack," she said loudly into the radio, the words shaky from the irregular road surface. "Abort and retreat. I repeat, abort and retreat. We've been made!" There was only a crackle of static so she boosted the gain. "Louie to the Dog Pack. Do you copy?"

"Roger, we receive you," a garbled voice replied. There was more, but the signal faded away.

Steering with one hand, Caramico tried to fiddle with the frequency. Damn, the reception was poor around here. "Do not try to kill the DOD agents! Repeat, do not kill! Retreat to the rendezvous point." There was no reply. "I said do not kill the Americans. Do you copy?"

There was a crackle of static. "I copy," the voice replied. "But we have a problem."

"What's wrong?" Caramico demanded, leaving the road and heading into the cool greenery of a golf course.

"Playtime is over, bitch. This is the FBI. Surrender, or die like the rest of your men!"

Biting back a curse, the lieutenant released the transmit switch, terminating the conversation and any hope of the FBI triangulating on her signal. Leaving the golf course, Caramico drove into a copse of trees and throttled down the motorcycle to park beneath a shady pine. For a long moment, she reviewed the situation; the only sounds were the distant fire bell and the chugging syncopation of the lawn sprinklers.

Lifting the radio once more, Caramico switched channels. "Louie to Top Kick, come in." There was no answer. "Mendoza, respond!" But there was only silence. Which meant the sergeant was either dead or his radio had been broken. Unless the FBI was jamming their frequencies. The Americans were very clever in such matters, she knew. It would probably be wise not to use the radio anymore.

Turning off the radio, the lieutenant scrambled the code on the keypad, then shoved the device into the recharging sheath built into the bike. The voice on the radio had claimed to be FBI, but that was obviously a lie. It would require Special Forces, maybe even the legendary Delta Force, to take out her troopers. The hunters had just become the hunted. Her troops were most likely captured or dead…no, they had to be dead.

Why would they try to trick her into surrendering if they already had prisoners to torture in their secret dungeons? Thank goodness her men didn't know enough details about the Great Plan to hinder its completion in any way. Wheels within wheels, that was how you won a war. What a soldier didn't know, couldn't be forced from him by any amount of brutal torture. This mission had turned ugly fast, but things were going to get a lot worse when the nuclear bombs finally started to fall.

In the far distance, smoke was rising from the burning jail. Police sirens could be heard, or possibly ambulances, the wails too distant to ascertain.

Then a black dot rose into the sky from the direction of the airport. Helicopter. The civilian authorities had arrived. Soon, there would be roadblocks and military helicopters on search-and-destroy missions. She had only a few minutes to leave the area. But where to go? Weeks ago the Forge soldiers had established a camp at a cave inside the western foothills. It held clothing, fuel, new identification papers, weapons, money…everything they needed to get back to Black Fortress mesa. She couldn't use any of that now. After her men talked, the FBI would be waiting there with nets and stun guns to take her alive. Better arrange for a supply drop and reinforcements.

With no choice, the lieutenant pulled out a cell phone and hit a programmed number. The connection was swiftly established, and the screen became illuminated with a swirling color pattern indicating the signal was being scrambled. If the pattern fluctuated, or went still for even a moment, that meant the call was being traced. Lord knew, the Snake Eater had his faults, but the hated little hacker was a genius with electronics, no doubt about that.

"Report," a stern voice commanded.

There was no mistaking the person on the other end. General Calvano himself.

"Sir, we have a problem," Caramico reported crisply.

CHAPTER EIGHT

Rolling at exactly the speed limit, Able Team's unmarked van crested a low rise in the paved road. Shifting gear, Lyons saw that there was nothing ahead of them but a two-lane road slicing through the reddish landscape like an ebony sword thrust.

Seated at the small electronics workbench in the rear of the armored vehicle, Schwarz gave a dissatisfied grunt and closed his laptop.

"Anything?" Blancanales asked from the passenger seat. An M-16/M-203 combo assault rifle sat across his lap. The big weapon was expertly held below the window, just out of sight from any passing cars.

"Well, I got a picture of one of them," Schwarz answered, studying the crystal-clear JPEG of the startled woman, her features visible inside the motorcycle helmet. "A woman, a real beauty and there's no denying that. But man, she's crazier than a rabid snake. Blew up the entire building in retaliation."

"That means we can find out who she is with the photo," Lyons rationalized. "No other reason to get that mad otherwise."

"Unless she's insane."

"True."

"Try Interpol," Blancanales suggested, watching an SUV roll by. It was full of civilians laughing and singing. A family on vacation. A little girl in the back waved her fingers, and Blancanales grinned back in reply. Kids, an endless source of new hope in a tired old world.

"Already tried Interpol," Schwarz replied, slinging the portable computer over a shoulder. "So I sent it to Bear. The cybersquad can do a global search in just a few minutes."

"Fair enough," Lyons said, slowing a little to let the SUV get farther ahead of them and allow for some combat room. "I just hope the sheriff did as we requested and stayed out of town. He's just the sort of lawman to take matters into his own hands and try to capture these assholes alive."

"My money would be on the sheriff," Blancanales said, keeping a careful watch on the shadows alongside the larger sand dunes. When the expected attack came, it would most likely be from that direction. "I know the type well. He's tougher than a boiled steak."

Adjusting his sunglasses, Lyons snorted. "Rousting Saturday-night drunks and arresting the occasional drug smuggler doesn't train you for dealing with paramilitary operatives. And anybody trying to start World War III isn't going to assemble an army of greenhorns and wannabes."

Resting an arm on the back of the two front seats, Schwarz started to speak when he caught a movement out of the corner of his eye. Snapping his head to the left, the man cursed at the sight of four big BMW motorcycles speeding away from the roadway and heading deep into the desert. A moment later the men and machines dipped into a long depression and were gone from sight.

"Nine o'clock," Schwarz announced, pointing a finger. "There, just past that big copse of cactus plants!"

"Yeah, I see them," Lyons replied, already edging across the highway. The big van jounced across the low concrete median dividing the lanes, hit pavement, then raced over the berm, spraying loose gravel out behind. He'd been afraid of this happening. When they tricked one of the enemy into getting photographed, the rest decided to run. Okay, the ambush was canceled. Time to get hard.

"Remember, we need them alive," Blancanales said, checking the clip inside his Colt pistol.

Instead of the usual .380 hardball ammo, he had loaded rubber bullets to try to take the terrorists alive. The vulcanized rounds hurt like the devil, but wouldn't kill a man, even if delivered at point-blank range. However, all of the other clips in his ammo pouch held illegal Talon bullets, Teflon-coated, armor-piecing rounds that went through conventional police body armor like it was bare skin. Grimly, Blancanales worked the slide, chambering a round. One way or the other, the only way the terrorists were leaving Sonora was in the rear of the Stony Man van. Either wearing handcuffs or a body bag.

Schwarz went back to the workbench to grab his own M-16/M-203 combo. Quickly, he thumbed a fat tear gas grenade into the 40 mm launcher, then tucked a star shell into a pocket. Normally, the round was fired into the nighttime sky to slowly parachute down, the magnesium charge throwing out an incredible amount of light. However, Schwarz had a different use in mind this day. There were a lot of caves in this area, and if the bike riders tried to take refuge inside one, the blazing illumination of the star shell, plus the reek of magnesium smoke, would force them out into the open again.

Accelerating steadily, Lyons zigzagged the van across the irregular terrain, avoiding gopher holes and tumbleweeds. The ride was rough, but then the depression came into view, long and wide. A riverbed! The dust was still swirling along the bank where the bikes had crossed.

"Hold on!" Lyons shouted as the van went over the edge at full speed.

The vehicle was airborne for a full second, then it crashed hard onto the dried mud. A taillight shattered at the impact, the men rocked in their seats and some loose tools on the workbench went flying to clatter noisily. Fighting to regain control, Lyons tromped on the gas as the military tires dug into the ground and the vehicle raced forward with renewed speed.

The sharp banks of the ancient river rose to about six feet in height on either side of the van. The bikes and van were trapped like water in a sluice until the slopes got smoother or a lot lower. Perfect for close-quarter vehicle combat. Lyons could simply ram the bikes from behind.

"If we can just get close enough," Lyons muttered, reaching down to check the position of his Atchisson shotgun on the floor. The automatic weapon could fire several times faster than the best military-model shotgun, and carried more 12-gauge shells. The recoil was mind-numbing, but in the right hands it could level a small forest in seven seconds.

Reluctantly, Lyons reached up to open a hidden compartment in the ceiling and take down a Neostad shotgun. Built and designed by South Africa to quell riots, the oddball weapon had a pair of tubular magazines set above the main barrel. One of them carried stainless steel fléchettes, and the other canvas stun bags. A thumb switch on the stock allowed the gunner to switch from magazine to magazine, killing with this stroke of the trigger, but only stunning with the next.

There was no dust rising behind the van, the hard mud firm and solid. Slowing to take a gentle curve in the meandering river, Lyons tightened his grip on the steering wheel as the four bikes came into view. The BMW motorcycles were in a loose formation and rolling along at under 50 mph. The riders obviously thought they were in no danger.

"Hell, this is almost too easy," Schwarz said with a worried grin, working the arming bolt on his weapon. "I don't like it."

At that precise moment, one of the bikers turned to glance over a shoulder. The mirror-bright shield of his helmet hid the rider's features, and the Stony Man commandos got a distorted view of their own van in the tinted Plexiglas.

Jerking a weapon from a holster set alongside the frame, the rider started firing short bursts from an odd, futuristic machine gun. A hail of bullets peppered the front of the van, the 5.56 mm rounds bouncing harmlessly off the armor plating.

"That's an FN-2000!" Blancanales said in astonishment, returning fire out the side window with his combo. "Absolutely state-of-the-art. I didn't even know that Belgium had those on the market yet!"

"Who are these guys?" Schwarz demanded suspiciously, shooting out the other window as the rest of the riders pulled their modular assault rifles from holsters and began to hammer the racing van with converging streams of bullets.

Savagely twisting the wheel, Lyons sent the vehicle veering wildly back and forth, the incoming rounds tattooing the chassis but failing to achieve penetration. A 40 mm grenade was launched and missed, violently exploding alongside the van and throwing a tidal wave of dirt over the vehicle. Cursing bitterly, Lyons hit the wiperblades, and one of the arms snapped off from a well-placed round. The sons of bitches are getting our range! The Able Team leader raged.

Suddenly, the lead rider dropped back and sent a long burst from his weapon at the Stony Man commandos. The 5.56 mm bursts dented the chassis, smashing a headlight and punching straight through the Lexan plastic windshield. Loud bangs came from the aft as the armor-piercing bullets ricocheted off the rear doors and bounced around for a moment.

"You okay?" Blancanales shouted over the wind whistling through the holes in the windshield. Dropping a clip, he hastily reloaded.

"Nope, I'm dead," Schwarz retorted, rubbing a bad bruise under his body armor. "Send flowers!"

Sticking his head and shoulders out the left window, the angry man triggered the M-16 at the speeding bikes, but the rubber bullets were doing nothing to these men. Maybe they also had body armor? Not good news. Switching his grip, Schwarz gave them a taste of the M-203. The stun bag hit a rider, and he wobbled, almost falling off the bike from the impact, then turned and started blasting again with the FN-2000.

Fishtailing, Lyons avoided the incoming 40 mm shells, fiery explosions bracketing the van. In ragged unison, Blancanales and Schwarz cut loose with their weapons, the cacophony sounding louder than doomsday inside the battered vehicle. As they reloaded, both men switched to standard hardball ammo.

Now lines of hits spurted dust between the bikes and along the banks of the river. One of the bikers cried out, throwing his arms high as the rear tire blew. The bike veered out of control and smashed into the hard bank. Thrown over the handlebars, the man crashed through the windshield and smashed his face into the wall of dried mud at sixty miles per hour. He left a long crimson streak on the rough sandstone, and fell limply to the bed in a crumpled heap.

Passing the corpse, the Stony Man commandos checked the body for a split second, then concentrated on the other riders.

"Time to end this," Lyons growled, feeding more gas to the powerful Detroit engine.

Ahead of them, the three remaining BMW motorcycles were weaving back and forth, making it impossible to track on any of them accurately.

These men are combat soldiers, not just some street muscle hired for a job, Blancanales noted dourly. Just who the hell are we up against, the Red Star? Would the Chinese Intelligence agency fire missiles on their own homeland? He knew the Red Star operatives hated America, but that kind of action bordered on insanity.

Unexpectedly, two of the bikers went wide, exposing the leader, and he tossed a small canister over a shoulder.

Even as it bounced along the riverbed toward them, Lyons started evasive maneuvers. Briefly, he wondered what it could be. Obviously that was a specialty grenade of some kind. But sleep gas or BZ gas would never reach the occupants of the speeding van, they would be long past any thermite or white phosphorous before it had a chance to damage the vehicle, and that only left...shit!

At the very last second, Lyons desperately veered sharply to the right, grinding along the sandstone bank, as the canister exploded on their left. A hellish spray of fire filled the depression, orange tendrils of flame extending into the van through every bullet hole. Then they were through the fireball, but the flames suck to the chassis, burning fiercely and sending out volumes of black smoke.

"Napalm!" Blancanales shouted, withdrawing inside and closing the window. "Smart bastards." On a regular vehicle the napalm would have cooked the men inside, but the van was armored against such standard tactics, and aside from removing the paint, the charge of jellied gasoline did scant damage.

"Our turn," Schwarz countered, leaning between the two men in front and shoving the barrel of the M-16 through a hole in the windshield.

As his partner fired, Blancanales ducked from the arching brass raining down everywhere. Stoically, Lyons kept driving, steadily edging closer to the terrorists. Just a little bit more….

The lead rider was hit several times by the chattering barrage, and his left arm went limp, blood spraying from a direct hit. But that was when the ancient riverbanks flattened out and the four vehicles were racing across the flat bottom of a huge lake, a leftover from when Mexican glaciers retreated through America on their way to Canada about ten million years ago.

Instantly, the three bike riders separated into different directions. Tightening his grip on the steering wheel, it took Lyons only a single heartbeat to make a decision.

"Take 'em!" he commanded, stomping on the accelerator and shifting gear to head straight for the rider ahead of them. If these boys were paramilitary, or the real deal, this would be their commander.

Dropping BZ rounds from the M-203 grenade launchers, Blancanales and Schwarz slammed in AP rounds, leveled their weapons and fired.

The double thumps seemed to fill the speeding van, and seconds later the two departing bikes stridently exploded, men and machines annihilated by the high-explosive rounds.

The remaining rider turned his head at the noise, his body language registering shock at the sight. Then, twisting the handlebar throttle, he urged the BMW motorcycle on to greater speed and faced forward one split second before driving through a large stand of fat cacti.

The windshield shattered and the rider screamed as he

plowed through the thorny plants. Arching around the copse, Lyons saw the bike come out the other side, the gloved hands of the rider covered with the barbed quills. Weaving erratically, the biker hit a lump of rock on the lake bottom, completely losing control. The front wheel turned sharply, the bike jackknifed and the man went flying to land yards away, limbs flailing.

Throwing off a hail of bright sparks, the bike scraped along the rough stone. Moving in the opposite direction, the rider tumbled along, his leather jacket shredding on the rough material until he began to leave a crimson trail across the field of prehistoric sandpaper.

Jamming the van to a halt, Lyons and the others burst from the vehicle before it stopped rocking back and forth. They needed the biker alive!

But before they could reach the supine man, two more black BMW motorcycles charged over a swell in the vista. Dropping fast, the Stony Man commandos dived for cover among the low rocks and stubby cacti.

The silent bikes raced past the fallen man, the riders ruthlessly putting rounds into the still form with their assault rifles. Then they opened fire at Able Team.

Moving constantly, Lyons answered with the Neostad, trying for a capture. Again the stun bags did nothing. Then he grunted from a hit, but his own NATO body armor easily stopping the 5.56 mm rounds.

Popping up into view, Blancanales and Schwarz laid down suppressing fire, while Lyons switched magazines with a flick of a finger and cut loose with a thundering AP cartridge.

The targeted biker seemed to literally fly apart from the hellstorm of stainless steel fléchettes. Then the fuel tank of the destroyed machine loudly detonated. Covered with flames, the tattered human corpse tumbled off the bike to land facedown, the spare ammo for the assault rifle in the pockets of his leather jacket beginning to crackle like popcorn as the live rounds cooked off from the intense heat of the blaze. Jerking and twitching with every explosion, the burning corpse was torn into grisly pieces in a fusillade of internal gunfire.

Snarling something in a foreign language, the second driver braked to a fast halt with a squeal of brakes, grabbed the FN-2000 with both hands and fired a 40 mm grenade. But the Stony Man commandos were already separating, and the shell only hit the copse of broken cacti. A writhing fireball of white phosphorous engulfed the plants, the needles sizzling like fuses, the circular trunks splitting open wide, the damp spongy interior oozing outward like warm blood.

Seared by the wave of heat, Blancanales and Schwarz fired back, taking refuge behind the smashed motorcycle. Lurching into action, the rider answered with the assault rifle, arching behind the burning cactus to disappear for a split second, then coming back again firing nonstop. Obviously, he was reloading where Able Team couldn't get a bead.

Charging the last bike rider, Lyons fired the Neostad, flopped to his belly and fired again, then started rolling and shooting. The rider was battered, but undamaged. However, the windshield of safety glass shattered into a million tiny green cubes.

The rider flinched from the explosion and nearly went into the burning plants. Dropping the FN-2000, he grabbed the handlebars with both hands and steered away from the growing conflagration.

Suddenly Schwarz stood directly in front of the rider. Revving the big engine, the terrorist charged, and Blancanales fired his M-203 from the side, the high-explosive shell hitting the man in the ribs. But the distance had been too short for the warhead to arm and the man was sent flying sideways off the motorcycle. He rolled back to his feet in a martial arts move, a 9 mm Bersa automatic pistol brandished in each gloved fist. Darting among the rocks, the terrorist banged away with both weapons, not hitting much of anything.

Instantly, Lyons fired his .357 Colt Python, the big-bore rounds hitting the terrorist in the chest. The Magnum rounds failed to penetrate the body armor, but the savage beating made it impossible for the fellow to accurately aim.

Leveling his .380 Colt with both hands, Blancanales inhaled, paused and stroked the trigger. The black Talon rounds punched through the leather jacket and the body armor underneath, coming came out the man's shoulder in a gush of red blood and white bones.

"Give it up!" Lyons shouted in his best cop voice, honed from years of working on the L.A.P.D. "Be smart and live!"

Dropping a smoking Bersa, the terrorist continued firing the other gun, then stopped as if making a decision. Turning to face the sky, the man shoved the barrel of the Bersa under his jaw and yanked the trigger. The muffled report blew the helmet off his head in a grisly eruption of bones, brains and blood.

Caught by surprise, the Stony Man operatives could only watch as the gushing corpse teetered, then collapsed, spilling warm life onto the cold desert stones.

"Son of a bitch," Lyons said in disgust, reloading the Neostad. "These people are goddamn fanatics."

"They're trying to start a nuclear war," Schwarz added, working the arming bolt of his M-16 to clear a jam. The dented brass went spinning away to land with a musical tingling on the ground. "What the hell else would you expect?"

Blancanales shouldered his weapon. "All right," he growled. "Let's find out who these assholes are. Damn!"

Plumes of black smoke were rising from the burning motorcycles, and softly in the distance they heard the wailing siren of a police car. The Stony Man operatives knew that the sound would carry for miles in the flat desert, but time was short. Moving fast, the three men began the odious task of checking the mutilated corpses.

"Grab and git," Lyons directed. "We can do the analysis back on board the Hercules."

Getting bags and latex gloves from the van, the other men nodded agreement and went to work. Schwarz took their fingerprints, while Blancanales washed their faces with moist towelettes from the field kit and took pictures of the least damaged features. With no compunction, Lyons went through their bloody pockets.

"Their prints are gone," Schwarz announced glumly, proffering a sheet of paper. "I'd say burned off with acid."

"Expected as much." Blancanales snorted, pocketing the digital camera and going to the least damaged motorcycle. "I'll check the VIN on the bikes."

"They'll be listed as stolen, of course," Lyons said, busy at his grisly task.

Kneeling at a smashed motorcycle, Blancanales shrugged. "Most likely, but mistakes have been known to happen."

Rifling through the blood-smeared objects, Lyons found the new wallets were full of American money, five grand each, along with the mandatory driver's license, insurance card, registration—just enough ID to get them past a cursory check by the highway police. Any deeper examination would probably get the curious law officer a bullet in the back of the head. As expected, there were no personal items at all; photographs of family or friends, movie stubs, lock of hair from a girlfriend, business card from the local dry cleaner…not even a credit card or ATM card. The riders were all men and wore no jewelry, not even a wedding ring. The wristwatches were good, but mass-produced models, nothing special, and there were no personalized engravings on the backs.

"Find anything useful?" Lyons asked, tucking the items into a nylon bag for later analysis. These men were starting to resemble a CIA incursion team more than a group of terrorists. Military ghosts. Men who never officially existed.

"Not a damn thing," Blancanales stated ruefully, rising from a crashed motorcycle with a cell phone in his hand. "These bikes have vehicle-identification numbers registered for members of a motorcycle club in Houston, none of which have been reported stolen."

"Aha!" Schwarz beamed in delight.

"In fact," Blancanales continued, unabated, "one of them just got a ticket this afternoon in downtown Houston."

"A thousand miles away," Schwarz muttered.

The man nodded. "Yep, duplicate numbers of legitimate bikes. The license plates haven't come through yet, but I'm expecting they match the Houston bike club."

"Seems to be the same with the guns," Schwarz said slowly. "The serial numbers have been rubbed off with a file."

"What about the ammo?"

The man grinned. "They seem to have forgotten about that."

"Probably also listed to the Houston bike club," Lyons retorted. "But as the man said, mistakes have been known to happen." Spent shell casings were a detail that few people ever considered. The base of every bullet carried the logo of the manufacturer, along with an ID number showing when and where it was made. Stony Man ammunition was an exception. It was smooth and featureless on the base, with nothing that could give anybody the slightest hint which nation had dispatched the teams. The CIA did the same thing for their field agents, as did the British SAS, the Israeli Mossad, and quite a few other secret government agencies around the world.

"Well, even if the casings are also blanks, the guns themselves tell us something," Lyons said, hefting one of the recovered pistols. All of the men had the exact same sidearm, a compact 9 mm Bersa Thunder. "These are made in Argentina, and aren't well-known outside of South America."

"Yeah," Blancanales said, "it's an odd handgun to issue to your people. Why not steal something more commonplace like a Beretta or a Glock? Those sell internationally."

"Unless these are the specific weapons the men had been trained with to fight," Lyons said, working the slide to check inside the automatic pistol. This weapon hadn't been fired in the fight and was spotlessly clean. Oiled and ready for combat.

"These guys are beginning to sound like regular military," Schwarz said, furrowing his brow. "And to the best of my knowledge no country in the world issues Bersa handguns as a sidearm to their army except Argentina. And they certainly do not issue FN-2000 assault rifles to their troops."

"Unless these are Special Forces," Blancanales countered. "Or a rogue unit. Which would mean—"

A loud crack of thunder interrupted the man, the noise coming from the distant sand dunes. Pivoting fast, the Stony Man operatives turned to see a roiling mushroom cloud of dark smoke majestically ascend toward the heavens.

"Anybody care to bet that was the bolthole those last two bikes came from?" Lyons asked, holstering his Colt Python. The Bersa had been dropped to the ground, his own gun drawn without conscious thought. Slowly, he holstered the

Colt at his hip. "The riders had stopped reporting, so the high command decided to destroy their base camp to remove any possible trace to the headquarters."

"Time to go," Blancanales suggested, slinging the M-16 combo over a shoulder. "We'll find nothing useful in those ruins. Any blast that generated a cloud that big must have blown their camp off the map."

Stroking his mustache, Schwarz started to agree, then frowned. "Map," he repeated. "Blew it off the map, you said."

"Yeah. So what?"

The man grinned. "Tell you in a sec." Sprinting over to a smashed motorcycle, Schwarz checked the cargo compartments on the rear fender for booby traps, then warily opened the lid. Inside was the usual effluvia of the desert: high-energy snack bars, salt pills, bottles of water, some MRE food packs, spare ammo, snake bite kit and a road map atlas of America. Tucking the atlas into his nylon evidence bag, Schwarz checked the other wrecks and recovered another two more of the spiral-bound books. The rest were too badly burned or covered with gasoline to be of any use.

"Those aren't going to tell us anything," Lyons said. "If they're smart enough to remove their fingerprints with acid, then there's no chance these men jotted down the location of their headquarters in a margin."

"Ah, but there's a big difference between smart and clever," Schwarz replied, patting the bag. "You forgot to consider—"

The wailing sirens came again, definitely louder.

Moving fast, the members of Able Team returned to their battered van and clambered inside. Lyons needed two tries before the engine finally caught, and he raced away from the combat zone, heading off at a tangent to the riverbed and the rising mushroom cloud. Once he got them behind a couple of sand dunes, the locals would never be able to find them again.

Just in case, Blancanales gathered the weapons and hid them in disguise compartments around the vehicle, then started throwing the spent shell casings from the floor out the windows. There was nothing he could do about the bullet holes or burn marks. But they would abandon the van near the airport, and set the self-destruct charges before walking back to Grimaldi and the waiting Hercules. Fifteen pounds of strategically placed thermite in the chassis of the van would reduce the armored vehicle to a glowing puddle of steel in about sixty seconds.

Assisting his friend with the cleaning, Schwarz then sat at his workbench and pulled out the four road atlases, laying them down side by side on the smooth counter. "Here we go," the man said, reaching under the bench to extract a plastic spray bottle.

Warming the liquid ninhydrin in his hands, Schwarz began to carefully spray the front covers of the books. Not much, just a light spray. He knew this was a total shot in the dark, but his wild gambles had paid off before. And if the ammunition proved to be stolen like the motorcycles, this might be their only clue to the location of the headquarters of the terrorists.

Nothing was happening, so he added another treatment. Of course, if the paper had gotten too hot, or too damp, since it was last used, this wasn't going to work. His preference would have been to use an argon laser, but the delicate devices had the bad habit of constantly breaking down in the field, or worse, losing focus and setting the target paper on fire. Hermann Schwarz was an electronics expert, but the man wisely acquiesced to the tried-and-true method of bringing out latent prints from paper. The ninhydrin reacted to the amino acids present in human sweat and nine times out of ten…

A slow smile grew as purple splotches began to appear along the edge of the covers. The splotches were totally useless for the purpose of identification, but that wasn't his goal. Using a knife blade, Schwarz began to turn the pages and treated each atlas individually. As expected, most of the state maps were blank, or with just a few random dots here and there—although New York, Los Angeles and Washington, D.C., had been circled. Ominous. But a few pages showed streaks along major interstate highways where sweaty fingers had traced travel routes: Kansas…Nebraska…South Dakota… and that was all.

"Any luck?" Lyons asked, glancing curiously into the rearview mirror. It was cracked slightly from a ricochet, but still serviceable.

"Tell you in a few minutes." Dutifully, Schwarz finished the rest of the books, even checking the indexes, but there was no more.

Two of the books had highways marked in the middle of the country, the third only a few dots here and there and the fourth was blank. Probably the atlas of the leader. Kansas, Nebraska and South Dakota. The three states had nothing really in common, but when placed in order, the stained highways created a path that went from the border of Texas. A terrorist, or spy, would know better than to touch the location of a strike, or a hidden base, on a map that might fall into the hands of the FBI. But a combat soldier wouldn't. There were very few forensic labs on the battlefield. Even then, the bike riders hadn't touched anything inside of the map of Texas. But if the trail ended there, then it had to have begun at—

"North Dakota," Schwarz announced, looking up in triumph from his work. "They have a base in North Dakota."

CHAPTER NINE

Argun River Valley, China

Moving fast across the cloudy sky, a pair of Chinese J-6 Farmer jetfighters streaked over the sylvan battleground, the reconnaissance cameras in their bellies clicking away madly.

Old, but highly functional, these sleek, single-engine fighter-bombers were brand-new from the sprawling war complex in Shenyang. The People's Liberation Army of China had many models of jetfighters, some stolen from America, others purchased from Russia, or even wholly designed by their own scientists, but the J-6 was considered the most versatile military jet in existence. The nickname Farmer came from the fact that the nimble jets were deadly dogfighters, and always made their enemy "buy the farm." Aviation slang for a fiery crash.

On their control boards the video cameras zoomed on a nightmare. Thick, acrid smoke covered the landscape, and dead bodies lay strewed about everywhere in the horrible tapestry of unbridled warfare. Blast craters dotted the churned soil, and a dozen Russian Hind-class helicopters were burning wrecks along the river and on the sloping hillside. In a field of flowers were several Chinese APCs and MRL trucks. Banking sharply for another look, the three pilots said nothing as the delicate microphones picked up the sporadic crackle of small-arms combat in the thick woods. Somewhere out of sight, a man screamed, another cursed and an assault rifle chattered. But whether it was a Chinese QBZ or a Russian AK-101, it was impossible to tell.

"So it's true," Lieutenant Tzu said into his helmet microphone, banking the J-6 Farmer in a circle. The ground flashed by underneath in a near blur. "The Great Bear has awakened and come calling at last."

"So it would appear, wing leader," Captain Dee commented dryly, his heart hammering. "Activate your digital cameras, comrades! I want video of everything! And double check for any radio messages on the encoded wavelengths. Some of our men may be trying to contact us."

"Radio is clear…look, sir!" Lieutenant Chiu cried. "Twelve o'clock low! Russian tanks!"

Squinting into the distance, the lead pilot saw a dozen Russian T-90 battle tanks moving into the Argun Valley from around a hillock. Almost at once, the audio pickups detected a sizzling hiss and something lanced out of the trees toward the invaders. The RPG bounced off the prow armor of the lumbering T-90 and detonated in the air, the halo of shrapnel harmlessly peppering the other squat tanks.

Instantly in motion, all of the Russians swung their massive 125 mm cannons toward the forest and cut loose with a strident volley.

A score of majestic pine trees was reduced violently to splinters, and a roiling sea of orange flames surged through the dense woods. Briefly, there came some screams, and then there was only the crackle of the burning thermite.

"They used antitank shells on our men," Tzu said softly, his voice tight with emotion. "Burned them down like mangy dogs."

"Dirty bastards," Chiu snarled, one hand on the joystick, the other resting on the touch-screen weapons control panel.

"Stay tight, comrades!" Dee snapped, banking the J-6 around a soaring mountain peak. The snowy crest was shiny with ice, fleecy white clouds surrounding the rocky tor like the nimbus of a candle flame. "We have strict orders to not, repeat not, engage the Russians unless attacked! This is a recon flight only."

"But, sir…"

"I said no, Tzu!"

"Incoming!" Chiu cried, his F-6 Farmer doing a quick evasive barrel roll, then streaking upward, the aft turbofan ablaze with raw power.

Spreading out fast, the other two pilots briefly checked the status of their comrades and actually saw a blurry shape rise from below and punch through the belly armor of the J-6 and detonate inside the jetfighter. The craft exploded into a writhing fireball, and a moment later the thundering concussion buffeted the other two Farmers, rattling the war planes hard as they raced across the clear blue sky.

"Arm all weapons," Dee said in a deceptively calm tone, his hand dancing across the control board. "Follow my lead, and fire upon my command only!"

"Yes, sir," Tzu growled, putting a wealth of emotions in the simple words. With the flip of a switch, he activated the HUDWAL system. A targeting grid appeared on the windshield of the cowling, along with missile status, fuel pressure, distances and GPS bomb guidance. This was a recent upgrade and seemed to be working perfectly.

Streaking high into the sky, the Chinese fighters moved into an attack vector, activated their radar jamming, dropped defensive flares and chaff, then dived back into the valley at full speed, rapidly building velocity until the G-forces crushed the chests of the men, making it almost impossible to breathe.

The battleground swelled with nightmarish speed on the forward video screens and the Chinese pilots saw the tanks start to move quickly away from each other, thick fumes pouring from the aft smoke generator, the 87 mm mortar throwing out smoke grenades in every direction in an effort to mask the vehicles, but it was far too late for such simplistic tactics. The two Chinese J-6 Farmers released a full salvo of PL-12 AA missiles from under their wings, and a few seconds later three of the Russians disappeared in fiery detonations, the riddled chassis lifting off the ground from the sheer force of the titanic blasts. The smoke screen was dissipated, but soon replaced by the smoke generators and banging mortars.

Swinging their cannons skyward, the foggy T-90 tanks retaliated again and again, the antiaircraft rounds hitting nothing. Then on the IR screen, the Chinese pilots saw a squad of soldiers poured from underneath one the armored vehicles. Taking a defensive position among the boulders, Chinese dead lying at their boots, the Russian soldiers lifted long, slim tubes that puffed smoke from the front and flames out of the aft end.

Supremely confident, the Chinese pilots replied with long bursts from the twin 30 mm cannons, the wall of high-velocity lead tearing apart the missiles in midair. Trying to track after the fighters, the Russian tanks boomed once more. But the F-6 Farmers rolled over to slip apart, then twisted to nimbly return. Stuttering fire extended from the 57 mm rocketpods under their wings.

The armor-piercing rockets stitched across the tanks like the revenge of an angry God, the thermite warheads filling the entire valley with a blinding glare. On the microphones inside their helmets, the grim pilots heard the Russian invaders shriek in unimaginable agony. Then, unexpectedly, one of the T-90 tanks exploded, the blast shoving another tank across the grassy field to tumble down the river embankment and crash into the rushing water. The armored vehicle lay in plain sight for a split second, and then it was gone beneath the churning waves.

"Again!" Captain Dee said, trying to keep a smile out of his words. He hated the filthy Russians, and was secretly delighted for a legitimate excuse to slay the murdering cowards. He glanced again at the video monitor, relishing the sight of the enemy sheathed in Chinese fire.

Then something flashed between the two Farmers.

Both pilots cursed at the sight of a full wing of Russian MiG-31 jetfighters appearing from around the Argun Mountains, the angular warplanes spreading out in a search formation.

"The fools haven't seen us yet," Dee shouted, quickly tapping the VR buttons on the glowing touch screen. "Fire the heat-seekers!"

"Yes, comrade!"

With their hands tight on the joysticks, the Chinese pilots pressed the safety with their thumbs, then pulled the triggers. From the wings of the J-6 jetfighters there dropped four gleaming white needles of advanced technology. The AA missiles fell for a dozen yards, then ignited their engines and streaked away, spiraling madly in a hunting pattern before aiming at the oncoming MiG-31 fighters. Locked on target, the heat-seekers surged in speed.

Caught by surprise, the Russians began to spin rapidly along their axis in an evasive maneuver, their PANDA system trying to blind the incoming missiles to no avail. In desperation, the MiGs spread out and fired a full salvo of GRAVIS antimissiles. Three of the Chinese warbirds were aced. But the fourth found a target and the tail of a MiG blossomed into radiant hell.

Spinning crazily, the burning fuselage slammed into another MiG, the combined explosions seeming to fill the sky. The burning wreckage tumbled down to smack into the side of a mountain and disappear in the raging forest fire.

Banking sharply, the Chinese J-6 Farmers dropped their wingtip fuel tanks and drastically cut power, coming dangerously close to stalling their turbofan engines in an effort to turn around and directly engage the enemy. From every direction, dotting lines of green fire moved between the J-6 Farmers as the Russian MiGs cut loose with their own 30 mm cannons, the tracers clearly visible even in the bright daylight.

Circling each other in complex patterns, the Russian and Chinese warplanes launched more missiles and antimissiles, their cannons firing in prolonged bursts. Metallic chaff and sizzling magnesium flares pumped from the fighters, the visible combat counterpointed by the on-board computers automatically engaging in silent electronic warfare. The Russian tanks boomed from below, the shells missing the Chinese to detonate on the sloping hillside starting more fires and a small avalanche of loose boulders.

Suddenly, the cowling of the Russian planes turned dark and the MiGs broke formation to leave the river valley at top speed.

"Cowardly dogs!" Tzu sneered, starting to peruse the retreating planes. He was out of missiles and low on ammunition, the fuel pressure gauges hovering near the danger level, but the man was grimly determined to repel the invaders from his beloved homeland at any cost.

"Cover your eyes!" Dee barked, scrambling to don a pair of mirrored glasses. The face shield on the helmet was designed to protect his eyes from shrapnel and flying glass, but not this sort of attack.

On the misty battleground, a soldier clambered into view from a tank, his arms full of a stubby weapon that resembled a WWII flamethrower, except that the flared end was made of glass and crystal. Switching on the gasoline-powered generator inside his backpack, the Russian grinned fiendishly as he swept the sky with the UV laser.

A thousand feet high, Tzu screamed as everything turned a solid black. "I can't see!" he wailed, clawing at his face. "I'm stone blind!"

"Yes, comrade, I know," Captain Dee said gently, squinting against the invisible light stinging his eyes in spite of the protective glasses and tinted shield of the helmet. He felt furious over the other man's failure, and wanted to chastise the fool, but what was the point? A blind combat pilot couldn't land a jetfighter. Nobody could. When the fuel ran out, the other man was dead.

As the violet glare receded from the cockpits of the F-6 Farmers, the Russian MiG fighters returned in combat formation, every weapon firing.

"I wish we had a nuke," Dee whispered harshly, firing the last rounds from the nose cannon. When the dwindling ammunition was gone, he would boost to supersonic and depart the valley, leaving his friend to the cold mercy of the Russians. There was nothing else he could do.

"What was that?" Tzu gasped, his jet starting to loll slightly. "The Russians have a nuke?" He touched his throat mike. "Firebird Two to Cold Dragon base! Alert! Alert! We are under nuclear attack!"

Incompetent fool! Furiously, Dee grabbed for his throat mike to override the transmission when a salvo of Russian missiles appeared from above, arching downward fast. The Chinese pilot shoved the joystick to the maximum, insanely accelerating to try to escape. For a split second, he saw the red tips of the missiles stab through the resilient plastic cowling, then his world was filled with fire and flame for an even shorter period of time. Then there was only peaceful blackness.

A few minutes later, the Citadel in Beijing sent out a coded message to all of its Western air force bases. In short order, hundreds of Super Seven interceptors, J-6 and Foxhound fighters, along with a dozen Xian nuclear-strike bombers, streaked into the sky heading for a nameless valley in the Argun Mountains.

Stony Man Farm, Virginia

SITUATED DEEP UNDERGROUND, the subterranean Computer Room was cool and quiet, the four Stony Man hackers hunched low over their consoles, hard at work. From a small coffee station off to the side came the powerful smell of fresh coffee. The only discernible sounds were the steady tapping of fingers on keyboards and a low hum from the wall vents.

Sipping strong black coffee from a ceramic mug the size of a beer stein, Aaron "The Bear" Kurtzman watched his staff and rubbed a hand along the rubber-edged wheel of his chair. His calloused palms caressed the worn material with hated intimacy. The man knew every inch of the wheelchair the way an ordinary man knew the contours of his face.

"Anything yet?" Kurtzman asked, draining the coffee and placing the mug aside on his console.

"Nothing on the shell casings," Akira Tokaido replied, popping a piece of gum in his mouth. "According to the files at Interpol headquarters, the ammunition was sold to the Chilean army, but then stolen by some Communist guerrillas in the Alps, and has never surfaced again until now."

The young Japanese-American youth was a natural-born hacker. Tokaido was wearing loose clothing, the items mismatched as if the social concept of fashion didn't exist. The heavy beat of thumping rock music seeped from the earbuds pressed into his ears.

"How about our pinup girl?" Kurtzman asked, frowning.

The JPEG of the raven-haired woman was taped to the side of his computer monitor. Her black eyes sparkled like diamonds inside the motorcycle helmet, her pretty face a snarl of bestial rage as she raised the FN-2000 assault rifle into a firing position. She was gorgeous, and had gunned down a dozen civilians. Beauty and the beast combined.

"Still working on it," Carmen Delahunt answered. "If she's a professional mercenary, then she must have a police record somewhere."

Her long red hair tied off in a ponytail, the beautiful woman was neatly dressed in a green cotton blouse and loose black skirt, shapely nylon-clad legs tucked under her chair. On her workstation desk were numerous pictures of her children.

"Also check with NATO. She could be part of a terrorist group."

"Already doing so," she said with a cold smile. "Nothing so far. I'll try the Mossad and then British Intelligence."

"Don't forget the S2 in Brazil," Kurtzman suggested. "They could be hiring out their people as muscle. Lord knows the bastards have a finger in every other dirty enterprise in South America. Why not this?"

Delahunt only grunted in acknowledgment as she returned to her task.

Kurtzman watched her for a moment, then turned as he noticed the colored lights change on the main monitor. Things were getting nasty along the Russia-China border. Hundreds of ships were jammed at the Panama Canal, and several fights had started and been stopped, but nothing serious yet. However, Uganda had activated its entire army, and downtown Japan was still on fire, the rioting getting worse all the time.

"Akira, any chance of tracing that cell phone call?" Kurtzman demanded, lifting his mug and scowling at finding it empty.

Thoughtfully, Tokaido paused to blow a pink bubble. "No way," he decided, chewing back in the sticky confection. "Whoever these folks have as their computer support is very good. Almost too damn good."

"Anything from the Dirty Dozen?" Kurtzman asked hopefully, rolling to the kitchenette and pouring himself a fresh cup of coffee. The Dirty Dozen were his invention, instituted long ago. They were a collection of artificial personalities the cybernetic team maintained as sources of information. They posted fake arrest reports in newspapers, and then denied them on the Internet, which made everybody believe the reports had to be real. The Dirty Dozen covered the full spectrum of criminal activity from racketeering to assassinations, with a little arms smuggling on the side.

"Yes and no," Tokaido said, sounding annoyed. "Nobody is offering to sell, rent or lease control of the GPS network, or even claiming that they could do it, either. However, somebody is trying to hire mercenaries from Larry Dixon in Omaha for an unspecified job."

Dixon was one of the Dozen. "Omaha is on the escape route of the Texas bikers," Kurtzman said slowly, chewing over the possibilities. "Okay, hire out some muscle, then have Jack fly Able Team to Omaha for the meeting. With any luck, it'll be our mystery woman and they'll capture her alive to squeeze out some hard information."

"And if it isn't the terrorists," Tokaido asked pointedly, "just some crime lord making to take over more territory?"

Kurtzman dismissed the matter with a shrug. "Then Able Team leaves, and they're still on the escape route. Those people left Texas with their asses on fire. They must pop up somewhere for supplies before reaching North Dakota—rob a bank, loot a gun store, raid a police station, whatever. And when they do, Able Team will drop on them like a ton of bricks."

"Unless they were killed when that cave exploded in the foothills," Tokaido said, starting to type away.

Having no reply to that possibility, the chief computer expert wheeled himself back to his console and slid underneath smooth as a docking space shuttle. A soldier did what he could, nothing more. "Hunt, talk to me," Kurtzman commanded gruffly.

"Almost done," Huntington Wethers announced, turning from his console. "And...there. Okay, good news, bad news." The slim, dapper man had silver highlights at his temples and was chewing on a briarwood pipe. "There seems to have been a great deal of research into the possible modification of the GPS network by the United Kingdom, Germany, Japan, China, all of the superpowers, including America, but so far, nobody even has an idea how it could be accomplished." Placing the pipe on a rosewood rack, Wethers took another and tucked it into his mouth. Smoking was forbidden near the delicate computers, but the former university professor still liked to chew his old pipe as an aid to concentration.

"Who was the first, and who's the most recent?" Kurtzman demanded, a laser printer built into his console scrolling a top-secret report, the sheet of paper traveling under a sheet of glass and going directly into a shredder that reduced the paper into tiny flakes. An experimental long-range antimissile fired at

Port Woomera in Australia had just crashed outside of Santiago, the capital city of Chile, which sure as heck, he knew, was not the intended target. Thankfully, there were no civilian deaths. However, their luck couldn't hold forever, and the next time…

Removing the pipe again, Wethers tapped the monitor. "The first person to publish a paper on hacking the GPS network was…" He smiled. "Hermann Schwarz."

"Gadgets?"

"Exactly. He claimed it was impossible. The most recent was our old friend, Virgil McPherson, who also claimed it was impossible."

"Yet it has been done," Kurtzman noted, a dark scowl furrowing his brow. The big man took a slurp of the scalding coffee. Okay, if a frontal assault failed, then it was time to try the back door. "Any recent work done on protecting the network?" he asked sagely. "There's no better thief than a locksmith."

"Way ahead of you, Chief," Wethers said, tapping a button to scroll the monitor. "It seems that the UN Security Council authorized such a project several years ago. The head of the project was a…just a moment….Professor Sigerson von Reinhold."

"Von Reinhold," Kurtzman repeated thoughtfully. "So he's a member of the German royalty."

Wethers shrugged. "Well, a very long time ago, yes. But the professor just goes by his family name these days, sans the honorific."

"Any chance he's alive?"

"Sadly, no," Wethers said with a frown, reading the bottom of the classified report. "Reinhold died in a plane crash last year in the Argentine Alps."

"Where was that again?" Kurtzman asked, raising an eyebrow.

"Argentina," Wethers said, then stopped cold. "Yes, I see the connection. Curious."

"Like hell it is," the computer expert growled, setting aside the mug. He started pressing buttons to slave their consoles to his own. The bullets were stolen from Argentina, and the professor was killed in the same country.

Quickly, Kurtzman scanned the assorted reports and files. There was scant data about Reinhold, and no death certificate. Only unconfirmed newspaper reports. "Wethers, drop everything else and make sure this man is dead."

"Already doing that," Wethers said, hands moving across the keyboard like a concert pianist playing Mozart.

A long minute passed. Another.

"Well?" Kurtzman demanded gruffly.

"The official files in Argentina were deleted," Wethers announced with obvious satisfaction. "But I tracked down the off-site backup files in Staten Isle."

"New York?" Tokaido asked in shock, looking up from his typing. "The Argentine government kept their backup files in another country?"

"That's Staten Island," Wethers said tolerantly, as if lecturing to one of his classes. "Staten Isle is off the coast of southwest Argentina."

With a nod, the others returned to their work.

"So you were able to rebuild the deleted files?" Kurtzman asked, checking his monitor.

"Nobody could rebuild those files," Wethers stated, crossing his arms. "The deletion was thorough, with no remaining fragments or pieces. A triple-layer erase of ones and zeros, you know the drill."

Yeah, Kurtzman understood. That was the procedure that the White House, the Pentagon and even Stony Man itself used.

After each deletion of a file, the medium would be overwritten by random numbers, then deleted again and overwritten again. After the third time, nobody could bring back those files.

"Odd that the main files were deleted, but the backups were in good shape," Kurtzman said suspiciously. Then he saw the truth of the matter. Most of the files for the Argentine military weren't on computers so that an enemy couldn't hack the system and steal them. Okay, that was clever. But while the military records were in poor shape, the Accounting and Receiving Department of the Argentine government kept detailed files on everybody in their employ.

Tapping the scroll button, Kurtzman skimmed the files. Both parents were of German extraction and moved to Argentina after World War II. His father was believed to have been a member of the Third Reich, but cleared of all charges because of fire-damaged papers. Reinhold was born in Argentina, and graduated Buenos Aires University magna cum laude. Then he went to Oxford University for his postgraduate work in cybernetic communications and advanced theoretical electronics. The perfect man to invent a way to hack the GPS network, Kurtzman thought.

"And before his untimely death, Reinhold spent a year at Fort Peron, working on code-breaking software for a General Rolf Calvano," Kurtzman said, reading out loud. "Anything on this Calvano?"

"Hmm, his army personnel file is in the military archives at the capital, but it's protected by a very impressive firewall," Wethers said with a frown. "This may take me a moment... Interesting design, actually...." His voice faded away as the man became engrossed in the task.

"Stay on it," Kurtzman directed him. "Let me know when—"

"All right, General Rolf Bolivar Calvano is a pure-blood Argentinian," Wethers interrupted, relaxing his tense stance. "The man appears to be a real hard case, but is fanatically patriotic to his country. Wounded four times in battles with the Communist insurgents, four medals for bravery during their infamous Dirty War of 1983 and has two demotions for excessive brutality in interrogating prisoners. A wife and two kids in Cordoba, but believed to have several mistresses scattered about the country, almost no friends, not in the military. Doesn't belong to any political parties, bowling leagues or anything else that I can find. The army is his life."

"Where was he born?"

"In the slums of Buenos Aires, raised in an orphanage, worked in a factory making cars until he ran away and faked ID papers to join the army. He got disciplined a lot in boot camp, but then got his act together and had been a model soldier for the next three decades."

"Until now," Kurtzman ruminated, stirring sugar into the thick coffee. This was exactly the sort of man who usually was on the same side as Stony Man. A soldier standing bold against the night. He bent the rules a lot, but never outright broke them. However, it was starting to seem that was a cover. In truth, he had been working on some project since before he joined the military forces. But why would he want to start a world war? What would it accomplish aside from killing most of the world's population? Something glimmered in the back of his mind at the thought, but the more Kurtzman tried to nail it down, the more the notion slipped away.

"Is Calvano also listed as deceased?" Kurtzman asked expectantly.

"Oh, no, very much alive," Wethers replied. "At the present, he is the base CO for Fort Peron, nicknamed Firebase Alpha by his troops. No reason cited." The man worked away in silence for a while.

"Alpha," Kurtzman muttered, rubbing his jaw. That certainly seemed to indicate there were other bases somewhere, which would make sense. Calvano would need one uplink in each hemisphere to cover the entire world. North Dakota was looking more and more important by the minute.

"Well, well, there are classified reports that Communists claim he took huge sums of money from their war chests and turned in nothing," Wethers continued. "His civilian apartment was checked but they didn't find any money, or a fancy sports car. There are a lot of accusations, but no indictments."

"He might have kept the money to fund this uplink project," Kurtzman theorized, starting to take a sip of coffee, then putting the mug back in place. "After all, a pound of food stolen from the enemy is worth ten pounds of your own supplies. This is the twenty-first century and every general worth his salt has read *The Art of War* by Sun Tzu."

"Absolutely," Wethers agreed, massaging his wrists. "However, I wonder if—"

"Got her!" Carmen Delahunt yelled in triumph. "Bear, I found our mystery woman! Her name is Henrietta Caramico, no middle name, which is rather odd for a Spanish woman. Caramico is one of the very few female officers in the Argentine army…" A smile slowly grew on the woman's face. "And her last known billet was at Fort Peron, under the command of General Rolf Calvano."

"Hot damn, now we're talking," Tokaido said with a grim smile, but his hands never paused in the endless typing.

"What's more," Delahunt continued, "according to the official records, Lieutenant Caramico died two years ago in a plane crash."

"Another ghost soldier," Kurtzman said, rubbing a hand along the wheel of his chair. "All right, this could just be a coincidence, but we have to check it out thoroughly. I want a full dossier on Calvano ASAP. What he eats for breakfast, his favorite comic books as a kid, everything!" He paused. "Including everything you can get on this Firebase Alpha. If this pans out, we're not sending in Phoenix Force to do a recon without as much information as possible."

Without a word, the two hackers got busy.

"There seems to be something quite bizarre going on at the firebase," Wethers said slowly, his frown deepening. "It appears to be on red alert."

"So what? Considering what is happening in the world, that only makes sense," Kurtzman stated, rubbing the wheels of his chair and wondering where the hacker was going with the observation. "Most of the military bases in the world have closed their gates and gone hard as a prayer in hell."

"Quite true," Wethers answered, removing his pipe to gesture at the screen. "However, Fort Peron went on alert status a full day before the Texas warehouse exploded."

Silence surged through the Computer Room.

"Are you sure?" Delahunt demanded.

"Absolutely," Wethers stated, giving a nod. "Almost twenty-four hours exactly. They claim it was for war games. But none were scheduled for a couple of months."

"It's them," Tokaido declared. "It's gotta be." Unless this was an incredibly clever red herring to make them waste valuable time while civilization continued to fall apart.

Kurtzman considered the matter from every angle and made his decision. Reaching for a telephone, the man tapped in a few numbers. "Barbara? Me. We may have a hot lead for Phoenix Force…."

CHAPTER TEN

Ezeiza International Airport, Argentina

Slowly, the sun rose on the horizon, banishing the night and heralding a new day. Inside the DC-3 airplane, the muted rumble of the twin engines was barely discernable to the men of Phoenix Force as they ate a hurried breakfast or dutifully checked over their weapons. This mission was just a recon for the Stony Man team, but they were preparing for combat anyway. There were old soldiers, and lazy soldiers, but no old lazy soldiers.

Leaning out the small side window in the cockpit, David McCarter was buffeted by the rushing wind as he clung to the brass sextant with a white-knuckled grip.

Muttering under his breath, McCarter focused the antique navigational aid on the sun, then cut it by half and quickly ran the mathematical calculations. Going back inside, he slid shut the window and sighed in relief.

"Okay, we're just passing Punta del Este in southern Uruguay," McCarter declared, placing the sextant into a velvet-lined wooden box. "Right on course."

"Just a few hours behind schedule," Hawkins said, sitting in the copilot's seat, the yoke tight in his hands.

"Close enough," McCarter said resolutely, taking the pilot's seat and buckling on the safety belt. "I never realized how much we depend on the bloody GPS network these days. It's a bleeding nuisance to find out where we are with a sextant and compass. But we should reach Buenos Aires in about an hour."

"And then the fun starts," Hawkins said, releasing the yoke as the other man took control of the aircraft.

Although every member of Phoenix Force knew the basics of how to fly most planes, McCarter was a properly trained pilot and Hawkins had no problem letting the Briton have the stick. Only the ace Stony Man pilot Jack Grimaldi was better at flying. But then, it was said Uncle Jack had been born wearing wings and could pilot anything from a box kite to a space shuttle. And so far, that had proved to be true. Not very surprisingly, his favorite plane was the huge C-130 Hercules, the largest propeller-driven airplane in existence, affectionately called the "Herc" by every airman lucky enough to pilot one of the colossal sky monsters.

Opening a thermos, Hawkins poured himself a plastic cup of hot broth. Unfortunately, their C-130 Hercules had been abandoned at Puerto Rico to help maintain the illusion that they had all been killed by the San Juan mercs. The DC-3 was a replacement found by Kurtzman and his team. Their present DC-3 was almost a toy in comparison to the mighty Herc, only a hair more than half the size, with a third of the range. But the DC-3 was a classic, a workhorse of the clouds.

Invented way back in 1930, the DC-3 had been in production, on and off, ever since. It really said something special about the sturdy skytrain that after seventy years, modern-day avionics couldn't design a better all-purpose airplane than the old "Gooney Bird." A DC-3 was able to take off, and land, on rough ground that would crash any other airplane. An important factor in their covert work, exponentially expanding their choice of landing zones. The craft could easily hold the entire team with their equipment and munitions, although not their Hummer. But much more importantly, the DC-3 didn't make use of the GPS network. It was strictly a directional-radio, dead-reckoning and compass craft, complete with a library of maps stored in the tight causeway between the cockpit and the aft cargo hold.

"Sure hope a Hummer is waiting for us," Encizo said, spooning some stew from the open Mylar envelope of an MRE pack.

The man was sitting on a wooden bench bolted to the portside fuselage. There were a lot of steel rings set into the flooring, and nets festooned the curved walls of prestressed aluminum. Clearly, this particular Gooney Bird had been used for hauling freight, with no consideration given for passenger comfort.

"It's going to be rough country in those foothills," Manning agreed, adding a touch of silicon lubricate to the bolt-action of his Barrett sniper rifle. He worked the bolt with a subdued click. "Be even worse if we have to go into the mountains. The Argentine Alps make the Shenandoah Mountains look like sand castles."

"Worse than Pakistan?"

"There isn't anything worse than the Pakistan mountains on this Earth." Manning paused in thought. "Well, maybe Mars. Or the big moon—what'sitsname?—Ganymede. You know, the one that is constantly exploding?"

"I just hope this gamble pays off," James added, a cloth cap pulled low over his face. He was lying on a stack of camping supplies lashed to the deck under a canvas sheet. Any good soldier knew to grab some extra sack time whenever possible. It had been part of their basic training, along with defusing high explosives and peeling potatoes. "If Calvano isn't controlling the GPS network, then we're shit out of luck."

"I hear that, brother," Encizo muttered, shoving the Mylar envelope into a plastic garbage bag hanging from a nearby stanchion.

Pulling out a tiny packet from his shirt pocket, Encizo ripped it open with his teeth and carefully wiped his hands before consigning the moist towelette also to the garbage bag. Clean once more, the man pulled a Walther PPK .38 from the shoulder holster under his white linen jacket to check the draw. Anybody stupid enough to touch an automatic pistol with greasy hands, he thought, deserved the unmarked grave he or she was surely about to be shoveled into.

Satisfied with the draw of the Walther, Encizo holstered it once more and adjusted his jacket to cover the deadly weapon. In an effort to stay low-key, the team was going into Argentina as tourists, civilians on a fishing trip to Mar Chiquita, famous for freshwater trout. Every man was dressed in colorful Hawaiian shirts, denims and sneakers. Their considerable arsenal of weapons was carefully hidden among the plastic boxes full of camping supplies. This was something the team had done before. Kurtzman had couriered them German diplomatic passports, which made inspecting their possessions virtually an act of war, so they expected no trouble slipping the weapons past the customs inspectors, or even the hard-nosed Federal Police.

Slowly, noon arrived and departed, before the DC-3 broached the sprawling coastal city of Montevideo. Staying out of the way of the commercial jetliners, McCarter saw that the dockyards were full of big cargo ships and oil tankers, cargo cranes rising above the vessels like the skeletons of dead giants. Black rock formations dotted the white sandy beaches.

"Looks rather nice," Hawkins commented, finishing off the broth.

"Why not?" McCarter snorted. "Who the hell goes to Uruguay for their vacation?"

As there was no answer to that, Hawkins went to use the small lavatory, and came back smelling of military soap. "Spell you for a while?" he offered, slipping back into the copilot's seat.

"Thanks," McCarter said, gratefully releasing the steering yoke. Then he rose to shuffle into the back for some chow, his stomach softly rumbling in harmony to the engines.

Less than an hour later, the DC-3 was skimming above the crystalline-blue waters of the Rio de la Plata bay. Dipping a wing, Hawkins angled toward Buenos Aires. Twenty minutes later, the sprawling metropolis rose into view over the horizon, gleaming skyscrapers and stone office buildings spreading outward for miles. There were a lot of good reasons that Buenos Aires was called the Paris of South America. Aside from the sheer size of the bustling city, there also were countless art museums, night-clubs, universities, casinos, opera houses, sports arenas, and the usual cadre of grim international corporations safely ensconced in their shining towers of glass and steel. Green parklands dotted the cityscape, and concrete highways wove an impossible maze throughout the buildings and across the wide rivers.

Reclaiming the pilot seat, McCarter lowered their airspeed as Hawkins donned a set of headphones and contacted the control tower at Ezeiza Airport, giving their fake flight number and fake ID. The tower accepted the falsified identification and assigned them a place in line with the other planes

waiting to land, along with a private runway set at the absolutely extreme far end of the mammoth airport.

Circling the isolated landing strip a few times to get the feel
of the wind, McCarter feathered the propellers, dropped the
airfoils and headed in for a landing. The tires touched once
and bounced, squealing in protest. Then he tried again, and
the DC-3 lightly touched down without any protest and rapidly rolled along the runway, until McCarter angled the airplane off the macadam and onto a grassy field. A tan Hummer
was parked near some laurel bushes, a white cloth tied to a
wiper blade showing it was for them.

"Bear doesn't miss a trick," Hawkins noted, threading a
sound suppressor to the barrel of his 9 mm Beretta pistol. Then
the man scowled and reached out fast to adjust the gain on
the radio headphones. "Say again?" he demanded.

Suddenly alert, McCarter said nothing as he set the brakes,
but kept the twin engines gently turning over in case they
needed a quick departure.

"Get hard, people!" Hawkins called, yanking off the headphones and turning toward the causeway. "The Federal Police are on the way!"

In the cargo hold, the rest of the team moved fast, acquiring weapons and looking out the small windows. Nobody
was in sight yet.

"How did they make us?" McCarter demanded angrily,
drawing his own 9 mm Browning Hi-Power pistol. "Our papers should have fooled anybody."

"They did," Hawkins retorted, casting off the seat belt.
"But airport security says that because of the recent rash of
international incidents, all planes must be searched."

"And they tell us after we landed?" James demanded from
the hatchway leading to the cockpit. The lanky man filled the

causeway, an MP-5 submachine expertly balanced in his hands, the bolt thrown back and the safety off.

"Which makes it a tad bit harder for us to leave, my old china," McCarter said gruffly, temporarily lapsing into Cockney rhyming slang.

That took James a second to decipher. Old china, china plate, mate, as in friend.

"I gather our diplomatic immunity means nothing?" Encizo added, pressing a U.S. Army monocular to his face. There were some vehicles moving along an access road about a thousand yards away, but if they were coming this way he couldn't tell yet.

"They couldn't care less," Hawkins stated. "They say it's a case of national security."

"Now where have we heard that phrase before?" James muttered under his breath. "Sounds more like Calvano wants to make sure nobody is coming after his ass."

Adjusting the focus on the monocular, Encizo started to speak when he caught a glimpse of the people inside the four…no, six camouflage-colored Jeeps heading their way. The men were all wearing the same uniform, grenades festooning their military webbing, and they carried FN-2000 assault rifles. One Jeep had an M-246 mounted atop a universal symbol, a bald man loading the 7.62 mm machine gun expertly swaying to the motion of the speeding vehicle.

"Federal Police my ass. Those are soldiers," Encizo announced, slinging the monocular over a stanchion and swinging around his own MP-5 to work the arming bolt. "These boys are packing some serious heat, and look ready to rock."

For a split second McCarter debated taking off into the air again, but then realized the futility of the move. On the ground, they stood a fighting chance. Up in the air, the slow DC-3 would be an easy target for the Argentine jetfighters. No choice, then.

"T.J., Rafe and Cal, load the Hummer!" McCarter barked,

grabbing a coil of nylon rope hanging on the wall. "Gary and I will rig a diversion. We leave in sixty seconds. Now move!"

Everybody lurched into action.

By the time the three men had the Hummer packed with everything it could hold, the engines of the DC-3 were roaring with power, the entire airplane shaking as it struggled to take off, held to the earth only by the locked wheels.

"Here they come," Hawkins said calmly, unwrapping the safety tape from a grenade.

Jumping out the side hatch of the Gooney Bird, Manning raced to a position behind the shuddering airplane and unlimbered the deadly Barrett. As if in reply to the action, a lieutenant in the lead Jeep lifted a bullhorn to his face and shouted something in Spanish, the words booming across the grassy field.

In reply, Manning leveled the Barrett and stroked the trigger. The colossal rifle boomed and the windshield on the Jeep shattered. Instantly, the six Jeeps took evasive maneuvers. Working the bolt to chamber another round, Manning waited until he had a clear shot, then fired again. The windshield on a second Jeep was annihilated, along with the windshield on the vehicle traveling close behind. The Jeeps braked to a halt, and the soldiers started to shoot back, the FN-2000 assault rifles spraying bullets in a ragged barrage.

Without comment, Hawkins threw the grenade, which landed between the two groups and began to leak dark smoke. Now, the rest of Phoenix Force started to throw smoke grenades in every direction, along with a few stun grenades, the harmless flash-bangs sounding infinitely louder than the real thing.

When the billowing smoke was thick enough, McCarter jumped from the DC-3, the end of a rope in his hands. Partially closing the hatch, the former SAS officer yanked hard on the nylon length, then slammed the hatch shut. The rope caught in the jamb, holding it in place even as the brakes were released and the straining DC-3 surged forward, rapidly building speed as it moved across the neatly mowed field.

The soldiers immediately began to shoot at the escaping plane, the 5.56 mm hardball ammo peppering the aluminum fuselage of the runaway plane. Then the M-274 machine gun cut loose, armor-piercing rounds punching a line of holes through the DC-3 with contemptuous ease.

As the rest of the team continued to toss smoke grenades, McCarter pressed the contact on a radio detonator and a dozen Willie Peter charges flared inside the Gooney Bird, illuminating the craft like a Halloween pumpkin, tongues of flame licking out the broken windows.

The soldiers stopped shooting as the burning airplane rolled past them trailing thick smoke. Dripping flames, the DC-3 smashed through the wire fence edging the airport field, and crashed into the trees. A wing buckled, and engine cowling came off. But the two propellers kept spinning, sending a wave of chopped greenery high into the sky.

Climbing into the crowded Hummer, James tossed away the last of the smoke grenades as McCarter pressed the second switch on the radio detonator.

Buried in the foliage, the burning Gooney Bird flared with blinding light as a dozen thermite grenades cut loose, the waves of explosions making the craft begin to sag as the metal started to melt.

Shouting curses, the soldiers dived for cover and a moment later, the fuel tanks of the DC-3 erupted, closely followed by the ample stores of ammunition. The irregular crackling of discharges sounding like rattling leaves for a hundred yards in every direction. An alarm began to howl from the airport.

Slipping the Hummer into gear, Hawkins started to drive toward the city, the military vehicle easing through into the roiling clouds of dark smoke to disappear like a ghost in the night.

CHAPTER ELEVEN

Firebase Omega

His eyes closed to mere slits, Hasuraya "Mongoose" Metudas closely studied the bank of sixteen video monitors forming a curved wall on the wide console. Each screen had text crawling across the bottom, detailing troops' movements and replaying the top news reports from around the world.

A skinny, rat-faced man, Mongoose was wearing a heavy sweater and a knit cap against the cold. The computer room he nicknamed the North Pole, for obvious reasons, was sealed airtight to help the laboring air conditioners keep the temperature just below freezing. Located at the back of the room, the massive Cray SVG supercomputer worked faster in the cold. However, regularly buying liquid nitrogen was a telltale giveaway to anybody searching for an enemy hacker. And somewhere along the east coast of the Untied States was a group of fellow computer experts, probably CIA or NSA, the government electron-riders almost as good as he was. They had helped direct the destruction of the former employer, Mohad

Malavade in Calcutta. But the clever bastards weren't going to stop Forge. There was too much at stake.

And as soon as I learn their location, Mongoose added grimly. I'll drop enough burning jetliners on them to flatten Mt. Everest!

On the run from Interpol and Indian Intelligence, Mongoose had started off working for Calvano just for the paycheck, but over time the general had convinced the hacker this was the only way to save humanity. Now he worked free of charge, bringing about the end of the old world, to help create a new world order of sanity and peace.

But like any radical surgery removing cancer, Mongoose sagely mused, using fingertips to up the rheostat of the electric jumpsuit situated under his bulky turtleneck sweater, there's going to be some blood and pain. That couldn't be helped. Aside from getting the nuclear war over as soon as possible.

Softly murmuring headphones dangling around his neck, Mongoose listened with an unfocused mind, absorbing the torrent of data and deciding where to have the GPS network malfunction next.

Hacking into the GPS network had been relatively simple in comparison to overriding the security codes of sixteen nations to use their own spy satellites against them. And Mongoose needed the spy satellites to orchestrate the cresting waves of destruction. Even a nuclear warhead was useless without some way to aim the thing.

And the fools constantly tell me where to strike all by themselves. The little man called "Snake Eater" by the soldiers of Forge smirked in pleasure. Keep broadcasting live news reports, and soon I will level the world!

Typing away on a silent keyboard, Mongoose transferred the last payment to a group of mercenaries in Nebraska, crashed a Cessna jet and sent French artillery shells into Germany, blowing up a fuel depot and setting a factory complex on fire.

Tulsa, Oklahoma

RIPPING OPEN HER SEQUINED vest, Darla Crane cast it aside, exposing her full jiggling breasts. Wearing only a flimsy G-string, every inch of the nearly nude woman was either covered with tattoos or pierced. Immediately, the crowd of men in the strip club went wild, whistling and applauding.

On the second lighted ramp of the Kit Kat Club, Lorna Morgan moved sensuously to the heavy beat of the pounding music, then bent over to yank off her white-satin hot pants, revealing that she wasn't wearing a thong and had recently been to the beauty salon for a Brazilian wax. Once again, the crowd roared its frank approval.

Sitting quietly in a dim corner, Caramico and Mendoza forced themselves to cheer at the naked dancers on the stage as they waited for the FBI to arrive.

After getting the sergeant patched up, the Forge operatives had been on the run nonstop since Texas, sleeping in ditches, hijacking random cars and stealing the lunch bags of construction workers at a building site. And every moment they were braced for the American secret police to attack and try to haul them off to an interrogation cell where they would be slowly taken apart by the CIA until betraying General Calvano. But the Forge soldiers had decided to kill themselves before allowing that to occur. But that was the contingency plan. Hopefully, the mercs that Snake Eater had arranged to meet with them at this club were as good as they claimed.

Strangers in a strange land, the Forge soldiers had chosen

the establishment more for its notoriety than anything else. Even halfway across the globe in Argentina, the soldiers had heard about the infamous Kit Kat Club. Framed posters of past performers adorned the walls, all the way back to the legendary Betty Paige and Gypsy Rose Lee.

Moving through the crowd like an eel, a slim man sat opposite the Forge soldiers in the booth. Without a comment, the newcomer poured himself a glass of warm beer from a pitcher. He took a sip, grimaced in disgust, then put the glass aside and wiped his mouth clean with a pressed white handkerchief. His initials were embroidered on a corner.

"The cost is five grand, per man, per day," Warner Bronson said, straightening the cuffs of his lavender shirt. The middle-aged man was nattily dressed in a Hugo Boss suit and Italian loafers. His nails were manicured, shiny with clear polish, and there was a definite aroma of lilacs wafting about the man.

"That is acceptable," Caramico replied, easing down the hammer of the Bersa pistol hidden below the table. With a deft movement, she tucked the deadly pistol into the shoulder holster under her windbreaker. After the wholesale slaughter of her team in Texas, the lieutenant didn't give a damn how much the mercenaries cost. Just as long as they were the best.

"How soon can they be here?" Caramico added, running a hand along her cropped hair. It was strange to touch her neck, and she felt oddly vulnerable, more naked and exposed than the girl dancing on stage.

"They're already on the way, dear lady," Bronson boasted, smiling widely. "I anticipated your needs and arranged for them to come here post haste."

"Excellent."

Dismissing the matter with a cavalier smile, Bronson

waved for the waitress, his other hand clicking back on the safety of the silenced Remington .32 pistol in his pocket.

Staying alert, Mendoza said nothing, his hand still out of sight under the table. There were a lot of people in the world that the soldier didn't like—lawyers, Communists, Americans—but at the top of the list were middlemen: pimps, union negotiators, fences and black marketeers. He hated them all. The leeches made nothing, and did nothing, except buy and sell other people's property for a hefty profit. Somehow, it seemed cowardly, almost unclean, like robbing a friend. The soldier tried not to grimace at the smeary fellow sitting across from him, but could only manage a sneer of disdain.

If Bronson noticed, he made no comment.

As the performance onstage ended, the crowd applauded loudly, and Caramico leaned across the table to pour the sergeant a beer, even though his glass was almost full.

"Try to smile more," she whispered to him. "And try to act like you're enjoying the show. I've seen fresh corpses with bigger grins."

"I am a soldier, not a spy," Mendoza retorted, trying not to bend from the waist. He was covered with bruises from the brief fight with the sheriff, cheek slashed, bullet hole in his shoulder, but the soldier didn't want anybody to know how difficult it had been to take the old man. And having a suicide dynamite pack strapped there wasn't helping matters.

"Besides, this is not entertainment," the sergeant added, looking at the new group of busty dancers taking the stage. "These woman look like cows waving their big udders about. Big, fat, ugly cows."

"Prefer young girls, eh?" Bronson chuckled. "Well, to each his own."

"I like an honest whore," the big sergeant said stiffly. "Which is infinitely better than mounting little boys, *maticone*."

Pretending to be puzzled by the Spanish word, Bronson tilted his head in a questioning manner, but there came a subdued click from under the table.

"Do you really need this man?" he asked. "I can easily find you a trained monkey with twice his intelligence. It would probably smell better, too."

Clearly annoyed, the lieutenant started to reply when the waitress arrived.

"Hi, I'm Sheryl. What can I get you?" the young girl asked, the question punctuated by the snap of her chewing gum. Barely out of her teens, she was dressed in fish-net stockings and spiked heels that had to have been agony on her feet. Black hot pants seemed to have been sprayed on her trim body, and a silver-striped vest pushed up her small breasts until they appeared several times their original size. Her hair was teased into a beehive and streaked with several different colors, none of them natural. A small tattoo of a flowery vine encircled her left ankle, a butterfly was on her stomach and a coil of barbed wire went around her left arm.

"Chivas, on the rocks," Bronson said with a smooth smile, folding his hands in his lap to hide the gun.

"More beer," Mendoza snapped, stroking the cut on his cheek, which had been expertly repaired with a form of surgical glue. It itched like crazy, but there were no stitches to come loose in a fight. He considered that a fair trade-off.

"Cancel both of those orders, please," Caramico corrected. "Take away the pitcher and bring us cold bottles of beer. Cold, mind you. And they'd better still be sealed."

"Oh yeah, sure, no prob there," Sheryl said, chewing away contentedly. "We run a class joint here, ya know? No hookers in the shitter, let me tell ya. The boss likes class." She touched her beehive of hair with fingernails the color of a freshly slaughtered pig.

"Class," Sheryl repeated proudly.

"That's why we came," Caramico said, stuffing a fifty-dollar bill into the teen's garter. Her fingers lingered on the smooth nylon, savoring the warmth for a long moment before letting go reluctantly.

The large denomination of the bill allowed such intimacy, and Sheryl giggled in response, then turned and headed for the bar, her petite hips swaying in time to the loud music.

"Too young," the sergeant scoffed.

"Too dirty," Bronson countered.

"No time," the lieutenant stated, fondling her fake wedding ring. "There's just never enough time."

Suddenly the soldiers became alert as several large men walked into the strip club. The newcomers paused, allowing their eyes to become adjusted to the darkness.

"That's them," Bronson said, raising a finger.

"Yes, we know," Caramico replied.

One of the strangers at the door, a tall bald man, caught the gesture and nodded in return. A burly man paid the entrance fee to a muscular bouncer nearly bursting from a tuxedo, while the third stood back, almost as if he were standing guard. Offering their hands to be stamped, the grim trio entered the club and brushed aside a couple of off-duty dancers trying to cage drinks from the new arrivals. The girls accepted the rebuff and moved on to find fresh victims.

Moving with the ease of panthers, the men of Trinity started across the crowded room. The three hard cases had the look of professional killers, their expressionless eyes as hard and cold as Christmas in jail. Their gaze swept the crowd of drunk patrons once, then ignored them completely. The nude dancers onstage never got a glance.

Trying not to show it, Caramico was impressed. These men were moving in a combat formation, watching each other's backs as if on a battlefield. She assumed the mercenaries were armed, but couldn't tell it from their stance or clothing. There were no bulges under their loose jackets or telltale slumping of the shoulders from carrying heavy ordnance. Yet the mercs had to be carrying machine pistols, or something bigger. They seemed far too confident of being able to handle any trouble to be armed with only automatic pistols.

Mentally, the lieutenant reviewed the data sheet faxed for her by Snake Eater to the local library. Based in the state capital, the three mercs called themselves Trinity, after the nuclear bomb project built way back in the 1940s. She found that amusing. The tall bald man was Mike Potvin, his shaved head gleaming from the stage lights so that it almost appeared as if he had a halo. The handsome man smiled a lot, talked little, and was wanted in four countries for a wide variety of crimes, ranging from kidnapping to arson. He had escaped twice from federal prison, killing guards both times, and was supposed to be an expert marksman with any pistol.

The short, ugly man was Tom Smith, a hulking gorilla with coal-black hair and an acid-scarred face. A master of the martial arts, he often killed with his bare hands, but seemed to prefer a crowbar or sledgehammer.

The last member of Trinity was Kurt Sakeda. Middle-aged with wavy hair and a deep artificial tan, Sakeda looked like an aging Hollywood actor. But his green eyes flashed with hints of madness, and the waitresses steered clear of the former Mafia assassin.

Staggering through the array of crowded tables, a drunk

man accidentally bumped into Potvin. Mumbling a slurred apology, the fellow started moving away when the mercenary grabbed him by the collar and slammed a fist into his stomach. The drunk went pale and gasped for breath. Twisting a grip on his shirt collar, Potvin dragged him over to an empty booth and shoved him behind the table. The drunk tried to rise and Potvin slammed an elbow into his throat, then ground a thumb into an eye, until the terrified man looked as if he was going to start screaming.

"All of it," Potvin said softly, tightening his grip. "Not just mine, but all of it."

With trembling fingers, the pickpocket dug inside his coat and handed over a wallet and a small collection of bills and credit cards.

In cold fury, Mike Potvin slapped the man twice in the face, oddly keeping in time to the pounding music. Bleeding from the mouth, the pickpocket reached into another pocket and extracted a wad of bills as large as a soup can.

"Get out," Potvin said, tucking the money away.

Nodding weakly, the pickpocket quickly shuffled for the exit, leaving a trail of crimson droplets on the floor tiles. The bouncer held the door open for the man and closed it promptly behind him. His job was to maintain the peace. If nobody was complaining, and the crowd was still buying drinks, the bouncer really didn't care what the customers did to each other.

Reaching the table, Trinity stood for a moment looking at the Forge soldiers sitting there, then they took their seats.

Without a word, Bronson handed them a fat envelope, and Sakeda tucked it inside his jacket without checking the money. The little man knew what would happen if he shortchanged them.

"What's the job?" Potvin asked softly. "Need protection from Warner here? He likes soldier boys."

"Shut your mouth, merc," Mendoza muttered under his breath.

"You want some, Frankenstein?" Sakeda asked, watching a topless girl walk by, her heavy breasts swinging to the roll of her ample hips. The dancer was covered with glitter and a few tattoos that looked real until you noticed her sweat was making the henna stain run slightly. It looked as if her barbed-wire tattoo was bleeding.

"Yes, we do," Caramico replied. "Prove to us that you are not FBI plants."

"No problem." Potvin chuckled. "Tom, kill somebody that won't be noticed."

The hulking Smith didn't answer, but from under the table there came the subdued cough of a silenced pistol, the noise nearly lost in the music and cheering. Over in the far corner, an old man was sitting alone in a booth, sipping a beer. Suddenly, he jerked, then slumped over in his seat and went still.

"Good enough?" Potvin said, pulling out a toothpick and tucking it into his mouth. "Or you want more?"

"Good enough for now," Caramico agreed. She would never have shown it, but she was very impressed. A shot that fast, from under a table, past a dozen moving people, in this low light?

"So, back to the original question. What's the job?" Potvin asked, throwing his arms across the back of the booth.

Caramico started to speak when the waitress delivered the beer. Potvin flashed her a hundred. "Keep the change, and don't come back every few minutes," he said, not even looking her way.

Going pale, the girl nodded and hurried away. It had been a long time since the Mafia had conducted any business here.

These days they only seemed to want Oriental girls, and the Kit Kat specialized in big, busty blondes. Damn few of which ever came from Japan or Korea.

"We got some Feds on our ass and need them removed," Caramico said succinctly.

"Done. Got a description?"

"Just follow us and kill anybody who comes our way."

"No problem," Potvin stated. "When you do want to—"

But Caramico and Mendoza were already rising. "Time is of the essence," the lieutenant said, brushing back her short hair uncomfortably. "We have a car big enough for all."

"No, we ride behind," Sakeda corrected harshly. "Gotta stay mobile to watch your ass."

The Forge soldiers exchanged knowing glances, and relaxed. That had been the final test. This Trinity team seemed more than capable for the job of escorting them to North Dakota. Pity they would be killed the moment they crossed the border.

"One more thing," Caramico said, moving away from the table. "I'm in charge, not him…" She pointed at the sergeant. "Or him!" She jerked a thumb at Bronson. "Your orders come from me."

"Whatever you say, boss," Smith stated, turning to face her for the first time. "Why? Got something you want done?"

"Yes," the lieutenant said, looking at Bronson. "He knows too much, and can be bought. Kill him."

"Wha…" the man gasped, a hand darting under the table. "But I've never betrayed a client in my life! My whole business depends upon my silence!"

"Then shut up," Potvin commanded in an icy voice, a 9 mm Beretta in his fist. There was an acoustical silencer on the end. "Now bring them out nice and slow. There's a world of difference between dying and dying slow. That's knowledge you don't want."

His eyes darting about in fear, Bronson licked his lips. "Look, lady, maybe we can make a deal," he whispered hoarsely, his empty hand rising into view.

Unexpectedly, a loud explosion shook the entire building, and a flare of white light filled the club brighter than a thousand suns, or so it seemed. The patrons and performers went motionless in shock and confusion as a dark cloud of smoke expanded across the tables from the direction of the lavatory.

"Everybody freeze!" a voice boomed. "This is the FBI! You are under arrest!"

Instantly, Potvin fired at Bronson, the man jerking and falling from the coughing hail of bullets as he slipped out of sight beneath the table.

"Fucking feds!" Sakeda snarled, pulling two handguns from under his shirt and starting to bang and boom away.

Dropping to the stage, the dancers began to scream, the cursing audience knocking over the tables to rush for the front door. The bouncer tried to get out of the way, but the mob plowed onward, shoving him outside with them.

"You are under arrest!" the stern voice bellowed again. "Surrender or die!"

"Fire exit," Potvin whispered hoarsely, his silenced weapon coughing into the roiling cloud of smoke.

The Glock .45 in his fist booming thunder, Sakeda grabbed Caramico by the blouse and yanked her into motion. "Get moving! We'll handle this!"

Holding their Bersa pistols, the Forge soldiers both paused only for a heartbeat, then turned and ran. The men of Trinity were right behind them, firing steadily. As the group crashed through the fire exit, an alarm went off and the shouting inside the smoky club actually got louder.

In the parking lot, frightened people were running in every direction, and several fistfights had started for unknown reasons. Firing from the hip, Potvin coolly took out the halogen light clusters above the lines of cars, and darkness descended.

"This way!" Sakeda said with a grin, dropping a spent clip into a pocket and quickly reloading.

His silenced gun sweeping for targets, Potvin took the lead, with the others close behind.

AS THE FIRE DOORS automatically swung shut, the old man sprawled in the booth across the chaotic club raised his head from the table and wiped the fake blood from his face with a sleeve.

Checking the screaming crowd to make sure nobody had been hurt by the fusillade of blank cartridges, Jack Grimaldi eased from the booth and raced through the thinning fumes of the stun grenade. Casting a brief glance over a shoulder, Grimaldi saw that Bronson was already gone, having quickly figured out all by himself that the mercs were firing blanks for some reason and taking the opportunity to leave as soon as the others were outside. Smart man. Unfortunately, there would be no way for him to question the fellow now. Bronson would crawl into a nice deep hole and pull the cover over until further notice. Pity. But there was only so much Able Team could do without blowing its cover.

A flash-bang grenade is always handy, in case a hasty retreat is needed, the pilot noted. Damn things sound like a nuke inside even a large room like the nightclub. Pelting down a short corridor, Grimaldi could see that every mirror in sight was shattered from the stun grenade. In an open field they were deafening; inside a building, the harmless charge sounded louder than doomsday.

Charging into the empty manager's office, Grimaldi shot off the lock on a steel door and slipped into the night. Heading across a weedy lot, the man hopped a fence and paused to whip out an EM scanner. When he was sure that the replacement van for Able Team was undisturbed, he disarmed the door and quickly got inside. Pushing down a panel on the dashboard, Grimaldi grabbed a microphone and started flipping switches. He heard the circuits get warm and thumbed the transmit button.

"Rock Garden, this is Sky King," the chief pilot for Stony Man said quickly. "Three into two makes five, but I lost six. Repeat, six has done a Houdini."

The military radio hummed softly as it condensed the words in a one-second squeal, then broadcast it at a commercial telecommunications satellite overhead. The squeal would be picked up by a NSA listening post and relayed directly to the private comsat in geosynchronous orbit above the Farm. Their nameless enemy had top-notch hackers, but early this morning Hal Brognola asked the President to direct every FBI field team in the nation to randomly fire off squeals about any damn thing they wished: favorite recipes, childhood memories, sports scores. No matter how good the terrorist organization was they couldn't possibly track down one squeal among the hundreds of others. The plan was foolproof.

"Confirm, Sky King," Price replied less than a minute later. "Find six if you can. But please be advised that the Einstein Boys have left the party of sad men."

That took a moment for Grimaldi to unscramble. The Einstein Boys…Trinity. Sad men…they were blue? The police. Damn, the mercs had escaped from the police station!

"Understood, Rock Garden," the man stated calmly. "Will watch for a surprise party."

"We're soon going to have a party of our own, and everybody is invited," Price said tersely, her voice crackling for a moment with static. "Move fast. Over and out."

Turning off the radio, Grimaldi started the big Detroit engine and activated a small homing screen. Each member of Able Team was wearing a beacon, just in case they got separated. But three blips immediately appeared in the lower-right side of the screen, heading away from the club at roughly ninety miles per hour.

Shifting into gear, Grimaldi started after the escaping terrorists and their Stony Man escorts. If this worked, they would be lead directly to the North American uplink dish.

Swinging the unmarked van into traffic, Grimaldi sincerely hoped that Trinity was nowhere as good as the rumors said. There was too much at stake for the mission to be derailed by some lunatic mercs seeking revenge. I'll have to do something about that, the pilot grimly noted, and pulled out a cell phone to start placing a long-distance call.

CHAPTER TWELVE

Buenos Aires, Argentina

Once far away from the airport, Hawkins maneuvered the Hummer into an alley between a couple of office buildings. Warily, the team checked to see if anybody was pursuing them, but everything seemed to be clear. Just in case, McCarter directed Hawkins to zigzag through the maze of back alleys until coming back out on a major boulevard. The traffic was a steady parade of cars, trucks, motorcycles and delivery vans. A river of metal.

Forcing an entry into the congestion, Hawkins maintained the speed limit in an effort to stay inconspicuous. But he needn't have bothered. Nobody noticed their arrival. All of the drivers seemed to be talking on cell phones while eating lunch. The scene was so much like every other major city in the world, the members of Phoenix Force had to smile. New York, Berlin, Perth—people were people, concentrating on their personal errands and the trivia of life. Nobody would probably have noticed if they stripped naked and launched a rocket attack on a cymbal factory.

Staying with the flow of traffic, Hawkins followed signs for the continental highway. It wasn't an easy task. The man could read Spanish, but bright neon lights blazed everywhere and taxicabs whizzed constantly, obviously attempting to break light speed. The city was crowded to the burst point, the sidewalks jammed with noisy people in a wide spectrum of clothing, ranging from high fashion to gaucho cowboys in leather chaps and fringed hats. Every store was packed solid with customers, every parking spot along the curbs was taken, every parking garage was full, and in some areas the cars were triple-parked at fire hydrants. A low rumble of thunder proved to be a cheering crowd inside a gigantic sports arena. The ivy-covered entrance to the Argentine Museum of Natural History was mobbed with excited people, the hundreds of flash cameras resembling lightning strikes as the TV crews tried to get closer to the poised skeleton of a Tyrannosaurus Rex and a huge map showing where it had been unearthed in the southern regions of the nation. Clearly, this was some special day of celebration, or else the population of Argentina was truly staggering.

"Unless the army is using helicopters, there is no way they could be following us," McCarter growled, easing the grip on his Browning Hi-Power pistol held alongside the seat and out of sight. "Let's head inland."

"Absolutely," Hawkins drawled, shifting gears and heading around a opera house.

Traversing the spaghettilike maze of streets, the Hummer soon reached the continental highway and started directly out of town. Several times, the team passed a highway patrolman issuing a ticket to a speeder, or arresting a drunk, and once they saw a heavily armed group of Federal Police handcuffing a group of bloody men. Through the open rear doors of their van could be seen stacks of clear plastic bags full of a white powder. Plus, a lot of AK-47 assault rifles.

"Drug dealers," James commented.

A couple of hours later, Phoenix Force was still on the highway moving through the colossal city. The offices and skyscrapers had slowly changed into suburbs, homes and schools, and parks stretching forever. There didn't seem to be an end to Buenos Aires. But eventually the suburbs thinned into rolling farmlands and finally wild woods, the forest thick and deep.

"The Paris of the south, my ass," Encizo snorted, massaging a bullet scar on his temple. "This is more like The City That Never Stops."

"How far away is Fort Peron?" Hawkins asked, glancing sideways.

"Fifty more miles," McCarter replied. "But we turn off the main road at the next exit to travel overland."

"We're not going to drive up to the front door and politely ask to come inside and look around?" Hawkins asked, almost smiling.

"Hardly." Exhaling slowly, McCarter snapped open the lid of a PDA, the tiny screen displaying an aerial map of the countryside. "I downloaded this before we landed. We head due west, turn north at the abandoned rock quarry, then follow the river, and there's Fort Peron."

"Smack in the middle of nowhere," Hawkins commented, spotting the exit and slowing down. He started to add something, then cursed. Blocking the entry to the side road was a Federal Police car.

"On my mark," McCarter said out of the corner of his mouth, even while smiling in confusion at the two stern officers climbing from the police car.

Gently applying the brakes, Hawkins stopped the Hummer

a few yards away from the police, wisely keeping both of his hands in plain sight. "Something wrong, sir?" he asked politely.

"Nobody is allowed to use this road by order of the military," the older policeman said. His uniform was wrinkled from sitting in the parked car for a long time, but the 9 mm Bersa pistol in the holster at his hip gleamed with oil.

"But we have permission from General Calvano," McCarter declared loudly. "Now, get out of the way, fool!" This was a calculated risk. If Calvano was behind the hacking of the GPS network, he would have to be a fool to have honest policemen guarding his back door. These men were either his own troops in disguise, or else cops that he owned, body and soul. Either way, using his name should invoke an immediate response.

But at the mention of the general, the two Federal Police exchanged quick looks, then clawed for the guns on their hips.

Instantly, the members of Phoenix Force fired the stun guns in their hands. The tiny barbs hit the two men in their chests, easily punching through their shirts to reach the bare skin underneath. The second contact was made, the accumulators discharged 200,000 volts along the hairline wires trailing behind the barbs. Twitching for a moment, the Federal Police dropped their guns, went limp and collapsed to the ground.

Using an EM scanner, Encizo checked to make sure there were no hidden video cameras watching the policemen from the bushes. "We're clear!" he announced, turning off the device.

The rest of Phoenix Force got out of the vehicle and checked the two cops to make sure they were okay from the aftereffects of the stun gun. They were fine. Then the unconscious men were thoroughly searched, but there was nothing interesting in their clothing aside from the usual items. Taking the wal-

lets and watches, James then administrated a powerful seda-
tive that would keep the men asleep for almost a day. The Stony
Man operatives handcuffed the snoring police and locked them
inside the trunk of the patrol car.

Snapping the key off in the lock, the men got back into
the Hummer and proceeded swiftly into the woods. The
numbers were falling. Sooner or later, the police would be
found, and the attack would hopefully be attributed to a simple mugging. There was always somebody who hated the
local cops, no matter how politely they conducted themselves. But if it wasn't, then the blood would really hit the
fan. Time was short, and the sooner they did a recon on Fort
Peron the better.

"Hate to leave the bastards alive," Hawkins muttered, leaving the side road and taking an old logging trail. "Cops know
how to escape from a locked trunk. Even when handcuffed."

"If they were the police," McCarter countered. "If they're innocent, they'll wake up in twenty-four hours with a bitch of a
headache, and one hell of a story to tell their buddies over beer."

"And if they work for Calvano?"

"Drive faster," McCarter urged, checking the clip in his
MP-5 submachine gun.

Flashing a grin, Hawkins did his best, but the ground was
rough and uneven, filled with gaping potholes left behind
from the huge trucks hauling trees to the lumber mills. Trained
professionals, the members of Phoenix Force remained calm
even when their speed slowed to a bumpy crawl.

Thankfully reaching a fire road, Hawkins paused the Hummer while Manning and Encizo hopped out to cut the entry
chain blocking unauthorized entry. Killing the headlights,
Hawkins continued onward through the thickening gloom
wearing a Starlite visor.

THE DAY FADED INTO NIGHT and the stars came out by the time Phoenix Force found the rock quarry. Leaving the Hummer in a cave, the men threw a thermal blanket over the machine to help hide the radiant heat signature. Then they changed into jungle-colored ghillie suits, gathered their backpacks and weapons and took off at an easy lope toward the river. The team was carrying plenty of explosives, including LAW rocket launchers and satchel charges.

The moon had risen above the land, shining down a cold blue light, by the time they found the isolated military base. The glow of the searchlights was distinguishable a mile away.

Leaving the open bank of the river, the six men faded into the greenery. Judiciously, they unleashed the EM scanners to check for hidden video cameras, proximity sensors and land mines. The men found a lot of them and it was slow going having to constantly circle around, zigzag and backtrack to avoid the ample electronic defenses, but eventually Phoenix Force made it around the side of the hillock.

Ever so slowly, David McCarter pushed aside the leaves of a flowering bush and down below was a military compound.

Fort Peron, aka Firebase Alpha, lay before them like a diorama of some famous battle at a military convention. The searchlights were positioned at the opposite ends of the parking lot, far away from everything else in case the beams drew in enemy fire. A double fence encircled the base with dogs running in between, pillboxes and guard towers dotted the compound, and armed guards rode in a Hummer constantly on patrol outside the fence. There were additional sniper posts on the tops of the squat concrete buildings of the base, and two white radar domes resembling golf balls towered above everything. Three MRL trucks were positioned in a triangle formation around a large object covered with a fluttering canvas sheet on the parade ground.

The Stony Man team also noted several armored personnel carriers parked in various locations, not simple transport models, but U.S. Army M-113 Gavin vehicles. The lightweight APC was deadly fast, and while the original models had possessed some serious engineering flaws, those had all been fixed over time. McCarter could see that these were the upgraded versions. The fuel tanks were mounted externally and heavily armored with reactive armor laid over louvered aluminum. Instead of a standard .50 caliber machine gun on top, these boasted a 25 mm Bushmaster rapidfire, plus a 12.7 mm coaxial machine gun.

But what really caught his attention was the cage. Resembling an array of open Venetian blinds, the slat-armor shield completely surrounded each squat vehicle from the middle of the tires to the armored hatch on top. Only very recently developed in the Iraqi war, the outer preshield would detonate an RPG or LAW early and stop the enemy explosives from achieving penetration. The slat-armor shield was dirt cheap, weighed next to nothing and worked like a battlefield dream.

A smooth paved road lead from the main gate to a prefab bridge crossing the deep river valley. There was a guard kiosk on the other side, along with two additional Gavins and a TOW missile launcher capable of stopping an Abrams M-1 battle tank.

"And if the TOW fails, they blow the bridge," James whispered into his throat mike. "Any of this standard issue for the Argentine army?"

"Not a piece of it," Hawkins replied, sweeping the base with the passive IR goggles. There were a lot of hot spots— kitchen, generator bunker, garage, shower stalls—but no cold areas to mark the location of any Cray supercomputers. But those could have easily be hidden far underground.

Sweeping the base with a directional microphone, Encizo listened to the idle talk of the guards, soldiers and the officers. The base personnel seemed a lot more friendly than was usual among the military, and suddenly he learned why. These men weren't part of the Argentine Defense Forces anymore.

"Forge," Encizo subvocalized in his throat mike, the single word clearly discernable to the other team members in their earphones. "This base hasn't got anything to do with Argentina anymore. This is Calvano's personal army for something called Forge. Hell, they're boasting about the ICBM attacks."

"Keep talking, assholes," McCarter whispered, checking the sleek pneumatic pistol nestled in a shoulder holster. There were three additional darts tucked securely into loops on his canvas gun belt. Forge. At least now the enemy had a name.

Adjusting the radio on his belt, James gave a brief report on the recent discovery by the team, along with a picture of the moonlit base, then sent off a squeal.

Continuing a sweep of the firebase, Encizo upped the gain of the parabolic microphone in his grip. "This is odd. The rooftop guards are talking about what they're going to do after Forge saves the world."

"Saves it?" McCarter shot back, raising an eyebrow. "Bloody strange way to save the world by causing a bleeding nuclear war."

"You know, I've always wanted to ask," Hawkins said, focusing his field glasses on something behind the administration building. It was another TOW missile. This place was armed for major combat. "What's the difference between bloody and bleeding over in jolly old England?"

"Britain," McCarter corrected automatically, watching the route of the outer guards in the Hummer. "And it's the difference between golly-shucks and motherfucker."

"Really? Ain't that a bitch," Hawkins said with a hard chuckle. Save the world, eh? Forge sounded like another group of fanatics, similar to Unity or the Brigade. Well, the big Texan knew of a fast cure for their dementia: several doses of subsonic lead delivered directly into the head. Worked every damn time.

"This base should have a battalion strength," James muttered uneasily. "But there are only thirty civilian cars in the parking lot. There can't be more than a hundred people here."

"That's a long way from battalion strength," Manning agreed, listening to the rustle of the leaves around them. "Maybe most of the soldiers live on the base, and don't need cars." His tone suggested that the man didn't believe it. There was no sign of a PX, school, day care or playground. This was a military hardsite and nothing else. The code name of Firebase Alpha was making more sense. This had to be where the terrorists planned to ride out the nuclear storm while they…what? Forged a new world? It was a chilling thought, but still circumstantial.

"There's a satellite dish hidden in that copse of trees across the bridge," Hawkins noted dourly. "But that's bullshit. Whoever designed this base wasn't stupid enough to put the uplink array out in front where it could be easily destroyed."

Looking at the base through the powerful telescope on the Barrett rifle, Gary Manning grudgingly agreed. That had to be a dummy satellite dish to lure invaders into a trap. The damn thing was probably sitting on top of a ton of high explosives, enough to remove the dish, trees and the invading forces off the face of the planet. The real dish was most likely a hundred miles away connected to the base by hard lines buried deep underground. His respect for Calvano increased, along with his certainty that this was the headquarters for the enemy. Phoenix Force could blow the whole installation off the map, and accomplish nothing.

"Okay, this place looks as suspicious as bloody hell, but we can't tell a thing from up here," McCarter said, tucking away the glasses. "We need to get inside and do a hard recon."

Sitting back from the bushes, Hawkins crouched on his heels, his camouflage-painted face raised toward the sky lost in thought. "Well, there's no way we're going to sneak inside," he declared harshly.

Reaching smoothly over a shoulder, James pulled a LAW rocket into view and extended the tube, the sights popping up into view. "Of course, since they've already admitted their part in the ICBM strikes," the man said, aiming the antitank weapon downward, "then there's no need for us to be subtle anymore."

BLOWING A SMOKE RING at the full moon, the Forge soldier walking along the outer perimeter of the firebase smiled contentedly, then frowned as he caught a flash of light from the nearby hillside. Oh no, was it another news reporter? The general would be furious!

Reaching for the radio at his hip, the soldier flinched as something flashed past him to strike the bridge. There came a loud explosion midway across the structure, flames and smoke rising from the impact point.

Turning frantically, the soldier tried to race for safety behind one of the stout pillboxes when thunder filled the night as the entire bridge erupted, the self-destruct charges and hidden land mines all cutting loose together. The concussion hit the running man with stunning force, throwing him pell-mell forward for a dozen yards. He hit the ground hard and lost the radio. He started to rise, but then heard the sharp whine of shrapnel flying by overhead. Dropping low, he hugged the dirt and prayed for deliverance.

An indeterminate amount of time passed and there was only chaos and noise, the roiling crescendo of the annihilating bridge covering the firebase with fiery light like morning thunder.

As the force of the explosion slowly began to dissipate, the Forge soldier weakly rose and saw a dozen men rushing his way carrying assault rifles. From the parking lot, the alarms on the civilian cars began whooping, the headlights flashing for attention.

"What the fuck happened?" Major San Martin demanded, a 9 mm Bersa in his hand. A napkin was tied around his neck, greasy food stains fresh on his chin. "Are we under attack?"

"I don't know, sir," the soldier replied, clutching his aching stomach. Contrary to popular belief, the concussion of a big explosion always seemed to hurt a man worst in the gut, not the head. "I saw a flash of light and then the bridge blew up. I...think it was a rocket, sir."

Rocket? Suddenly alert, the major studied the dark hills for any suspicious movements. A minute passed, then another, and nothing happened. No gunfire, no more rockets, no crashing of tree limbs from armored vehicles forcing a path through the dense foliage.

"You sure it was a rocket?" the major demanded, lowering the weapon. Why would anybody blow the bridge, and then do nothing? That made no sense. Unless this was a diversion. Glancing at the pillboxes, the major saw the soldiers inside the bunkers standing at their guns, ready for trouble. Nobody was getting past them.

Rubbing his aching stomach, the Forge soldier started to speak when the bridge gave the terrible sound of tearing steel, a metallic scream of pain that increased in volume until it was deafening. Tearing loose from the anchors on both ends, the bridge broke apart, the flaming ruins tumbling into the river valley below, the echoing crash throwing a maelstrom of burning sparks into the smoky air, making the valley briefly resemble a portal into hell.

Limping to the crumbling edge of the ravine, the badly bruised Forge private craned his neck to look down. The remains of the bridge lay smashed and burning in the shallow water, the steel support beams still groaning like a giant animal slowly dying.

"A rocket? I don't know, sir," he demurred uncertainly. "Maybe it was just lightning."

"Idiot," the major growled, and lifted the radio from his belt. He pressed the transmit button and started to speak when he saw a footprint in the churned dirt. A boot print, and not the style used by Forge. It was pointing toward the base. Just one print. But it should not have been there, and it was fresh, the dust not yet settled into the marks obscuring the details. Cold logic said this was impossible, but the combat veteran decided to go with his gut instincts.

"Red alert!" Major San Martin said quickly into the radio, crouching slightly and raising his pistol. "We have intruders on the base. Repeat, the base has been invaded!"

CHAPTER THIRTEEN

Omaha, Nebraska

The Daughters of American Liberty cotillion was in full regalia when the black limousine rolled to a stop at the front doors.

The hall was colossal, with marble columns lining the patio, stained glass windows arching ten feet high and completely surrounded by a manicured lawn and lovingly sculptured hedges in a dazzling array of artistic shapes. The dance music coming from the full orchestra was sprightly, and even the liveried doormen were unconsciously tapping their feet as they approached the limousine.

Then the door opened and Trinity stepped out with guns in hands.

"Hey!" a doorman said in surprise.

Which was as far as he got before Potvin shot the fellow in the throat, red blood spraying across the other two attendants. Both men promptly raised their hands in surrender, but Smith and Sakeda gunned them down without even pausing to check the bodies.

Moving inside, the men of Trinity took out a startled butler and the pretty girl in the coat check room. Sweeping along the hallway, their guns never stopped coughing and a score of people fell to the plush carpeting gasping out their life.

Reaching the main ballroom, Trinity holstered their handguns and pulled out Heckler & Koch MP-5 submachine guns. Everybody dancing on the crowded floor was wearing either a dapper tuxedo or a beautiful taffeta gown. Flowers were everywhere and the air was redolent with the aroma of champagne, expensive perfume and power. The Daughters of American Liberty was the Midwest version of the Daughters of the American Revolution based in Boston. It was a hundred years younger, but just as rich, and possibly even more powerful.

A hundred smiling faces turned to shock at the arrival of Trinity, and the music raggedly ground to a stop as the mercs worked the arming bolts of the deadly weapons.

Instantly, several bodyguards rose from the crowd of people sitting at the tiny tables. They didn't know these men, but the bodyguards knew the type. Hammers. What the old school would call a hit man. The three strangers radiated death like cold from an iceberg.

As the guards reached inside their tuxedo jackets, the mercs cut loose, gunning down the armed men without qualm or pause.

Now everybody started to scream, but Trinity blocked the main doorway and there was nowhere to run. The throng milled about, seeking escape, but any movement toward the kitchen doors or fire exit only brought another chattering burst from the machine guns.

Dropping the spent clips, Trinity reloaded, and Smith stayed in place at the door, while Potvin and Sakeda moved into the crowd of horrified people like savage machines. Some fool took their picture with a video phone, and Potvin shot the elderly woman in the belly at point-blank range. The rich society matron could only gasp as she fell off her chair to land sprawling on the petal-covered marble floor.

The killers went past the twitching body and grabbed a young woman sitting at the next table, cruelly yanking her to her feet. Terrified, the woman started to ask a question and Smith backhanded her across the face, then did it again. Blood dribbling from a broken nose, the trembling woman burst into tears and started to shake.

Several men sitting at other tables nearby began to rise and Smith, at the door, put a long burst of 9 mm AP rounds into the ceiling. A moment later, metal groaned, and the ornate crystal chandelier violently crashed onto the dance floor. That kept everybody motionless.

Pulling out a cell phone, Potvin tapped in a number, his hard eyes constantly on the move over the squirming crowd of millionaires. These were exactly the types of idiots to try something heroic.

The phone gave a fast series of clicks, then a voice answered.

"Give me Bronson," Potvin demanded. He waited a second, then grimaced. "What? Don't gimme that shit, bitch. I know he's alive, and he sure as hell wasn't going to go to Condel Hospital. We found wads of paper all over the floor at the club. That asshole was shot with blanks. He may have a few broken bones, and probably a load of bruises, but he isn't dead, and you're the best doc in town that handles our kind of people. So put him on, or else."

There was a short pause.

"Bronson here," the man replied, his voice blurry from pain medication.

"Listen to this," Potvin commanded, and thrust the cell phone at the young woman.

Still sniffling in her hands, the teenager started screaming as Sakeda pulled out a knife and ran the blade along her arm, slightly breaking the skin.

"Recognize the voice?" Potvin asked. "That's your daughter, Victoria."

Over the tiny speaker, Bronson gave a strained laugh. "Have you seen the way I dress? I'm gay! I've never been with a woman in my life!"

"Yeah? Then you won't mind if we play with her a little, will ya?" Potvin snapped back. "Okay, nail her hands to the table!"

A lot of people in the crowd jerked at the pronouncement, and Smith fired another burst, setting them put into place.

Chuckling, Sakeda grabbed the young woman and dragged her to the heavy buffet table. A sweep of his arm cleared away the pheasant and caviar, antique china and sterling silver pieces flying madly. Then, bending her over the table, Sakeda slung the MP-5 over a shoulder and pulled a hammer and some steel nails from inside his clothing.

"Daddy, help me!" Victoria cried. Then she shrieked hysterically as the first spike was driven through her flesh.

"Stop! Stop hurting her!" Bronson cried out, tears in his voice. "Yes, okay, she's my daughter! I act like a homosexual to stop anybody from even looking for her. How the hell—"

"Every whore in this state answers to me, and you talk in your sleep, moron," Potvin declared, walking over to hold the cell phone closer to the weeping teenager. "Besides, I don't do business with anybody unless I know how to hurt them. Really and truly make them wish for death."

"You bastard," Bronson whispered hoarsely.

"Nail her other hand!"

"No! Please, dear God, whatever I have is yours," Bronson gushed. "Money, drugs, weapons… Just ask!"

"Better," Potvin said, narrowing his eyes. "Now unless

you want to hear us rape this bitch, and then set her on fire—" he paused to let the threat seep into the other man's mind "—then put us in contact with the man called Snake Eater, and I mean right now."

There was no response from Bronson.

"You hear me, Bronson?" Potvin snarled, tightening his grip on the SMG. "Give me Snake Eater, or she dies right here and now!"

"Betray a client? B-but that would put me out of business forever!"

Whimpering softly, Victoria squirmed as Sakeda drew a knife blade along her jawline.

"Last chance," Potvin declared in a no-nonsense tone.

"A-a-agreed." There came a series of clicks and a pleasant voice came on the phone, the words heavily accented.

"Good evening, Mr. Potvin, and what can I do for you this lovely evening?" Mongoose asked politely.

"Somebody just kidnapped your last client by pretending to be us," Potvin retorted, barely in control of his monumental rage. "I want the impostors dead, and you want the client protected. If you know where they can be found, let's cut a deal. Interested?"

There was a short pause.

"Absolutely," Mongoose whispered. "I think that we can do quite a bit of business together, my friend."

Stony Man Farm, Virginia

MASSAGING HER STIFF NECK, Carmen Delahunt was studying a blacksuit field report on her VR helmet when a tiny icon for NATO appeared on the bottom of the visor overlapping the factory schematics and railroad graphics. It took her a full second to react to the sight, and as she quickly reached for the symbol with her cybernetic gloves it suddenly began to flash a bright red. Cold adrenaline flooded her body as the woman tapped the icon to access the encoded message.

"Red alert!" Delahunt yelled from her console, dropping her stocking feet to the floor to lean forward. "We have intruders at NATO Depot 75. That's 75!"

"The nuclear weapons cache in Turkey?" Kurtzman asked, quickly slaving his console to hers.

As the machines dovetailed, he saw the main screen begin to scroll with the NATO data flow, a submonitor flicking into pictures of the interior of the subterranean warehouse, relayed via fiber-optics of pinhead cameras hidden in the vaunted ceiling.

Kurtzman cursed at the sight. There were a dozen men in antigas gear working with laptops on a door to the large cage. The thieves were surrounded by megatons of military ordnance, but ignored it all to just concentrate on the cage. The men were surrounded by unlimited explosives, and there was an oxygen/acetylene torch nearby just begging to be used. But they weren't falling for the trap. Any attempt to force open the cage would cause the immediate and automatic release of VX nerve gas. But more importantly, thermite charges would ignite, reducing the plastic boxes and their precious contents to slag in only seconds.

"Damn, they must know what's inside," Tokaido said, spitting out his gum. He hit a macros file and a submonitor became illuminated with the contents of the long-term storage facility.

Trying to stay one step ahead of their nameless enemy, Tokaido had a host of sensitive files already accessed and ready. With all of the recent disasters, it had only made sense to check on the status of certain NBC weapons systems, nuclear, bacteriological and chemical. At the top of the NATO inventory for

Depot 75 was a list of tactical nuclear weapons: two artillery shells, two bombs and two CIA-style suicide backpacks.

"How soon until NATO can get some troops there?" Wethers growled, moving his pipe to the other side of his mouth.

"Hours," Kurtzman replied gruffly, his hands flashing across the silent keyboard. "They're already busy handling all of the other mysterious crashes and explosions across Europe."

"But these are nukes being stolen!"

"Yeah, but they don't know that yet," Kurtzman stated angrily, sending a priority-one alert to NATO headquarters in Brussels. "And by the time they get some people there it will be too late. The sons of bitches have already cracked the second door lock!"

"Which leaves four to go," Delahunt said, then she flinched. "No, only three! They just got another!"

"I'm attempting to hack the system," Tokaido said in forced calm. "Damn these firewalls. They're good."

"Should be," Wethers said gruffly. "I helped make them."

"Did you leave a back door?" Kurtzman demanded hopefully.

"No, too risky," Wethers replied curtly, banging a fist impotently on the console. "Besides… Damn, these people *are* good. They just ripped out the auxiliary communication lines buried under the floor. There's no way we can activate the self-destruct charges now."

"Are you positive?" Delahunt snapped, struggling to cut the power to the depot or release the VX gas. But nothing was working. The depot had a lot of defenses, most of them automatic, but the primary defense of a nuclear arsenal had always been total secrecy. A thief couldn't steal something if nobody knew where it was.

"Positive," Wethers replied, the single word spoken like a death sentence. The Farm had fought for decades to keep nuclear weapons off the black market, but with this theft six of the latest and most powerful models would be unleashed upon civilization. It really didn't matter if this was al Qaeda, PLO, Unity or even Hamas. The death toll would be staggering, and with the planet already teetering on the edge of world war, this was just the sort of push that could send them over the brink into Armageddon.

Already the invaders were starting up forklifts and beginning to move crates of supplies out of the way to clear a path to the exit.

Think, man, think! Wethers raged internally. I could set off the fire sprinklers. Those released inert argon gas that would eventually suffocate men wearing gas masks, but on the monitor he could see that these versions had small air tanks attached to the masks. Self-breathers. The argon gas would do nothing but let the thieves know somebody was trying to stop them. Totally useless.

Then the professor narrowed his eyes into hard slits. He had a wild idea that just might work if he had enough time....

"Come on, we've got to find a way to seal those bastards inside," Kurtzman declared, savagely hitting keys. He tried again to cause a massive short-circuit in the electrical system and ignite the munitions, but failed once more.

"I'm trying to activate the failsafe by radio control from a NATO satellite. It's long shot but…" Delahunt paused, her gloved hands fondling the air as if kneading bread dough. "It worked! I'm in. Shit, they used the debris from the main door to block the tracks of the secondary doors."

"How the hell did they even know about those?" Kurtzman raged, then something clicked in his mind. "Akira, run a probe! These assholes must have some serious computer support. If they've hacked the security system through the telephones or through the power lines…"

"Then the enemy might be watching what is happening by using a piggyback signal," Tokaido finished. "On it! Just give me a minute…"

"Don't lose him!" Kurtzman commanded.

"Okay, the signal isn't coming from anyplace in Europe," Tokaido said, the slow words counterpointing his flashing hands. "That was a fake. Clever fellow, he's using the Atlantic long-lines instead of a satellite relay…."

Unexpectedly, the intercom buzzed. "Kurtzman, what the hell is going on down there?" Barbara Price demanded.

"Tell you later!" Kurtzman yelled, clicking off the device so that his team wouldn't be disturbed again.

His mind a whirlwind, the chief hacker struggled to come up with something, anything, to stop the would-be thieves. On his screen, an indicator blinked as the fourth lock disengaged and the fifth fell right behind it. Only one more to go and the cage would be open. "Carmen, can we access the nukes?"

"Not to set them off, no," the redhead answered curtly. "Way ahead of you there, Chief."

"He's not in North America," Tokaido continued, sweat dripping off his face in spite of the coolness of the room. "The signal is being bounced off a couple of telecommunications satellites…and a weather satellite…" The man snarled as he detected a bounced signal. "The bastard knows we're trying a trace, and now is attempting to find us!" This was now a race. The hacker who was the fastest would win; the loser would be bombed out of existence.

"Are the sensors live?" Kurtzman demanded. His heart pounding, the man dredged up everything he could remember about NATO procedure for the handling of nuclear weaponry.

"Absolutely," she replied. "But what good are they?"

"The inspection program!" Wethers announced, swiveling in his chair. "Use the inspection program!"

At the cry, Kurtzman's eyes went wide. By God, that just might work!

"Carmen, access the UN override and blow open the seals for an on-site inspection!"

"The seals? But that would…" Delahunt gave a hard smile under the VR helmet. "God, that's clever."

Staring anxiously at the screen, Kurtzman watched as plastic carrying cases snapped open displaying the six nuclear charges.

Still working on the door, the men jerked at the noise, and one of them moved quickly away. But it was already too late. Set in a wall niche, a Geiger counter started to click wildly as the outer casing of the six nuclear bombs opened wide for a visual inspection, closely followed by the internal armor plating and then the primary shields. A soft glow began to infuse the air as the subcritical charges of radioactive U-235 were fully exposed.

Instantly, the thieves sagged their shoulders and dropped several of the laptops. The machines crashed on the concrete floor, the screens going blank. One of the thieves reeled drunkenly and clutched the bars for support, while another turned to loudly retch behind a forklift.

In grim satisfaction, the Stony Man hackers watched as the dozen would-be thieves began to slump, two of them shuffling for the exit. All of them soiled their clothing, and most tore off the gas masks and bulletproof vests. Their faces were deathly pale, their slack mouths flapping for air like fish on a sidewalk. But the intruders got only halfway there before limply collapsing, thin red blood dribbling from their blind eyes and deaf ears.

With a muttered curse, Tokaido slapped the keyboard. "Lost them!" he cried. "I was getting close so the other hacker cut and run. The source was in South America, but that's as far as I got."

With every living cell in their bodies rapidly breaking down from the waves of hard radiation, the twelve men began wetly coughing out their dissolving lungs in a shockingly similar manner to the innocent civilians they had ruthlessly murdered with mustard gas only a few minutes ago outside.

"More than enough," Kurtzman said. "South America means Calvano."

"Most likely."

"I'll inform Phoenix Force," Wethers said, turning back to his console. "If the general has a computer expert that good, he must be the person who hacked into the GPS network. We really could use him alive!"

"If possible," Delahunt agreed grimly, closely watching the monitor for any signs of treachery from the dying thieves. On the wall, the Geiger counter was clicking so fast it almost sounded like a single continuous tone, the rads nearly off the scale.

It took a full hour before the men stopped moving completely. Ruthlessly, Kurtzman then released the argon gas, flooding the depot way past the safety level to where nothing could breathe. One of the figures on the floor stopped twitching, and he let more argon flow into the depot until he was well and truly satisfied that every one of the invaders was dead.

Every monitor in the room turned into hash.

"What the… We've lost the satellite feed," Tokaido stated, working his console to no result. "Damn, I was afraid this might happen! Calvano didn't know exactly where we were located."

"So he used the GPS network to slightly shift every satellite above the East Coast," Delahunt finished. "We can't talk to our teams anymore!"

"And the nation is stone blind against an enemy attack," Wethers said.

"Telecommunications, NASA weather satellites, NSA spy sats, Watchdogs, Keyholes, cell phones—everything is gone!"

"Carmen, find that sat!" Kurtzman commanded, sliding back a panel on his console and grabbing a joystick. "Akira, get the feed back! Wethers, steal us a landline and then another satellite!"

Moving frantically, the team went to work, and for a very long time there was only the soft sound of tapping fingers and the loud crackle of static from the dead monitors.

IN THE NATO DEPOT, misty with argon gas, the shipping containers for the nuclear weapons still lay open, even though the shielding for the devices was closed once again. In the heated rush of the aborted theft, nobody on the Stony Man team seemed to have noticed that all six nuclear weapons had opened wide for a core inspection. But only five of them had softly glowed with live uranium.

CHAPTER FOURTEEN

Omaha, Nebraska

Moving steadily along Route 29, the dark blue SUV holding the Forge soldiers carefully maintained the speed limit. A dozen yards behind the vehicle, a large black Cadillac stayed precisely in position, the armed men inside watching for treachery from every direction.

"Well?" Lyons snapped from behind the steering wheel.

"We've lost the Farm," Schwarz declared, placing aside the compact radio transceiver on the backseat near a box of ammunition. "I caught a squeal about Trinity busting out of jail, and General Calvano running Forge with Phoenix Force invading his Argentine base, then nothing."

"Trouble with the equipment?" Blancanales said hopefully, running a finger along the scar on his face. The spirit gum holding the prosthetic in place itched like crazy; he had to force himself to keep from scratching it off.

"No way. Even the cell phone is dead," Schwarz answered, chewing a lip. "I would venture a guess that Forge must have shifted every telecommunication satellite above eastern

America, if not the whole continent, to try to knock Kurtzman and his people off the air. Everything seems to be down in this whole area."

"Except for the GPS network," Lyons said, glancing at the glowing computer screen set into the ornate dashboard. The icon for the Caddy was moving northward along Route 29 through northern Nebraska. "That seems to be fine."

"For the moment." Shifting his position on the backseat, Schwarz frowned darkly. "But Forge will need that up and running to keep making things veer off course at the last second."

"So we're on our own," Blancanales said, working the arming bolt on the M-16 assault rifle cradled in his arms. Luckily, Trinity was known for using a wide variety of weapons, so the team didn't have to leave their preferred weapons behind with Grimaldi.

Outside the tinted windows, Able Team saw only the endless Nebraska farmlands on both sides of the highway, the lush fields of corn extending for miles in every direction. Aside from the few cars on the black highway, the only objects visible were a billboard advertising a local restaurant that specialized in honey-fried chicken, a sprawling farmhouse with an unpainted grain silo rising high and shiny like a SCUD missile and a hulking combine harvester, the colossal farm machine resembling a mobile factory with its array of rotating thrasher blades, serrated cornheads, conveyor belts, swing arms, chains, hydraulic lifters and pneumatic augers. A glass-lined booth was perched high on top, the driver nestled inside like some sort preserved specimen on display in a museum, instead of the highly trained operator of a quarter-million-dollar piece of farm equipment.

"Anything on the CB?" Lyons asked, adjusting the cloth cap covering his shaved head.

"Clear," Schwarz said, touching the earplug worn under his bushy wig. "But it only has a range of about a hundred miles."

"Any way to boost that?"

"Not with what we have onboard," the man said, spreading his arms wide. "I stuffed everything possible into the trunk, but this civilian boat doesn't have half the storage capability of our modified Chevy van."

"I just hope the Farm still exists," Blancanales commented, tightening the grip on his weapon. "Forge might have taken out our Comsat. Or it could have had a 747 plowing into the base at five hundred miles per hour."

"That wouldn't damage the underground computer annex," Schwarz stated confidently.

"Unless it was carrying a nuke," Lyons said succinctly.

With those words, tense stillness filled the luxury car until there was only the soft crackle of static on the radio and the soft hum of the tires on the smooth highway.

"This is Alpha." Lieutenant Caramico spoke suddenly over the Kenwood radio, her words almost lost in the hash. "I want a sitrep."

"Roger. This is Beta, all clear," Lyons replied, accelerating the Cadillac to move past the dark blue SUV containing the Forge soldiers. He nodded in passing, they returned the gesture and Able Team took the point position again.

The two cars had been rotating around each other every fifteen minutes or so, since Kansas. A three-car formation would have offered infinitely better protection, but Caramico was in a hurry and didn't want to chance tangling with the police by stealing a third car. The concept of simply buying a used vehicle from a dealer seemed to never have occurred to her, and Able Team wasn't offering any suggestions. They much preferred to keep thing this way and keep the Stony Man team intact.

Especially since we're driving into an ambush, Lyons noted dourly. He felt sure Forge would attack them the moment they reached a secluded location, most likely in the northern territory of South Dakota. Lots of desert up there, with countless arroyos and ravines to hide the burned wreckage of a car and lifeless corpses.

Lost in contemplation for a moment, Lyons came fiercely awake as the four cars ahead of the Cadillac started to jerk, veering wildly in every direction. Rubber chunks shot off the shredding tires and bounced randomly along the pavement. The drivers fought to control their shuddering vehicles, but a Volvo sedan and a Yugo violently slammed together. Fenders crumbled, headlights exploded and windshields cracked. With horns blaring loudly, the cars smashed into the concrete divider. The airbags of the Volvo deployed, but the driver of the Yugo was thrown against the dashboard with grisly results.

Wondering if there was a sniper shooting out the tires, Lyons concentrated on the surface of the road and saw the carpeting of dark objects a split second before plowing into the middle of them. Hundreds of four-point stars covered the asphalt, the needle-sharp tips jutting up like barb spears.

"Caltrops!" the former L.A. cop yelled, as all four tires on the Cadillac blew in unison.

The large car dropped to the pavement with a hard crash. The windows cracked, the exhaust system flattened, and a geyser of bright sparks flew from behind the vehicle like a fireworks display as it scraped along the pavement.

Twisting the steering wheel with all of his might, Lyons fought the shuddering Cadillac into the right-hand lane and managed to stop only inches from the berm.

But the other vehicles on the highway weren't as lucky, and several of them went off the road and onto the loose gravel.

The first car to reach the berm exploded into flames, broken pieces of passengers and chassis flying every which way. Close behind came an old pickup truck, the vehicle flipping high into the air from the AT land mine buried in the berm. Sheathed in flames, the smashed truck came crashing down to disappear in the lush cornfield. A sports car was next, and then a delivery van, body parts and broken glass splaying across the highway and field.

"Those are antitank land mines!" Lyons snarled, yanking off his seat belt. "I thought Forge wanted their people alive?"

"They do," Blancanales countered, stuffing his pockets with spare ammo clips. "This must be somebody else."

"Could be Trinity," Schwarz muttered, scanning the surrounding area with a monocular. "But how did they find us? I disabled the low-jacks on both vehicles myself."

"Forge must have told them," Lyons rationalized, pulling the Atchisson shotgun special from the floor. He clicked off the safety. "This isn't a hit, but a rescue attempt. Trinity wants to save its reputation by fulfilling the original contract."

"Good. That gives us an edge," Blancanales said grimly, sliding a satchel of grenades over a shoulder. "The mercs will hesitate to use heavy weapons until the Forge soldiers are in the clear. That'll let us—"

At that second, the dark blue SUV came into view, wildly fishtailing across all three lanes in an effort to avoid the spiked stars. But the tires blew anyway, and the top-heavy sport utility vehicle flipped over to skid for yards along the littered highway, pushing a mound of the deadly caltrops ahead of them.

The members of Able Team sighed in relief at the sight. Then a sleek Corvette came streaking down the highway, obviously trying to get past the obstructions by sheer speed. As the tires blew, the nose of the sports car dropped hard to the pavement, the airbags deployed and the car blindly rammed directly into the overturned SUV. The two vehicles bent around each other, metal crunching and glass exploding. Then the SUV shockingly detonated, the fireball expanding across the divider to wash both sides of the highway.

Buffeted by the concussion, the Stony Man operatives couldn't believe what they were seeing. The Forge soldiers had been fine, virtually unharmed by the crash.

"The stupid assholes must have had a self-destruct bomb," Schwarz raged. "Rigged to blow if they were captured alive."

"And the crash set it off," Blancanales finished. "There goes our only way of finding the American uplink site!"

"Not necessarily," Lyons countered. "If this was a rescue mission, then Trinity should know where to take Caramico and Mendoza afterward."

"And we still look like them," Blancanales grunted.

"Sounds good," Schwarz said, dropping the monocular and pulling a combat knife. He quickly began to slash apart the seat cushions and soon had cut a hole through to the trunk.

Tense moments passed as Schwarz passed the backpacks to the other men. Trinity might know their duplicates were riding escort, but it was highly doubtful that they knew which car contained Able Team. That gave the Stony Man operatives a small advantage. But as soon as the mercs decided to do a clean sweep…

Just then, the hood of the Cadillac buckled and a heartbeat later there came the rolling boom of a high-powered sniper rifle. A split second later, a fiery dart streaked across the top of the corn and slammed into the disabled Volvo, blowing it to smithereens.

Bursting out of their car, Able Team threw smoke grenades to give them some cover as they shuffled through the blanket of caltrops. The men were wearing civilian shoes, and the sharp spikes would stab straight through the soft soles.

Another LAW rocket streaked by and the sniper rifle boomed again, a chunk of pavement cracking away. Flipping the arming leveler on a smoke canister, Blancanales saw several men laying on the berm, ruined hands clutching their bloody feet. A woman was facedown on the asphalt, a caltrap embedded into her forehead, a pool of red spreading around her long tresses.

Their assault rifles chattering at the berm, a loud explosion only yards away rocked Schwarz, but he kept running, his tattered shirt exposing the NATO body armor underneath. Lyons and Blancanales got past the gravel without incident, and all three men jumped over the drainage ditch. They hit the soft loam and crawled away into the green stalks, only to converge again a hundred feet away. The corn randomly jerked from the passage of high-velocity bullets, and from somewhere there came the roiling blast of an HE grenade.

Checking their throat mikes and weapons, the Stony Man operatives listened carefully to the sounds of the enemy gunfire. The cross fire was coming from different directions. Choosing targets, the three men separated and charged down the paths between the rows of upright stalks.

Alternately running and crawling to try to hide his passage through the tall corn, Blancanales zigzagged across the farmland at his top speed. The young corn seemed to go on forever.

Unexpectedly, he stopped at the sight of a figure lurking in the greenery. He saw it was only a farmhand, and started to leave when he noticed that although the man was wearing dirty overalls, he had on dress shoes, the patent leather shiny and clean. Leveling the M-16 assault rifle, Blancanales fired a short burst across the man's legs, trying to only wound the stranger in case he was wrong. With a strangled cry, the farmer fell into plain sight, an Ingram MAC-10 machine pistol tight in his hand. Ruthlessly, the Able Team warrior stroked the trigger once more, stitching the fake worker from throat to groin. The man twitched and dropped, lifeless.

Immediately, the silken tufts of the corn stalks overhead began to shake from incoming rounds, the green leaves wrapped around the corn jumping with juicy thwacks.

Staying low, Blancanales knelt in the soft loam and briefly checked the warm body. There was civilian clothing under the bloody overalls, and an S&W .357 revolver in a holster behind his back. A compact Kenwood transceiver was clipped to his belt, but a stray 5.56 mm round had accidentally blown the radio apart, loose wiring dangling. Clearly this was one of the men from the ambush, but the fellow was of African ancestry, and the three known members of Trinity were Europeans. Only one possibility made sense.

The mercs had hired some mercs! Blancanales scowled, touched his throat mike. "Alert," he subvocalized, "our friends have friends. Number unknown. One down."

"Two down," Schwarz whispered in his earphone.

"Three," Lyons panted, as if running. "Stay sharp! We have no idea how many we're facing. Watch out for civilians."

"And me, too," Blancanales responded, when the rows of corn around him started to tremble.

For a long tick of the clock, he thought the snipers had located him and were hammering the area with a barrage of hot lead. Then the ground began shaking, and Blancanales cursed as he sprinted for his life. A shadow covered the man, and the titanic combine loomed before him like a wall of doom, the chainsawlike cornheads cutting down the plants in an endless stream. It was like looking into the working maw of a woodchipper.

Firing a long burst from the M-16, Blancanales retreated as the 5.56 mm rounds ricocheted harmlessly off the heavy frame of the sturdy farm equipment. Then the whining noise of the cornheads changed to a thumping as the thrasher came to life, the thirty-foot-long drum of shiny blades spinning to a blur. The fallen corn stalks were annihilated and flew upward into the auger like confetti to be sucked out of sight and blown out the rear vents.

At the chilling sight, Blancanales knew this was part of the highway trap. There was no conceivable reason to attach the wheat thrasher to a combine in a corn field. But Trinity had done both, turning the ordinary piece of farm equipment into a rolling death machine.

Trying to shoot backward, Blancanales tripped on the exposed roots of the corn, but went into a barrel roll and came up running. The machine was closer now, the air throbbing with the beat of the thrasher and the roar of the massive 500-horsepower diesel engine.

Gaining a little distance, the Able Team warrior turned and put a 40 mm grenade directly into thrasher. The spinning blades detonated, shrapnel flying off to the sides, but the remaining couple of blades kept going 'round and 'round, now hacking the plants into chunks instead of tearing them completely apart.

The shell had exploded prematurely. He fired a long blast at the dimly seen driver, hidden behind dangling chains and tufts of corn silk. In response, the combine harvester accelerated, twin columns of black smoke from the mighty diesel engine pouring into the blue sky.

Frantically reloading the grenade launcher on the run,

Blancanales aimed for the driver again. This time the barrage of double-aught buckshot smashed apart the windshield and the driver cried out, falling from his chair. The machine turned to the right. But a moment later, the driver reclaimed his seat, blood on his right arm, the tattered shirt revealing the molded body armor underneath.

"Another damn merc," Blancanales growled. Shooting the M-16 nonstop, he tried to get around the huge machine, but the thrasher blades extended yards past the harvester on both sides. The brief glimpse of the side he got was of smooth metal. There wasn't a vulnerable fuel line, hydraulic line or anything else in sight. Designed to work under the most adverse conditions, the combine was a tank in everything but name.

Then he'd fight it like any other tank.

Slinging the assault rifle under a shoulder, Blancanales paused for a dangerous length of time as he extracted a grenade, ripped the tape off the arming lever and pulled the ring. The cornheads were moving along the ground, destroying everything in their path. The former Black Beret threw the grenade as high as he could, then turned and ran. As the combine harvester moved after him, the grenade came down again and exploded in the air, a fiery rain of thermite falling over the colossal machine.

Almost instantly, the driver screamed in pain and the combine shifted off to the side. Without warning, a sharp hissing heralded the sizzling launch of a dozen LAW rockets from inside the burning cab, the warbirds streaking away in looping spirals. One of the rockets nosed into the dirt alongside Blancanales, and his heart stopped beating until he realized the distance from the cab had been too short for the warhead to arm.

By now, the writhing chemical flames completely covered the chassis, the unstoppable thermite burning through the industrial grade steel as if it were balsa wood. Hydraulic lines came loose, spraying red fluid about like severed arteries. Pneumatic hoses burst, whistling and hissing. The auger sighed to a halt, and the thrasher stopped with a jerk. Only the deadly chained blades of the cornheads continued processing.

With the thrasher out of commission, Blancanales pumped another 40 mm shell into the booth and the control room violently exploded, grisly bits of man and machinery blowing skyward. As the thrasher collapsed onto the cornheads, the blades jammed the chains, and the entire front of the combine seemed to tear apart. Sprocket assemblies audibly broke, support struts bent, the conveyor belt burst at the seams, and the auger cracked free. Then the diesel engine whoofed into flames, the smoky orange fire mixing oddly with the searing blue-white glare of the military thermite.

RUNNING FAST ALONG THE PATH between the waving field of corn, Schwarz encountered two farmhands in the wrong clothing and took them down fast.

Checking one of the bodies, the Stony Man commando found a Kenwood transceiver, but with a million possible combinations on the alphanumeric keypad, he would need the laptop back in the Cadillac to bust the encoding. He could hear the enemy, but not what they were saying. The words were garbled squeals and chirps. Useless. But tucking the radio away just in case, Schwarz dropped out of the way of a LAW rocket that came from out of nowhere. The warbird arched high, then dived straight down and detonated in the loose soil, the blast throwing loose dirt and cornstalks for dozens of yards. Taking advantage of the chaotic moment, Schwarz fired a long burst from one of the dropped MAC-10 machine pistols, then loudly cried out in pain. But the other mercenaries didn't buy the clever trick, and responded with a hail of lead that peppered the green stalks all around him.

Dodging out of the way, Schwarz crawled along the soft soil until reaching an unexpected zone of smooth grass. Directly ahead was a large billboard. Dropping the partially loaded clip packed with imbalanced tumblers, he quickly reloaded the M-16 with armor-piercing rounds and emptied the entire clip, sweeping back and forth across the billboard.

The AP rounds punched through the wood with snapping sounds, and mercs dropped into view from behind the billboard, their machine pistols chattering once before going silent. In short bursts, Schwarz took out the would-be snipers, then reloaded and waited. The mercs might be dead, but every combat instinct he had said that these were merely the flankers for one of the Trinity team. Warily alert, Schwarz stayed low and waited for the real enemy to appear.

PAUSING AT THE EDGE of the cornfield, Lyons tugged his cap on tighter and studied the farmhouse. The building was mostly made of brick, but with a freshly painted trim, almost all of it speckled with bullet holes. He didn't have to check inside to know that the legal owners were long gone.

There didn't seem to be anybody inside the farmhouse, and now Lyons could see a previously unnoticed barn that had been converted into a garage. Probably for the combine harvester, the big man guessed, trying to stay motionless. Come on, guys, show yourselves.

A thunderous blast erupted from atop the silo, followed by a lance of flame. Spinning, Lyons saw a car on the highway buck from the arrival of the incoming round, then the gas tank ignited flames. That was a Barrett! Somebody atop the silo had a Barrett sniper rifle!

Swinging up his Atchisson autoshotgun, Lyons almost smiled as he flipped the selector to full-auto. Creeping through the rustling corn, he got behind the garage, then boldly stepped into view and cut loose with the shotgun, the 12-gauge cartridges of steel fléchettes ripping through the corrugated aluminum of the grain silo. The weatherproof metal opened wide as the entire structure shook from the thundering fusillade. A man cried out from on top, then the badly damaged side buckled and the silo collapsed, falling on the ground into a pile of rending metal and swirling dust clouds. From somewhere inside the wreckage the Barrett boomed. Lyons replied with another blast from the hammering Atchisson, and there was only the muted groaning sound of the silo settling upon itself.

That was when a trio of shiny humanoids stepped out of the farmhouse and onto the wooden porch.

Thumbing cartridges into the Atchisson, Lyons could see that the three men were dressed in silvery heat-resistant suits that covered every inch of their bodies, a hood with a reflective faceplate masking their features. Two of them carried flamethrowers, with bulletproof vests draped over the pressurized fuel tanks strapped to their backs. Stubby MP-5 submachine guns were slung at their sides. The third man carried a massive XM-214 electric minigun, the enclosed Niagara-style ammo feed going over his shoulder and out of sight inside his thermal suit.

"Heads up," Lyons subvocalized in warning. "Trinity is here and they're packing flamethrowers and a minigun."

"Flamethrowers?" Schwarz's voice crackled in his earphone. "In a field of green plants? That doesn't make any sense."

"But the minigun does," Blancanales retorted. "Any more mercs about?"

"Not a sign," Lyons replied, tracking the shrouded men with the Atchisson. "But they could be in hiding."

"They usually are, brother."

Leveling their weapons, two of the men took aim at the thick fields of corn. The third man turned around to watch their backs, one gloved hand tight on the support handle, the other on the joystick. He pressed the trigger to the first click and the six barrels softly whined as they began to rotate to operational speed.

"Here it comes," Lyons warned.

Steadfast, the two men with flamethrowers pulled the triggers and moved the vented barrels around, sweeping back and forth as if spraying insecticide, but nothing seemed to happen.

Then Lyons saw some crows flutter from the sky to land hard on the ground. Squawking angrily, the black birds flapped their wings madly, constantly bumping into each other.

"Turn around fast!" Lyons whispered hoarsely, shoving his face into the dirt. "Don't look at the farmhouse! Those aren't flamethrowers, but laser rifles!"

"Fuck! How the hell do we fight an enemy we can't look at?" Blancanales demanded, annoyance strong in his voice. "Shoot randomly and hope for a lucky strike?"

"Gadgets, will the smoke protect us?" Lyons demanded.

"No."

The single-word response told the other members of Able Team all they needed to know. In the movies, the hero would use smoke to block the laser beam, or don mirror sunglasses, but Hollywood often got weapons wrong. In the real world, neither of those ploys would do a damn thing to stop the lasing ultraviolet beam.

"Okay, those aren't fuel tanks on their backs, but power generators," Schwarz theorized. "Probably NASA hydrogen cells. Those supply plenty of power for a really long time. The minigun uses the same thing."

"Don't tell us how it flipping works," Blancanales snapped. "Tell us what to do, boy genius."

"Yeah, well, I'm working on it. Give me a minute."

Barely daring to breathe, Lyons risked a fast peek. Two of the men were starting to move into the rows of corn, separating as they began a hunt for Able Team. The third stayed near the edge of the trimmed grass, the XM-214 still spinning, ready to unleash a hellstorm of lead at the touch of a finger.

Mentally, Lyons reviewed his ammunition supply. He was out of grenades and fléchette rounds. There were plenty of aluminum drums of double-aught buckshot cartridges for the autoshotgun, but he would have to get a lot closer to be sure of an instant kill. That meant charging across the flat lawn toward the minigun, which discharged 166 rounds a second. Not a good idea.

"How many shells do you have left?" Lyons demanded curtly, slowly easing the Atchisson into position. A quick move could reveal his position, and then he'd be fighting blind, to keep from going blind. There was the gritty feel of dirt in his mouth and he tried not to imagine that it might be the last thing he ever tasted in this life before they shoveled him under the grass.

Suddenly the two mercs began firing their MP-5 submachine guns into the corn in an effort to draw out their hidden foes, the twin lasers constantly sweeping the plants. The third man braced the minigun, taking a half step forward in his eagerness to start the one-sided battle.

"I've got…two HE shells and one Willie Peter," Schwarz replied.

"Two AP rounds and one HE," Blancanales added. "That's enough to do the job, but how do we aim?"

"You don't, I do," Lyons said, closing one eye and sneaking a peek at the sky, then at the three members of Trinity. "Keep facing the billboard. Now check the position of the Volvo on the highway, see the smoke plume? Track fifteen degrees toward the burning combine. Note the bend of the smoke from the breeze. Take that into account. Gadgets, aim for two o'clock high. Pol, four o'clock, and add ten degrees toward the highway. That should do it." The man knew the triangulation was purely guesswork, but when there was no other choice, a soldier took a gamble and hoped for the best.

"If we miss, we'll hit you," Schwarz said in a monotone. "I'd rather risk a charge with my eyes closed."

"And that minigun would cut you down in a nanosecond," the Able Team leader reminded him harshly. "Take it easy, and stay loose. You've got plenty of time…fire."

Dull thumps from the M-203 grenade launchers sounded from the field, and Trinity instantly replied with everything it had—lasers, MP-5 subguns—before the XM-214 minigun burst into action. A stuttering flame extended from the top barrel as the deadly superfire vomited a maelstrom of high-velocity lead. The corn stalks didn't fall, they disintegrated as the .223 rounds plowed through the growth, searching for the hidden men.

Then a whistle came from above, and the shells arrived, landing alongside one of the mercs and hitting the other directly. The men screamed as the 40 mm rounds cut loose, blowing them into fiery chunks. The double blast was still ringing in his ears when Lyons stood and charged the last member of Trinity, holding back the Atchisson until he reached point-blank range.

The minigun was still vomiting hot lead, the merc trying to track toward the new foe, but the inertia of the massive seventy-two pounds of spinning metal resisted any quick movements. Chewing a path of destruction along the ground, the .223 rounds almost reached Lyons when he triggered the Atchisson, all seven 12-gauge cartridges firing in under a second. The merc was cut in two, the minigun tracking high as his torso fell away. The monster gun went silent as the dead hand released the trigger on the joystick.

Dropping the exhausted Atchisson, Lyons drew his .357 Colt Python and shot the bisected man in the shocked face, then did the same to the other mercenaries. This was no mercy shot to ease their pain. The grim warrior was just making sure that Trinity was truly dead.

"All clear," Lyons said, pulling air into his lungs. The whole fight lasted only a few moments, yet it seemed as if it had taken hours. Turning, he hawked and spit the taste of dirt from his mouth. Not in the grave yet, he thought.

Less than a minute later, his teammates appeared from out of the cornfield at opposite ends of the lawn. Checking to make sure the combat zone was secure, the Stony Man operatives rejoined their friend, easing tense fingers off the triggers of their hot weapons.

Removing the gore-splattered hoods, Lyons revealed the faces of Trinity. Smith and Sakeda had their eyes closed, death softening their features until it appeared that they were merely asleep. Only Potvin still glared hatefully at the universe, his teeth fully exposed in a feral rictus of fury.

"I'll check with Bear to make sure these are them," Blancanales said, sliding a cell phone from a pocket. Tapping in a memorized number, he waited a few seconds, then flipped the phone closed. "Goddamn it, the Farm is still off-line."

"Expected as much." Schwarz sighed. "It takes a while to realign a satellite."

"Much less all of them," Lyons agreed, dropping the thermal hood over the angry face of the insane merc. Looking over the battlefield, he saw that the lasers were smashed and the XM-214 minigun was reduced to a pile of twisted metal. There was nothing here to salvage, except the bodies. "Okay, let's get this over with."

Lacking the usual protective latex gloves, they knelt on the grass and used their bare hands to start searching through the blood-splattered pockets of the dead men. They unearthed a huge amount of cash, several 10 mm derringers, a lot of knives, cell phones, a couple of maps of South Dakota and a GPS unit. Schwarz took the electronics. The redial on the cell phones yielded nothing, which wasn't surprising. Only a rank beginner would leave an important number live on his telephone. However, the recall button on the GPS brought up the state map of North Dakota.

"Let's see how smart these assholes were," Schwarz said with a humorless grin, and breathed on the tiny screen. The plastic fogged, revealing a couple of smudges near the border, as if somebody had tapped the screen with a finger to show the location to others.

"That's probably the dropoff point for Caramico and Mendoza," Blancanales said, rubbing the scar on his cheek. Irritably, he started to yank it off, but then stopped his hand. "So why don't we?"

"What, deliver corpses?" Schwarz asked, raising an eyebrow.

"That might just work," Lyons muttered thoughtfully, running a hand over his bald scalp.

Schwarz got the idea. "I see. How could Forge possibly know that their people, or that any of the mercs, are dead? None of the cell phones are working."

"Exactly," Blancanales said, resting the stock of his assault rifle on a hip. Then the man scowled. "Damn, we got company."

Turning toward the highway, Lyons grunted at the sight of several cars and a Mack truck parked near the crash site, excited people moving among the smoky debris, obviously checking for survivors. There was no sign of the police yet, but they would arrive pretty soon. Route 29 was the main highway in the state and regularly patrolled by helicopters.

"Rosario, get those civilians out of there," Lyons said brusquely. "Tell them we're the FBI and this was a terrorist attack."

"No problem," Blancanales said over a shoulder, starting for the highway. "I'll say they were smuggling anthrax. This is farming country, and that'll put the fear of God in them."

"It always does for me," Lyons agreed with a snort.

"Gadgets, go blow the last of those landmines. I'll find the car, truck, whatever Trinity used to get here, and load up the least damaged of the bodies."

"See you in five," Schwarz said, taking off at a run.

Standing alone amid the destruction, Lyons studied the grisly remains of the mercenaries. If we put enough bandages on the faces of the dead men, he thought, nobody would be able to tell that the people were actually corpses. At least for a few minutes, and that was all the edge my team would need to get close to the terrorists. But after that, the Stony Man team might need a bargaining chip to make the Forge terrorists talk.

With a dour expression, Lyons nudged one of the laser rifles lying on the grass with his shoe, then savagely crushed the delicate focusing lens under a heel. It shattered with a splintering crackle.

Turning away from the cornfield, Lyons headed toward the makeshift garage. His duty was clear. A soldier killed the enemy. Period. Using torture only reduced a man to the level of a beast. There were other ways to extract needed information: bribery, intimidation, psychological warfare, recruitment, amnesty, drugs…. If they had to fight fire with fire to save the nation, then America had already lost the war on terrorism.

Reclaiming the Atchisson, Lyons reloaded the weapon before going into the garage. A nebulous plan was already forming in his mind. Of course, to make it work, Able Team would require some specialty equipment. Trinity had a rendezvous set with Forge on the border of North Dakota, which gave Able Team very little time and distance to acquire the needed equipment.

Working the slide to chamber a cartridge, the Able Team leader briefly wondered how difficult it would be to rob the Homeland Security field office in Sioux Falls, South Dakota.

CHAPTER FIFTEEN

Firebase Alpha

In an explosion of glass, the searchlight on top of the administration building winked out and darkness covered the western side of the military compound. A single moment later, the lolling boom of a large-caliber rifle rolled down from the woody hillside.

"Snipers!" a Forge soldier yelled, pointing at the dark trees.

Firing their assault rifles, the soldiers boldly charged for the forest when there came a soft thump from the darkness.

Recognizing the muffled sound, Major San Martin cursed and sprinted away. But the rest of the soldiers paused for a moment in indecision. Had that been a grenade or...

In strident fury, the ground near the front gate loudly erupted into flames. Ragged pieces of men and metal went flying. Another deadly blast closely followed a few yards to the right, then a third detonation occurred several yards to the left in a classic bracketing pattern.

"Mortars!" Major San Martin shouted, banging away at the

woods with his Bersa pistol. But if the copper-jacketed 9 mm rounds hit anything it wasn't readily discernable.

The dull thumping of the hidden ordnance continued unabated, the remains of the front gate and the concrete pillboxes becoming wreathed in flames. Shrapnel filled the night air, humming past the soldiers who weren't torn to pieces.

The other searchlight crashed and went out. A second boom echoed from the hills. Now the firebase was shrouded in blackness, the deep gloom illuminated only by the glow of a few windows, the reflected light from the bottom of the ravine and the flickering flames of burning fuel on top of the concrete buildings. The dancing shadows distorted the familiar structures of the military compound into a nightmarish appearance. Covered with fire, a howling sniper raced off the edge of the barracks roof to fall from sight, his weapon discharging at the meaty impact.

Unsure of where the enemy was coming from, the remaining Forge soldiers charged in every direction, unleashing controlled bursts from their FN-2000 assault rifles into the treetops.

Unexpectedly, the softly thumping mortar paused, and soldiers raced to take cover. Then the deadly rounds came down again in exactly the same locations as before. A dozen soldiers were blown into horrid gobbets of ragged flesh having foolishly taken refuge in the earlier blast craters under the mistaken notion that incoming shells never hit the same spot twice.

An alarm started howling from atop a tall pole, and lights came on in a score of windows. Doors were flung open and soldiers appeared in various stages of undress, their hair tousled from sleep, but deadly Bersa pistols and assault rifles tightly held in calloused fists.

Scrambling into the cabs of trucks, other men started the engines and the MRL honeycombs raised into firing positions.

Stuttering irregularly, the honeycombs spit fat rockets into the starry sky, their radar desperately searching for enemy helicopters or jet fighters.

In dark harmony, a corner of the perimeter fence erupted into a lambent geyser, the concertina wire shattering into a million pieces as the metal support posts toppled over, creating a ragged opening in the barrier.

Crouching on the open ground, Major San Martin snarled as he identified the sound of M-2 plastic explosives. Forge stocked only C-4 satchel in the armory, so nobody was trying to escape. But the front gate was already down, so why make another entry point? Then his blood ran cold. Could the attack on the fence be another trap?

"Back! Keep back!" the major bellowed in warning, starting that way. "It's a trick!" But it was too late.

A handful of Forge soldiers was standing at the breech, assembling a .50-caliber machine gun to repel any possible invasion when they vanished in stentorian hellfire.

Aghast, the major stopped in his tracks, unable to believe the amount of death and destruction done to the vaunted base in only a few minutes. Half of his troops had to be dead by now. Who the hell was attacking them, the entire U.S. Army?

TOSSING SMOKE GRENADES and flash-bangs everywhere, Phoenix Force moved low and fast through the shadowy darkness, darting from building to building, shooting anybody they encountered that was wearing the uniform of Forge.

Supremely confident that the secret base would never actually see any combat, the Forge soldiers were totally surprised by the attack. Pandemonium filled the night, with rockets brightly streaking into the sky overhead. Clouds of smoke and acrid fumes floated along the streets of the base, somewhere a man screamed in pain, and assault rifles were chattering nonstop, although exactly what the soldiers were shooting at wasn't very clear.

Dedicated to a seek-and-destroy mission, the Stony Man commandos were taking total advantage of the situation and penetrating deep into the heart of the terrorist camp. All they had to do was to find the uplink array and blow it apart, or at least smash the operating computers. A simple enough task, but every building they checked that registered a cold blue on the thermal scanners of their IR goggles proved to be a fake. Somebody in Forge had expected a night attack, and liquid nitrogen containers were all over the base, the frigid exhaust masking the location of the real supercomputers. And worse, with every tick of the clock, the shock was wearing off the Forge soldiers. Soon there would be organized resistance. The clock was ticking, and the Phoenix Force team had only a few minutes of protective confusion remaining before they were pushed back into the forest. After that, they would be running for their lives, and there would be nobody to stop Calvano from wreaking untold destruction upon the helpless world.

"Firebird to Rock Garden," McCarter tersely subvocalized into his throat mike. "Come in, Rock Garden!" But there was still only crackling static on the radio transceiver. Either there was trouble with the Stony Man Comsat or the Farm no longer existed.

"Anything?" Hawkins asked, firing down a dark alleyway. An answering cry told of a mortal hit.

"Nothing," McCarter replied with a snarl, shooting through a closed window. The glass shattered and a Forge soldier inside fell away from the wall rack holding an XM-214 mini-gun. James fired again, blowing the backpack generator into rubbish. Without power for the electric motor, the minigun was useless.

Pausing at an intersection, Encizo lifted his IR goggles to read a signpost when a soldier on a rooftop chattered a long burst from his FN-2000. The 5.56 mm rounds stitched Encizo across the chest, and the man staggered from the hammering blows on his NATO body armor. Then he sent back a hail of 9 mm rounds from the deadly MP-5 SMG, moving in a tight figure-eight pattern. With a strangled cry, the Forge soldier dropped from sight clutching his ruined neck.

Just then, a trooper carrying a combat shotgun rushed around a corner and paused to gawk at the sight of the strangers. Dressed in camouflage ghillie suits and IR goggles, the Stony Man operatives looked like invaders from Mars.

Caught in the act of reloading, Encizo moved fast, lashing out with a steel-tipped combat boot to kick the man in the groin, then the belly and throat. With a muffled grunt, the terrorist collapsed unconscious.

"This way," Encizo directed, slapping in a fresh clip and jerking his weapon to the right.

Crossing the street, Phoenix Force reached a small brick building. Taking flanking positions, McCarter and Hawkins stood guard while James went to work with a key-wire gun on the lock. It yielded in less than a minute, and they quickly slipped inside. But the offices were empty, dark and deserted.

Briefly checking with an EM scanner, McCarter got no reading of an electromagnetic field from either computers or an uplink. The only thing of interest was a poster on the wall of a pretty Spanish girl in a string bikini skiing down a snowy mountain.

Grunting in annoyance, McCarter shoved the scanner into

a cushioned pocket on the leg of his ghillie suit, and moved outside with the rest of the team close behind.

"Where next?" Hawkins started to ask, but turned to fire his MP-5 in the middle of the sentence.

High overhead, a Forge soldier was swinging a flamethrower their way, the lance of reddish-yellow fire moving along the street in hellish majesty, the lashing flames splaying along the black asphalt. As the rest of the team hammered at the soldier with 9 mm rounds, his chest suddenly burst open. The flamethrower died away as the dead man went flying backward. A few seconds later, the boom of the distant Barrett arrived.

"Thanks," McCarter whispered into his throat mike, working the arming bolt to clear a jam from the ejector port.

"Screw that, you've got incoming!" Manning replied curtly. "Big steel, three o'clock and moving fast!"

The men of Phoenix Force spun around just as a lumbering Gavin APC turned the corner. The halogen headlights briefly illuminated the team in harsh clarity before they dived for cover. Instantly, the coaxial chain gun on the side of the Gavin unleashed a barrage of 12.7 mm rounds. Then the chattering weapon exploded into pieces, the distant Barrett announcing Manning's deadly marksmanship.

There was movement inside the Gavin and the armored top hatch flipped open, a Forge soldier grabbing for the 25 mm Bushmaster cannon. Expecting that move, Phoenix Force tore the man apart with concentrated volley fire, and Hawkins flipped a grenade into the air. It hit the hatch and rattled down into the APC. The enemy gunners inside cursed in horror, then the Willie Peter charge flashed and the anguished voices went silent forever.

"This is taking too bleeding long," McCarter growled,

checking his wristwatch. "Everybody spread out and find the base security bunker. They'll know the location of the uplink array."

Without comment, the Stony Man operatives took off in different directions, swiftly disappearing into the murky shadows.

THE DOUBLE DOORS to the security office slammed aside, and a rumpled man in a bathrobe strode into the room with a monstrous .50 Desert Eagle pistol in his fist.

Looking up from their consoles, the Forge soldiers said nothing, and went straight back to work, issuing fast orders over their VOX mikes, directing men and machines in a rescue mission for the wounded, and trying to block the two holes in the fence with anything that could be found. Wearing helmets and body armor, armed guards stood nervously in the corners, twisting their hands on the FN-2000 assault rifles, clearly wishing they were outside and mixing in the fight. Grenades festooned the web harness on their chests, and one man carried an XM-214 minigun.

"Shut off those damn alarms!" General Calvano shouted. "OD, what is happening on my base?"

"We're being attacked by unknown forces, sir!" the Officer of the Day announced. "Mortar fire from the hillside, along with a sniper." The man paused awkwardly.

"And?" the general prompted harshly. "Speak, man, or I'll have your balls for breakfast!"

"There have been some reports of commandos actually inside the base," the soldier continued doggedly. "But nothing confirmed yet."

"Reports from where?" Calvano demanded suspiciously, walking along the banks of video monitors.

Most of the screens in the woods surrounding the base showed nothing of interest, a moonlit forest glen, a babbling brook, the main access road. But an entire row of screens was blank, the feeds terminated, and several more displayed the burning bridge collapsed into the Otonio River, and the ruin of the front gate.

Dead bodies were strewed everywhere, blast craters dotted the landscape and dozens of soldiers were running about firing their weapons. One corporal was moving through the cars in the parking lot, smashing windows with the butt of his gun and turning on the headlights. The rows of beams were starting to brighten the smoky gloom, showing more dead soldiers and the same burning buildings.

"From where? All over, sir," the soldier reported, swallowing with difficulty. "The old offices, Storage Shed 5, the abandoned barracks—"

"The cold spots," Calvano interrupted, tucking the Desert Eagle into a pocket of his robe. Somebody was trying to find the supercomputer that ran the uplink. "All right, recall everybody outside the base! I want a wall of men surrounding the—"

Something flashed across the video screen showing the parking lot and several cars violently exploding, flipping into the air and turning over to crash on their crumpled hoods from the sheer force of the detonation. All of the headlights winked out, and darkness returned with a vengeance.

"That was a LAW rocket," the general stated in cold certainty, advancing upon the console as if about to attack the screen. He paused in the realization of what he was doing, and stood casually erect. Always be calm in front of the troops, especially when everything was going to hell. "OD, are there any people still on the roofs?"

"No, sir, all dead."

"All?" Calvano bellowed, arching an eyebrow. "How is that possible?"

"My best guess is a Barrett rifle, sir," the soldier began, gesturing at the blank screens. "Every shot kills one, or two, of our troops. Even the men wearing heavy armor."

"What about the Gavins?"

"I have six blocking the holes in the fence. Three are being held in reserve, and one is not responding."

"That means it's been destroyed," Calvano muttered, furrowing his brow.

Then he scowled. "You there, private! Zoom in on that screen!"

The soldier did as requested, until the view of the foggy intersection filled the monitor.

"That's a smoke grenade," the general stated, pointing at an object lying on the pavement. "And not the model we carry."

Just then a loud bang drew his attention to a monitor. Puzzled, the general stared at the sight of the buckled door to the garage coming free from the hinges and falling to the ground. Now why in the world would the sniper use the Barrett to smash down the door to the garage? Unless...

"Get the Gavins out of there!" Calvano barked. "Now! Right now!"

A security officer hastily began speaking into the VOX throat mike when another LAW rocket streaked across the tumultuous base and went straight through the man-size opening. A muffled blast filled the garage, then a moment later the entire building erupted, the windows exploding and the roof rising on a staggering fireball as the emergency stores of gasoline and munitions simultaneously ignited.

"So much for the reserve Gavins," Calvano snarled, hunching his broad shoulders. "OD, get the Ashanti helicopters into the air! Bomb those hills until the forest is leveled! But kill that sniper!"

"Already on the way, sir!" the OD reported in grim satisfaction, cracking his knuckles.

Glancing at the side monitor, Calvano smiled at the sight of four black ghosts rising into the air from the small helipad in the center of the firebase. Recently purchased on the black market by Snake Eater, the sleek Italian gunships were armored killers, carrying more firepower than a dozen Gavins. Then he sharply frowned as one of the helicopters turned on its running lights as required by standard safety precautions.

"Combat mode, idiot!" the general snarled, reaching for the screen. He turned around. "OD, have that moron go black at once!"

But before the soldier could act, the distant Barrett spoke once more. The windshield shattered and the helicopter wobbled, then listed sideways and touched rotors with a second. In a shattering microsecond, the sixteen spinning turboblades of the two gunships were shredded into shrapnel. The deadly halo of fiberglass and steel radiated outward to hammer the other two gunships. Both exploded, and in ragged order, the four crippled helicopters dropped a hundred feet to crash on the concrete helipad. The blast shook the beleaguered base, shattering windows, the detonating fuel and ammo of the gunships combining to form a writhing mushroom cloud that rose to mask the silvery moon. Illuminated from below by the scattered fire, the roiling cloud made it look as if the military compound had been nuked.

"Mother of God," a private whispered, making the sign of the cross.

"OD, warm up the *Pegasus*," Calvano ordered, tightening the sash on his robe. The base was lost. Time to leave. They would continue the Great Project from their main firebase in the Andes. "And sound the retreat. Everybody is to gather at the parade ground in five minutes, or be left behind."

Everybody knew what that meant and quickly began issuing the recall orders into the VOX throat mikes.

"But, sir, the bridge is gone," the officer said, nervously glancing at a flickering screen showing the fiery ruins in the valley. "Our people across the river can't get back here in that short a time!"

"Yes, I know," Calvano said, pulling a chain from around his neck. A small hexagonal key was attached.

The OD stood. "Sir, please, there must be another way!"

"No, there is not." Calvano sighed, going to the main console and inserting the key into a hole. Twisting hard to the right, then the left, there came a soft hiss and a panel slid aside on the control panel, exposing a sheet of glass with a keypad underneath.

Smashing the glass with his balled fist, the general tapped a long code sequence into the keypad, then pressed his thumb to a sensor plate. Immediately, every video screen in the security office was filled with bright light, and the room trembled as the tons of high explosives situated under the fake uplink dish hidden inside the copse of pine tress thunderously detonated.

As the reverberations slowly faded, nobody spoke for a long moment, the grim reality of the situation turning their faces hard as stone.

"Our brothers have made the ultimate sacrifice," Calvano loudly announced, massaging his cut fist to make the blood flow faster. The glass had sliced his bare flesh, but that was a small price to pay to maintain the goodwill of his troops. "Now we must do our part," he continued, brandishing the bloody fist. "We've lost a battle, but not the war! Death to America! God bless Argentina!"

Rising from their seats, the Forge soldiers repeated the

rally cry and exited the control room in an orderly fashion. The emergency drill had been practiced only a couple of times, nobody ever thinking it would come to pass. But this was fast becoming a night of impossible events.

As the OD closed the door behind the last soldier, a strong smell of burning plastic tickled his nose, and several of the consoles began to glow a dull red from deep inside. The magnesium charges had already destroyed the feeder circuits to the controls, rendering them inert, removing any possibility of an enemy tech trying to deactivate the automatic self-destruct. Thirty seconds after that, the thermite charges inside the walls would cut loose and the entire brick building would be swiftly removed from existence.

Twisting the key in the lock to jam the door solidly in place, the Forge officer turned and raced along the access tunnel to rejoin the general and rest of his brothers. Firebase Alpha was lost, and dozens of Forge soldiers were dead. Just incredible. But nothing could stop the Great Project, and when the coming nuclear war was finally over, Forge would emerge from their underground bunkers to seize control of Argentina and lead the way to a cleaner, saner world of peace and prosperity! But at the moment, there was other work to accomplish first.

Bursting out of the tunnel, the OD paused, then grabbed an assault rifle from a dead Forge soldier lying sprawled on the sidewalk. Checking the clip, the officer worked the arming bolt and headed into the swirling smoke for the parade ground. Everything depended on the general now. But time was short.

Three minutes to go, and counting.

CHAPTER SIXTEEN

Havana, Cuba

The tropical sky was heavily overcast, the black clouds threatened to unleash a torrential rain at any moment. But that did nothing to mar the excitement on the parade grounds.

Numbering more than fifty thousand strong, the entire Revolutionary Armed Forces were assembled in full combat regalia, their rapt attention turned upon the old man looking down on them from a review stand. His hair and beard were gray, his back slightly stooped from age, and a cane was held in his left hand. But his lined face burned with the same revolutionary fervor that let him seize control of the island nation more than fifty years ago. His voice was still strong, steeled by the strength of his political convictions.

"Are you prepared to fight for victory?" the president for life shouted into the microphone, his words booming across the crowded field. "To repel the invaders and force them into the sea?"

The endless rows of Cuban soldiers roared in response, shaking their AK-47 assault rifles in the air.

Stroking his gray beard, the president smiled and gave the massed troops a brisk salute. Taking that as their cue, the military orchestra surged into action playing the national anthem of the tiny Communist nation.

A thousand diesel engines revving in unison, the 1st Rocket Brigade began to roll into motion, the former Soviet Union MRL trucks moving past the review stand in a stately procession.

Adjusting his grip on the cane, the president nodded in frank approval. It had taken him decades to smuggle enough parts past the American Navy to repair the machines, but now they were fully operational, ready for battle. The rockets were crude by modern standards, lacking heat-seekers and GPS guidance. Just plain rockets, the warheads packed with twice the recommended amount of C4 high-explosive, along with an outer layer of steel fléchettes. More than deadly enough to blow Guantanimo Base off the island. His island! Leasing the land to the Americans was merely a political sham. He traded them oil for freedom, like those fools in the Middle East. But no more!

"I am no man's dog," he snarled, quickly changing that to a beaming smile at the troops below. Then a flotilla of ships would haul the advanced troops to the nearby Florida keys, seize control of the secret Hawkins missile bases there and turn the weapons upon Washington and New York. Any attempt by the Americans to repulse his troops would result in untold civilian deaths. After that, a second wave would attack Haiti, Jamaica and every other island in the area forging a huge United Cuba.

True, his air force was weak, only 250 jetfighters, and half of those were more than ten years old, but the MiG jetfighters he possessed would fight to the death for their president. Besides, there were SAM bunkers located around the entire coastline, and there were over a thousand gunnery emplacements hidden around the island nation, 53 mm and 67 mm antiaircraft rapidfire cannons in the countryside, and power-ful 100 mm howitzers located smack in the middle of every major city. Nothing could penetrate the defensive umbrella of hammering AA fire that covered his beloved Cuba. Plus, the army had ten thousand Stingers to help them in the coming air battle. U.S. Army Stinger missiles, the very best. The Cubans would turn their own weapons against the Americans. Fire fought with fire.

Now the filthy capitalist pigs would know how it felt to have invaders on their sovereign soil, the president thought defiantly, his chest swelling with pride. Let them drown in the sour bile of frustration!

As soon as the world war began, America would be far too busy defending itself against the other nuclear superpowers to bother with tiny Cuba. And that would give the island presi-dent a brief window to burn the hated Americans off his is-land, and establish a firebase of his own in Miami, supported by the Hawkins missiles in the keys. The cowardly American president certainly would never have the nerve to use thermo-nuclear weapons on his own soil.

"Victory, or death!" the old man shouted into the micro-phone, and the troops bellowed their agreement. Yes, the plan was perfect, and the time was coming. In a day, maybe less, vengeance would be his at last! And there was nothing any-body could do to stop the coming invasion. Nothing!

Sioux Falls, South Dakota

SLOWING DOWN SLIGHTLY, Carl Lyons took an exit and drove into downtown Sioux Falls. The traffic was sparse at that time of the day, a few newspaper trucks dropping off stacks to con-venience stores, a couple of pickup trucks piled high with boxes of new computers, a yawning man on a motorcycle and a handful of assorted civilian cars, the drivers talking on cell phones and drinking from plastic coffee mugs. Thankfully, there were no police in sight.

As it turned out, Trinity had brought along three Hummers full of supplies, most of which had been given to the other mercs. After disarming a couple of traps, Lyons took the best of three Hummers, reclaimed his fellow teammates on the highway and headed north on Route 29. Keeping a careful watch on the skies when state police helicopters appeared in the distance, Lyons drove the Hummer off the interstate and took refuge under the trees of an apple orchard until the coast was clear once more. Their cell phones had begun working a few miles ago, which seemed to indicate that only the East Coast Comsats had been moved. Briefly, Blancanales tried a number dedicated to a restricted government landline, and found it jammed solid with calls. But that had been expected.

Crossing over the border into South Dakota, Lyons stopped at a rest area to refuel the Hummer while Blancanales got them food from the restaurant, and Schwarz did things to the pay telephone. Getting back on the highway, Lyons drove swiftly into Sioux City, and started searching for a construction site. It took a while, but the team finally found a small strip mall being built near a new Native American casino. Parking the Hummer, Lyons went to the phone and began attaching another electronic device to the mouthpiece. A lounging street gang eyed the men in the new car with interest and began to saunter over until Blancanales and Schwarz displayed the M-16 assault rifles through the car windows and worked the arming bolts.

"Move along," Blancanales said in a bored tone.

Without missing a beat, the street gang angled away and left the area.

At the pay phone, the Able Team leader finished attaching the device to the receiver. Schwarz swore that this Jumper would make anybody trying to trace the call believe it was coming from the sister unit near the border.

"Any way to test this?" Lyons asked, screwing the mouthpiece of the handset back into place.

"Nope," the electronics wizard said languidly from the Hummer.

"Then here we go," the man muttered, and started tapping on the keypad. There came a click, and then silence for a moment.

"Homeland Security," a woman said in a calm, professional tone. "How may I direct your—"

"C-code nineteen," Lyons gasped, then broke into a fit of hard coughing.

The woman's cool demeanor was instantly gone. "Ident code?" she demanded brusquely.

Haltingly, Lyons gave a number. There came some soft taps as the woman on the other end of the line fed it into her computer. Then she audibly gasped.

Damn well should be startled. Lyons grinned. The code he gave would bring up the top-secret dossier of a member of the Thirty, the elite group of Secret Service agents assigned to personally guard the President of the Untied States.

"Is the Traveler in danger?" she asked hurriedly.

Traveler, one of the many code names for the President. "Yes." Lyons coughed. "Must get… Christ, my guts…"

"Is Traveler hurt or compromised?"

Compromised meant kidnapped. "Traveler is…" Lyons panted weakly, then groaned. "My guts are on fire…they tell us how bad it'll be at Q, but mother of God." He broke into tears.

"You're shot in the stomach? Son of a… Location!" she snapped, trying to cut through his fog of pain. "Special Agent Fielding, report your location!"

Slurring the words, Lyons gave an address a few miles away from the rest stop. Then he fired his gun twice into the air, grunted with pain and dropped the receiver. Walking in place, Lyons then lifted the receiver again and gently hung up.

Glancing about to see if the pistol shots had drawn any unwanted attention, the man saw Blancanales's choice of locations had been spot-on. Construction sites were always full of noise, and after only a few days the neighbors stopped paying attention to anything they heard.

Returning to the Hummer, Lyons got behind the wheel and deftly started the big engine. "Done," he announced, slipping into gear. "A wounded member of the Thirty in distress will have Homeland send everybody they can scrape together to that rest stop and start a house-by-house search."

"One of them being a known crack house that will not want to be searched," Blancanales added, "so I wish them luck there."

"My money is on Homeland."

"Agreed. But we'll only have a maximum window of five hours before they realize it's a trick. Possibly only four."

"After which they'll call the National Guard and fill the city with troops expecting a terrorist attack," Blancanales added grimly, laying the assault rifle across his lap. "So we'd better be long gone by then." In case of trouble with the local police, the M-203 grenade launcher was loaded with a stun bag. But the ammo clip was full of 5.56 mm HEAT rounds—high-explosive, armor-piercing tracers. A gift from the dearly departed Trinity.

"This never would have worked if the East Coast satellites weren't down," Schwarz noted, tucking his assault rifle away and pulling out his U.S. Army laptop. "In this sort of situation, the first thing Homeland will do is try to contact the White House. But with the cell phones down and the landlines jammed…"

"They'll go ape shit," Lyons finished, moving into the traffic. A semi rumbled by carrying steel beams for a bridge. "Got the correct address of where we're going?"

"Think so," Schwarz muttered, flipping up the screen. Already accessed, the plasma monitor showed a detailed street map of Sioux Falls. "Take the next left, and then go straight for a mile."

Nodding acknowledgment, Lyons followed the directions to outside the city limits. Even for a President in trouble, there would still be a skeleton staff staying at the HSA office. The place was never totally empty; there were far too many important files to keep from falling into criminal hands. On the other hand, the secret Homeland armory should be totally deserted. Hopefully.

In short order, Able Team reached a storage facility near the beginning of the rocky desert. Parking at a gas station across the street, Blancanales got out to refuel their tank while Schwarz watched the EM scanner and Lyons swept the area with enhanced field glasses. There was a weedy lot alongside the storage facility, home to a Pontiac Firebird slowly disintegrating back into the soil. The other side was an abandoned drive-in theater, the silver screen peeling away from the metal framework behind.

Checking his pocket EM scanner, Lyons found no hot spots in the storage facility. So unless there were people inside wearing NASA spacesuits, or drenched in ice, the armory was deserted. Good.

"Anything?" Blancanales asked, climbing back inside the Hummer.

"Everything is clear as far as I can tell," Schwarz said, busy with his own EM scanner, a cable attaching the delicate device to his laptop. "No chatter on the radio bands, passive

radar is clear, no unusual EM spikes. The place looks clean."
He paused. "Except that the fence around this storage facility isn't galvanized steel, but military-grade titanium. The
same stuff the Farm uses to halt incoming missiles."

"Then let's move," Blancanales said.

Driving casually across the road, Lyons read a Closed notice posted in the window of the small office. Ignoring that,
the Stony Man operative carefully maneuvered the entry keypad alongside the rear passenger window.

Rolling down the window, Schwarz slid a data card into
the slot, the plastic rectangle covered with exposed circuitry,
thin wires attached to the end also trailing back to his laptop.
The screen illuminated with binary codes and Schwarz hit a
few keys in rapid sequence. The control box gave an answering beep and spit out the card. A moment later the heavy gate
rumbled aside and Lyons drove inside the complex.

"Easy as pie," he boasted, slinging the laptop over his
shoulder, tucking the key card and wiring into a pocket.

"Try making a pie sometime," Blancanales retorted, watching the passing rows of locked doors. There were no alleys or
back doors, or any other conceivable hiding places. Just a flat
apron of black asphalt surrounding the neat rows of painted
steel sheds. If the team was attacked out here, it would be a
slaughter. They were already trespassing on a secret government installation, and any guards would shoot first and never
ask any questions at all.

"Which storage unit is it?" Lyons asked, driving along
slowly, trying to appear as if they belonged here.

"B-13," Schwarz said, closing the laptop.

Blancanales pointed. "And there it is."

Heading in that direction, Lyons noted a cluster of propane
tanks at the end of the row of sheds. Heating and cooking?

They seemed strangely out of place, and he made a mental note of their location.

Parking in front of B-10, Able Team slipped on hardhats and picked up toolboxes before stepping out of their Hummer. The three men were dressed in dull gray coveralls and bright orange safety vests marked with the letters DPW, department of public works. Stretching as if they had been driving for a long time, the Stony Man operatives warily surveyed the area. Everything seemed peaceful and quiet.

Going to B-12, Lyons pulled out a keywire gun and tricked open the padlock. It yielded easily, but as he swung open the door there was seamless sheet of plastic blocking the entrance. Damn! He had planned to open a joining unit and listen for any movements inside B-13. Suddenly he had a feeling that there were no individual storage units, but just one huge unit two hundred feet long. That wasn't an armory; it was a supply depot.

Closing the door, Lyons went to B-13 and tricked the padlock. As the door swung away, a ferruled slab of steel was revealed, resembling a bank vault door. There was a keypad and a flat screen roughly in the shape of a hand, a state-of-the-art palm lock.

Stepping aside, Lyons and Blancanales blocked any casual view as Schwarz went to work on the door with his U.S. Army laptop and some electronic probes. A tense minute passed, then another, before they heard a soft whirring noise and the internal bolts nosily disengaged.

Retrieving the probes, Schwarz pushed against the metal door and it smoothly swung aside on silent hinges, revealing only inky blackness. Pulling small flashlights from their vests, Able Team probed the darkness with their white beams, revealing rows of gleaming assault rifles and huge pallets stacked with trays of grenades.

"Jackpot," Schwarz whispered, sweeping an EM scanner across the area. There were some background readings for the power lines, but nothing else. There were no working video cameras, proximity sensors or live microphones in the lab.

With his Colt Python in one hand and a flashlight in the other, Lyons took point and eased inside the disguised building. Warily, he took a sniff, but there was no smell of cigarettes or coffee. Good enough.

"Okay, you know what we need," he said, holstering the gun. "Let's find a handtruck and start loading the Hummer."

"We have—" Blancanales checked his wristwatch and tapped the alarm function "—four to five minutes, and counting."

Unexpectedly, they heard the sound of a flushing toilet, and a door blocked by a pallet of satchel charges swung open exposing a uniformed HSA guard zipping up his pants. The guard and Able Team exchanged startled looks for a split second, then everybody clawed for weapons.

Lyons drew first and fired at the guard, trying for a shoulder wound in case the man wasn't wearing any body armor, which he knew was highly unlikely in such a secure location.

The round tore through the man's flesh, spinning him, blood spraying into the air. But he came to a stop in a crouch, firing a big-bore .357 Magnum Glock pistol. A booming lance of flame extended from the pitted muzzle and scored a bloody furrow along Blancanales's cheek, missing removing the man's head by the thickness of a prayer. Dropping flat, he returned fire, trying to drive the guard back into the restroom. But the guard stood firm and kept throwing hot death at the Stony Man team.

The fire extinguisher exploded on the wall behind Lyons, gushing out a torrent of chemical foam across the racks of assault rifles, combat shotguns and ammunition trunks.

Swinging up his Beretta, Schwarz dropped a bead on the man, then saw from the bloody rip in the shirt of the guard that the man indeed wasn't wearing any body armor. Shit! Rapidly shifting his aim, the electronics expert stroked the trigger and hit the door. It violently swung shut, slamming into the HSA guard and driving him against the jamb. As bones cracked, the HSA guard cried out and wildly fired his weapon, taking out a fluorescent light fixture in the ceiling. Swinging downward on chains, the light swept between two racks of weapons, and Lyons dropped just in time to miss being beheaded.

Moving fast, Blancanales surged through the exit and out of sight.

Still gamely firing, the HSA guard took refuge behind the pallet of satchel charges, the Magnum rounds plowing through a case of gas masks and a pile of parachutes.

"Alert!" the guard whispered, quickly reloading.

But before he could say any more, Lyons stood in plain view and fired at the bulge on the crouching man's hip. The radio transceiver there was blown into pieces, and the snarling guard caught Lyons twice in the chest. Slammed backward from the heavy Magnum rounds pounding onto his body armor, the Able Team leader hit the wall and cracked his head. Everything went fuzzy for a heartbeat, and the man instinctively dropped to the floor a split second before a .357 round dented the metal wall exactly where his head had just been located.

Firing into the washroom, Schwarz shattered the toilet and got a geyser of water that the HSA guard completely ignored. Only now the man was firing at the pallet of grenades, trying to blow up the armory rather than let it fall into enemy hands. Even as cold adrenaline flooded his body, Schwarz had to admire the guts of the fellow. This was one tough son of a bitch.

Streaking back in through the doorway, Blancanales appeared with his M-16/M-203 combo. Firing a long burst of 5.56 mm rounds all around the door to the flooded lavatory, he forced the guard into position and unleashed the grenade launcher. The 40 mm barrel belched smoke and the guard slammed against the wall, dropping his gun.

Weakly sinking to his knees, the man groaned as if dying, one hand on his chest, as the stun bag dropped away. Then his other hand came into view holding a wallet.

"Please," the guard wheezed, holding out the thick folded wad of leather. "I surrender! Here, take my money!"

Having encountered this sort of thing before from drug dealers back in Los Angeles, Lyons ducked behind a plastic crate of MRE food packs as the deadly .44 derringer hidden inside the wallet fired, the double explosion shredding the leather.

But Schwarz caught both rounds in the chest. It would have been a killing blow, except for the NATO body armor underneath. The guard seemed shocked that the Stony Man operative wasn't dead, and Schwarz used the distraction to level his Beretta, but stayed his hand. In spite of the urgency of the situation, he couldn't gun down a man simply doing his job. The crazy son of a bitch was fighting as if terrorists were trying to raid a Homeland Security arsenal. The HSA guard was only doing what any of them would have done in a similar situation. Fight to the death, to keep the enemy from stealing the weapons.

Bracing himself, Lyons hopped over the MRE boxes, charged across the empty floor and slammed a shoulder into a tall gunrack. The rows of combat shotguns rattled, the metal shelving bent. The big man put everything he had into shoving harder, and with a tortured groan, the floor bolts tore free and the entire rack came crashing down on the floor, sounding like a detonating locomotive.

A dozen shotguns came loose and buried the guard under

a hundred pounds of unloaded steel. As the man fought to get clear, Blancanales closed the breech of the M-203 with a hard snap, and fired again.

Caught directly in the stomach, the HSA guard doubled over with a ghastly exhalation, then violently retched, shuddering and shaking all over before limply collapsing.

Quickly reloading in case the man was faking, the Stony Man operatives rushed over to the guard and kicked away his Glock before turning the groaning man over.

Blancanales checked the unconscious guard for any serious injuries. "He'll be fine," he said at last, feeling the man's chest for any broken bones. "Thankfully, that's only a flesh wound in the shoulder."

"Wasn't trying to kill him," Lyons said gruffly, dabbing the back of his neck with a handkerchief. The cloth came away red from the earlier blow to his head.

"We came damn close, though," Schwarz retorted, sliding a satchel charge of M-2 plastic under the guard's head to make him more comfortable.

But Blancanales eased it away. Any niceties or succor from them would look bad for the guard, as if friends had attacked the secret armory.

"Use this," Lyons said, passing over a roll of gray duct tape.

Stoically, his teammates bound the guard at the ankles and wrists, and laid a strip loosely across his mouth.

Just then, Blancanales's wristwatch beeped softly. "That's the thirty-minute warning," he said, slinging the assault rifle. "We'd better move fast."

"And hope there are no more of these guys," Schwarz added.

LESS THAN AN HOUR LATER, Able Team drove away from the storage facility, the rear of the Hummer jammed full of boxes and canvas bags. As they headed back onto Route 29, a fleet of National Guard helicopters flew across the skyline of Sioux Falls. Sirens began to howl across the metropolis, warning of impending danger.

CHAPTER SEVENTEEN

Sahara Desert, Middle East

The side door of the Hummer opened, and a slim man dressed in a three-piece suit climbed from the military vehicle and strode to the side of a sand dune. A pair of large boulders formed a sort of natural recess, and the dapper man stooped to enter the cool darkness.

Here the ground was hard and firm, a sprinkling of loose particles covering the sand-colored concrete. Armed men stood guard nearby and they saluted the newcomer by snapping their assault rifles to their chests. Impatient with the useless protocol, the man nodded in return and went around a bend to a plain steel door set into a concrete wall. Placing his hand on a pad, he waited until the device scanned his palm and fingerprints, then flashed a green light. The steel wall split apart, revealing an elevator, a line of U.S. Army Claymore mines circling the box at waist level.

Stepping coolly inside, the man did nothing, ignoring the row of buttons. After a moment, the elevator automatically engaged and began to descend to the bunker that existed two hundred feet below the burning surface of the Sahara. Touching any of the buttons would instantly set off the ring of antipersonnel charges hidden inside the floor and ceiling, the double blast totally destroying the elevator, along with anybody inside, no matter how much body armor he or she was wearing.

The elevator eventually stopped moving and the doors opened with a soft sigh. Briskly exiting the car, the young man strode down a long corridor, passing rows of doors marked with project names. There were no departments in Unity, only goals. Whatever resources were needed for a mission were assembled and unleashed. But the destruction of a single group in no way hurt or hindered the other teams. Each was totally autonomous once activated. This had afforded the terrorist organization safety from the Great Satan, British and the hated Israelis, for decades. It was the secret to their success. Not cells of communication like the Communists, but cells of power. Independent teams with no knowledge of the others. Only the Supreme Council knew everything, and it could never be reached this far down in the middle of nowhere.

Proceeding to the end of a long hallway, the man passed in front of a titanic pair of bronze doors flanked by a set of concrete pillboxes, the sort of fortifications that had been so popular during World War II. Inside the stout redoubts were teams of men who operated the 40 mm Vulcan electric miniguns and twin .50-caliber machine guns. The weapons were chosen for their ability to stop the charge of most armored personnel carriers, or even a light tank. However, it would be impossible for those war machines to make it down the slim elevator shaft. Any team of invaders fast enough to reach the Command Center of Unity wasn't armored enough to withstand the heavy weaponry of the pillboxes.

Standing in front of the doors, the man waited, knowing that sensors and probes were sweeping over his body for weapons, recording devices or anything else on the long list of contraband material. This was the nerve center of Unity, and no chances would be taken with the safety of the men behind the big doors. If they fell, so did the entire terrorist network across the globe.

A soft click came from the doors and then the massive portals ponderously swung aside with the soft sound of working hydraulics. Stepping inside the conference room, the man felt the breeze of the doors cycling shut, then heard the magnetic bolts thud into place.

"Well?" the leader of Unity demanded from the head of a long table.

A score of other men, and two women, sat in chairs along the table, the smooth, polished surface covered with papers and documents, small computer monitors built flush into the surface for each member of the Supreme Council.

"Hamas failed," he announced. "Our spy in Forge has informed me that something went wrong in Turkey and the Hamas are all dead from radiation."

"Then they didn't steal the bombs," a man growled angrily, crumpling a sheet of paper in his hand. "We were idiots to trust such an important task to those bombing buffoons!"

"No, Hamas is loyal to the cause," the leader replied softly, his face an impassive mask of control. "And they did their best. Failure comes to us all in spite of the most detailed planning and expert people."

"What are your new instructions?" the man asked, clasping both hands respectfully behind his back. He would have liked to sit down, but that honor was reserved only for members of the council, people whose hands could safely be hidden out of sight below the polished mahogany wood inlay.

The old man leaned slightly on his cane, adjusting his position in the soft chair. "In spite of this new development, I think that we should proceed with the planned attack on America."

The words were said casually, but the result was galvanizing.

"Are you insane?" the representative of Libya shouted, nearly standing. "We have only this one nuke, and you have no idea what our people had to do to get it!"

"On the contrary, I know in precise detail," the old man snapped, narrowing his dark gaze. "After all, it was my plan that obtained us the nuclear device from the NATO storage facility in Turkey. Plus, it was my Russian and Chinese scientists who modified it from a simple atomic explosive into a powerful hydrogen bomb, a thousand times stronger."

"But Hamas failed…" Syria rallied.

"Irrelevant," the leader snorted, dismissing the matter with a wave of his hand. "It would have been best for America to blame Hamas for the coming attack, but no matter. My people assure me that there is no way the strike can be traced back to our launch facility here."

"But—"

"Enough!" the old man roared, slamming his cane on the table. The crash was louder than a pistol shot. "The time is right, and we finally have the weapons needed to strike hard and deep into America. Not a mere show of force, but hard enough to wound them to the very core!"

"Do we?" the representative of Kuwait murmured, running her long red nails along the surface of the table. A burnoose was draped over the back of her chair, but here in the private chambers she wore Western-style clothing designed for comfort and ease, instead of dehumanizing neutrality. "To the best of my knowledge the kill range of a Class Nine warhead is four city blocks, maybe six under the precisely right circumstances."

"Six blocks?" Going to a map on the wall, the newcomer took a slim tube from the vest pocket of his suit and played the red dot of the laser pointer across the East Coast of the United States. "This is not some pitiful tactical nuclear weapon," he stated proudly, as if he had invented the weapon. "This is now a thermonuclear device, boosted by a tritium injector! The fireball alone will be ten blocks wide, and the blast will spread over a hundred miles!"

"That large?" Saudi Arabia whispered, sweat on his thin lips. The tip of a pink tongue licked it off. "Praise be to Allah!"

No known god had anything to do with their plans of destruction, but the leader of Unity nodded in reply. War was a matter of politics, nothing more.

"With a kill zone this large," the newcomer said, continuing to move the red dot across on the map, "we can easily avoid the impressive air defenses of Washington, and have the missile strike, say…Richmond, or even the farmland outside of Lynchburg. There's nothing there of any importance to protect, so the defenses will be minimal."

"Minimal does not equate easy," Iran warned, furrowing his forehead. His hair was a glistening white, a shocking comparison to his dark skin.

"True," the newcomer agreed. "But even if antimissiles were to detonate our stolen ICBM high in the air, the shock wave would still kill a million Americans. Maybe twice that number. And if it hits the ground…" He grinned, exposing rows of perfectly white teeth. "The blast wave would destroy every prime target on our kill list—CIA headquarters, FBI headquarters, Dulles Airport, the Pentagon, Congress, the Senate, the White House… Everything from the Atlantic Ocean to Kentucky would be obliterated, reduced to radioactive debris."

"Show me the figures," the old man commanded, leaning closer, his eyes alive with excitement.

The young man clicked off the laser pointer and right on cue the wall map receded into the ceiling to reveal a black-board covered with complex mathematical equations.

All of the men frowned in concentration, struggling to process the staggering figures. Only the leader of Unity leaned back in his chair, slowly smiling in pleasure. The math was far beyond his simple education, but he knew people. If the young man had the figures ready for their inspection, then they had to be true.

"Yes, I see," the leader said. "Most impressive."

The young man gave a bow. "Thank you, sir."

"With this new information, I withdraw my objection," Libya said. "Let us proceed immediately."

"But make haste," Qatar warned, raising a stiff finger. Her hand was badly discolored from acid burns. "The Americans are not fools! We should fire the missile the instant it is ready, give them no time to find us and to stop it from being launched."

A murmur of agreement went around the table.

"And what should be the target, sir?" the newcomer asked, standing straighter. When America fell, his would be the name attached to the great victory. Who would remember the old men and women who laid the plans? Only the men who did the work would be praised by the people, hailed as heroes from the Arabian Sea to the Atlantic Ocean!

"Where indeed?" The leader of Unity looked over the map of the area: West Virginia, Maryland, Delaware, Washington, Virginia. This was the very heart of their hated enemy. A blow anywhere would do incalculable destruction. Did the exact target really matter? Not in the least. The youngster was merely trying to curry favor with the council. Fair enough. He would accept the meaningless compliment with dignity and grace, even though privately marking the ambitious fool for later execution.

"There," the leader of Unity declared, pointing with the tip of his cane. "Right there in the middle of a forest, where there are no missiles or interceptors to hinder us in any way whatsoever. We shall strike there, and let the atomic blast roll across the farmlands of Virginia to destroy Washington forever!"

The council erupted in a ragged cheer as the young man pulled out a PDA and marked the kill zone for their thermonuclear ICBM. An unknown forest preserve called the Shenandoah National Park.

Firebase Alpha, Argentina

MOVING STEALTHILY THROUGH the smoky darkness, McCarter finally located the parade ground, and scowled at the sight of the monstrous helicopter. The huge craft was a CH-53 Super Stallion, just about the strongest and largest cargo helicopter in the world. The craft was a hundred feet long, with three colossal turbo engines, and could lift over fifty soldiers, plus a ton of supplies. This was no patch job or old good left over from another war, but pure state-of-the-art and top-of-the-line. Near the prow was the picture of a winged horse painted on the metal with the name *Pegasus* underneath in a flowing script.

A couple of Forge soldiers were still dragging the canvas sheeting away, and the pilot was in the cockpit flipping switches in a preflight check. The general had to be trying to escape! Which meant the bastard was coming right into the gunsights of McCarter. Perfect.

"Red alert," McCarter subvocalized into his throat mike, moving deeper into the shadows of some trees edging the parade ground. "There's a Super Stallion on the parade ground getting ready to leave. Cargo must be Calvano."

"Can't see it," Manning said in annoyance over the radio link. "There's too much flame and smoke!"

"We're on the way," Hawkins replied crisply. "Stay loose and—"

A sudden loud squeal sounded over the earphones and McCarter cut off the radio. Somebody at Forge had detected the radio transmissions and was jamming the airwaves. Took them bloody long enough! he thought. However, the response lag rather confirmed that whoever was running their computers wasn't located here.

With a low rumble, a dozen Gavins appeared around the mess hall, and McCarter quickly took cover.

The three sets of propellers of the *Pegasus* were beginning to slowly rotate when the convoy of armored personnel carriers rolled to a halt alongside. General Calvano climbed out of a vehicle closely surrounded by armed troops.

Out of grenades, McCarter could only track the mob of people with the sights of his MP-5, hoping for a shot at the leader of Forge. But the bodyguards knew their business and the general reached the *Pegasus* safely.

Still trying to maneuver into position to get a clear shot at the general, or to find some way to cripple the huge helicopter, McCarter was forced to take cover again as dozens of armed Forge soldiers began to arrive at the parade ground. In orderly procession, the soldiers climbed inside the colossal helicopter, the overhead props turning ever faster. Desperately, McCarter checked again for even a single grenade. But he was completely out, and the soft lead 9 mm rounds in the MP-5 would do nothing against the armored hull of a Super Stallion.

More troops arrived, then the hatch was closed and the door shut. They were getting ready to leave!

"Come on, guys, where are you?" McCarter muttered, dropping the submachine gun. Drawing the pneumatic pistol from his shoulder holster, McCarter aimed and fired.

The first dart veered off into the night, deflected by the mounting turbulence of the three sets of spinning blades. Reloading, McCarter shot again, then again, finally getting one of the barbed darts lodged into the soft rubber of a landing wheel.

The wash from the blades suddenly increased noticeably as the engines revved in power and the *Pegasus* lifted gently off the grass. A moment later, Hawkins, Encizo and James appeared out of the darkness.

"Any grenades?" McCarter demanded, but he could see that the others were completely out of high explosives. Damn, damn, damn!

"Check a Gavin! See if you can turn one of the 25 mm Bushmasters on that flying office building!"

Nodding, the men melted into the darkness, but just then the *Pegasus* lifted high into the nighttime sky above the burning firebase and angled off toward the west.

Suddenly, three of the Gavins came to life, the top hatches flipping up and members of Phoenix Force rising into view to swivel the Bushmasters at the departing airship. The trio of miniguns cut loose in ragged formation, the phosphorescent tracers among the 25 mm HE shells dotting the sky only to strive for the Super Stallion as the huge helicopter continued to rapidly climb higher.

There came the sound of a machine gun from above, and the rear of the Super Stallion sparkled as the aft brace of 12.7 mm rapidfires was brought into action. Blasting hot lead death in every direction, the weapons stitched glowing tracer rounds into the swirling mists covering the base, smacking into the ground and ricocheting harmlessly off the armored Gavins.

Moving behind a flagpole for protection, McCarter rode out the wave of hot lead, then stepped out with his SMG chattering at the dark sky. But if the 9 mm rounds could even reach the helicopter there was no way of knowing.

After the team reloaded, the 25 mm Bushmasters chattered again, the Stony Man operatives expertly moving the weapons in tight circles, but the shaking weapons were impossible to accurately aim at the fleeing helicopter. Then the side of the *Pegasus* visibly dented, a small window cracked, and there came the telltale sound of the distant Barrett.

Instantly, defensive smoke poured from a series of vents around the Super Stallion, and the three sets of turboprops spun to full power as the chopper angled away from the potential danger, slipping into the clouds of roiling smoke to disappear from sight.

Angling at the maximum height, the men operating the Bushmasters tried again for a kill, and the Barrett spoke again with no result. But after a few moments, the 25 mm rapidfires went silent, and McCarter dropped the empty clip from his MP-5 to shove in another. They had missed killing the general by only a few seconds.

Glancing around the fiery desecration of the military base, McCarter shouldered his weapon and pulled a small device from a cushioned pocket of his ghillie suit. With the press of a thumb, the tiny screen became illuminated with a map of Argentina. Four blinking dots showed on the screen, one of them moving steadily to the west. Touching the controls, he blanked the darts that had missed the Super Stallion, and now there was only one winking icon on the screen. Gotcha.

"All right, let's move out!" McCarter subvocalized into his throat mike, carefully tucking the tracking device away. "We're going after the bleeding bastards, so grab any useable weapons from the dead, especially any explosives. We rendezvous with Gary in ten minutes!" Lifting an FN-2000 from the bloody form of a dead Forge soldier on the ground, he checked the clip, then slung the assault rifle.

"And don't forget fuel," Hawkins said over the radio. "The tanks on this APC are only half full."

"Mine are almost dry," James added. "But there're plenty of rounds for the Bushmaster."

"Half full," Encizo finished, the headlights of a Gavin coming on to shine brightly across the parade ground. Spent brass from the Bushmasters littered the grass like golden dewdrops.

"Then we'll drain two to fill the one with spare ammo," McCarter directed. "Gary, any sign of activity?"

"All clear, David," Manning replied smoothly. "I think that explosion across the river took out all of their reserve personnel."

"Come again…what explosion?" McCarter asked, the muscles in his stomach tightening.

"The fake satellite dish hidden in the trees across the river," Manning explained. "It went up a few minutes ago. You probably didn't hear it among all of the other detonations."

Sputtering curses, McCarter charged for the nearest Gavin and clawed open the rear hatch to scramble inside. "Full speed, three on three formation!" he barked, striding to the front of the armored vehicle.

"Calvano is crazy, but he wouldn't mine the whole base," James said hesitantly, starting the engine of the Gavin. "Aw, what am I saying? Haul ass, people!"

"And stop for nothing!" McCarter added, dropping into the seat alongside Encizo. "Now, move!"

"I'm on point!" Hawkins declared, his Gavin rolling over dead bodies to plow through some hedges and jounce onto the littered street. The other two armored personnel carriers were close behind.

But as the heavy machines began to race through the burning military compound, a powerful blast shook the ground and a distant building broke apart as it rose into the night on a writhing fireball. Then a Quonset hut detonated, closely followed by the armory, the barracks, the laundry, commissary, pillbox and guard tower.

Hammered from every direction, the Gavins brutally rocked back and forth as they desperately charged along the buckling roadway that went directly into the heart of rampaging destruction.

CHAPTER EIGHTEEN

Johannesburg, South Africa

Nobody spoke inside the concrete bunker, all eyes upon the detailed relief map covering the large table like a child's board game.

The hundreds of cities were black circles, a chalk number showing the population, and little metal bridges spanned painted rivers. Miniature versions of hydroelectric dams, oil derricks and nuclear power plants resembled toys in spite of the amazingly precise details. Tiny plastic ships sat motionless on the painted blue sea, while plastic tanks and artillery dotted the rolling hills and farmlands. Little jet fighters, helicopters and missiles were equipped with folding flags that could be raised to show if the equipment was airborne or still on the ground, and a score of human figures carrying rifles were scattered about the war map, white cards on their backs bearing a number to show how many South African soldiers each represented.

A wooden disk bearing a satellite photograph lay to the west showing the approach of a rainstorm, and in the north-eastern Kalahari Desert a score of plastic tanks and soldiers bore the hated flag of their ancient enemy of Angola.

"Are you sure they have broken through our defensive line?" the president of South Africa asked, licking dry lips. The politician was only thirty years old, but seemed to have aged drastically in only the past few hours.

"Confirmed, sir," a colonel in intelligence replied. "Their tanks are rolling along the major highways and destroying everything in their path. This is a full-scale invasion."

"Do we have any idea how many are dead?"

"Unknown, sir," the man replied, checking a clipboard tucked under his arm. "The enemy is killing everybody they encounter, soldiers, civilians, farm workers, school children…"

Reaching out with a wooden stick, an aide silently moved the Angola markers deeper into South Africa.

"Bastards," a grizzled general muttered, puffing away on a cigar. His left leg was gone at the hip, replaced with a titanium skeleton, a grim souvenir from the war for independence.

"Sir, we have no choice," the Minister of Defense said. "They've invaded our nation without cause, killed thousands, maybe ten of thousands of our people, and are driving a wedge right into the heart of our nation. If we don't stop them in the desert, we may never stop them!"

Saying nothing, the president bowed his head in somber contemplation. How could this have happened? South Africa had a colossal arsenal of weaponry, everything from a neutron bomb down to German 88 cannons from World War II!

"I've asked America for assistance," the general said, "and they're sending ships. But by the time those arrive, there may not be a South Africa anymore.

"Sadly, you are correct, old friend," the president said wearily, sitting in a chair. "I have no choice. General, the action code is Nine, Omega, Fourteen. Firing code is Zulu Tango Five. Repeat, Zulu Tango Five."

"Yes, sir," the general said solemnly, and turned to relay the order to his aide.

Nobody spoke in the war room for a long time, the only noise coming from the gentle hum of the air purifiers.

Then an aide touched the radio receiver in his ear, nodded and used the stick to sweep all of the Angolan tanks from the map, replacing them with a small red disk marked with the atomic symbol for uranium.

"And may God grant mercy on my soul," the president whispered, closing his tired eyes.

The bunker was deep underground, protected by hundreds of yards of concrete and steel, but the man could imagine the raging hellfire of the tactical nuclear bomb in the Kalahari Desert. The mushroom cloud would be visible for thousands of miles, and he knew for a fact that the deafening thunder of the nuclear detonation would be heard around the entire world.

North Dakota

CRAWLING OVER THE BLISTERING hot rocks, Carl Lyons crested the escarpment and looked down upon the five men. The Forge soldiers were all carrying LAW rockets, with an FN-2000 assault rifle slung across their backs. Staying low behind a row of loose boulders, the gaps filled with sage bushes, the soldiers were sitting on folding canvas stools and drinking from canteens, while keeping a sharp watch on the nearby roadway.

A hundred feet away, Route 29 cut through the bleak landscape like a black river. The highway curved near the boulders, forcing any traffic to slow down considerably, making the location a perfect spot for an ambush.

Unless you're looking in the wrong direction, Lyons mentally noted, easing the safety off his Neostad shotgun.

A recent acquisition from the HSA armory, the left tubular magazine of the deadly weapon held four stun bags of the newest variety. More than just wads of cloth with soft jelly beads inside, these also contained breakable capsules that released an anesthesia compound that could put a down a charging rhino. And just in case those didn't handle the problem, the other magazine held four 12-gauge cartridges of stainless steel fléchettes, which didn't knock a man unconscious, but cut the poor bastard in two.

Knowing they were heading into a trap, Able Team had wisely turned off Route 29 a good hour before reaching the North Dakota border, and swung far out into the rocky badlands to circle around to try approach the Forge soldiers from behind. It took a while, but they found the ambush.

Retreating to a safe distance, the men discussed the matter and quickly headed in different directions. Lyons stayed with the soldiers, while Schwarz and Blancanales drove far into the desert on rented motorcycles. The big black BMW bikes had been acquired in Huron, outside of Sioux Falls. Utilizing a transmission instead of a chain, the motorcycles were extremely quiet and it took less than an hour to coat the machines with industrial glue, then liberally apply a thick layer of sand. Now the black bikes were a dull, rusty color, and even the windshields had been removed to make sure there was nothing shiny to accidentally reveal the presence of the silenced machines.

Just then, his earphone gave soft beep, closely followed by another. Lowering the Neostad, Lyons checked his wristwatch. Excellent. The others were finally in place and the Forge soldiers should be reporting to their headquarters any minute now. Regular as clockwork, the men stationed below Lyons used their Kenwood hand radios to report to somebody. The same as back in Texas, the radio signals were heavily encoded, but knowing the frequency used by the enemy gave the Stony Man commandos all they needed. With Schwarz and Blancanales about a hundred miles away to the west and east, when the Forge soldiers sent off their hourly status report, the three men could use loop antennae to triangulate on the broadcast, and when their hidden base responded, they would have it located within a few yards.

"Unless they're smart enough to change frequencies every time they talk," Lyons muttered, adjusting the controls on a directional radio with a loop antenna on top. The portable radios of Stony Man changed frequencies automatically, just like the transponders used by the Navy SEALs and Delta Force. It all depended upon how savvy their commander was with counterintelligence technology. Calvano knew computers and satellites, but either way—

Covering a yawn, a Forge soldier laid aside his LAW and lifted a radio.

Swinging up a monocular, Lyons dialed for maximum enhancement and got a crystal-clear view of the Kenwood as the man tapped in the code.

Punching the code into another Kenwood stolen from the HSA armory, Lyons clearly heard the lieutenant report that nothing had happened yet. Anxiously, the Able Team leader waited, almost holding his breath, then the base replied with an acknowledgment and clicked off the air.

"Got them," Schwarz said triumphantly. "Their base is at…Black Rock Mesa in McHenry County, about fifty miles deep in the heart of the Badlands."

Tucking away the loop antenna, Lyons turned his head in

that direction. The barren landscape was rough and rugged, a vast rocky vista of irregular stone.

"Any back doors?" he asked, lifting the monocular and thumbing on the solar filter. The view dimmed slightly as the glare of the sun was removed and he had a clear view to the horizon.

Tabletop mesa and craggy mountain peaks stood like castles on the flat ground. Driving their Hummer across that in broad daylight would be suicide, and there was no time to wait for night. The Internet was buzzing with news from around the globe of ever-increasing military conflicts. The world was poised for war and every minute counted. If they took too long seizing control of the uplink array, or failed in their mission, the civilization death toll could be astronomical.

"Checking," Blancanales said, obviously busy with something. "Okay, according to this topographical map I bought at the mountaineering store, there should be a rill we can drive behind to hide our approach until about a mile away from Black Rock. Then we only have to cross about a few yards of open space before we can duck behind another mesa. That will let us get within two hundred feet."

"If this approach is so good, Forge should have the area heavily mined—" Lyons began, then cut himself off. "No, forget that. This state is full of hikers and tourists. If a troop of Boy Scouts got blown apart, the National Guard would seal off the entire territory and do a rock-by-rock search for any more explosives."

"They could use remote-control landmines like the Farm," Schwarz suggested. "Fiber-optic cables wouldn't leak any magnetic field for a park ranger to detect. But our EM scanners will let us know if the cameras are live or not."

"Good enough. But we still have to cross two hundred feet of open space in broad daylight," Blancanales noted dourly. "Can we do that in under ninety seconds?"

"Not without dropping a lot of equipment," Schwarz declared.

"Or we can give them something to look at," Lyons said, pulling a knife and starting to hack at the loose soil. When the hole was large enough, he laid an M-2 satchel charge inside and loosely covered it with dirt, leaving only an inch of the ebony antenna sticking up from the reddish ground.

"Leaving them a little gift, Carl?" Schwarz chuckled softly.

"Biggest one I have actually."

"Make sure it isn't going to start a rock slide and take out a lot of civvies on the road."

"No danger of that," Lyons said confidently, patting the solid granite ledge supporting the escarpment. "I just hate to leave them alive."

"Unfortunately, killing them now would only alert the people inside the mesa when they failed to make their hourly report."

"Yeah, I know. So let them keep waiting for Trinity."

"You know, there's still going to be some kind of surveillance along the perimeter of the mesa," Blancanales added pragmatically. "Even if it is only more armed guards."

"Too bad for them," Lyons said with unaccustomed savagery, checking the arming circuit on the military explosive. When he got an answering beep, the man tucked the remote detonator into a pocket of his ghillie suit. The damn things may give excellent camouflage, but they were hotter than summer in hell.

"All set here," Lyons subvocalized into his throat mike, beginning to carefully slide down the escarpment. "We rendezvous at the northern rill in an hour."

"Roger," his teammates replied.

"Sir?" a Forge technician asked, looking up from his console in Command and Control.

"Yes, what is it?" Erica Sabot asked, reading the result of the latest GPS attacks. The computerized clipboard in her hand was equipped with a Bluetooth, and relayed a steady stream of data from the Internet. On the master console was a monitor scrolling with constant reports from Snake Eater, and while not officially part of her job, Sabot considered it only good sense to make sure the foreigner was telling them the truth about the assorted strikes. So far, so good.

"I caught a radio transmission a few seconds ago," the man said hesitantly, removing a set of headphones. "It was localized, scrambled and not from one of our sentry outposts."

"Are you sure?" Sabot demanded, placing the clipboard aside and swiveling her chair. The minicomputer turned itself off with a low hum.

"Absolutely," the technician said, and reached out to press a button. From a wall speaker came a short burst of gibberish.

"That's an encoded transmission, all right," she acknowledged uneasily, tapping a finger on her jaw. "I don't like this. Better inform Professor Reinhold, and double the guards at all entrances."

"At once, ma'am."

"Also send out a reconnaissance party to check the perimeter," Sabot amended. "Especially the rill to the north."

"Should the troops take prisoners if they find anybody?" the man asked, his hands busy flipping switches.

"No, the time for secrecy is nearly over," Sabot said, leaning back in the chair and reclaiming the clipboard. "Better have the guards kill anybody they find."

"Yes, ma'am."

"And activate the land mines," she added, turning the minicomputer back on and searching for any fresh news from China.

CHAPTER NINETEEN

Argun Valley, China

A huge mushroom cloud of roiling black smoke rose to above the river valley in hellish majesty. Red flames licked about inside the boiling column and lightning crackled about the decimated landscape, adding to the general destruction.

A glowing deathwind polluted with unstable isotopes howled like insane demons above the fused soil. The nearby river was boiling. The thunderclap of the atomic blast echoed among the shuddering mountain peaks, and a hundred small fires dotted the distant horizon in a shotgun pattern.

The entire forest was gone for almost a mile, the closest trees reduced to mono-atomic vapors for a thousand yards. Gradually, chunks and blackened lumps appeared, and finally the tall pine trees were merely uprooted and smashed into kindling from the exothermic concussion of the tactical nuke.

Every trace of the recent combat between the Chinese and the Russian soldiers was completely eradicated, the men and machines totally annihilated, leaving only a few fist-size lumps of molten steel that had once been million-dollar tanks splashed across the distant hillsides. The squadrons of jet fighters were gone from the rumbling sky, the smashed wreckage strewed randomly across a thousand miles.

The fused ground still trembled from the pile-driver impact of the uranium blast, the tortured wind constantly becoming louder and more forceful from the growing hurricane of furious thermal currents lashing upward from the lambent slag pit.

Very far away in Beijing and Moscow, the military leaders of both nations congratulated themselves for stopping the enemy invasion, even if it had taken desperate measures to get the job done. Hopefully, it would be enough. But just in case, the politicians and generals began stoically preparing a salvo of long-range missiles, the warheads tipped with hydrogen bombs, the thermonuclear charges ten thousand times more destructive than the pitiful little tactical nukes used this day.

At the first sign of further aggression from the detested enemy, the missiles would fly. Not at isolated mountain valleys but at the major cities: St. Petersburg, Peking, Vladivostok, Chungking, Simbirsk, Canton.

In a cataclysmic maelstrom of nuclear fire, the long-expected China-Russia War would finally begin. The outcome of which both sides faced with dark apprehension and a dreadful eagerness.

Andes Mountains, Western Argentina

A GENTLE SNOW WAS FALLING on the windshield of the Hummer, the double set of wiper blades maintaining a rhythmic arc of clarity. The wall vents gushed hot air and the defroster audibly moaned. The halogen headlights stabbed into the dancing flakes and soon vanished; visibility was only a dozen yards.

Shifting gears, McCarter fed more power to the big engine

and kept a sharp watch on the edge of the steep road only a few feet away. Far below was a deep crevice, the bottom masked in lazy fog. There was nothing ahead of them, or behind. Only the snow and mist. It was as if the APC was driving through a dream.

Escaping from the exploding Fort Peron had proved to be simplicity itself for the Stony Man operatives. The Gavins were tough war machines and plowed through the cascading detonations as if designed for that very purpose. The slate armor around the APCs had proved its worth, getting battered and bent outrageously from the endless barrage of shrapnel in the mad dash for safety. However, the M-113 vehicles crashed intact through the sagging ruin of the front gate, the men inside shaken and bruised by the rollicking journey, but still very much alive.

Reaching the forest, Phoenix Force kept on going, plowing deep into the morass of trees, leaving the thundering legacy of General Calvano far behind. One of the APCs passed by the empty auto-mortar set by Manning. There were several dead Forge soldiers lying around the weapon, but none of them had managed to broach the protective ring of Claymore mines encircling the mortar.

Cresting the ridge of the woody hillock, the team rendezvoused with Manning in a small clearing, the man rising from the bushes like a pagan god. Exchanging grins of relief that everybody was alive, Manning climbed into the APC driven by McCarter and the three vehicles left the decimated battle zone to reclaim their stash of supplies in the old mine. That was all of the food and ammunition the team had remaining, and the Stony Man commandos knew that they'd need every pound for when they tangled with Forge again.

After checking over the fuel and munitions, McCarter decided they would use the Hummer instead of the APCs. The Gavins could carry more, but an armored personnel carrier was painfully noticeable in civilian traffic. There was no way they could remain covert driving a Gavin on a public road. Besides, the Hummer got better gas mileage, and there was no telling yet where the *Pegasus* was flying. The blip on the tracking device was still in motion, proceeding ever deeper into the rugged expanse of the Argentine Andes Mountains.

After banding some minor wounds, the team shifted everything useable into the Hummer and took off immediately, heading back to the Continental Highway rather than smashing their way through the dense forest. They'd make better time on the paved road.

Passing the roadblock, McCarter noted that the police car was gone, which meant the cops had escaped, and there would be an APB out for the Hummer. Not good news. He debated going back for a Gavin, but decided to keep going. The numbers were falling and there was no time to waste. In preparation to go EVA, the team started removing their camouflage paint and got into their civilian clothing once more.

Driving the Hummer until the needle was almost on empty, McCarter refueled at a roadside gas station, while Hawkins bought as many cans of fuel as they could without being conspicuous. James and Manning depleted a roadside restaurant of whatever consumables were available, and Encizo emptied a small hunting store of as much spare ammunition for their military weapons as possible. There was a cornucopia of 9 mm bullets and 12-gauge shotgun shells, but only a single box of .357 Magnum rounds for Manning's Desert Eagle, the same for Encizo's .38 Walther PPK, and nothing for the 5.56 mm FN-2000 assault rifles. Wisely, he didn't even ask the happy clerk about ammunition for the Barrett sniper rifle.

Delivering the supplies to the Hummer, Hawkins and James went to a corner market to purchase several bottles of ammonia and a large plastic bucket. Just in case of trouble.

Taking turns behind the wheel, the men of Phoenix Force drove through the remaining darkness and all the next day, doggedly keeping track of the *Pegasus* and Calvano. The blip had finally stopped in a hotly contested section of the mountain range, the area claimed by Argentina, Chile and the Communist guerrillas. That was good news. There would be few civilians around and plenty of combat room for the coming battle. The general had managed to escape from Phoenix Force once, but it would never happen again.

The long day slowly faded into night, and the farther Phoenix Force drove into the mountains, the steeper and more narrow the roads became. The air got colder by the mile. Soon, their breath was fogging, then the windows became frosty, and then the first snowflakes appeared.

A sign near a town warned this was the last chance for gas in a hundred kilometers, so McCarter turned off the highway and the team judiciously hit the local shops for additional supplies. The snow was an unexpected complication.

Woolen longjohn underwear, boots and gloves were available, but the only parkas for sale were a bright orange color to make lost people easier to find in the mountains. However, an hour at the local laundry with a couple of bottles of bleach rendered the parkas a muddy fleshtone close enough to white to serve as winter camouflage. Next came skis and poles, then snowmobiles and snowshoes, plus a lot of beer, the last item added to make them seem like a group of gringo tourists just there for a drunken weekend.

The snowmobiles had powerful motors that could propel the sleek machines at well over 60 mph, but they made more noise than a wood chipper. On the other hand, the auxiliary electric motors were nearly dead silent, but only had a top speed of 25 mph. Stealth or speed. It was good to have a choice.

Heading back onto the highway, McCarter had Hawkins take the next exit and follow a long, winding road into the foothills. The ice-covered roads were slippery, but the Hummer traversed them with little problem, the rough military tires digging in hard.

Snow was falling soft and silent from the white sky, and it seemed to McCarter that a blizzard was coming. That was both good and bad, he decided, zipping up the new parka. The weather would help hide them from the Forge troops, but would also make it tough to find their hidden base in the first place. Then the man sneezed. He only hoped the Forge didn't have any more guard dogs. The bloody parkas reeked of bleach so bad the team members could have been tracked through a sewage plant.

Stopping to dump the beer off a cliff, the team decided to have a fast meal, probably their last before the assault on the Forge firebase. Ignoring the beef jerky and MRE packs, they extracted the handful of U.S. Army Self-Heat Meals they had brought along. Popping open the tops on the lumpy bags, they poured in some water from their canteens and tightly closed the tops again. As the crystals inside the envelopes reacted to the water, the packages became warm, and soon wisps of steam rose from the tiny vents. Eagerly, Phoenix Force tore into the bags for their first hot meal in days.

"Best thing ever invented," Manning said with his mouth full of beef stew.

His face smeared, Hawkins swallowed some steaming lasagna. "Amen to that, brother!"

Starting to add a comment, McCarter jerked around with

the Browning Hi-Power pistol in his hand. A moment later, a llama walked out of the snowy bushes and casually strolled past the Hummer as if it weren't there.

"Wonder what those taste like?" James grumbled, retrieving his meal from the floorboard. The stew had spilled and was gone. Mopping up the mess, he tore open an MRE and started chewing down a cold turkey dinner.

"Rather a lot like emu," Manning said, trying not to smile.

Holstering his sidearm, Encizo lifted an eyebrow. "Emu?"

"Close enough, anyway."

"God, you're a weird bastard." Encizo chuckled, going back to the interrupted meal.

Finished eating, the team got to work. Driving the Hummer into the bushes, they cut down branches to cover the vehicle, then slid the snowmobiles off the trailer. Checking over their weapons one last time, Phoenix Force started across a snowy field and darted into the misty expanse of trees.

Constantly checking a compass, McCarter led the other men through the forest and up a gentle foothill. Cresting the top, they started down once more and immediately the snowmobiles started increasing speed, slipping and sliding dangerously along the icy slope. Quickly, the Stony Man commandos threw the vehicles into Reverse to try to slow the wild descent. Unfortunately, the weight of the men and the supplies kept the machines going at a breakneck pace.

Biting back curses, McCarter fought his snowmobile around an outcropping of black rocks, then swing wide around a smooth patch of white that might have been a snow bridge. Those often covered deep holes, or even rivers, and at their present speed that would be lethal.

Zigzagging frantically to dodge trees, rocks and miscellaneous lumps, the team fought the streaking machines down the slick expanse until finally reaching the bottom. Gliding across a smooth field, they coasted for while to regain their breath, and checked the compass and started off once more, heading toward the northwest.

Long, slow, cold miles passed when suddenly Hawkins jerked his head upward.

"Plane!" the man subvocalized into his throat mike, and the team scattered for cover.

Minutes later, there came the sound of a single-engine plane moving through the storm overhead.

"Might be a mail plane," Manning said, swinging up the Barrett to try to track the noise. "Or a delivery service ferrying supplies to mountain resorts. We do that all the time in Canada."

Encizo worked the arming bolt on an FN-2000 assault rifle. The longer barrel gave the weapon much greater range than the MP-5, and would count for a lot when fighting with an aircraft.

"Or it might be a reconnaissance plane for Forge," McCarter countered, pulling out a monocular to check the clouds. IR showed nothing so he switched to UV. Now he got a blurry image. "Okay, she appears to be a single-engine Cessna, but it's impossible to tell for sure." Adjusting the focus, he frowned. "However, it's armed with a bleeding rocket pod on each wing."

"Forge," Hawkins growled, an FN-2000 balanced in his gloved hands. A finger rested on the trigger of the 40 mm grenade launcher.

"Or the Federal Police, Argentine army, Chileans or the goddamn Commie guerrillas," Encizo stated. "Good thing we reached the trees. Those antitank rockets would have blown us into the next world."

"And then some," James agreed, tracking the airplane with a 9 mm MP-5 machine gun. Hopefully the pilot wasn't checking the landscape with infrared scanners. The blazing engines of the snowmobiles would show up brighter than a road flare in a broom closet.

Adjusting their woolen ski masks, the Stony Man commandos anxiously watched the clouds, waiting for the attack to begin. But the buzzing noise wavered and lowered in volume, then moved off to the north.

"Base is to the west," McCarter said, checking his compass. "It must be doing a perimeter sweep."

"Okay, we go silent from this point," the Briton directed, starting the electric motor of the snowmobile. The dashboard meters flickered to life, but that was the only indication that the engine was operating. "We'd better get far away from here before it comes back for a second pass."

In ragged order, the men slid forward and the silent machines darted into the falling snowflakes.

Suddenly coming out of the storm, the men of Phoenix Force found themselves crossing a frozen lake. Every member of the team knew that they were incredibly vulnerable to attack out in the open, and increased their speed. Then they heard a soft crinkling sound. A spiderweb of cracks appeared under Manning and Hawkins, then all of them.

Instantly the men separated and revved the snowmobiles to maximum speed. But behind the team, the cracks were extending in every direction, and getting wider, water appearing in a few areas. Switching on the noisy gasoline engines, the men frantically raced across the shattering lake and breathed a sigh of relief when they were reached the shore at last.

"Kill them!" McCarter ordered over the radio, and the men went back to the slower electric motors. Their speed dropped noticeably, but they slid through the wintry landscape with only the hush of the treads discernable.

By now the cold was seeping through their civilian parkas, and the men hunched low, trying to absorb some of the heat coming off the deactivated gasoline engines. Icicles hung thick from the tree branches, and from somewhere there came a splintery crash as a branch cracked apart from the accumulated weight.

A few miles later they saw a low swell in the ground, and judiciously braked the vehicles. Throwing thermal blankets over the machines to hide their heat signatures, the men then donned the bulky snowshoes. Moving fast and low, the team left only light tracks in the freshly fallen powder, and the windblown snowflakes should fill those in very quickly.

Darting from tree to tree, the team constantly checked for landmines and proximity sensors. Hawkins found the first, a Claymore hidden inside a bird nest made of fiberglass. Manning found the next, a video camera slowly sweeping across the icy landscape. The lens was partially covered with the freshly fallen snow, so Manning added another layer of ice from a spray bottle kept warm inside his parka. That would give them the necessary cover, and if somebody came outside to clean the camera lens, so much the better. The team only needed that door to open for a single moment.

From that point onward, the team moved easily through the boobytraps, thankful for all the hours Chief Greene had made them practice over and over in trying to penetrate the multiple layers of defensives around the Farm.

Reaching a clear zone, Phoenix Force found themselves standing in a strange sort of arbor. The trees branches overhead had been lashed together, additional branches woven into the lacing to make a crude dome over a squat concrete dome. The featureless walls were covered with ice, and there was only one door, slightly recessed into a steel-edged alcove. The door was a seamless slab of burnished metal, and there was no sign of a handle, lock or keypad.

"No way we're getting through that quietly," McCarter stated, pulling out his IR goggles. "Everybody search for thermals."

Looking through the infrared goggles, Hawkins noted that on the side of a nearby escarpment, the snow was moving against the wind, bending in toward a ragged opening in the rockface. That could only be the air pumps for the underground base. If there was an attack, the subterranean bunker would seal itself tight against a nuclear, chemical or bacteriological strike. But for the moment, Forge was still taking in outside air. Obviously, secure in the knowledge that nobody knew where they were hidden again.

Touching his throat mike, Hawkins changed his mind and raised a gloved hand to sign "follow me." There were very few deaf soldiers in any army, and American sign language was a perfect way to silently communicate. Even with the cameras blocked, there could be hidden microphones, as well.

Stealthily crossing the arbor, feeling as if their every footstep was as loud as cannonfire, Phoenix Force reached the cave and quickly checked for traps before easing inside. The walls of the cave were rough hewn and appeared natural, but situated behind a stout steel fence was a large piece of machinery covered with pipes and conduits.

We're screwed, Encizo signed, jerking his chin at a louvered cowling set deep among the machinery. *That's a biofilter.*

Removing the useless bottle of ammonia from a pocket, McCarter tossed it aside. Encizo and James did the same. The plan had been for the team to relieve themselves in the plastic bucket, add the ammonia and pour it liberally all around the air-intake vents. With luck, the Forge soldiers would think some wild animal had used the cave as a lavatory and would send somebody to shovel away the reeking mess. Phoenix

Force would then follow the man back inside the bunker. But the biofilter canceled that idea. Even if the team had some VX nerve gas, it would never reach the troops underground. At the first sign of any unusual infusion, the biofilter would automatically shut down the air vents and sound the alarm.

Okay, there are too many trees around here, McCarter directed, using both hands to sign. *So spread out and find where the Super Stallion landed.*

The computers? Encizo asked silently.

It's our only hope now.

Moving fast, the team swept through the woods in a three-on-three defensive formation. They found more land mines and video cameras hidden among the trees, but there was a corridor through the forest and they moved alongside the outside of the clear path, deactivating each explosive charge in turn.

Leaving the woods, the men found a large open field, the ground dotted with tree stumps rising a few inches from the snow. The crude landing field was covered with hundreds of boot prints, the white snow stained with oil and gas.

Raising a clenched fist, McCarter rotated it once, then splayed his fingers. The rest of the team nodded and spread out in different directions. A few moments later, James appeared from behind a snowbank and waved the others closer.

Gathering quickly around, the rest of team saw a few drops of red blood on the snow, and the boots of a Forge soldier were visible behind a large rock. The boots shook once, then went still.

Slipping around the snowbank, they found a copse of trees, a disguised door in the fake trees swung open wide. More machinery could be seen inside. Warily entering the artificial copse, McCarter grinned at the sight of several large, pressurized tanks embedded with thick insulated pipes leading into the ground. This had to be part of the cooling unit for the massive Cray computers operating the uplink. The complex machines were extremely sensitive to heat, and were kept cold with a liquid nitrogen refrigeration system. The computers at the Farm used the same arrangement, only the nitrogen tanks were kept immediately alongside the computers for safety. The deadly material was nonexplosive, but incredibly dangerous in the right hands.

Rapping a quivering gauge with a gloved knuckle, McCarter found the tanks almost full. They had to have been freshly recharged from the *Pegasus*. Exchanging their skiing gloves for cumbersome welding gloves, the men got to work with adjustable wrenches and shut off one of the tanks, then released the locking clamps. With the other tanks full, nobody should notice the missing tank for days. More than enough time.

It took all of them working together to manhandle the cumbersome canister out the tiny door, and then roll it along the cleared pathway to reach the concrete dome. Positioning the canister directly in front of the door, the entire team put their shoulders against the tank for support, and McCarter used a wrench to work the exhaust valve on top.

The pressurized canister savagely recoiled as a thin watery spray blasted from the nozzle, and a biting wave of preternatural cold slapped the men in the face. Turning their faces away, they fought to breathe, the frigid air stabbing their lungs with icy knives.

Hitting the armored door, the liquid nitrogen splashed about, turning the door and surrounding concrete dull in color, then becoming shiny as a mirror.

Finally, the stream eased to a trickle as the tank was depleted, and McCarter closed off the valve. Gratefully moving away from the empty canister, Phoenix Force pulled on their flexible gloves once more and readied their assorted weapons.

Slinging the 9 mm MP-5 machine gun over a shoulder, Hawkins checked the 40 mm round in the FN-2000 assault rifle. There was one shell from the grenade launcher, so he would have to make it count.

Nodding at the others, McCarter raised an arm to protect his eyes and triggered a single shot from his MP-5 machine gun. As the 9 mm bullet hit the discolored metal, the entire door shattered as if made of glass, the military armor crystallized by the incredible cold of the liquid nitrogen. Sprinkling to the ground, the concrete crumbled away, a large hole forming in the resilient dome. Buried inside the jamb, a dozen Claymore mines were briefly exposed before they also fell away, frozen into inert dust.

With a soft wind blowing loose flakes around their snowshoes, Phoenix Force moved swiftly into the Forge base, their weapons at the ready. Ahead of them was a long corridor, winding steps leading almost straight down.

Easing off the snowshoes, the team started to proceed down the corridor when a Forge soldier walked into view on the stairs, an FN-2000 assault rifle slung across his back. The burly soldier gasped at the sight of the masked invaders and went for the Bersa pistol holstered at his side.

Without a qualm, McCarter shot the man in the throat.

Gurgling, the terrorist collapsed, partially on the concrete floor, one boot dangling over the stairwell. Sweeping forward, the team then stopped in its tracks at the sound of laughing children coming from below.

"The sons of bitches brought their families with them," James snarled, tightening his grip on the MP-5. "What the hell do we do now?"

"Our job," McCarter replied coldly, his voice sounding as if the man aged ten years with the grim pronouncement.

The men of Phoenix Force said nothing in reply, then straightened their shoulders and started down the spiral stairs into the very heart of the enemy fortress.

CHAPTER TWENTY

Royal Oil Field #9, Saudi Arabia

The heavy pounding was a palpable thing in the warm desert air. The loud noise of the nineteen massive pumps handling the colossal flow from the 114 oil derricks almost sounded like a beating human heart. Rhythmic and steady. It was as though an invisible giant stalked among the hundreds of workers, towering derricks, pumping stations, repair shops, storage tanks and barracks.

Without warning, a violent explosion erupted and one of the derricks blew apart, the black crude soaring high into the air before another blast destroyed a second derrick, the blast igniting the column of oil into a towering geyser of flame. Alarms began to howl and men ran in every direction as a dozen more oil wells erupted into vertical flamethrowers.

Unexpectedly, a tool shed was thrown backward as the sand began to bulge upward. Soon, the loose sand flowed away to reveal an enormous metal tube rising from below the desert.

Then the tube broke apart, the two halves of the metal lid folding back. Icy steam hissed into view for a single moment, then a soft rumble began, swiftly increasing into a roar of controlled power. A missile rose majestically into the air, the fiery launch of the illegal rocket hidden from the sight of any NATO WatchDog or Keyhole satellite by the growing conflagration of the burning Saudi oil field.

Unseen by the world, the Unity ICBM lifted swiftly skyward on its long journey to the East Coast of the United States of America.

McHenry County, North Dakota

BRANDISHING ASSAULT RIFLES, a dozen Forge soldiers arrived at the rill. They got a brief glimpse of three gringos wearing gigantic backpacks and covered with weapons when there was a large explosion. Coughing and sputtering, the men recoiled from the whirlwind of sand, then a second detonation tore their world apart. Battered and bloody, only one soldier at the rear of the group survived and struggled to move his broken hand to radio the ambush back to headquarters.

Moving swiftly through the sky, Able Team mentally urged their NASA jetpacks to move faster. They were still a long distance from the Black Rock Mesa, and the fuel supply was dropping fast.

Caught by surprise by the Forge soldiers, Able Team had acted in unison and instantly taken flight, the triple blast from the jetpacks creating a silent hurricane of loose sand. Then Blancanales dropped a satchel charge in the middle of the terrorists and the blast had ripped the enemy apart.

"Come on, baby," Lyons muttered, trying to make the device move faster by sheer willpower.

Invented by NASA, the jetpacks were worn by astronauts over their spacesuits and used to maneuver in the zero gravity of a high orbit, or even deep space. However, down here at the bottom of the gravity well of Earth, the powerful monochemical thrusters had a service life of only ninety seconds.

The U.S. Marine Corps had experimented with the jetpacks, and used them several times successfully in covert infiltrations. So successfully, in fact, that the machines were quickly adopted by the FBI, and then by Homeland Security. The esoteric devices were the main reasons the Stony Man operatives had raided the HSA armory. However, the operator-pilot had to be razor sharp. There wasn't room for a parachute, so unless the flyer was on the ground when the fuel ran out it was pancake city.

"It's no good. We're too far!" Schwarz called over the radio. "Start dropping supplies!"

The other two men paused in consternation, then swiftly obeyed. The rest of the satchel charges went first. That made them move faster across the sky and gave a touch of hope. The bulky flamethrower went next, along with the XM-214 minigun.

The distant ground was flashing below their boots in a blur, as the top of the mesa came into view. Suddenly, a group of Forge soldiers appeared from a clump of bushes working the arming bolts on their assault rifles. Able Team cut loose with their weapons and the terrorists died before getting off a shot.

As Lyons approached the edge of the mesa, the jetpack sputtered slightly. Crushing the joystick in his fist, he tried to get every drop of fuel out of the weakening engine. Just a little bit more…

With a sputter, the jetpack died and Lyons dropped onto the edge of the mesa, the impact of the landing rattling his teeth. Then the dead weight of the jetpack started to make him tip over backward. Slapping the release buckle on the chest harness, the Able Team leader dug in his heels as the equipment came free from his shoulders. He lurched forward to safety just as his teammates landed in a crouch a few yards away.

Unlimbering the Atchisson autoshotgun, Lyons fired twice into the bushes, then reloaded. The first couple of cartridges had been stun bags in case they needed a sentry alive. But Forge knew they were there by now, so stealth was no longer a consideration. Grimly, the former L.A. cop attached a cheesewheel clip to the bottom of the weapon, the aluminum magazine loaded only with stainless steel fléchettes. There was absolutely no chance of any civilians being inside the mesa, so this was going to be a straight-out blitz. Kill everybody they found until reaching the computers. No prisoners, no surrender.

Shrugging out of his jetpack, Schwarz pulled out an EM scanner and swept the area for land mines. Almost immediately the device gave a low warning beep right alongside the man. Warily, he peeked into the nearby weeds and saw a metal hatch, the kind used for a SAM missile pod. Damn, this wasn't just the secret lab, it was a Forge hardsite! Boosting the power to the scanner, Schwarz redoubled his search for traps.

Checking the suppressor on his Colt Model 1911, Blancanales paused at the sight of ants swarming on a series of dark spots on the rock. He bent closer and recognized spilled blood. And a lot of it. His guess would be that some poor bastard had gotten his throat slashed.

"Clear," Schwarz declared in relief, tucking away the device.

There was a movement in the bushes and Lyons cut loose with a short burst from the Atchisson. A man cried out and fell into view, the chest of the Forge soldier a gory mash of bones and organs.

Instantly, Blancanales armed a grenade and flipped the bushes. More men cried out in pain.

Rushing to the area, Able Team fired down into the access tube, a couple of Forge soldiers dropping off the ladder to hit more men below until there was a tangle of bodies at the bottom.

Lyons fired a long burst down the shaft, and everybody in the pile stopped moving. Shouldering his M-16/M-203 assault rifle, Blancanales started down the ladder by putting his combat boots on the outside and cupping the metal with fingerless gloves. He dropped away fast with Schwarz standing guard from above. Before he was halfway down, his teammates followed.

Landing in a crouch on top of the tattered corpses, Blancanales moved away from the ladder, his assault rifle sweeping for targets. A thump announced the arrival of his companions.

A squad of men charged around a corner, shoving clips into the assault rifles, and Blancanales fired the M-203. The thumping 40 mm shell vomited a deathcloud of double-aught buckshot tearing off heads, arms and legs. Only the torsos protected by body armor hit the gory floor intact.

Sweeping down the long corridor in a three-man defensive pattern, the team slapped disposable thermometer stickers on the walls. Suddenly, one of them turned a cold blue, and Lyons moved to the door, then stopped when he saw it was actually an airtight hatch made to resemble an ordinary door. There was no latch, only a keypad with a thumbprint scanner.

"Cover!" he subvocalized into his throat mike, hitting the wall.

Blancanales took a position on the other side, and Schwarz knelt in front of the door, swiftly attaching a wiring harness to the scanner. Swinging around his laptop, the man started working the keyboard, his fingers making soft patting sounds.

The screen began flashing a wild series of circuit diagrams, microchip connections and command prompts, the images almost blurring together they were coming so fast. There was a subdued clank, and with a hydraulic sigh, the door unlocked to open with a sigh of escaping air.

"Alakazam," Schwarz whispered, closing the laptop. Now only the thumbprints of Able Team would be recognized by the Forge security computer, and not those by anybody else. The virus was a little something special he had cooked up with Hunt Wethers and Akira Tokaido. This was its first trial in combat, and so far, so good.

The room inside was icy-cold, long banks of Cray supercomputers humming in the swirling mists. Yanking open a service panel, Schwarz shoved in a probe searching for the main feeds. Then he clipped a black box around the bundle of wires and pressed a red button on top.

"Come on, Bear," he whispered, waiting for the green light on top to flash. "I know you've been playing possum to fake out Forge. There is no way that moving a satellite could take out your team for more than a couple of hours...."

The light flashed twice, then winked out.

"Yes!" Schwarz said in victory, closing the panel and running a tube of military epoxy along the edge. Nobody was getting inside again without a welding torch, which would kill the circuits.

"Well?" Blancanales demanded anxiously from the doorway.

"The Farm now controls the North American uplink," Schwarz said, closing the door. It sealed with a hiss and loudly locked.

"So they were playing possum, eh?" Lyons said, almost smiling as he slapped a Claymore mine to the outside of the door. "Good, now let's clean house. Nobody leaves this mesa alive, except for—"

Jerking alert, Blancanales stared at his wristwatch. The biohazard sensor in the compact device had just buzzed on his skin. With bated breath, he waited for the results and the dial blinked a series of tiny yellow LEDs.

The wall vents could be heard softly hissing.

"Nerve gas!" Blancanales cried, clawing a combat syringe from a sleeve. He jabbed the metal tube onto his arm, the needle inside automatically injecting him with the antitoxins for a dozen deadly compounds. A terrible warmth filled his body, and his stomach convulsed, almost making him retch.

Turning, he saw his teammates with the syringes clutched in their hands slowly slumping to the floor. Had they injected themselves or not? There was no way to tell.

Moving as if in a dream, Blancanales reached for the tubes and tried to shove them against his friends again, but everything was so blurry the man wasn't sure if he was using the correct end.

The noise from the wall vents seemed to get louder.

Falling from his limp hands, the biohazard tube fell to the floor with a clatter and Blancanales lost consciousness.

CHAPTER TWENTY-ONE

Stony Man Farm, Virginia

In the Computer Room, Hal Brognola leaned against the wall, a telephone in his hand. The phone was a dedicated hardline that went directly to the Oval Office, and a soft crackle of static told that the line was open.

"No, sir, Mr. President," Brognola stated, closely watching the wall monitors for any changes. "Nothing to report from our people in the field yet."

Barbara Price scowled darkly as she walked back and forth behind the four cyber wizards hunched over their consoles. Somehow, Able Team had managed to seize control of the uplink for the Northern Hemisphere and linked the controls to the Cray supercomputers of the Farm. Excellent news! Now all the men had to do was keep that link operational at any cost.

Unfortunately, restoring the military systems for America, Great Britain, Russia, China and the rest of the world was only half the problem. According to the President, the political situation at the United Nations was almost completely in chaos. Ancient feuds and grudges had come boiling to the surface, and several of the smaller nations had walked out of the Grand Council, and in the Security Council a terrible feeling of war was in the air, like a cold wind from a distant graveyard.

Nobody trusted anybody at the moment. Thus, whatever country suddenly got the control of their missiles and satellites before anybody else would immediately be attacked by every other nation under the natural assumption that they were actually the source of the worldwide technological failures. Missiles would start crisscrossing the globe, and soon entire cities would begin vanishing in nuclear detonations. The end of the world.

The political situation was delicate. One wrong move by Stony Man and billions would die. There was only a single solution to the matter. Everybody, absolutely every nation, not just the Northern Hemisphere, had to regain control of all of their systems and satellites at exactly the same moment. That would defuse the tension, and buy the United Nations diplomats some precious time to calm things down and restore sanity. But if Able Team or Phoenix Force failed in their mission objectives, or if Kurtzman and his people fumbled restoring the GPS network to perfect working condition at the same precise instant…

"Easy does it, people," Kurtzman said soothingly. "I'll give you the signal. There's plenty of time. No worries, eh? Get everything ready, and triple check your landline connections."

Making no sign that they even heard the man, Tokaido, Delahunt and Wethers remained motionless at their consoles, their hands hovering over the keyboard. Volumes of data flashed by their screen and submonitors at dizzying speed.

Pausing by Kurtzman's workstation, Price stared at the blank computer monitor bearing the designation for Argentina.

"Come on, David, where the hell are you?" she demanded softly, the words somehow sounding like a desperate prayer.

Firebase Omega, Argentina

WARM AIR FROM THE WALL VENTS banished the cold from the shattered front door as Phoenix Force continued down the spiral stairs checking for traps and video cameras. But the stairs were clean, and after only a few yards, the metal staircase ended in a long tunnel, the walls, ceiling and floor sheathed in a soft metallic substance.

The men glanced at the material and kept moving. They knew what lead looked like. The material was obviously here to keep out radiation from above. There were also discolored bands of lead in the walls, and radiation sensors nearby. Clearly these were blast doors, set to slam shut the second they detected any incoming radiation. But why hadn't they been closed and sealed yet? Strange.

After several yards, the tunnel sharply angled to the left, and then immediately to the right in a classic antiradiation zigzag. Once past the safety break, the men could clearly hear the voices again, along with a child's laughter. It sounded like a small boy. There came another antirad zigzag, and the voices could be heard much more clearly. Some people were having an argument.

"But I want to play in the snow!" the boy whined in Spanish. "Please, Mother?"

"Now, Juan…" a woman began patiently.

"I told you before, not today," a man said firmly. "You can…er, play in the snow tomorrow. But not today."

Staying close to the lead walls, Phoenix Force crept closer and encountered a second spiral staircase leading downward. Bright lights were coming from the next level. Pulling out a flexible probe, James crouched low and eased a fiber-optic cable along a lens the size of a pencil down the stairs, turning a dial over the edge, using the dial on the handheld control to move the tiny camera lens around. On the screen, there was only confusion, then a clear shot of the lead floor, the ceiling, and then a sandbag nest came sharply into view. A Bushmaster 25 mm minigun was resting on a stout tripod, and a couple of armed Forge soldiers were standing near a pretty young woman, holding the hand of a small boy.

"But, Mom," the boy insisted, nearly dancing with frustration. He was wearing winter clothing and holding a sled.

The adults all shared knowing looks.

"Obey your father," the woman said sternly, then she addressed the taller of the soldiers. "I'll see you tomorrow, my love."

The private turned his back to give the married couple a moment of privacy as they briefly kissed. Then the woman walked around a corner, dragging the protesting boy along by the hand. A few moments later, there came a dull boom.

"Children!" the private exhaled, wearily shaking his head. "I just can't understand why anybody would want to have children these days."

"That's because you don't have any." The corporal smiled contentedly, lighting a cigarette.

"Those are illegal down here, my friend," the private warned with a stiff finger. "Once the blast doors close, that is."

"Which is why I asked for guard duty today," the corporal replied, blowing a smoke ring at a radiation sensor in the gray ceiling. "One final goodbye cigarette."

"Addict."

"Shithead."

Using both hands, James brought back the fiber- optic cable and tucked it away in a shoulder bag. "On the left," he reported.

Nodding in acknowledgment, McCarter worked the slide

on a silenced pistol and jumped into the hole in the floor. He missed the stairs by a scant inch and landed in a crouch, his weapon coughing a fast three times.

The private was thrown backward, most of his face splattering on the lead wall from the arrival of the soft-lead dumdum round. The corporal lost the cigarette as he was slammed against the opposite wall, both hands clutching his stomach from the bullet slamming into his Forge body armor.

Fighting for breath, the corporal tried to focus his eyes as he heard the sound of running boots. Clawing for the radio on his hip, the soldier found it was gone, along with his Bersa pistol and combat knife. He pulled in a breath to shout and a wad of cloth filled his mouth, carrying the odd flavor of gun oil. Rough hands dragged the huffing corporal erect and lashed his wrists behind his back with plastic cuffs.

Doing a fast sweep with an EM scanner, James declared the area free of hidden microphones or video cameras. Just past the sandbag nest, a branching tunnel ran to the left and right of the main access tunnel, both passageways ending in another antirad zigzag.

"You get a chance for life only because your son is behind that door," McCarter said in flawless Spanish, nudging the bound man with the hot tip of the Browning Hi-Power.

The Forge soldier grunted in understanding, but his eyes glared in raw hatred.

"Only civilians, your families and children behind those?" McCarter asked, indicating the big doors. "Barracks for the single men in the other direction?"

Breathing slowly, the prisoner did nothing.

Dropping the clip from the Browning, McCarter let the soldier see the soft lead dumdum rounds inside so that he would have no misconception the weapon might be loaded with blanks to merely scare him into talking.

Scowling fiercely, the prisoner flexed his arms to test the plastic handcuffs then nodded ever so faintly.

"Family quarters?" McCarter asked again, gesturing with the pistol.

Easing his defiant stance, the corporal nodded.

"Okay, seal it," McCarter ordered out of the side of his mouth.

Hawkins and Manning moved past the break and found a set of sliding metal doors sheathed in lead. Manning sniffed and caught the faint trace of a woman's perfume and the sickly sweet aroma of bubblegum.

"Smells like Akira was here," Hawkins said in dark humor, pulling out welding patches from a shoulder bag.

Hiding a smile under his woolen ski mask, Manning helped the man slap the U.S. Army patches directly onto the seam of the two doors. Designed by tank crew for emergency repairs on armor, the patches were composed of soft iron with alternating strips of epoxy and thermite paste underneath.

As the patch adhered firmly to the two doors, Hawkins yanked off the activating strip from the side, and the minuscule amount of thermite briefly flared, softening the iron until it started to flow down the lead. Then the thermal charge died away, and the combined metals began to cool and harden. The patch was only a crude weld, but opening these doors would now be difficult without an acetylene torch or high explosives. Manning slapped on two more, while Hawkins added a couple to the tracks on the concrete floor. No matter what happened next, there weren't going to be any civilians wandering through the middle of the battle. The UN Peacekeepers could release the women and children later. If there was a later for the world.

"Now, as for you," McCarter said, tapping the bound man

with the sound suppressor. "Why are the outer blast doors still open?"

The Forge soldier was good, but his eyes still widened in fear at the question.

"They were waiting for somebody," Encizo said thoughtfully. "Somebody important enough for even the little kids to know he wasn't here yet… Oh shit, it's Calvano!"

"That Cessna!" McCarter growled. "He must be on the Cessna doing a final recon of the perimeter before sealing off the base!"

At the English name of the plane, the Forge soldier kicked out a boot at Encizo and tried to escape, but McCarter clubbed the fellow on the back of the head with the Browning. He crumpled with a sigh, a tiny trickle of blood seeping through his hair.

"He'll live," Encizo said, kneeling to briefly check the unconscious man.

Charging into view, Hawkins and Manning appeared from behind the zigzag with their weapons sweeping for targets.

"Got brave, I see," Hawkins noted, loosening his grip on the FN-2000.

"Yeah, he grew some extra balls when we figured out Calvano is on the Cessna," the Cuban said, grabbing the man by the collar and dragging the limp body out of sight behind the sandbags.

"The Cessna must have skis instead of wheels," Manning rationalized, casting a glance at the spiral staircase. "Which means Calvano is going to use the clearing where the *Pegasus* landed before."

"And see the remains of the front door," James added with a dour expression. "No way he'll come inside… No, wait, this guy is a field general, not a desk jockey. He won a ton of medals in combat. General Calvano is going to lead the charge right down this corridor."

"A Cessna that size doesn't hold a lot of people," McCarter said, still holding the Browning. "We're talking six, maybe ten, guys at the most."

Looking blandly to the right corridor, Encizo added, "And a couple of hundred from below."

"Hundreds? Nothing I hate worse than a fair fight," Hawkins said in a pronounced Texas drawl. "What's the plan?"

"Rafe, mine the stairwell," McCarter said, holstering the pistol and bringing up his MP-5 machine gun. "Gary, bust the Bushmaster. T.J., jam those external blast doors so that we can leave. Calvin, with me. We have a computer to find."

Without comment, everybody went to work.

Going to the first rad break, James checked around the zigzag with the fiber-optic cables again. "Clear."

Sweeping into the next tunnel, McCarter saw a series of blast doors ending at an elevator. There was another 25 mm Bushmaster minigun suspended from the ceiling, a red light blinking from a small video camera on top. Remote control.

With no other choice, McCarter pulled the Browning and fired once. The cough was barely audible, but the crash of the video camera lens sounded like an explosion.

Instantly, the Bushmaster came online, the deadly weapon sweeping the corridor, but nothing else happened. The operators obviously unsure if there was a technical problem, or not, and having no wish to fire upon their returning leader.

Advancing toward the machine, McCarter pulled out a wire cutter and snipped the power cables, killing the Bushmaster, while James slapped a couple of welding patches onto the floor to block the blast doors. Then easing to the sides of the elevator doors, the men set off smoke grenades and placed them on the floor. Minutes passed.

Suddenly there came a musical ding and the elevator doors parted.

"What the...there's a fire out here!" a man said, breaking into a ragged cough.

Swinging into view, McCarter fired the Browning and the four men inside the elevator died with shocked expressions. Leaving the bodies where they fell, McCarter and James waited until the rest of the team joined them, then once again did nothing as the doors automatically closed.

After a few minutes, the elevator started to descend, summoned back to whatever level the technicians had originally left from. Pulling off their ski masks, the Stony Man operatives donned gas masks and set off several BZ canisters, the elevator filling with the mildly hallucinogenic fumes.

With another ding, the doors separated and the BZ gas rolled forth, making the group of men standing in the corridor recoil slightly. One started to raise his assault rifle, and McCarter shot him in the belly, the man doubling over to moan and gasp in pain, sounding as if he was merely choking on the thick fumes. Then the rest of the team moved swiftly into the gas cloud, using fists and rifle stocks to silently remove the Forge soldiers from the equation.

Going to a wall panel, James broke the lock with a small pry bar and ran a quick check on the exposed cables with an EM scanner.

"Well?" McCarter asked, trying to watch both directions of the corridor at the same time.

"Useless," James cursed, pocketing the device. "These are auxiliary cables. But the Cray must be close. They feel cold, and that doesn't travel far along wiring."

Scowling, McCarter started to ask a question when there came the crackle of an intercom from somewhere close by in the BZ gas. "What's with all the smoke?" a man demanded in oddly accented Spanish. "Is there a fire?"

Moving through the thickly swirling mists, McCarter and Hawkins went toward the new voice and weren't surprised to find a large window set into the whitewashed brick wall.

Pressing their faces to the glass, they discovered it was icy-cold, and in the room beyond was a huge Cray supercomputer, along with a small dark-skinned man in a turtleneck sweater sitting at a complex console. Suddenly, they understood completely why Forge called their chief hacker Snake Eater.

Ever so gently, McCarter lightly rapped the window with the barrel of his MP-5 machine gun. The short man inside looked up at the tiny noise, then recoiled in horror.

"You!" Mongoose gasped, just as McCarter and Hawkins began to fire the weapons point-blank at their old foe.

CHAPTER TWENTY-TWO

Black Rock Mesa

Sluggishly coming awake, Lyons felt something cold go around one of his wrists and instantly could tell it was a steel handcuff.

Reacting instinctively, the former L.A. detective jerked his arms apart to keep from being shackled and lashed out with an elbow. A startled cry announced a hit, and the Able Team leader charged at the nearest blur. The man was still weak, but his strength was returning fast. Slamming the other person onto the rock wall, he rammed a knee into the guy's crotch, then butted hard with his forehead. With a death rattle in his crushed throat, the other man fell limply to the floor.

His vision starting to clear, Lyons saw his teammates lying nearby, their hands already lashed into place. And across the corridor were three Forge soldiers wearing gas masks. One of them worked on the Claymore mine attached to the cold door. Two others turned toward him.

Risking everything, Lyons started forward, but both of the armed soldiers expertly leveled their FN-2000 assault rifles. The man reluctantly stopped, his heart pounding.

"Hold it, gringo!" a sergeant commanded, raising the assault rifle slightly. "Private, bind his hands properly!"

As Lyons slumped his shoulders in defeat, the other soldier pulled out a set of the disposable plastic cuffs. They were military design, more than capable of restraining a gorilla, much less the weakened Stony Man operative.

But as the Forge private touched his arm, Lyons moved fast. Spinning, he grabbed the barrel of the sergeant's assault rifle and yanked hard. The motion made the sergeant inadvertently pull the trigger, and the stuttering assault rifle stitched the private across the chest, red blood spraying into the air.

With a curse, the sergeant released the weapon and clawed for a Bersa pistol at his hip. Swinging up the rifle by the barrel, Lyons slammed the stock against the side of the big man's head. There was a ghastly crunch and the sergeant dropped the Bersa, then collapsed alongside the fallen gun.

Throwing a pair of pliers as a distraction, the third man pulled a Bersa and fired. The slug missed Lyons completely. He replied with the FN-2000, the 5.56 mm rounds tearing the technician apart.

Taking a knife from one of the fallen men, Lyons sawed through the bonds that restrained his teammates when a tall, lanky man walked around the corner. Immediately, Lyons recognized the fellow as Professor Reinhold, the brains behind the hacking of the GPS network.

"Freeze!" Lyons bellowed in his best cop voice.

But the professor dived to the side and came up firing the dropped Bersa. The 9 mm round knocked the assault rifle from Lyons's grip, a second round slamming into his chest. The Able Team leader grunted from the impact on his NATO body armor, and kicked the gun from the grip of the scientist. Even as the weapon went sailing away, Reinhold seemed to crumple, then rose, driving both fists into Lyons's stomach. Again, he only grunted from the martial arts blow, and tried to knee the man in the face. Reinhold blocked with a forearm and dived sideways ramming an elbow into his adversary. The sledgehammer blow knocked the air from his lungs, and he grabbed for the gas mask, yanking it free and hurtling it away.

Grinning in amusement, Reinhold angled his body oddly and lashed out with an open hand. The move almost caught Lyons by surprise. The gas had no effect, eh? Swaying out of the way just in time, he felt the fingernails of the Forge scientist scrap his throat.

On the floor, Blancanales and Schwarz began to stir sluggishly.

Circling each other, Lyons and the professor each made a couple of tentative grabs that were blocked, then Reinhold kicked a pistol off the floor, sailing it past Lyons's head. He didn't even try for a grab, but instead dived for the dropped knife. He came up in a roll, and steel clashed on steel as Reinhold blocked with a hidden blade of his own.

Slashing for throats and groins, the two men moved in a deadly ballet of thrust and parry. The professor got a crimson cut along the side of his neck, Lyons's blade missing the vital carotid artery by less than a millimeter. Then Reinhold sliced the Stony Man operative across the chest, only the NATO body armor preventing it from opening his stomach. But he pinked the man on the wrist, and they retreated slightly, panting for breath and looking for the other to make a deadly mistake.

Bobbing and weaving, Lyons lashed out with a kick, the steel toe of the U.S. Army combat boot catching the other man in the ribs. Bones cracked, and the professor winced noticeably. Then Reinhold flipped his knife in the air, catching it by the blade and whipping it forward. Lyons tried to dodge, but the blade slammed deep into his shoulder, an inch away from the body armor. Hot blood oozed from the wound. Stumbling backward, Lyons tried to do the same, but Reinhold caught the spinning blade and threw it back, this time hitting Lyons in the upper thigh. Crumbling to the floor, the Able Team leader grabbed the handle jutting from his flesh, but didn't try to pull it free. That would only make the wound bleed ten times worse, and probably kill him.

Yanking the trick wallet from his pocket, Lyons didn't pretend to beg for clemency, but simply fired the two booming .44 rounds from the derringer. They drilled into the wall alongside the professor, tiny rock chips flying.

Pulling a pen from his shirt pocket, a grinning Reinhold pressed the button on top and a six-inch steel spike clicked into view from the bottom, a drop of greenish fluid appearing from the needle-sharp tip. Poison!

Moving in for the fast kill, Reinhold suddenly jerked backward as machine-gun fire filled the corridor. Dropping the trick ice pick, Reinhold hit the wall hard and spun away from the incoming bullets to sprint around the corner and out of sight.

"Carl, are you hurt bad?" Schwarz asked, kneeling by his friend. Blood was everywhere, and he wasn't sure how much of it came from Lyons.

Ripping open his parka, Blancanales pulled out a small field surgery kit and flipped open the top, but Lyons smacked the med kit away.

"N-no t-time," he whispered hoarsely, slumping against the cold door, the Claymore mine only inches above his stubbled scalp. "S-stop him…b-before…" The man went limp.

Slowly standing, Schwarz understood. Before he blew up the computers controlling the uplink.

Pausing for only a split second, the two Able Team warriors looked down upon their friend, then turned and took off down the corridor at a run. All for one, and one for all, was a child's game. This was the real world, and the mission came first. They didn't like it, but it was part of a soldier's burden.

Reaching the end of a long corridor, they found three elevators, but only the middle one in operation. Ignoring the obvious trap, they hit the emergency stairs and raced pell-mell into the bowels of the rocky mesa.

BURSTING OUT OF THE ELEVATOR, Reinhold headed straight for the armed soldiers standing behind a low barricade of sandbags.

"Intruders!" the professor yelled, gesturing vaguely. "Kill anybody who gets off the elevators!"

"Is…is this another test?" one of the guards asked suspiciously.

"Code nineteen!" the professor snarled, limping past a section of the area lined with Claymore antipersonnel mines. Past them was the armored door to Command and Control. Wasting precious time cycling through the elaborate locking mechanism, the professor squeezed through the truncated portal before it had finished opening completely.

"Peterson, shut down the computers!" Reinhold yelled, lurching across the room, leaving a crimson trail on the terrazzo flooring. "Sabot, activate the self-destruct!"

"Are you insane?" Erica Sabot asked, rising from her wheeled chair.

"Code nineteen!" he snarled, reaching a weapons cabinet. The professor didn't bother to use his key, but simply smashed the glass with his bare hands and grabbed an HK G-11 caseless rifle from the rack. Checking the power level of the batteries, he clicked off the safety just as there came a familiar hum of working hydraulics.

In horror, the professor turned to see the armored door swing open, revealing a commando holding a laptop, wiring connected to the sensor pad, and another one working the arming bolt of an M-16 assault rifle. Red blood was splattered on the wall behind them, and there was no sign of the armed guards.

Swinging around the G-11, Reinhold jerked wildly as Blancanales shot first, the 5.56 mm rounds peppering the man's bulletproof vest, but doing no harm. Then Schwarz fired his 9 mm Beretta, the Black Talon cop-killer rounds stolen from the HSA neatly blowing through the vest and coming out the back of the startled man. Bloody gobbets of flesh smacked against the Lexan plastic wall overlooking the huge Cray supercomputer.

As the professor fell into a pile of his own intestines, several people began to scream hysterically. One man tried to hide behind a chair, and a raven-haired woman yanked open a desk drawer to haul out a Bersa pistol.

"Don't do it!" Blancanales warned, then put a short burst into the ceiling.

Her beautiful face contorting into a snarl, Ericá Sabot release her grip and the gun dropped back into the drawer.

"Is this command and control?" Schwarz demanded, holstering the Beretta and sliding the M-16/M-203 combo assault rifle off his shoulder.

Too furious to speak, Sabot dumbly nodded.

"Are there any civilians in the mesa?" Blancanales demanded, shaking her by the arm.

Angry, Sabot tried to pull away, but the man tightened his grip until she flinched.

The rest of the technical staff was still screaming, several of them trying to hide under their consoles.

"I said, are there any civilians in the mesa?" Blancanales repeated urgently. "Any hostages, prisoners, noncombatants?"

"W-we don't t-take p-prisoners," she said in halting English.

"That's not something to brag about, lady," Schwarz snapped, grabbing her by the collar and hauling the woman over to the main console. "Release the nerve gas."

She stared at him in total confusion. "What was that?" Sabot asked in whisper.

Blancanales fired the M-16 and the chair next to her spun wildly, smacking into the console and rolling away to crash into a file cabinet.

"Don't make me say it again," Schwarz ordered, placing the fluted barrel of the M-16 to the back of her neck. "Now release the nerve gas. All of it. Flood every level!"

"Or we'll find somebody who will," Blancanales added ominously.

Defiant words rose in her throat, then Sabot caught sight of Reinhold lying on the terrazzo floor, his blood following the rectangular outlines in the polished concrete. Whoever these people were, negotiation wasn't an option.

Pulling her chair in tight under the console, Sabot deftly worked the controls for a while, releasing the deadly gas. She also sent an emergency message to the general.

"Done," she reported, swiveling away from the console. "Shall you kill me now? Or is it to be rape?"

"Never on the first date," Blancanales said dryly. "Just show me what's actually happening."

Confused by the cavalier remark, Sabot went back to the console and flipped several switches. Soon, the computer screen was filled with a dozen frames, each of them showing

Forge personnel stumbling about drunkenly. Several people tried to don gas masks, but were never successful, their faces turning blue first, and they fell off screen.

"Monsters," Sabot whispered, a tear trickling down her quivering cheek. "You are monsters!"

"No, we're soldiers, and you're a terrorist," Schwarz corrected, nudging her with the M-16. "So shut up."

The woman scowled darkly, but obeyed. These American killers would never understand that they were trying to save the human race from itself. There was no other choice. Hopefully her message got to Calvano and he would respond soon. She didn't know how long she could last under torture. The very idea made her feel sick.

Repulsed by the scenes of death, Blancanales and Schwarz forced themselves to watch the monitors closely to make sure the deadly gas was reaching every level, every room, until there were only motionless forms sprawled on the rock floors.

"Good enough," Blancanales decided. "Okay, go join your buddies over in the corner. Stay quiet, and you'll probably live through the day."

"And then?" Sabot demanded.

"Jail," Schwarz replied bluntly. "If you're lucky."

"I see," the woman demurred. Reaching up to take a pencil from behind her ear, she looked at it thoughtfully, then bit down hard on the wood. There was a sharp crack; she went stiff, then slumped limply in the chair.

Jerking her around, Schwarz yanked the broken pencil from her slack mouth, but it was too late. The body was limp, and there was a strong smell of bitter almonds on her breath.

"Cyanide," Blancanales said. "A suicide pencil. These people are insane!"

"Were insane, you mean," Schwarz said softly, looking off to the side.

The screaming and wailing from the rest of the staff had ceased a couple of minutes ago, and now they were all lying prone on the floor, broken pencils clenched between their teeth.

"Sweet Jesus." Schwarz exhaled, resting the stock of the M-16 assault rifle on a hip. "Okay, now what?"

Blancanales wasn't sure. There was no way of telling if the gas used was the same stuff that had nearly killed them before, and they were out of antitoxin. Until they got the word to leave from the Farm, their job was to stay right safe inside the command and control room and guard the computers.

"We hold our position," Blancanales said stoically, looking at a tiny picture of Lyons on the computer. The big man had toppled over onto the dirty floor, a pool of dark blood slowly spreading around his still form.

CHAPTER TWENTY-THREE

Firebase Omega, Argentina

The hammering barrage of 9 mm rounds hit the thick Plexi-glas window and buried themselves in the resilient material, hanging suspended like flies in amber.

Mesmerized by the sight, Mongoose didn't seem able to move a muscle. The window was eight inches thick, and the armor-piercing rounds were almost six inches deep into the material. If he had chosen a slimmer window, the commandos would have blown him into pieces.

Just then, the armored door clicked and swung open, James holding a keywire gun in one hand and an MP-5 machine gun in the other.

"Hiya, buddy," the Stony Man operative said sardonically. "Long time no see."

Swallowing hard, Mongoose tried to smile. "Well, I—"

"Shut up, moron," Hawkins snarled, entering next. "Just move away from those controls." There was an FN-2000 balanced in his hands, the heat coming off the barrel visible in the cold air.

Licking dry lips, Mongoose wanted to order them to stop

letting in the warm air, but wisely refrained. Moving with exaggerated slowness, the hacker raised both hands and used his sneakers to push the wheeled chair away from the console.

Entering the cold room, the rest of Phoenix Force checked for hidden guards and video cameras, but found the area clean.

"T.J., more smoke. Rafe, close the door," McCarter said, studying the array of blade servers filling the rear of the room. "We want the Cray nice and cold. At least for another few minutes."

Wisps of fog seeped from a ceiling vent above the Cray, and in the corner was a small tank of liquid nitrogen, the metal container painted a brilliant yellow.

Pulling a smoke grenade from the bag at his side, Hawkins pulled the pin, dropped the spoon and tossed the bomb outside into the corridor. Fresh smoke rose to mask the bodies and brass on the floor. Resting his MP-5 on a shoulder, Encizo gave a nod and shut the door, the jimmied lock reengaging with a sharp click.

"Are you the new prison soldiers?" Mongoose asked, trying to sound pitiful. He gave a little shiver that had nothing to do with the cold.

"Cute. But cut the shit," McCarter said, putting the barrel of his machine gun to the side of the hacker's head. "You're the chief hacker for Forge, so don't waste my time trying to pretend you're a prisoner forced into working for these assholes."

An arsenal of lies coming to mind, Mongoose started to speak when the silenced gun pressed harder into his soft skin. Dumbly, he simply nodded.

Slinging his weapon, Manning expertly frisked the hacker. In spite of the multiple layers of sweaters and thermal underwear, the Stony Man operative retrieved a small collection of knives, derringers and a trick pen. Pressing the button on top,

Manning scowled as a steel needle jutted from the bottom, some sort of greenish fluid dribbling onto the floor. He dropped the pen on the tiles and crushed the weapon under his boot.

Forcing himself to stay silent, Mongoose cast a fast glance at the console, his sight resting on the red alarm button. Press that once and troops would arrive in force. Press it twice, and poison gas would flood the room. He was immune, but doubted highly that these commandos would survive the experience.

"Clean," Manning reported, stepping away, making sure his holstered pistol was out of reach.

"All right, do as you're told, and I may let you live," McCarter said. "Close every blast door below this level."

Without comment, Mongoose nodded and rolled closer to the console, to begin typing on the keyboard. The alarm button was only inches away. Overriding the security protocols was easy, since he had written them for the South Americans, and always left a back door that only he could find. Unexpectedly, an icon appeared on the bottom of the computer screen as an emergency call arrived from Black Rock, but he ignored it and continued activating programs. It wasn't his problem anymore.

Leaning on the console, James used a combat knife to pry open a panel, and reached inside to clip some wires. Beaming a smile at the bust, the Stony Man operative pressed the alarm button several times. Nothing happened.

"You seemed overly concerned," James said with a humorless smile. "Is this better?"

Hunching his shoulders as if receiving a beating, Mongoose stopped stalling for time and finished the task. On the main screen, several pictures within pictures appeared, showing the heavy blast doors sliding across the corridors and hallways, firmly locking into place.

"Done, sir," Mongoose announced wearily, a bead of sweat

trickling down his back in spite of the frigid air in the computer room. "But it is too late. General Calvano and ten troopers have just entered the elevator and are on the way to this level."

"They're not on the video screens," Hawkins said, swinging his FN-2000 assault rifle to point directly at the man. "Care to tell us how you know that?"

Mongoose pointed a finger at the Plexiglas window. "The elevator is coming down from the top level," he said calmly. "Who else could it be?"

"The bastards got past my Claymore," Encizo cursed. "These guys are assholes, but not stupid."

Rubbing an old wound on his right shoulder, McCarter agreed with the assessment, and quickly reviewed the tactical situation. A stand-up fight with Forge would almost certainly destroy the computers. They couldn't risk that. Okay, they had to do this the hard way.

"Calvin, hot link the Cray to our friends in the north," McCarter ordered. "Everybody else, we're taking down the general right here!"

"But the Cray…" Mongoose began, unable to stop himself.

Nudging the hacker with his gun, James pushed him in the wheeled chair over into a corner, far from the computer and door. McCarter stood guard while the others used the last of the smoke grenades inside the computer room, the cold air seeming to augment the dark chemical fumes. Visibility was reduced to only a few feet.

As the men took positions, they heard the muted ding of the elevator and humanoid shapes began moving through the thinning white BZ gas. Inside the computer room, the fresh gray smoke swirled along the air currents, ebbing and flowing like a cloudy river.

"These men are dead, sir," somebody announced from the floor.

"More nines," another soldier added. "Not our caliber."

"What's that sweet smell?" a soldier said, sniffing hard.

"Sleep gas! Use your masks!" a stern voice commanded. "Our antitoxins may not be enough." There came the sound of opening Velcro, and some murky movements.

Slowly, a shadowy figure walked closer to the window, then the intercom buzzed. "Snake Eater, are you alive?" the voice demanded. "What happened to my men? Did a nitrogen tank explode? Are we being attacked?"

When there was no reply, after a moment the door latch rattled.

"Check it!" the voice demanded.

Carrying assault rifles, several men pressed their faces to the Plexiglas window. "I think the Cray is on fire, sir," a corporal said hesitantly. "There's a lot of smoke in there."

"But the fire alarm hasn't activated," the unseen man replied. "It's a trap! Attack!"

Instantly the Forge soldiers opened fire, the FN-2000 assault rifles deafening in the corridor, the rounds slamming deep into the eight-inch slab of Plexiglas but failing to achieve penetration.

"Everybody, raise your guns threateningly, but do not fire," McCarter subvocalized into his throat mike. "Then look worried and pretend to search for spare ammo clips."

"Make them think we're out," Hawkins said, rummaging in an ammo bag full of loaded clips, his hand coming out empty. "That's not too far from the truth."

The hammering fusillade in the external corridor continued unabated, chips flying off the window from the endless barrage of hot lead. A small crack appeared in the corner.

Backing away from the hammering noise, McCarter knew the truth of the matter. Locked inside the room, their plan to take clips from the dead terrorists' stolen FN-2000 assault riles was moot. "Okay, they've noticed we're not returning fire. Now drop your weapons and start using handguns."

Doing as they were instructed, the team began to pull back from the Plexiglas shield, moving deeper into the thick smoke, their pistols banging away constantly.

"They're out of ammo, sir!" a sergeant announced, slapping in a fresh clip. "Down to handguns, and some of our weapons!"

"Cease fire!" the voice bellowed.

As the barrage raggedly stopped, a large man appeared at the window. He had grizzled hair, and the uniform bore the insignia of a general. A gas mask covered his features.

The Stony Man operatives did nothing, suspecting another trick, when the general leaned in close and lifted his mask for a good look into the smoky room.

"Take him," McCarter ordered calmly, feeling a rush of adrenaline to his stomach.

Rising into view from behind a humming server, Gary Manning rested the .50-caliber Barrett rifle on top of the machine, aimed and fired the last bullet. The Plexiglas window seemed to bulge outward for a prolonged microsecond before shattering into a million pieces. The explosion of plastic threw the startled Forge soldiers backward, their primed weapons firing wildly.

As the thick barrier fell away, McCarter raised his MP-5 and stitched the general across the torso, then kept firing, the 9 mm rounds forcing the man flat against the wall, the soft lead slugs ricocheting off his body armor.

Then Hawkins triggered the grenade launcher. The distance was too short to arm the warhead, but the 40 mm round hit Calvano between the eyes, and his head smashed apart like a dropped pumpkin.

Instantly, the Forge soldiers cut loose with their assault rifles, the 5.56 mm rounds hitting the Stony Man warriors and bouncing off their body armor as they returned fire with their 9 mm machine guns. The terrorists fell, blood pumping from a dozen holes in their arms, legs and throats.

"Check the dead for fakes," McCarter barked, advancing to the console. He brushed off the sparkling pieces of Plexiglas with a gloved hand. "Cal, give me a status report!"

Kneeling at the console, James saw that the Cray was still working; no ricochets had damaged the delicate circuitry. But clean air was flooding in through the ruined window, dispelling the military smoke. Warm air.

"She's overheating!" James snapped, looking at the temperature gauge. Yanking off his gloves, the man frantically worked the controls. "Block that window, and somebody turn the liquid nitrogen up all the way!"

"Is it still operational?" McCarter demanded, walking closer.

"Tell you in a second," James shot back, pressing the transmit button on the powerful military radio.

Stony Man Farm, Virginia

"HOT DAMN, WE HAVE THE SOUTHERN uplink!" Kurtzman boomed. "Move with a purpose, people!"

Flashing into action, the cybernetics team activated macro files by the score, their fingers flashing along the keyboards.

In heart-pounding anticipation, Brognola and Price watched anxiously as the wall screen flickered into a vector graphic map of the world, the military status of every nation indicated by a color bar. Almost all of them were in the red: war.

A slow minute passed, then in ragged formation the superpowers stepped down from red going all the way to green. The nations weren't at peace, but nobody was holding a finger on the nuclear button anymore.

"We did it." Price sighed in relief.

"Alert. Incoming missile," Tokaido reported, slaving his console to the master war computer at Cheyenne Mountain. "Six, no, five hundred miles off the Eastern Seaboard and heading for D.C." Then the young hacker paused. If he didn't know any better, he'd swear the thing was coming directly at the Farm!

"How in hell…" Price asked, then shook the question off and grabbed her cell phone. "Chief, we have a possible incoming nuke! Seal the base and ready the SAM launchers! Repeat, incoming nuke!"

"Mr. President, there's an incoming ICBM," Brognola said, speaking in a clipped tone. "Get into the bunker right now, sir!"

"No need for that," Kurtzman announced with a sense of pride as a bright flash lit up on the wall map and the incoming triangle vanished.

"Did it detonate early?" Price asked, the cell phone still tight in her hand.

"Negative. That was a conventional explosion," Delahunt said, gratefully removing her helmet. Laying it aside, she ran stiff fingers through her damp hair. "The Navy shot it down with a flight of antimissiles from…" She paused to smile weakly. "Actually, they launched antimissiles from every damn ship berthed at Virginia Beach. About two hundred of them."

"Thank God." Price then thumbed the cell phone. "Stand down, Chief, the danger is over."

"Where did it come from?" Brognola demanded, hanging up the telephone. His fingers opened stiffly, almost unwilling to let go after being clenched for so long a time. "Who sent it? Are there any more on the way?"

"Unknown at the moment," Kurtzman said slowly, reading an incoming transmission from Argentina. "No, correct that. David captured the Forge hacker alive, and he says it came from our old friends Unity."

"Mongoose?" Wethers said, taking an educated guess.

"Right the first time."

The professor thought he had recognized the man's handiwork. "Any chance he knows where their headquarters is located?" Wethers asked, sticking the cold pipe back into his mouth.

Turning in his wheelchair, Kurtzman gave a smile that came straight from hell. "Actually, he does."

EPILOGUE

Opening his eyes, Carl Lyons looked about the white room in confusion. Then the man slowly relaxed as he realized he was in a hospital room.

"Damn, you are a hard man to kill," Brognola said, hitching closer on a metal stool. "Nice to see you back among the living, Carl."

Lyons said nothing, letting his mind clear for another minute. Hanging from a stand, an IV dripped fluids into a tube that went into the back of his hand, and his shoulder was uncomfortably stiff. A sensation he knew all too well. Recent surgery and stitches. Bandages around his chest hinted at possible broken ribs, too.

"Mission…" was as far as Lyons got before his voice failed, dwindling into a croak.

"Everything is fine," Brognola said, taking a plastic tumbler of ice water off a table and proffering the flexible straw to the man.

Knowing it was going to hurt, Lyons took a tiny sip and

grimaced from the razor-blade feeling flowing down his throat. Then he took another sip, waited for the discomfort to ease, then drank freely for a minute before finally relinquishing the straw.

"Thanks."

"No problem," Brognola replied, refilling the cup and placing it in a convenient position on the bed table.

Summoning strength, Lyons looked at the big Fed. "Report," he whispered.

Caught by surprise, Brognola broke into a laugh. "Yes, sir! The world is back to normal, such as it is, and the Forge firebases have been destroyed. We had no breakage, aside from you, and caught all of the Forge personnel. The UN Peacekeepers freed the trapped families without any incidents. Thank God."

Fingering the neat row of stitches, Lyons nodded in relief.

"Anyway, the President has placed a rush order for inertial guidance systems for our ICBM defense," Brognola continued. "The NSA is assigning new safeguards on our Comsats, and the Pentagon is installing self-destruct mechanisms into all of our long-range missiles. Army, Navy, the works."

"Good." Lyons settled weakly into the soft bed.

"You'll be interested to know that Phoenix Force caught the hacker working for Forge. It was our old pal Mongoose from Calcutta."

His temper flaring, Lyons narrowed his gaze. Yeah, he remembered McCarter talking about the cowardly computer genius. Betrayed his employer, then did it again with his next employer, and then faked his own death to escape Stony Man.

"Is he dead?" Lyons whispered. "If not, he should be."

"Agreed," Brognola said with a palms-up gesture. "However, he's currently spilling his guts to Kurtzman about Professor Reinhold's work on the GPS network. With the detailed information, the network can be redesigned so that this sort of thing never happens again."

"Don't..." Lyons broke into a cough again.

Reaching for the tumbler and straw again, Brognola arched an eyebrow. "Trust him? Of course we're not going to trust him. Although, he has been very helpful. Even told us the exact location of his old employer, Unity."

Accepting the deliciously cold tumbler, Lyons said nothing, then questioningly tilted his head.

Grinning widely, the big Fed checked his wristwatch. "Oh, just about any second now."

Sahara Desert, Middle East

ARGUING LOUDLY OVER THEIR latest failure, the Supreme Council of Unity was still sitting around the large conference table when every video monitor on the base flickered into a picture of a large granite statue, the man of stone turning to face outward and slowly smiling with a grinding noise.

"Welcome from America," the voice of Aaron Kurtzman said. "Now say goodbye, assholes."

A split second later a Tomahawk cruise missile arched over a sand dune high above the subterranean base; it angled sharply, diving into the loose sand and penetrating almost to the concrete roof of the underground base when the massive warhead detonated. The entire isolated area erupted into a thundering volcano, the brunt of the blast directed downward by the shaped-charge of the special bunker buster.

The strident concussion seemed to shake the world, as sand dunes rose and fell like waves upon the sea, cresting and crashing in primordial chaos. Static electricity randomly crackled like wild sheet lighting as a roiling column of smoke rose to darken the sky.

As the colossal reverberations finally ceased, the loose sand began to trickle back down into the glowing blast crater, the mighty Sahara already starting to fill in the molten grave of the terrorist organization. Soon, there was no trace that Unity had ever existed.

* * * * *

ROOM 59

Welcome to Room 59, a top secret,
international intelligence agency sanctioned
to terminate global threats that governments can't touch.
Its high-level spymasters operate in a
virtual environment and are seasoned in the
dangerous game of espionage and counterterrorism.

A Room 59 mission puts everything on the line;
emotions run high, and so does the body count.

Take a sneak preview of
THE POWERS THAT BE
by Cliff Ryder.

Available January 8,
wherever books are sold.

"Shot fired aft! Shot fired aft!" Jonas broadcast to all positions. "P-Six, report! P-Five, cover aft deck. Everyone else, remain at your positions."

Pistol in hand, he left the saloon and ran to the sundeck rail. Although the back of the yacht had been designed in a cutaway style, with every higher level set farther ahead than the one below it, the staggered tops effectively cut his vision. But if he couldn't see them, they couldn't see him, either. He scooted down the ladder to the second level, leading with his gun the entire way. Pausing by the right spiral stairway, he tapped his receiver. Just as he was about to speak, he heard the distinctive *chuff* of a silenced weapon, followed by breaking glass. Immediately the loud twin barks of a Glock answered.

"This is P-Five. Have encountered at least three hostiles on the aft deck, right side. Can't raise P-Six—" Two more shots sounded. "Hostiles may attempt to gain access through starboard side of ship, repeat, hostiles may attempt access through starboard side of ship—" The transmission was cut off again by the sustained burst of a silenced submachine gun stitching holes in the ship wall. "Request backup immediately," P-Five said.

Jonas was impressed by the calm tone of the speaker—it had to be the former Las Vegas cop, Martinson. He was about to see if he could move to assist when he spotted the muzzle of another subgun, perhaps an HK MP-5K, poke up through the open stairwell. It was immediately followed by the hands holding it, then the upper body of a black-clad infiltrator. Jonas ducked behind the solid stairway railing, biding his time. For a moment there was only silence, broken by the soft lap of the waves on the hull, and a faint whiff of gunpowder on the breeze.

Although Jonas hadn't been in a firefight in years, his combat reflexes took over, manipulating time so that every second seemed to slow, allowing him to see and react faster than normal. He heard the impact of the intruder's neoprene boot on the deck, and pushed himself out, falling on his back as he came around the curved railing. His target had been leading with the MP-5K held high, and before he could bring it down, Jonas lined up his low-light sights on the man's abdomen and squeezed the trigger twice. The 9 mm bullets punched in under the bottom edge of his vest, mangling his stomach and intestines, and dropping him with a strangled grunt to the deck. As soon as he hit, Jonas capped the man with a third shot to his face.

"This is Lead One. I have secured the second aft deck. P-Two and P-Three—"

He was cut off again as more shots sounded, this time from the front of the yacht. Jonas looked back. *A second team?*

And then he realized what the plan was, and how they had been suckered. "All positions, all positions, they mean to take the ship! Repeat, hostiles intend to take the ship! Lead Two, secure the bridge. P-Three, remain where you are, and target any hostiles crossing your area. Will clear from this end and meet you in the middle."

A chorus of affirmatives answered him, but Jonas was already moving. He stripped the dead man of his MP-5K and slipped three thirty-round magazines into his pockets. As he stood, a small tube came spinning up the stairway, leaving a small trail of smoke as it bounced onto the deck.

Dropping the submachine gun, Jonas hurled himself around the other side of the stairway railing, clapping his hands over his ears, squeezing his eyes shut and opening his mouth as he landed painfully on his right elbow. The flash-bang grenade went off with a deafening sound and a white burst of light that Jonas sensed even through his closed eyelids. He heard more pistol shots below, followed by the canvas-ripping sounds of the silenced MP-5Ks firing back. That kid is going to get his ass shot off if I don't get down there, he thought.

Jonas shook his head and pushed himself up, grabbing the submachine gun and checking its load. He knew the stairs had to be covered, so that way would be suicide. But there was a narrow space, perhaps a yard wide, between the back of the stairwell and the railing of the ship's main level. If he could get down there that way, he could possibly take them by surprise, and he'd also have the stairway as cover. It might be crazy, but it was the last thing they'd be expecting.

He crawled around the stairway again and grabbed the dead body, now smoking from the grenade. The man had two XM-84 flash-bangs on him.

Jonas grabbed one and set it for the shortest fuse time—one second. It should go off right as it hits the deck, he thought. He still heard the silenced guns firing below him, so somehow the two trainees had kept the second team from advancing. He crawled to the edge of the platform, checked that his drop zone was clear, then pulled the pin and let the grenade go, pulling back and assuming the *fire in the hole* position again.

The flash-bang detonated, letting loose its 120-decibel explosion and one-million-candlepower flash. As soon as the shock died away, Jonas rolled to the side of the boat just as a stream of bullets ripped through the floor where he had been. He jumped over the stairway, using one hand to keep in touch with his cover so he didn't jump too far out and miss the boat entirely. The moment he sailed into the air, he saw a huge problem—one of the assault team had had the same idea of using the stairway for cover, and had moved right under him.

Unable to stop, Jonas stuck his feet straight down and tried to aim for the man's head. The hijacker glanced up, so surprised by what he saw that for a moment he forgot he had a gun in his hand. He had just started to bring it up when Jonas's deck shoes crunched into his face. The force on the man's head pushed him to the deck as Jonas drove his entire body down on him. The mercenary collapsed to the floor, unmoving. Jonas didn't check him, but stepped on his gun hand, snapping his wrist as he steadied his own MP-5K, tracking anything moving on the aft deck.

The second team member rolled on the deck, clutching his bleeding ears, his tearing eyes screwed tightly shut. Jonas cleared the rest of the area, then came out and slapped the frame of his subgun against the man's skull, knocking him unconscious. He then cleared the rest of the area, stepping over Hartung's corpse as he did so. Only when he was sure there were no hostiles lying in wait did he activate his transceiver.

"P-Five, this is Lead. Lock word is *tango*. Have secured the aft deck. Report."

"This is P-Five, key word is *salsa*. I took a couple in the vest, maybe cracked a rib, but I'm all right. What should we do?"

"Take P-Six's area and defend it. Hole up in the rear saloon, and keep watch as best as you can. As soon as we've secured the ship, someone will come and relieve you."

"Got it. I'll be going forward by the left side, so please don't shoot me."

"If you're not wearing black, you'll be okay."

Jonas heard steps coming and raised the subgun, just in case a hostile was using the ex-cop as a hostage to get to him. When he saw the stocky Native American come around the corner, Glock first, Jonas held up his hand before the other man could draw a bead on him.

Martinson nodded, and Jonas pointed to the motionless man in front of him and the other guy bleeding in the corner of the deck. "Search these two and secure them, then hole up. I'm heading forward. Anyone comes back that doesn't give you the key word, kill them."

"Right. And sir—be careful."

"Always." Jonas left the soon-to-be-full operative to clear the deck and headed topside, figuring he'd take the high-ground advantage. Scattered shots came from the bow, and he planned to get the drop on the other team—hell, it had worked once already. "P-One through P-Four, Lock word is *tango*. Report."

"P-One here, we've got two hostiles pinned at the bow, behind the watercraft. Attempts to dislodge have met with heavy resistance, including flash-bangs. P-Two is down with superficial injuries. We're under cover on the starboard side, trying to keep them in place."

"Affirmative. P-Three?"

"I'm moving up on the port side to cut off their escape route."

"P-Four? Come in, P-Four?" There was no answer. "P-Four, if you can't speak, key your phone." Nothing. *Shit.* "All right. P-One, hold tight, P-Three, advance to the corner and keep them busy. I'll be there in a second. Lead Two, if you are in position, key twice."

There was a pause, then Jonas heard two beeps. *Good.* Jonas climbed onto the roof of the yacht, crept past the radar and radio antennae, then crossed the roof of the bridge, walking lightly. As he came upon the forward observation room, he saw a black shadow crawling up onto the roof below him. Jonas hit the deck and drew a bead on the man. Before he could fire, however, three shots sounded from below him, slamming into the man's side. He jerked as the bullets hit him, then rolled off the observation roof.

That gave Jonas an idea. "P-Two and Three, fire in the hole." He set the timer on his last XM-84 and skittered it across the roof of the observation deck, the flash-bang disappearing from sight and exploding, lighting the night in a brilliant flash.

"Advance now!" Jonas jumped down to the observation roof and ran forward, training his pistol on the two prostrate, moaning men as the two trainees also came from both corners and covered them, kicking their weapons away. Jonas walked to the edge of the roof and let himself down, then checked the prone body lying underneath the shattered windows. He glanced up to see the two men, their wrists and ankles neatly zip-tied, back-to-back in the middle of the bow area.

"Lead Two, this is Lead. Bow is secure. Tally is six hostiles, two dead, four captured. Our side has one KIA, two WIA, one MIA."

"Acknowledged. Bridge is secure."

Jonas got the two trainees' attention. "P-One, make sure P-Two is stable, then head back and reinforce P-Five, and make sure you give him the key word. P-Three, you're with me."

Leading the way, Jonas and the trainee swept and cleared

the entire ship, room by room. Along the way, they found the body of the young woman who had been at position four, taken out with a clean head shot. Jonas checked her vitals anyway, even though he knew it was a lost cause, then covered her face with a towel and kept moving. Only when he was satisfied that no one else was aboard did he contact everyone. "The ship is clear, repeat, the ship is clear. Karen, let's head in. We've got wounded to take care of."

"What happens afterward?" she asked on a separate channel.

"I'm going to visit Mr. Castilo and ask him a few questions."

"Do you want to interrogate any of the captives?"

Jonas considered that for only a moment. "Negative. All of them are either deaf from the flash-bangs or concussed or both, and besides, I doubt they know anything about what's really going down today anyway. No, I need to go to the source."

"I'll contact Primary and update—"

"I'm the agent in charge, I'll do it," Jonas said. He sent a call to headquarters on a second line. "No doubt Judy will flip over this. Do you still have a fix on that Stinger crate?"

"Yes, it's heading south-southwest, probably to Paradise," Karen replied.

"Naturally. See if you can get this behemoth to go any faster, will you? I just got a really bad feeling that this thing is going down faster than we thought." He gripped the handrail and waited for the connection, willing the yacht to speed them to their destination more quickly, all the while trying to reconcile the fact that his son was involved in a plot that could very well tear a country apart.

* * * * *

Look for THE POWERS THAT BE
by Cliff Ryder in January 2008
from Room 59™.
Available wherever books are sold.

ROOM 59

CRISIS: A massive armed insurgency—
ninety miles off America's coast.

MISSION: CUBA

A Cuban revolution threatens to force the U.S.
into a dangerous game of global brinksmanship,
thrusting spymaster Jonas Schrader into an
emotional war zone—exacting the highest price
for a mission completed.

Look for

THE powers THAT be

by cliff RYDER

Available January wherever you buy books.

GOLD EAGLE®

GRM591

JAMES AXLER

DEATH LANDS

Desert Kings

Traversing the terrain of Utah, Ryan Cawdor and his warrior survivalists find new evidence that the past is alive and dangerous— with a score to settle. The brilliant and cunning cyborg known as Delphi is reborn and ready to continue his drive for domination. And he's eager for the keys to the kingdom that only the legendary Deathlands survivors—and their secrets—can help him attain.

Available March wherever you buy books.

TAKE 'EM FREE

2 action-packed novels plus a mystery bonus

NO RISK

NO OBLIGATION TO BUY

Look for

AleX Archer
SERPENT'S KISS

While working on a dig on the southern coast of India, Annja finds several artifacts that may have originated from a mythical lost city. Then Annja is kidnapped by a modern-day pirate seeking the lost city. But she quickly sides with him and his thieves to ward off an even greater evil—the people deep in the Nilgiris Mountains, who aren't quite human...and they don't like strangers.

Available January wherever you buy books.